The Shaft

The Shaft

Alex Graham

PIATKUS

To Mel who gave me the idea

Note:

This is a work of fiction. Any resemblance to actual events, locales, organisations, or persons, living or dead, is entirely coincidental and beyond the intent of either the author or the publisher.

Prologue

As the sun slid down behind the volcano, violet shadows crept over the surface of the lake. This was the time of day she loved best – when the shattering heat of the day was subdued to a sensual warmth. In a little while the evening breeze would coax the dust to rise like a mist and the lake would begin to ripple with waves. A tiny green lizard darted across the café's tiled floor, paused for a moment then vanished into a crack in the wall. She glanced at Daniel, deep in a crumpled copy of the *International Herald Tribune* he had found wrapped around a consignment of shoes sent out to the mission from the States. A crazy collection – platform boots, sequined sandals and patent leather clogs – which the Indians had found hilarious.

He looked up and caught the fleeting amusement in her eyes. 'What is it, Mel?'

'Nothing really. I was just thinking how incongruous things can be.'

'That sounds deep – too deep for an evening like this. Here, have another drag of this.'

She took the well-rolled joint and inhaled deeply, letting the fragrant smoke curl itself inside her body and take possession of her mind. 'Where are the others?'

'John had business in Antigua. He hitched a ride there this morning. Simon was called out to the Sanchez house. It looks like their little boy may have TB. Hey, Miguel!'

The man behind the bar had the fine, high cheekbones

1

and delicate honey-coloured skin of the Mayan Indian. He paused in his task of arranging bottles of beer on a narrow wooden shelf. '*Si, padre?*'

'*Dos cervezas negras, por favor.*'

Miguel pulled two black bottles from the fridge, wiped them vigorously and brought them over. He flipped the tops against the edge of the metal table, catching them in the same hand. '*Padre* . . . ' He looked hesitant.

'*Si, Miguel, qué es?*' Daniel leaned towards him.

He was going to ask Daniel for a favour, Mel thought. She kept telling him he was a soft touch. How ironic that the one area of their lives where the Indians didn't want him was their religion. OK, they knew he was a Catholic priest but their complex blend of Catholicism and idol worship held no place for him. After an emotional Mass, conducted in a choking cloud of incense, the Indians would pick their way through the drifts of lilies and other flowers cascading down the church steps and process up the mountainside. There, in a dark secluded gully they worshipped a small black stone statue with bright yellow eyes wrapped in a scarlet cloak

The barman's expression was troubled. '*Padre* . . . ' he began again hesitantly but got no further. A sudden shout caused him to veer away back to the bar.

'What a bitch of a day!' Simon lumbered clumsy and loose-limbed to their table and flung his medical bag to the ground.

'Get me a beer, will you, Miguel? And one for John. I picked him up on the road. He's just gone to make a phone call. The bloody jeep broke down on my way back from seeing the Sanchez kid. The distributor's knackered. I managed to patch it up but it won't last long. We'll have to get some spare parts sent out and make sure the customs officials don't steal them this time.' He raked a hand through an unkempt shock of blond hair, bleached by the sun. 'Well?'

Mel laughed. 'I was just thinking how serene and tranquil it is here, or rather it was.'

2

'I don't do serene and tranquil. You should know that by now.' Simon raised the bottle of beer Miguel had given him to his lips and drank greedily, the thick, dark liquid spilling onto his coarse cotton shirt with the words MEDIC AID printed in big letters. 'Luis Sanchez has TB and if we're not careful we'll have a serious outbreak on our hands. It'll be the devil's own job to persuade these people to get their kids inoculated – even if we could get the vaccine, which we can't.'

'I'll try the medical centre at the Embassy if you like.' They looked up at the tall man who had slid unnoticed through the side door behind them.

'Great in theory, John. But will they really help?' Simon looked like a great big eager Labrador. In a moment his tongue would loll out of his mouth with excitement and anticipation.

'Sure!' John shrugged his shoulders. He bent to kiss Mel on the lips and took the chair next to her. How tired he looked. There was an uncharacteristic weariness in the way he held his head. The skin over his lean cheekbones was drawn so tight she could see a pulse.

'You didn't tell me you had to go to Antigua today. Was the trip OK?'

'Yes, it was . . . OK.' A shadow crossed his face.

'We have another batch of clothes ready to freight to Miami – in the next couple of weeks, probably,' Mel said with a quiet pride. The clothing project had been her idea – a way of helping the women of the villages to become self-sufficient. She was permanently amazed by their energy and creativity.

'Let me know if you want someone to go with it,' Simon said. 'I could do with a bit of a break. Even a cesspit like Miami seems tempting right now!'

'But it's so beautiful here,' Mel protested. She looked with shining eyes at the lake, its surface stirred by the cool winds from the mountains and a path of silver etched on the darkening waters by the rising moon. Far out in the middle

3

of the lake a string of lights showed that a fishing boat was making for the distant shore where smoke was rising from the village fires. Looking up she met Daniel's eyes, thoughtful and serious. 'If only you could capture certain moments, just for a little so you could soak yourself in them. Everything passes so quickly . . . ' she whispered.

'*Sic transit gloria mundi*,' John remarked dryly. 'Is that what you mean?'

'I wasn't being so philosophical – and I didn't know you knew so much Latin.' Mel leant back in her chair, stretching long bare legs in front of her.

The night air was sweetly pungent with its mingled aroma of woodsmoke, beer and sweat. The little café was half-full now. The men of the village in their white shirts, striped high-waisted trousers and high-crowned straw hats were drifting in from the fields. Miguel turned on the radio and the initial crackling gave way to a raucous football commentary that made all the men suddenly silent and intent. The match was between Guatemala and Costa Rica. The commentator's voice rose to a crescendo: 'GOAL!!!' His frenzied roar went on and on as if he were immune from drawing breath. It bounced off the café walls.

Mel got up. Outside, the inky depths of the lake beckoned. Kicking off her sandals she wandered down to the edge and let the cool water flow over her feet. Kneeling, she picked up a smooth flat stone still warm from the sun and skimmed it across the surface of the lake. And then she heard it, a dull rumble. Thunder? No . . . something else.

Was it coming from the radio? The insistent roar grew louder. Putting her head to one side she listened. Something was coming up the road, and fast, which was what sounded so odd. Nothing in Tenango travelled at speed, and certainly not at night. Pulling on her sandals she walked slowly up to the road, peering cautiously in the direction of the noise. Behind her, the men in the café had noticed nothing. They were all grouped around the radio laughing and talking excitedly. It had even drawn Daniel

4

and Simon within its noisy ambit. She couldn't see John. He was unmoved by this passion for soccer and was probably reading in the quietest corner he could find until the strange ritual was over.

She turned her attention to the road again. The junction with the main highway to Guatemala City was fifteen miles away on the other side of the hills. The rutted dirt-track which branched off to Tenango wound precariously through them before snaking down to the lake below. Tiny jewels of light blinked on and off. It must be a convoy of vehicles making for Tenango. An odd time to travel. Probably one of those overland adventure companies. Every now and then, a truckful of eager kids would turn up to chill out on the shores of the lake before tearing off again on some crazy six-month tour of Central and South America most of them would never complete because of malaria, gut-rot and the complications of an over-active sex-life.

Christ, I'm getting old, she thought wryly. Only nineteen but I sound just like my father. The lights were drawing nearer. It would be nice to see some new faces. What nationality would they be? Probably Australians and New Zealanders with their insatiable appetite to see the world, and their enviable indifference to creature comforts, lusting after the big 'OE' – the 'overseas experience' – to tell their mates about back home.

While she waited, Mel traced her initials in the dust with her foot. A pale-furred dog that had been dozing under a bush got up, stretched, chewed a few tasty fleas from off its hind leg and wandered across. With a grunt it settled itself at her feet and gazed soulfully into her eyes. She acknowledged it with a gentle click of her tongue. 'You'll be in for a good time, pal,' she said gently. 'Lots of scraps. So many leftovers you'll need a doggy bag.'

'What are you doing?' John's voice made her jump.

'There's something coming along the road. Look, you can see it. I think it's one of those overland expeditions.' But even as she spoke a full-throttled roar shattered the night air. Whatever it was seemed to be speeding up, the approaching lights suddenly so bright they blinded her. An animal sense of imminent danger shot through her. Her first thought was to get to Daniel, but John was gripping her by the arms, holding her so hard she gasped with pain.

'It's the Army,' he said tersely, dragging her back into the shadows as a convoy of three olive-green jeeps swept up and jammed on their brakes in front of the café.

A young officer leapt from the first jeep and drew a pistol. He gestured the other men into the café. 'Daniel!' Her voice was a shriek as she tore herself from John's arms and ran inside. She heard him swear and follow after her. Inside the café the soldiers had kicked over all the chairs except the ones on which Daniel and Simon were sitting. Miguel's treasured radio lay in pieces on the floor and all the Indian men were spread-eagled against the white-washed walls, backs to the room, legs apart, arms outstretched. Their posture gave them a grotesque resemblance to rock-climbers. The soldiers were frisking them, even searching under their high-crowned straw hats. It was an absurd sight and glancing at Daniel, Mel saw the priest's lips twitch. She began to breathe more slowly again. This was just some routine security exercise. The authorities were always worrying about revolutionaries in the mountains. In a moment this ugly little incident would be over.

The officer gestured to the local men to leave and the soldiers helped them on their way with a few well-aimed kicks. Miguel hovered uncertainly until the officer saw him and shouted, '*Vamos!*' Miguel took to his heels. They heard him running away down the street, the sudden excited barking of a dog and then silence. The young officer was still holding his pistol. 'Please,' he said politely and gestured to Mel to go and sit beside her friends. She hesitated, trembling.

'Do as they say.' John's voice was taut.

She moved obediently towards the table and pulled out a chair next to Daniel. The calm expression in his blue eyes

6

was telling her not to worry: everything would be all right. She tried to swallow but her mouth was dry. John was standing to one side and slightly in front of the officer. Perhaps in a moment they'd be given an explanation. The authorities didn't usually behave like this in the presence of foreigners.

Daniel began to talk to the young officer in Spanish. asking: 'What's going on? What's the problem?' The officer half-smiled, half-looked away as if embarrassed. He held up a hand to signify, 'Be patient – in a moment you'll understand.'

Out of the corner of her eye Mel saw two of the soldiers move up behind Daniel and Simon. Still smiling, the officer looked enquiringly at John who nodded then turned away. There was the gleam of metal as the two soldiers stepped forward. They wrenched back Daniel's head, offering his muscular throat like a Mayan sacrifice to the bright blade which slashed across it. There was something warm on her face, on her arms. Looking down Mel saw Daniel's blood trickling down her body. She could taste the salt on her lips. She opened her mouth to scream but the sound wouldn't come. Simon's body lay sprawled back in his seat, his throat agape, his feet in a pool of already congealing blood. Daniel had fallen forward, head cradled in his arms as if he was just sleeping.

Mel sat rigid with terror, waiting for her turn, but the soldiers weren't interested in her. She watched them wrap the two bodies in tarpaulin, carry them outside and sling them into one of the jeeps. One even got a cloth and made a brief attempt to wipe up the blood on the café floor.

The officer spoke rapidly to John, then glanced around the bar, checking everything was back in place. '*Vamos!*'

Within moments the engines were revving again and the soldiers were gone.

'John . . .'

Slowly Mel stood up and held her hands out in front of her face, uncomprehendingly. She felt John take her by the

7

arm and lead her down to the water's edge. There, in the moonlight, he gently removed her clothes and held her in the shallows, rinsing the sticky blood from her hair, her face, her body. She felt like a doll with no will of her own. When he lifted her up again she fell numbly against him, devoid of physical feeling. It was like being dead.

'Here, take this and wait while I go and find you some more clothes.' He wrapped a coarse Indian blanket around her, sat her down against a slab of stone and stepped quickly away into the shadows.

She waited alone on the shore, impassive, for whatever might happen next. But nothing did happen. John didn't come back and she sat there until the silver dawn light filtered through leaden clouds and an old peasant woman leading her donkey down to drink found her.

Chapter One

Amelia MacDonald struggled back to wakefulness in one of the twin divans in the bedroom she shared with her husband John. They had decided on twin beds just after Ben was born. It had been a joint choice, hadn't it, not just John's idea? It wasn't the first time she'd asked herself that question. John was on the telephone, pacing up and down in the early morning light that was streaming through a gap in the curtains. It must have been the phone ringing that had woken her. Then she remembered it was Saturday.

'Christ Almighty! How many of them? . . . I'll be there in ten minutes at the West Gate. I may need your chaps to help me get in. Make sure someone's told the Minister. I don't want him whinging that he only heard about it on the *Today Programme*. And send a car for my secretary. I may need her.' John MacDonald bit his lip as the police sergeant gave him the details and then flung the phone down. 'That's all I bloody need,' he muttered bleakly.

'What is it, dear?' asked Amelia softly.

'Nothing. Go back to sleep.'

'Why are you getting dressed?' She sat up now in her Viyella Liberty-print nightdress − even in late spring it could be cold at night in the Scottish Highlands − and gazed at him with big distressed eyes like a bird.

'We've got demonstrators trying to break into the plant. It's getting ugly.'

9

'Surely you don't have to go. It's the Director's responsibility.'

'He's asked me to deal with it. After all, I am the Plant Manager. Fabian's hardly going to dirty his elegant Jermyn Street cuffs with this sort of thing. If anyone important rings, give them my pager number.' He clipped the neat black box of the paging unit to his belt and fastened his film badge to his lapel, frowning.

'But John . . .what about some breakfast or coffee at the very least? And will you be back in time for the Fair Trade Fête meeting? You know how much effort I'm putting into getting goods from every continent!' She ran a hand through her boyishly short hair.

'Don't fuss! I'm sorry but don't expect me back till tonight.' He grabbed the car keys and strode towards the stairs.

Amelia's face crumpled as she collapsed back on the pillows and contemplated the busy but lonely day ahead. She heard the car spurt into life as John turned the key in the ignition and then an ugly noise as he missed the gear. He was getting too uptight. They really must take a break . . .perhaps when the boys had gone back to school she'd be able to persuade him. Even a couple of nights at the Green Inn at Ballater would be good. The food there was marvellous and they could walk. He might relax. They might make love . . .

He knew he was taking the bends too tight. Prickles of perspiration all over his body added to his irritation and he could feel his armpits were wet under the navy linen suit. He dug in his pocket for his security pass as the West Gate of the Cape Wrath Nuclear Reprocessing Plant, cocooned in razor wire, came into view. Behind it was the familiar cluster of domes and towers and beyond them the foreshore and the dark blue sea. A few protesters holding banners and placards were blocking the entrance. Although there were a couple of elderly countrywomen in sensible shoes and Barbours, the group consisted mainly of middle-aged men with straggling beards and thinning hair and women in bright ethnic gear which flapped around their frames. Probably all *Guardian* readers, Liberals and vegetarians!

He slackened his speed, sounded the horn and the motley group parted obediently enough. The policemen raised the red-and-white striped barrier and he shot through.

Pulling over by the police lodge, John MacDonald stabbed at the Rover 800's electric button to lower his window. 'Is this why you called me out? Because of the usual crowd of superannuated hippies with nothing better to do on a Saturday morning!' He glared at the huddle of protesters who were doing nothing more threatening than getting some picnic chairs out of their cars and spreading rugs on the ground. A tall red-haired woman in a long Indian skirt was preparing to address them through a megaphone.

'I might have guessed Sarah Grant was behind this. Why can't that bloody woman get herself some HRT and do us all a favour. If there's one thing I can't stand, it's hysterical menopausal women looking for a cause.' But his anger was synthetic. Deep inside he felt real relief. Thank God it wasn't anything after all.

'Excuse me, sir.' The police sergeant cleared his throat. 'I think you'd better come and take a look at the TV monitors. We've got serious trouble down at the main gate and we've just heard from the coastguard that there's a ship out there and it's heading towards us. They may be going to try and land on the foreshore and get into the plant that way. Our own Chief Constable's on his way and we've requested reinforcements from the Highland Constabulary.'

MacDonald took a deep breath. 'I see.' Inside the police lodge the TV screens showed a scene of mayhem in miniature. A row of vehicles – trucks, camper vans and a double-decker bus with shattered gaping windows – had been drawn up like a barricade in front of the main gate, blocking it. MacDonald peered. What was going on among the jumbled figures surging around the vehicles?

A man in combat gear and balaclava stood on the roof of

11

an orange camper van. He was holding a metal spike, bashing it rhythmically against a metal dustbin lid and yelling at the line of Nuclear Police officers who had formed up shoulder to shoulder on the other side of the gate. MacDonald could just make out some slogans daubed in large jagged letters on the side of the van. The black paint was still running. *Nuklear heraus! Nuklear heraus!*

'Nukes out,' he muttered grimly. 'Who are they?'

'Security think it's the commando wing of Earth Alliance.'

'The what?' MacDonald stared at the screen in disbelief.

'Earth Alliance is a new European environmental group based in Germany. They believe in direct action.'

'I can see that. Bloody anarchists.' More masked men were running up to the gates and lobbing what looked like smoke bombs. Others were pulling ladders out of the vehicles.

'They think that Greenpeace and Friends of the Earth have gone soft. They travel around Europe targeting industrial plants they don't approve of.'

'Just nuclear plant?'

'No, sir, anything. Their target lists include oil installations and chemical plant.'

'What the hell brought them up here? We're miles from anywhere. What do they want anyway?'

'Their tactic is to break in and cause as much damage as possible – stop the plant operating and get publicity. The media are here already, sir.'

'I thought I could see that little shit from the *Wrath Courier*. You know who I mean . . .'

'Fergus Brown, sir. Yes, he's with them. And there's an Outside Broadcast van coming up from Inverness.'

'How many workers are on site?'

'The early shift had just arrived when the demo started. We've got a hundred and twenty men in the fuel-reprocessing and waste-handling plants, including the shift managers. They've been alerted and the special electric fences have been activated. Anyone who tries to get in

12

will be fried. And Dr Docherty's over in the admin building. He was there when it started.'

'Sean? What's he doing here on a Saturday morning?' MacDonald turned impatiently towards the sergeant. 'I want the Chief Constable and the Head of Security in my office as soon as possible. And I want to know more about that ship. My office will be the control point while this lasts, and any information must be channelled there at once. How long before the reinforcements get here?'

'The convoy's already on its way from Wrath and should be here in about ten minutes. They've summoned some more men from Inverness.'

'Good. And my secretary?'

'Miss McKeague's been picked up from her home and she's on her way, sir.'

MacDonald nodded curtly at the sergeant and headed for his car to drive the quarter of a mile to the admin block. From there he'd have a first-class view of what was going on. The knot of tension in his stomach was growing tighter by the second.

Twenty miles away Mel Rogers pulled over to consult the map. Ahead of her, a dark blue sea stretched away to merge with the paler horizon, while to one side granite cliffs, wet and shiny with spray, fell sheer to the surf below. How beautiful it was, this remote corner of Scotland. It had been worth the very early start from Inverness. Yawning, she glanced at her watch. She'd been on the road for over two hours. Time for a break. And there was a speck of dust under one of her contact lenses – that was part of the downside to driving an open-top car. She fished it out and cleaned it. Then she went for a stroll along the clifftop, enchanted by the immensity and beauty of the scenery as seagulls swooped and dived in the pale light of a perfect day.

Young bracken, tender and green, crunched beneath her feet and the honeyed scent of gorse hung in the air.

13

Reluctantly she turned her steps back to the blue MGF sports car and reached inside for the road atlas. 'Oh shit,' she muttered. 'Literally.' Taking the soft top down had been a mistake – a seagull had dive-bombed the cover of the atlas with surprising accuracy. She wiped it clean with a tissue and found the page she wanted. Cape Wrath.

Turning inland, Mel left the west coast and its deep sea lochs for a wild mountainous terrain. Herds of deer moved languidly in the shadow of peaks with soft Gaelic names – *Ghlas-Bheinn* and *Meall Na Cra*. This was the only road northwards and there was no chance of getting lost, but it wouldn't be a good place to break down. She hadn't passed a single car in the past hour, and goodness knew where the nearest garage would be. At last, just as the sea came into view again through a gap in the hills, she saw the turning for Cape Wrath. Someone had painted a skull and cross-bones and a gallows on the signpost in lurid green paint. She stopped the car and reversed back to get a closer look. Amateurish stuff, probably kids, but all the same . . .

The road was winding westwards again past tiny fishing hamlets where piles of lobster pots lay heaped outside whitewashed cottages. Although everything was basking in the ripe sunshine it was easy to see that this was, in reality, a harsh environment, stark and ungiving. The few trees grew at crazy angles, sculpted by relentless winds that blew in off the North Sea. She was lucky to have such a wonderful day for her first sight of Cape Wrath.

Mel slowed up as she approached a tight bend and suddenly, unexpectedly, there it was: the Cape Wrath Nuclear Reprocessing Plant. Bizarre, almost surreal, an industrial plant in the middle of nowhere. The small town of Wrath with its 10,000 inhabitants, its shops, its one cinema and its surprisingly sheltered harbour lay two miles west of the plant, hidden around the next headland. She had read all about it. But from here there was nothing to suggest that anything else existed. The sunlight glanced off the silvered surface of a strange golfball-shaped structure. Mel frowned as she tried to recall what it was. One of the prototype fast reactors they had experimented with at Cape Wrath in the 1970s and 1980s? At the other end of the site, a huge oblong building resembling an aircraft hangar and clad in reflecting glass sparkled like a vast mirror. What looked like an electric fence, twenty-foot-high gates and closed-circuit television cameras positioned all around it told her exactly what it was: the nuclear fuel reprocessing plant itself.

Something out at sea beyond the plant caught her eye. Mel reached into the glovebox for her binoculars and, narrowing her eyes, saw a bright orange inflatable with four people balanced on the edge in purple wetsuits. One of them seemed to be carrying a megaphone. As she watched, other inflatables in lurid Day-Glo colours came powering round the headland. They seemed to be converging on something about sixty yards from the shore. Men with divers' weights on their belts began somersaulting into the water. Another man was training a video recorder on the scene. What on earth . . .?

More inflatables were making for the shore itself. People were jumping into the waves with what looked like Geiger counters in their hands. In a moment they were swarming all over the beach. Some of them were taking samples of sand, rocks and seawater, putting them carefully into plastic containers. The plant itself looked deserted.

At that very moment an alarm sounded somewhere on the site – a high-pitched shriek that set Mel's teeth on edge. Simultaneously a convoy of black vans came round the side of a low building and raced down to the beach. As the men piled out Mel could see they were in police riot gear – visors over their faces and extendable batons in their hands. Presumably they were the Nuclear Police. Some had dogs – she could just hear their excited barking as they strained at the chains around their necks.

The police waited until they were down on the shore itself, slithering over seaweed-covered rocks in their heavy rubber boots, before they released the dogs. The protesters were running for their inflatables, jeering and screaming their defiance. They all made it except for one man, who was brought down by an Alsatian. He was picked up bodily by four policemen and slung into a van. Mel lowered her binoculars as a numbing coldness seeped through her. Far away and long ago she had witnessed another man being slung into a jeep like a sack of rubbish, only he had been dead . . . Christ, what a time to remember that . . .

Mel jumped into the car. Hands trembling, she tried to insert the key. Pulling onto the road, she almost collided with an Outside Broadcast van, aerials swaying crazily and the purple logo of *Highlands and Islands TV* on its doors. She followed so close she was in its slipstream and pulled up behind it about a hundred yards from the main gates. Running across she tried to push her way through the jostling, fighting crowds. The police of the Highland Constabulary had linked arms in front of the gates. Behind them, on the other side, stood the Nuclear Police, motionless in their black combat gear, light glinting and reflecting from their visors and Perspex riot shields. Surely someone could help her get onto the site? Dodging stray elbows and pieces of debris, Mel forced her way up to a tall policeman and put out her right hand to steady herself. Simultaneously she felt her left arm being gripped with practised efficiency and twisted up behind her back. A disabling spasm shot through her shoulder.

'For God's sake I'm an employee,' she gasped, red-hot pain making it difficult to form the words. Her arm was released and she turned to look up into the humourless grey eyes of a police sergeant.

'Is that so? Where's your pass?'

'I haven't got one. I don't start work until Monday.'

'Name?'

'Mel Rogers. I'm the new Public Relations Manager.' A bottle flying past her head accompanied by a scream of obscenities seemed to give her words a certain irony.

Chapter Two

'What?...OK, bring her over. She might as well see for herself what a shambles we're in.' John MacDonald replaced the receiver and ran an irritable hand through his thinning fair hair. 'The new PR's here. I was tempted to tell the police to throw her to the demonstrators. Let her try out her communication skills on those savages.'

'The new PR?' His companion gave him a quizzical look from under thick, dark brows. 'I'd have shaved if I'd known.'

'You always look a wreck, Sean. What were you doing here anyway? Saturday morning's hangover time for you, isn't it?'

'I'm a reformed character. In fact, you were the one who told me to reform, as I recall ... I've been catching up with some work. That research reactor fuel-reprocessing contract we're negotiating with the Germans needs watching. They're trying to insert a penalty clause at the eleventh hour about the return of waste that's quite unacceptable ... Bloody hell, look at that!'

A fishing vessel had appeared around the cape and was sailing parallel with the foreshore. The inflatables which had been playing cat and mouse with the police launches were now racing towards it for sanctuary. The two men stared at the scene through tinted windows that dribbled with condensation because the aircon wasn't switched on at weekends.

MacDonald gave silent thanks, for it looked as if the ship wasn't going to come in close. What would he have done if the protesters had attempted a landing in strength? They could have been all over the site before the police were able to do anything. His palms felt moist. He'd ordered all the drums of plutonium-contaminated waste to be secured in the special vault in the waste store, but they might have been able to get at it. If a drum of it was stolen, or if the waste discharge pipe were blocked . . . But there were still those yobbos at the gates to worry about.

The phone rang and he snatched it up. 'Yes, thank you, Inspector, I can see that for myself. What's going on at the main gate? Good . . . excellent. Tell the teams to stay put in the plant and carry on as normal. They're not in any danger and it's important to keep the plant running. But I want the next shift stood down until further notice. The Shift Manager has their names and home phone numbers. I'm not risking trying to get over a hundred men on and off site until those hooligans have been dealt with. Is that clear?'

'Well?' Sean Docherty arranged his features into an expression of concern.

'The Highland Constabulary reinforcements have arrived from Inverness and they've begun making arrests at the main gate . . . Sheena!'

'Yes, Mr MacDonald?' The neatly dressed middle-aged woman sitting quietly at the computer looked round and smiled devotedly at him.

'I want to e-mail an update to the Scottish Office, DTI, the Health and Safety Executive . . . and we'd better not forget Sir Angus. He has to do something to justify his existence.'

'That's a novel view of an MP's role.' Docherty yawned. He strolled closer to the window while MacDonald dictated a few terse sentences to his secretary, and gazed out with a detached curiosity.

The police launches were returning to the shore and the

18

brightly coloured inflatables which had been speeding across the water like a flight of tropical birds were gone, no doubt safely winched aboard the mother vessel now sailing away over the horizon.

Hearing the door open Docherty turned to see a tall, slim, dark-haired young woman in jeans and oversized pastel pink sweatshirt. She was around twenty-six or twenty-seven, he guessed, liking the delicate oval of her face and the way her short hair swung as she moved.

Mel stepped forward a little hesitantly. 'Good morning. I'm—'

'We know who you are,' MacDonald interrupted and resumed his dictating. Mel coloured.

Docherty quickly held out his hand. 'You must forgive us. We've been having a difficult few hours working with the Head of Security and the Chief Constable to get things under control. This is John MacDonald, the Plant Manager, and his secretary, Sheena McKeague. My name's Docherty – Sean Docherty – and I'm Head of Contracts. The Director told us about you at the last management meeting. Welcome to Cape Wrath.'

'I need to talk to someone urgently about what's been going on.' There seemed no point complaining that it had taken her two hours to persuade police and security to allow her on site.

MacDonald turned, stepping close. His eyes were remarkable – a deep violet flecked with gold around the periphery of the irises. 'This isn't the moment for a syrupy little chat about public relations. We've got a group of malicious vandals howling around our gates. I can't get staff in or out, and if the reprocessing plant has to shut down it'll cost us hundreds of thousands of pounds which I presume is exactly what those bastards out there want.' Hostility fizzed out of him like sparks from a firework.

'They also want publicity and you're giving it to them in spades. I've just seen a journalist comprehensively kicked in the balls by a laughing policeman. You'll be able to watch it

19

on TV tonight like the rest of Scotland. And you know what the public will think? They'll say, "There goes the nuclear establishment trying to bully its way to public acceptability".'

The silence that followed was almost tangible. Docherty was looking amused. Mel met MacDonald's eyes without flinching. 'I'm on your side, for heaven's sake. I only want to help . . . Please let me do my job.'

'OK, so what do you suggest?' MacDonald lit a cigarette and held the packet towards her. She was so surprised by his change of attitude she almost took one, although she didn't smoke anymore. His surrender was almost more unnerving than his aggression.

'We should issue a press release at once,' she began. 'It's too late to take the initiative but we can salvage something. We'll remind the media that this is a Government plant and that everything we do is regulated by independent safety authorities like the Scottish Environmental Protection Agency. OK? Then we'll say that our democratic right to carry out nuclear reprocessing is being threatened, putting hundreds of local jobs on the line. And I want a quote from one of the plant workers . . .'

'You'll be lucky.' Sean gave her a measuring look. 'Things aren't exactly rosy in the employee-relations garden just now. We're privatizing some of the operational teams and understandably they're not too keen on it.'

'That doesn't matter. I don't want them to say how wonderful the organization is. I just want them to show the pride they take in their work.'

MacDonald shrugged. 'Be my guest. Sheena, get the Shift Manager on the line.'

Half an hour later Mel had her quotes and was sitting at Sheena McKeague's computer. As her fingers tapped quickly on the keyboard her mind was already thinking about the next step. Pressing the command to print she sat back and looked levelly at the two men, wondering why one seemed so tense and the other so exaggeratedly laid back. They were a weird combination.

'I've got a list here of all the local and national Scottish papers I want the release sent to. I'd also like it to go out to the press agencies, please. All the details are here. Is that OK?' She turned to Sheena, who nodded.

'Thanks. And now I want to go and talk to them – the demonstrators,' she said firmly, watching MacDonald's eyebrows rise and his jaw clench.

'Why? You don't know anything about Cape Wrath yet!'

'No, but I can listen to their concerns. I can offer to get them some answers. And it will put them on the back foot. They won't be expecting that. And I can do some interviews with the media at the same time – about our commitment to open and honest communication.'

'What commitment?' snapped MacDonald.

She smiled at him. 'It's our new policy. And it's what is going to save your bacon.'

Sean Docherty smothered a laugh. 'Come on then, I'll give you a lift. You'll be safer in a car.'

Fine words but what did 'open communication' mean in a situation like this, Mel wondered wryly. It was like suggesting to the Bosnians that it was time to be more community-minded. The hundred yards or so beyond the main gates looked like a battlefield. The barricade had gone – presumably the police had towed the vehicles away, although the orange camper van remained and was now on its side. Many people were preparing to leave and a line of vehicles was already snaking its way down towards the town, but a hard core of seven or eight hooded agitators were still sheltering behind the camper van, darting out to hurl cans of paint through the acrid smoke-filled air that spiralled from piles of old tyres that had been piled against the perimeter fence and set alight. Pieces of metal and shards of glass littered the ground. The policemen from the Highland Constabulary were forming up, ready to force a path through for the fire engine which stood waiting, blue

21

lights flashing, siren blaring, to put out the fires.

Docherty pulled over by the paint-spattered main gate and shook his head. 'There's nothing you can do at the moment. Those people are anarchists. They haven't come here to talk and they'll take great delight in kicking your head in. I suggest you forget whatever textbook stuff you've learned about building a dialogue until the police have things under control. The people you really need to talk to are over there.'

Following his gaze Mel made out a tall woman with long red hair and the pallor of a figure from a pre-Raphaelite painting running over to the group behind the bus. She looked agitated and was shouting. What was she saying? Mel strained to catch the words. She seemed to be telling them to leave.

'Who's that?'

'Sarah Grant. She chairs the Cape Wrath Action Group. She originally organized this demo but then it got hijacked. She doesn't look too pleased, does she? Doesn't believe in violence, you see.' His mouth twisted wryly.

'Why do you find this amusing?' Mel couldn't stop herself asking. There was something profoundly puzzling about Docherty's attitude.

'It's a perfect example of the stupidity of man.'

'And of woman? Is that what you're saying?' There was an edge to her voice. If Sarah Grant had worries and concerns she had every right to express them without being patronized. It was high time the nuclear industry stopped being so arrogant and tried to find some common ground with its critics. From deep within her came a sudden memory of her father's favourite saying: 'The problem with most human beings is that they allow sentiment to hijack their judgement. It prevents them from thinking logically.' It was the scientist's view of life – a philosophy that decreed that all that mattered was the pursuit of scientific fact, with no room for emotional baggage.

'I wasn't slagging off Sarah Grant. The issues are deadly

22

serious to her. You see, her husband used to work here. Ten years ago there was a serious incident and he received a radiation dose ten times the annual limit. He was carefully monitored – urine, blood, faeces, the works – and his health didn't suffer but Sarah believes the radiation dose he received was responsible for genetic defects in one of her children.'

'What happened exactly?'

'The child died when it was only three months old and the strain broke up Sarah's marriage. Her husband didn't want to believe that the terrible things wrong with his child could have been anything to do with him, although it would hardly have been his fault. So he moved south to Glasgow and shacked up with another woman. They've had three healthy kids together. But Sarah's convinced that the Cape Wrath Reprocessing Plant is a danger to the people who work there and to the local community. She blames the plant for the leukaemia cluster here.'

'Could she be right?' Mel gazed at Sarah Grant, now arguing furiously with the anonymous hooded figures, with a mixture of sympathy and interest. Poor woman. Right or wrong – poor, poor woman.

Docherty shrugged. 'I doubt it personally. But the population's so small the statistics are difficult to interpret. It's hard to be sure of anything. And there are all sorts of theories, from electric power lines to demographic change. Some people argue that when a plant like Cape Wrath gets built and a lot of middle-class folk move in from another area, it changes the scenario.'

'But how?'

'According to the theories, the newcomers are specially susceptible to, and can activate, a leukaemia virus. But there's little real proof of— Get down! Now!'

His arm shot out and Mel found herself pushed down under the dashboard. She caught her cheekbone against the catch of the glovebox and almost simultaneously there was the sound of shattering glass. The windscreen burst into a thousand stars as a paint can burst through and thudded against the head-rest of Mel's seat, just where her face had been a split-second earlier. Green paint dripped down the seat.

'Are you all right, sir? Miss?'

Shaken, Mel looked up to see one of the black-clad constables of the Nuclear Police peering in at them through the jagged-edged hole that had been the windscreen of Docherty's car. He opened the door and helped her out. Her legs were shaking so much she had to cling to the side of the car for support. She tasted blood in her mouth and looking down saw drops spilling onto her shirt. For one moment she thought she was going to freak. *Keep calm.* Daniel's face swam before her, serene and reassuring. She took a deep breath, willing the panic to recede.

The policeman helped her into the gatehouse. Docherty followed more slowly, lighting a cigarette. His languid manner was assumed. Just now he'd moved with the speed of an international winger.

Sitting with a cup of tea in her hand, Mel could see what was going on outside the perimeter fence. Had that paint can been a random shot, or was it intended for the two of them, sitting snug inside Docherty's car observing the mayhem? The police were advancing on the few remaining demonstrators, who had formed up in a group behind the toppled van, banging on their riot shields with their batons. The noise drowned the chanting. The protesters held their ground for a moment then faltered and began to fall back, sensing they'd shot their bolt. Then they were in flight, running to their cars and bikes, screaming abuse over their shoulders.

Sarah Grant was standing on the edge of a group of onlookers. A young man next to her with blond dreadlocks was popping away eagerly but carefully with a Hasselblad. The press.

Mel put her cup down. 'I'd like to go outside the fence, please.'

A constable escorted her to the barrier and she walked through, feeling like a character in a film about the Cold War crossing over at Checkpoint Charlie. It didn't seem real. She was aware of curious looks from the people still clustered around the gate. Funny, really. She'd expected Docherty to offer to go with her.

As she picked her way through the pools of paint she scanned the crowd, trying to spot the journalists. The Outside Broadcast van had already left but she spotted the lanky blond locks of the photographer. He had exchanged his still camera for a video one and was now a little way off filming a tall, kilted man with long, thick auburn hair who was striking a pose against the entrance to the site. The pose seemed designed to draw attention to the slogan *Independence for Scotland* printed in bold blue letters on his white T-shirt. Knowingly or not, his pose also drew attention to his muscled torso. For a second Mel was distracted. Then she began to push her way through the crowd towards them. As she did so the kilted figure turned and, pulling on a blue sweater, walked quickly away towards the coastal path.

When she reached the photographer he was changing his film cassette and at first made no response when she asked, 'Which paper are you from? Can I help?'

At last he looked up. 'Who are you?'

'Mel Rogers. I'm the new PR Manager at the Cape Wrath Plant.'

He smiled wolfishly, showing very white teeth. 'I'm Fergus Brown, local freelance. OK, so answer me this. Why are you turning Scotland into a nuclear dumping ground?'

'We're not. Any waste that's generated from our reprocessing plant goes back to the customer.'

'Really. And how long does that take?'

'Our contracts specify that the waste should be returned as soon as practicable and within twenty-five years at the latest.'

'And what happens if a customer country can't take the

25

waste back because it's become politically unacceptable? Look what happened in Gorleben in Germany last year. There were 100,000 demonstrators. The police were powerless. What happened here today was a fucking picnic in comparison. Shame, really. I'd have got better pictures.'

'Fergus!' A slight girl with shaven ash-blonde hair, a stud in her nose and skintight jeans called across to him. She had long beautiful eyes like a lynx that were staring at Mel with undisguised hostility. 'The demonstration's going to carry on down in the town. Will you take me on your bike?'

'Sure.' Fergus snapped his camera case with a businesslike click. In spite of the dreadlocks Mel had the impression of a very organized and professional young man. He probably had no more interest in what had been happening here than in any good story. A raped granny or a raid on a building society would be all the same to him. She knew the type very well. They were much easier to deal with than the few genuinely, passionately committed investigative journalists.

'Come and have a tour around the plant one day,' she called after him as he made for a shining red BMW motorbike that he'd parked well away from the trouble.

'In your dreams, Miss Goebbels,' yelled the girl as she leapt nimbly onto the pillion behind him. She made an obscene gesture at Mel with a finger tipped with black nail varnish and burst into a peal of laughter that merged with the roar of the BMW as Fergus stepped on the throttle and accelerated away to Wrath.

'We want the facts, not propaganda. When is Cape Wrath going to accept fully its responsibilities?'

Mel turned to find herself face to face with Sarah Grant. Someone must have told her who she was. For a moment the two women took each other's measure then Mel held out her hand.

'I couldn't agree with you more. That's what my job is all about. I'm glad to meet you – Sarah Grant, isn't it?'

Sarah Grant's face was thin but it had a fine-boned

beauty. Although she was in her early forties, lines were only lightly etched on her pale freckled skin. She took Mel's proffered hand and held it fleetingly. Mel hadn't been sure she would.

'It's very hard to find real allies. What you saw just now – that wasn't my idea. That was just a group of Euro-eco warriors getting their kicks by cruising through someone else's problems.' Sarah looked close to tears. 'They make it easy for people like you to dismiss environmentalist groups as anarchists with their own agenda.'

'Look, I'm not sure what you mean by "people like you". It's true I support the kind of work this plant is doing. I think it's important for jobs and the local economy and that it brings some benefits for mankind. But that doesn't mean I think everything at the plant's perfect or that I'm prepared to tell lies about it. I'll do my very best to get you the information you want.'

'So you say now . . .'

'I mean it.'

'We'll see.'

Sarah Grant gave her a last appraising look then walked away, leaving something of her sadness and disillusionment behind her. It was depressing. What kind of community had she got into? Only a few bystanders were left now, waiting more in hope than expectation for something further to happen. All the journalists had departed. No doubt they were down in the town filing their stories, waiting for the next thrilling instalment or piling into the town's bars for the first of the many drinks that would go down on expenses.

Goodness, but she was weary! She'd touch base briefly with John MacDonald, then she was going to head for her hotel, a shower and something to eat. Her blood-sugar level felt alarmingly low and it struck her that she hadn't eaten since the previous evening.

It was one of those hotels you find all over Britain.

Adequate enough to make it difficult to complain, but grudging in everything. Still, she'd only be living here until she could find a flat to rent. The soap tray in the shower cubicle held one tiny piece of hard white soap wrapped in shiny pink paper. There was one sachet of shower gel but no shampoo. Two white towels were piled neatly one on top of the other. They were just big enough to allow her to twist one around her body and tuck in the loose ends as she stepped from the shower, but too thin to absorb much water. Already the towel was darkening. Using the other one to rub at her short hair, Mel padded over to the window and gazed out at Wrath.

Her small, Spartan room looked down towards what had once been just a small fishing harbour. Even so, there was little to announce that it now received consignments of nuclear fuel from all over the world. Beyond the harbour wall the sea glimmered, immense and grey. She was almost as far north as it was possible to go without falling into the sea and hitting Scandinavia. And it felt like it. The rays of light shooting out from behind the setting sun in long shining fingers had an ethereal quality. The sky seemed more luminous than down south. Perhaps it was because the landmass petered out here, yielding to the great sea beyond.

There was something surreal about Wrath itself. By leaning even further out, gripping the window-sill with its flaking paintwork and craning her neck at an awkward angle, she could see the handsome Victorian town hall built in a time of prosperity which had never returned. Directly below her lay Wrath's main street with its rows of low greystone houses and tiny individually owned shops with notices on the doors explaining their complicated opening hours. Not much chance of nipping out for some late-night shopping here, nor of finding what she wanted even if there was. So farewell to new-baked ciabatta, freshly made pasta and sun-dried tomatoes. There seemed to be no sign of any further demonstration; in fact the town was unnaturally quiet. She listened intently for a moment and was surprised at the stillness. What time was it? She glanced at her watch. Not even nine o'clock. The land where time stood still, she thought to herself and returned her gaze to the silvery planes of the sea.

It was then she saw something move in the shadows of the bus shelter in the street below. Something quick and insubstantial as a wraith until the street light suddenly came on and she could make out who it was – the girl with the pale blonde hair who had ridden off with Fergus. She had a can of pink spray paint and began to spell out in large careful letters FABIAN WILLIAMS IS AN ARSEHOLE. Her tongue was protruding slightly as she worked. After she'd finished her message she stood back from it for a moment and then embellished it with a few CND signs and a very bad cartoon of an arsehole.

The odd thing was that there was nothing furtive about what she was doing. She was taking her time, almost as if she wanted to be caught. Would she look up and see Mel watching at the window? Mel pulled back a little into the gathering darkness of the room behind her. The street remained deserted, and after a while Mel saw the girl slouch down the street. After thirty yards or so she stopped and hammered on one of the doors. A familiar figure with spiky dreadlocks opened it and the girl dived in under his arm, shrieking with laughter. Mel could hear his own laughter begin to mingle with it.

The image stayed with her as she walked slowly downstairs, like a scene from a play that you can't forget.

The austere dining room was empty except for an elderly couple eating chicken in the basket with a fierce concentration. At her polite 'Good evening,' they looked up, nodded, then resumed picking over the bones.

Somehow she'd never felt so lonely in her life. The limp cheese salad she ordered did little to change her mood which felt dangerously close to depression. Why had she ever thought that coming to the back of beyond would be the answer? The weak cup of instant coffee seemed to set the seal on her day.

29

Hands deep in her pockets she walked down through the purple dusk to the harbour. The soft but salty air was invigorating. Yes, that was better. Reaching the breakwater she paused, flung back her head and filled her nostrils with the briny scent. Her light footsteps made no sound as she wandered along the breakwater listening to the rhythmic motion of the sea.

Suddenly she was conscious of a figure standing in a patch of shadow. She gasped, recognizing the tall, kilted man she'd seen posing against the site entrance sign at the demonstration. Christ, he'd given her a shock. Her heart was thudding against her ribs.

'I startled you.'

'Yes.' She took a step or two backwards. His sheer physical presence was intimidating.

'I'm sorry. My name is Hamish Cameron. Didn't I see you at the demonstration?'

'Yes. My name's Mel Rogers. I'm the new Public Relations Manager at the Cape Wrath plant.'

'Public Relations? The job that's high on bullshit and low on integrity.' He gave her a measuring look. 'So what were you doing outside the fence at Cape Wrath?'

'I was just trying to talk to people, to find out their concerns.'

He shook his head. 'What's the point? Scientists are so bloody arrogant they always think they're right. Look at asbestosis. Look at BSE. And what about the nuclear industry? Permitted levels of radiation have gone down and down without a single scientist having the humility to admit that the previous ones may have harmed workers and the environment . . . I'd have more respect for scientists if they'd admit they're human and fallible like the rest of us, but pigs might fly.' He paused then added more softly, 'And what makes you think they're going to listen to you?'

'If they won't listen to me there's no point in them employing me. Even if you don't like scientists you shouldn't dismiss their achievements.'

30

'Why not?'

'Are you really that cynical?'

His tawny eyes twinkled. 'Not cynical. Realistic.'

'It's not realistic to hold science in such contempt. Where would mankind be without it?'

'We wouldn't have atom bombs or chemical weapons or thalidomide.'

'Or electricity or anaesthetics. But nothing comes without some kind of price. If the benefits are big enough we accept the risk and do our best to minimize it. Otherwise we'd still be living in caves.'

He laughed gently. 'That's the first time I've ever heard anyone from the plant admit that what goes on there is risky.'

'You know that's not what I meant. I was just trying to put it into context. To explain that nothing in life is risk-free.'

'At least with some things you get a choice − you control whether you cross the road or light a cigarette. The problem with nuclear risk is that it's forced on the public whether they want it or not. It's a kind of technological imperialism. Did anyone ever ask the people of Wrath whether they wanted a nuclear plant on their doorstep? No, of course not. No more than anyone asks passengers on an ordinary flight whether they mind that there's a cargo of nuclear material in the hold or that the plane's wingtips are weighted with depleted uranium as ballast. That cargo plane that crashed in Amsterdam in 1992 was carrying four hundred kilos of the stuff ... as well as those nerve-gas ingredients the Dutch government admitted to last year. But people don't get asked. They're just told to trust the scientists and the governments they serve.'

'What do you do? Do you work with Sarah Grant? You've only told me your name.'

'Why should I tell you any more?' He turned away, apparently now more interested in staring at the sea than talking to her.

31

'Because it's polite. And because you frightened me just now. You could have been the Wrath strangler, for all I know.'

He laughed again. 'I might still be. You should be more careful where you walk at night. And no, I don't work with Sarah. I just don't like the way the English exploit Scotland. Cape Wrath's a prime example.'

A leaden weariness was creeping over Mel, leaving her no energy to argue. She gazed out beyond the harbour to where spasmodic flashes from the lighthouse lit up the darkling sea. A fishing trawler was making for the safety of the harbour, its engine throbbing cosily. Dark figures moved on its decks preparing to berth and start unloading the catch that would soon be speeding southwards.

Looking round she saw that Hamish Cameron had vanished into the night. He seemed to make a habit of dramatic gestures. Turning to retrace her own steps she saw that the moon was now high above the headland beyond the town, pale and beautiful. But for some reason she found she was trembling.

Half a mile outside Wrath, in a large late-Victorian house on the headland a silver-haired man was reading contentedly beside a log fire he didn't really need but which contributed to his sense of well-being. He reached out for the glass of malt whisky he'd positioned carefully at his elbow and grunted to himself with satisfaction. It had taken two and a half years to track down this book, but Blackwells' Rare Book Department had come up trumps once again. He ran his slender fingers over the rich brown leather binding with its delicate gilt tracery as tenderly as if he was caressing a woman's bare flesh. In fact, more tenderly, he mused maliciously. It had been a long time since Christine's skin had had anything approaching the satin feel of Sir Charles Alban's *History of the First Crusade*.

As if his unkind thought had conjured her up, the door opened abruptly.

'Fabian!' the voice of command rapped out. She stood directly in front of him, her expression uncannily like that of the stag whose head was mounted on the wall above her. They both bore a distinct look of outrage. The stag had always amused him, Fabian reflected idly, and it wasn't even as if he'd shot the bloody thing. It was Christine's idea to furnish this great mausoleum of a house like that of a nineteenth-century country squire.

'What is it?' Better bow to the inevitable. Reluctantly he put the book down.

She placed an arm on the ornate white marble fireplace. 'The demonstration's just been on the evening news on television – on the BBC! It looked awful. Of course the BBC are so biased and left-wing that all they showed was demonstrators being hit with batons and dragged into police vans. What are you going to do about it?'

'About what? It's all over. John MacDonald handled it as I asked him to. He kept me informed.'

'But it looks so *bad*, darling. You can kiss your knighthood away if you get much more bad publicity like this. Or many more incidents. It's not even as if you can trust the work-force. Whenever anything goes wrong at the plant they're the first to leak it to the press. You must make a stand.'

'Does it never occur to you that I might have other fish to fry?' His expression behind his gold spectacles was diffi-cult to read. Christine felt her indignation falter in the face of some unspoken warning.

He pressed home his advantage. 'I didn't ask to come up to this Godforsaken place. All I want is to get back to Whitehall so that I'm within walking distance of the London Library. Or I want to take early retirement so that I can live somewhere civilized and forget that Cape Wrath ever existed. After I've gone it can blow itself sky-high as far as I care. In fact it probably will, given how old and decrepit the plant is.' The look of frustration on her face was highly entertaining. Like a cow unable to get into the milking parlour at milking time.

'Don't worry, my dear,' he relented and smiled blandly. 'We've just recruited a new Public Relations Manager. I believe she's due to start on Monday.'

'But how do you know she'll be any good? And wouldn't a man have been better in the circumstances? What can some silly girl know about the kind of problems we face up here?' Really, Fabian was sometimes so obtuse. Why she had ever married him remained a mystery to her. If only she'd married Paul Cavendish when he asked her she'd be a Cabinet Minister's wife by now instead of the wife of a man whose indolence and indifference had got him relegated to the sticks. And not only him but his wife and daughter as well. It's no surprise our daughter's turning out the way she is, Christine Williams brooded. He takes no interest in either of us or in our family's standing.

She stalked down to the other end of the room and began adjusting cushions vengefully. He'd never understood how much her job as an MP's secretary had meant to her. Although her office had been a dusty little place tucked away behind Parliament Street, she'd had free access to the House of Commons and had mingled constantly with the great and the good. The sense of power had almost been something you could smell. An aphrodisiac. And she'd given it all up for him. She looked back at her husband's long thin form stretched out in front of the fire. Damn you, Fabian, she thought with something approaching real hatred. *Damn* you!

Chapter Three

It hadn't been a bad night for customers. Not a bad night at all. Mushtaq Khan felt quite pleased as he checked the takings. It wasn't easy supporting two children at college and sending regular cheques to his brother's widow in Karachi. The responsibility of being a family man weighed heavy but he didn't grudge the effort. His business now was to run a restaurant and he did it well, he reflected with satisfaction.

The demonstration had been a bonus. Khan's Curry House had filled up early with protesters and with journalists. There'd been the usual crude jokes. A flabby middle-aged reporter from the *Inverness Advertiser* had quizzed him offensively about the spiciness of the food. 'Now see here, Abdul, or whatever your name is, I don't want any of your ringstingers. I'll want my arsehole back again this side of Christmas.' Mushtaq Khan had smiled politely and resisted the temptation to ask the cook to add extra chilli to his *chicken do piaza*.

The only really ugly moment had been when a group of young Germans, fired up by too much Kingfisher lager, began banging their cutlery on the table and bawling something about the Cape Wrath Nuclear Reprocessing Plant. Two local men had gone over to their table and the room had fallen suddenly quiet.

'We fight our own battles in this town. We don't want rich middle-class foreigners interfering in our affairs. So

35

why don't you sod off back where you came from before I rip that nice earring out for you,' one of them said slowly and deliberately to the leader. Even if the kids couldn't speak English they'd got the message all right. They'd paid up meekly and trooped out, leaving plates of half-finished food steaming gently on the table.

'Kasim!' he called over his shoulder to a tall, thin young man dressed in the waiter's standard garb of black trousers and white shirt. 'I want you to finish off and lock up for me. I'm tired and I still have the VAT return to work on at home.'

'OK, no problem, Mr Khan.' The boy was wiping tables down with quick efficient flicks of a cloth, long dark hair tumbling over his brow.

It was excellent how well Kasim had fitted in, Khan reflected as he walked slowly along the harbour front, the evening's takings snug in an inner pocket he'd had specially sewn into his suit. Even though unemployment was high in Wrath with all the recent cuts at the plant, it was hard to find anyone he could trust. Kasim had turned up out of the blue three months ago. Taking a year out from studies at London University and wanting work, he'd said, looking at Mr Khan with dark, intense eyes. 'Allah provides,' Mr Khan had replied, following his instincts that this serious young man would be a good worker. And he had been right. But it was a shame Kasim couldn't speak Urdu. Brought up in London with a Pakistani father and an English mother he'd confessed, half-embarrassed, that he'd never learned the language.

Kasim was polishing the cutlery. All he had to do now was re-lay the tables for tomorrow's lunch trade. He'd switched off all the lights except for one solitary spot directly above him. It cast a sharp arc of light over what he was doing but the rest of the room was in shadow. The prints of the Taj Mahal and the Red Fort at Agra were less strident in the gloom. He preferred it that way. Tiredness seeped through his body but also a sense of relief. Wrath

36

had been full of strangers today and it had unnerved him. But now everything would be back to normal.

The sudden bleeping of the telephone made him drop a fork. Retrieving it he glanced at his watch, frowning to see a speck of grease on the glass. Half-past midnight. Surely a wrong number.

'Hello, Khan's Curry House.'

There was silence on the other end of the line.

'Hello?' Kasim repeated. He heard a sharp intake of breath but still no words. As the seconds passed a demon seemed to whirl inside his head, screaming with panic, the sound beating into his brain.

'Who is this?' Nothing. Just the click of a receiver being replaced.

It was a wrong number – of course it was. But glancing in the mirror he saw the waxen quality of his skin which seemed stretched too tight over his high cheekbones. The expression in his eyes looked bruised.

With a trembling hand he reached in his pocket for the small torch he used to guide his steps homewards through Wrath's dimly lit back streets and switched off the light. The darkness soothed him. It felt soft and safe, something he could wrap himself in. A cloak of invisibility like he'd read about in fairytales when he was a child.

He pulled on his leather jacket and fumbled in his pocket for the keys to the restaurant. With his other hand he located the key to his boarding house. When he reached his doorstep he wanted there to be no delays. Once he was safe inside he'd consider what to do. Perhaps there would be some other sign, something to give him a clue about whether he was being paranoid. If there was anything, he would need to make a call.

Kasim turned the leather collar up around his face and stepped outside. Silence, except for the ugly yowling of a cat. He glanced around. Everything looked normal. So why this feeling that something was about to happen. Premonition? Sixth sense? It didn't matter what

37

you called it. The very air seemed heavy with expectation.

He set off along the street with quick, silent strides, keeping in the shadows. He turned the corner and there they were. Two of them, arms linked, swaying gently. He could smell the whisky fumes on their breath.

'Well, what have we here? If it isn't a wee toastie.'

Kasim waited, eyes watchful, fingers closing on the flick-knife in his back trouser pocket. 'Toastie' wasn't such a bad thing to be called. Better than 'wog' or 'Paki bastard'. And they looked too drunk to give him a kicking. One of them lurched at him and thumped him hard on the shoulder. 'Poor wee timorous toastie . . .' Then he turned away and threw up into the gutter. His friend helped him straighten up and the two men staggered on, pushing Kasim against the wall of a house.

Barbarians, Kasim thought, nose crinkling at the disgusting aroma. But harmless ones. The sinister miasma he'd been sensing around him lifted. You're a fool, he told himself softly, a fool.

He strode quietly along the alleyway that led to the lodging house. He'd have to creep in. Mrs McKeague got very irritable if any of her lodgers woke her or her evil-smelling spaniel. His hand was already on the garden gate when he heard a sound, soft and furtive and very close behind him. He turned, and what he saw made his lips pull back and his jaws crack wide in a great scream which never happened. A blow on the back of his skull made him crumple. Arms picked him up roughly and pulled him into the shadows. Inside the house Mrs McKeague and her stertorously breathing dog slept on.

'May I see your pass, miss?' The police constable on the gate scrutinized Mel's picture, which had been heat-sealed into a plastic identity card. It was an old passport photograph she'd sent to Security and it made her look like a first cousin of Countess Dracula. But at least she had a pass now.

38

It had taken her over two hours to get through the induction process in the personnel offices in Wrath that morning. Her briefcase bulged with folders about staff conditions and safety arrangements, most of it written in bureaucratic gobbledygook.

She followed the constable's directions to the carpark behind the administration block where she'd found John MacDonald the previous day. Certain bays were reserved for people whose names were painted onto little pieces of wood that looked like *Stay Off the Grass* signs. They announced that the gleaming maroon Rover belonged to John MacDonald and that the elegant, elderly grey Bentley beside it was the Director's. Did Sean Docherty merit his own parking space? She couldn't see his name anywhere. A telltale sign perhaps. Like not having the key to the executive washroom.

Electronic doors whooshed open to receive her. No receptionist, just a rather elderly chart stuck to the wall showing the lay out of the building and which departments were located where. Very welcoming, she thought. But she found the public relations office quite easily. It was located one floor below MacDonald's and just a few doors along from Sean's at the end of a long corridor.

'Good morning, Miss Rogers.' A pleasant-looking girl of about nineteen with hair in a thick plait and an honest freckled face was compiling press cuttings in a large open-plan room. 'I'm Ishbel Morrison, your assistant.'

'Hi. Please call me Mel. What's in today's press? I caught breakfast TV on BBC Scotland but I haven't seen anything else yet.'

Ishbel sighed. 'It's not very good, I'm afraid. The papers have majored on police brutality. Two of the protesters ended up in hospital, one with bruised ribs where he got kicked and one with a suspected fracture of the skull. Earth Alliance have put out a statement accusing us of an extreme reaction and saying it must be because we have something to hide. The *Glasgow Herald* has a leader condemning the plant's safety record and saying Earth Alliance have a point.'

'What about the people who were arrested?'

'One of the divers has been charged with causing criminal damage to the discharge pipeline.' Ishbel consulted her notes. 'Oh yes – two others who were arrested outside the main gate have been charged with obstruction.'

'OK then, let's get to work, shall we? I want you to fix up a briefing for the local press tomorrow morning at ten a.m. It's going to be a weekly event.'

Ishbel's grey eyes widened. 'Where?'

'Right here on the site. I'm not going to give them any excuse for complaining we don't talk to them.'

The phone buzzed and Ishbel picked it up and hooked it under her chin, carrying on sifting the cuttings while she spoke. 'Press Office . . . Yes, yes of course I'll tell her.' She replaced the phone with a clunk. 'Mr Williams wants you to join him in the Director's dining room for lunch at one p.m.'

She might have guessed there would be a Director's dining room. Mel paused for a moment outside a highly polished wooden door with elegant brass fittings. It had been an exhausting morning, dealing with a succession of press enquiries about the demonstration and fitting in a live interview down the line on a consumer programme. She needed just a moment's space to herself. A few seconds was enough. Taking a deep breath she tapped lightly on the door and walked in.

Fabian Williams was at the far end pouring out sherry. He was the same thin patrician figure she remembered from the interview in Glasgow and wearing the same double-breasted pin-striped suit and what she guessed was a college tie. His rather long silvery hair was swept back in two perfectly symmetrical wings. An elderly dandy of the old school. It was difficult to stop herself grinning as she recalled the graffiti on the bus shelter.

'Miss Rogers. Welcome to Cape Wrath.' Just three

strides of his long thin legs brought him to her side. 'I'm afraid you had rather a baptism of fire on Saturday.' She was looking tired, he reflected, as if she hadn't slept that well. Probably wondering if she'd made a mistake coming to Cape Wrath. At least she'd had the choice . . .

'Have a glass of sherry. I'm expecting John MacDonald and Sean Docherty in a moment. I know you've already met them. Our Head of Security will also be joining us.'

'Thank you.' She accepted the drink although she didn't really want it. The sherry was pale and dry. Just like Fabian Williams.

He fingered his tie. 'Whitehall are very keen we sort out our public relations at Cape Wrath. This constant barrage we're under from the media – it's . . . well, it's becoming an embarrassment. There have been questions in the House about our operations here. I'm not even sure we have the local MP on our side anymore. I'm looking to you to turn things around.'

He spoke like a character in an old black and white film. What on earth did the workforce make of him on an industrial site like this? 'I'll do my best,' she said cautiously. 'But I'm going to need every support from you. And free access to information.'

'What do you mean by "every support"?'

'You're the Site Director. People expect you to be accountable for what goes on here and they expect to see you. One of the first things I want to do is to audit your contacts – find out who you know in the local community and nationally. Then I'm going to put together a contact programme for you including regular meetings with the media. I want you to project your vision of Cape Wrath and what it means for the local community.'

'Ah.' Williams was looking shifty and she sighed inwardly. Another one who thinks that PR can all be done by somebody else. *Here's some money. Please go and buy me a shiny new image.*

'And I must know what all the live issues are,' she

continued. 'Sean said something yesterday about employee-relations problems. And the papers today are talking about the plant's poor safety record. I need to know as much as anyone can tell me about what's happened here recently and about your future plans. I need to be involved in all the plant's operational decisions.'

'You don't run the plant, Miss Rogers, at least not yet.' John MacDonald's dry tones made her start in surprise. She hadn't heard him walk into the room, and now here he was right behind her. Sean Docherty sidled in after him, neater than on Saturday, but with the same amused observer's air.

'I wasn't suggesting that for a moment,' she said gently and smiled at MacDonald. She was damned if she was going to let his brusqueness get under her skin. 'I'm simply saying I have to be a trusted member of the team and involved in the decision-making process here. You need to know the PR implications of any decisions you're thinking of taking. You may not change your mind because of them but at the very least you need to have an idea what the consequences could be.'

MacDonald poured himself a sherry while Sean helped himself to a glass of mineral water. The glance he gave her was conspiratorial.

Fabian Williams was rubbing his bony hands together awkwardly. 'I'm sure we can find a *modus vivendi*, John. We must give Miss Rogers the freedom she needs to help us rehabilitate Cape Wrath.'

The look MacDonald flashed at him was unmistakably contemptuous. 'I was merely suggesting that the plant should be run by people who know what they're doing,' he said in his clipped, precise voice. The jibe wasn't directed at her, Mel realised.

An embarrassed silence was broken by the simultaneous arrival of a waitress with the first course and the remaining member of the lunch party – a fit-looking man in his late thirties who introduced himself as James Everett, Head of Security.

42

'Shall we sit down?' Williams gestured to Mel to sit at his right hand. MacDonald, Everett and Docherty sat down opposite.

'What attracted you to working at Cape Wrath?' MacDonald asked in a more conciliatory tone.

'My father was a scientist – an astrophysicist at Cambridge University ... I grew up with an interest in science...and a realisation of how often it gets misunderstood. Scientists can't always find the language to communicate with ordinary people.' As Mel talked on, playing with the slab of pale pink pâté nestling on a lettuce leaf, her dead father's face floated before her again. He still seemed so real to her – the dry tones extolling the virtues of science. He thought he could manage people and emotions – even his wife – by algebra. A wistful longing for him pierced her, together with a sharp pity. She had loved him, for all his faults.

'I think the nuclear industry in particular is very misunderstood,' Mel heard herself saying as she snapped back to the present. 'People get very emotional about words like "plutonium" and "half-life" and "radiation" because they don't understand what they mean. They become frightened.'

'It's their own fault for not taking the trouble to find out that we believe in what we're doing and that we don't take stupid risks,' MacDonald interjected. 'That's why, with due respect, I don't have very much time for all this PR business. It's just froth and no substance. People are too lazy or apathetic to grapple with the issues. So they deserve what they get.'

'Surely if people don't understand it's the industry's fault,' she argued back. 'You've been arrogant and secretive for years. There may have been a time when you could get away with it—'

MacDonald opened his mouth but Mel denied him the chance to interrupt her. 'But that's not the case anymore. The world's moved on. People expect organizations to be

43

open and accountable, and perhaps it's been your failure to recognize that and respond to their concerns that's got you where you are today.'

The tension in the room seemed to expand as they ate their way through the uninspiring lunch. It centred on Mel and the Plant Manager. James Everett ate fastidiously, commenting only once on the dirty knife he had been supplied with and the general lack of hygiene displayed by the canteen staff. Docherty too stayed on the sidelines, merely observing their taut exchange, while the Director looked frankly distracted. She was beginning to suspect that Fabian Williams had no real interest in her or her task.

'If you'd handled things differently you wouldn't have had a demonstration like that in the first place,' she went on, disconcerted by her discovery, the knowledge of it sharpening her voice. 'And when the demonstration did happen you handled it all wrong. You made yourselves look defensive and aggressive at the same time. You must remember that the demonstrators may have a point. Just because you don't like their methods—'

'Those yahoos are nothing more than a collection of left-wing layabouts who hoodwink naive young people into joining their ridiculous and dangerous causes,' Williams rapped out as if suddenly recalled to life. His eyes were cold as he raised his coffee cup to bloodless lips. 'Take Miss Rogers around the reprocessing plant, John.' He rose, nodded curtly and stalked from the room.

Dougie MacBain replaced the receiver and resisted the temptation to swear. As a lay preacher as well as a shift manager he tried to set an example to the men but today his patience was close to breaking point. His eyes roamed glumly around the locker room. The afternoon shift had just clocked in and were pulling on white boiler suits that zipped from crotch to throat and adjusting the attached hoods and collars that left only their eyes exposed. They were dressing themselves in silence with none of the usual horseplay and ribald comments. Each man seemed self-contained and thoughtful, chewing over the news that had dropped on them like a bombshell out of a clear sky. It wouldn't be long before their mood turned to anger and resentment, and he was the one who'd have to handle it.

Those fools in Personnel had as much of a grip on reality and as much humanity as Pol Pot. Sitting in their snug offices away in Wrath, acting like little Hitlers. He pulled the crumpled piece of paper out of his pocket and read it again. In impeccable English it announced that some of the maintenance teams who worked on the plant were going to be 'divested'. 'Divested' was a typical Fabian Williams word; it had sent Dougie straight to the dictionary. When that hadn't helped he'd got on the phone to Personnel.

What it apparently meant was that the men would be transferred to a new employer who would work for Cape Wrath under contract and could play around with their pay and conditions. 'Like the bloody slave market,' he'd yelled in frustration down the phone at some self-righteous young personnel officer who'd tried to tell him it was in the best interests of the tax-payer. It didn't help that they'd announced it just when MacDonald was trying to extract every last ounce out of the teams to finish the Brazilian reprocessing contract ahead of time.

And to top it all they wanted him to show some public-relations bimbo around the plant. He crumpled the note in disgust and flung it in the bin.

'I'm sorry I don't have time to take you around the plant myself, but one of the Shift Managers will give you a tour. He can answer any questions you've got.'

They halted outside the plant's electric gates. At a look from MacDonald a constable came out of the police lodge on the left-hand side of them.

'Give me your pass, will you please? The constable needs it.' Mel unhooked it from her lapel and gave it to

45

MacDonald who handed it to the policeman. 'Dougie MacBain will be looking after her.'

'OK, Mr MacDonald. That'll be just fine.' The policeman's polite expression and deferential tones told Mel everything she needed to know about John MacDonald's position at Cape Wrath. Something a tad more important than God's. But at least he was being a bit pleasanter to her now. She shouldn't rush to judgement. He must be tired. Coping with the riot couldn't have been easy.

'You'll get your pass back when you leave. It's just a precaution. The safety regulators insist we know exactly who's in the plant at any given time. Come and see me after the tour if you have any questions.' There was even a suggestion of a smile as he took his leave.

Mel followed the constable as the first of two electric gates slid open. As they walked through it closed behind them. A five-second delay and the next gate opened with a whisper. Before them lay the building which housed the reprocessing plants, a long rectangular construction of panes of tinted glass. They reflected back the afternoon sunlight. A glamorous high-tech, film star of a building.

But not on the inside. Looking around it was clear that the glittering exterior was just a shell around something much older. She took in the shabby paintwork, the old-fashioned notice boards covered with messages, some so old the paper had turned yellow and curly at the edges. The constable gestured her towards a wooden counter presided over by a man in a blue boiler suit generously stained with ink leaking from the phalanx of biros poking out of his breast pocket.

'George there'll give you your film badge,' the constable explained. 'You'll have to sign for it.' She dutifully wrote her name in the kind of book her primary schoolteacher had used to take the daily register.

'Here you are, lassie.' George grinned at her over his biros. 'You'll need to pin that to your protective suit. It monitors whether you've been exposed to any radiation.

46

Come with me and I'll show you to the ladies' changing room.'

She followed George down drab corridors past the men's locker room. A poster of a nude woman with gigantic breasts was attached to the door with lumps of Blu-Tack and she could smell the acrid aroma of stale sweat. *Welcome to the testosterone zone.*

It was also like being caught in a time warp, she thought, as she hung up her jacket on a bent metal hanger and negotiated her way into a white protective suit with a pointed hood. Everything looked as if it dated from the 1960s, including the Formica-topped table. They were obviously not very used to female visitors at Cape Wrath. The one loo had a cracked black plastic seat while the shower cubicle's plug-hole was clotted with an unappetizing mess of hairs and pieces of bright pink soap. Her reflection in the mottled mirror showed her a white-robed pixie with every appearance of an unfortunate skin disease!

George was waiting. 'I'll take you to the barrier. Have you been across before?'

'No. What do I have to do?' There was something a bit surreal about this. *Alice Through the Looking Glass.*

'Don't you worry, I'll show you.' He grinned down at her like a friendly uncle as she padded along by his side. 'Here we are. Nothing to be scared of.' George pointed to a long wooden shelf with cubby-holes underneath full of shoes, extending right across a long, low room. 'But first of all we need to check you for radioactive contamination.'

'But I haven't been anywhere yet!'

'That's what you may think, lassie, but some parts of the site are contaminated. We need to make sure you're not bringing anything *in*, just as much as we need to check you're not taking anything *out*!'

Contamination on the site? No one else had mentioned this – not Fabian Williams or John MacDonald or even Sean Docherty or Ishbel. Why hadn't they told her? Because to them it was just something routine? That was a more disturbing thought than if they'd deliberately concealed it. She bit her lip, trying to make it out. MacDonald had said he'd answer her questions. It looked as if she might well have a few.

'Stand on this, put your hands into the sockets and grip the bars.'

She did as George told her, stepping onto the metal plate of what looked like a Speak Your Weight machine. Pushing her hands into the two holes facing her at shoulder level she could feel a cold vertical bar at the back of each and grasped them tightly. After a couple of seconds the display panels on the machine flashed up a row of red zeros and it gave a ping.

'That's OK then. Now sit on the barrier, lift your feet off the ground and put these over your shoes.' George handed her some white plastic overshoes and she slid them over her loafers.

'Swing your legs across.'

She did as she was told and stood up, facing him on the opposite side of the barrier.

'Mr MacBain will be waiting for you just through that door there.'

In the corridor outside, a tall, sandy-haired man was waiting. He looked tired and edgy but summoned a smile as he introduced himself and politely invited her to follow him down a cavernous concreted corridor, all painted in the same flaky magnolia as the entrance. A strange noise, like a dripping tap, echoed around them, reverberating off the walls.

'Excuse me, but what's that?'

'That's the criticality monitor. It tells us everything's OK,' MacBain said, walking quickly on. But glancing back he caught her look of puzzlement and sighed. 'If certain categories of nuclear material come into contact with each other they can go "critical" which means they could trigger a nuclear chain reaction. That's what is deliberately engineered to happen in nuclear power reactors to produce energy. But if it happened in uncontrolled conditions –

here, for example – it could cause an explosion.' He was talking too fast, barely hiding his impatience at having to give up part of his afternoon when he was so busy. Get a grip, MacBain, he told himself. After all, she looked a nice wee thing. Not what he'd been expecting at all.

'What's the risk of that happening here?'

'Very, very low. We take great care how we plan the various campaigns in the plant. We know exactly how much uranium and plutonium we have at any given time and we keep them apart.' He wished he felt as confident as he sounded. Things had been happening recently that he couldn't quite explain but which made him uneasy. And there'd been some stupid careless mistakes. Radioactive liquid had been spilled while it was being transferred between two flasks, and two radiation workers had ducked out of the health physics checks and carried radioactivity off site with them. Patches of it had been found on the seats of one of the site buses during routine monitoring. Still, who could blame the workforce if they were getting careless? Management treated them like mushrooms – kept them in the dark and poured manure on them.

He paused at the first of a series of grey metal doors. 'Right then, the tour starts here.'

Mel's head thudded with the facts she was trying to absorb as she followed MacBain's tall figure through the series of plant rooms. It was like a visit to the Underworld – a grey, bleak, bloodless place. The plant operatives were moving slowly and silently, some of them in pressurized suits with special breathing apparatus. Treading carefully in her overshoes she walked past a series of caves, sealed off by thick glass. Inside each cave metal manipulators operated by remote control moved like giant crabs nudging lead canisters of radioactive material along to the next stage of their journey.

The process MacBain was describing sounded complex. 'When the consignments of fuel arrive we open the flasks, take out the fuel rods, chop them up and then dissolve the

49

pieces in a bath of hot concentrated nitric acid. This and the following chemical processes enable us to separate out the ninety-seven per cent of valuable plutonium and uranium from the three per cent of waste. We use the plutonium and uranium to fabricate new fuel or we simply return it to the customer. If we didn't reprocess it all the fuel, not just the three per cent, would have to be treated as waste.'

'What happens about the waste?'

MacBain shrugged. 'It's not a problem. We treat it depending on what category it is. Low-level waste is stored in pits. Intermediate-level waste is mixed with concrete and stored in drums and the highly active waste that emits the really significant levels of radioactivity is stored in liquid form.'

She had just opened her mouth to ask him another question when a siren began to whine, building quickly to a pitch which set her teeth on edge.

'What's that?'

'It means there's been another incident,' he said with more weariness than emotion. 'Dear God, what is it this time?' Around them the plant seemed to spring into life as men came running down the corridor, their anxious voices crescendoing around them. 'Mr MacBain,' one of them called, face sagging with relief as he spied the Shift Manager, 'you'd better come quick. The lads've spilled some radioactive liquid in Cave Four.'

MacBain pulled a mobile phone from his pocket and banged in some numbers. 'Dougie MacBain here. Get me a health physics team to Cave Four *now*!' He gave Mel a fatalistic look. 'You'd better come along and see for yourself . . .'

50

Chapter Four

'I've read the incident report but I'm still not clear what happened.' Fabian Williams removed his glasses and looked irritably around the table at his assembled managers. Why could he never get a straight answer to a straight question?

Most of them were avoiding his eye. Mike Gordon, the balding Senior Site Engineer, was making notes on a pad. Jock Maitland, the Head of Personnel, was gazing out of the window, smugly aware that this was nothing to do with him. Janice Griffiths, the trendily dressed thirty-something Head of Information Technology was playing with her three-stranded necklace of oversize pearls which took up most of her short neck. Dougie MacBain was looking uneasy and shooting anxious glances at John MacDonald. James Everett was waiting expectantly, like a lean hound quivering for a stick to be thrown, and Sean Docherty was wearing his usual expression.

But the young Head of Safety, Paul Carter, looked as if he wanted to say something. He cleared his throat but John MacDonald got in first. 'It was a simple error.' He leaned forward in his chair. 'Two shift workers were moving a bucket that had been used to catch the drips from that slow leak from the radioactive effluent tank. It hadn't been properly sealed and a tiny amount of the liquid spilled onto the floor of Cave Four. They became contaminated, setting off the alarms.'

'Do we need to report this to Government Departments, John?' There was an edge to the Director's voice. There'd been too many examples of carelessness recently.

'Yes, but we don't need to make too much of it. There was no release of radioactivity into the environment and the health physics people have given the workers the all-clear. I'll prepare a suitably worded report for you to send Whitehall. More importantly I'll make sure we deal with the tank leak at the next shut-down. We've been using buckets for four years. It's not ideal but we're so understaffed – we never get time for some of these good-housekeeping activities.'

'Very well. Let us move on.'

This was the first of Fabian Williams's fortnightly management meetings that Mel had attended and she was finding it weird. It wasn't really a meeting at all. Just a dialogue between Fabian Williams and John MacDonald with the others spectating.

'I'm sorry, but I have a question.' She smiled at her colleagues, trying to bring them in. Anything to get a reaction. 'What about explaining to the workforce what happened? Everyone on the site knows that there's been an accident. It's much better to give them the facts than let the rumour machine run riot. Rumour always exaggerates things. And we ought to tell the press as well. They're always complaining they never get any official information. It's wrong that they pick up all their news by hanging around the bars in Wrath.'

Mel looked enquiringly at Fabian Williams. The room had gone quiet. She braced herself for a storm, remembering the Director's reaction the last time she'd expressed her ideas. But he seemed in a more reasonable mood today.

'Isn't that a little over the top? After all, as John's just explained, nothing serious has happened.'

'In that case there's nothing to be afraid of in admitting it. I don't see the problem. What does everyone else think?'

Dougie MacBain stirred uneasily beside her then cleared

52

his throat. 'I think you're right. We shouldn't carry on as if we've something to hide.'

MacDonald gave him a sharp look then shrugged. 'I think you're being naive. I've never seen the point of hanging out our dirty washing in public.'

'But times are changing. People want and expect freedom of information. There's legislation going through Parliament about open government at the moment. If Cape Wrath isn't more open we'll begin finding ourselves in court. It's much better to take the initiative ourselves,' Mel argued.

The circle of faces around her covered every expression from disapproval to dismay. James Everett looked particularly alarmed as he surreptitiously trimmed his already neat nails with some stainless-steel clippers.

'And I'd like to take things a step further, to be really proactive. I want to develop a range of scenarios based on potential incidents, setting out how we would handle the PR aspects. We shouldn't be dealing with each occurrence as a "one off". What we need are well-developed communication plans covering every eventuality and the bottom line must be that we will always make information available.'

'I think she has a point,' Docherty said slowly, a look of sly amusement on his rugged features.

An ally? No, he's hoping there'll be a row, Mel realized with a flash of insight. He's just trying to stir things up so that he can sit back and watch the sparks fly.

'Well, I don't object. I only hope you won't regret what you've started, Mel,' MacDonald said tartly. But there was a malicious gleam in his eye as if he too had understood exactly what Docherty was up to and had decided to spoil his fun. He and Docherty seemed slightly ill-matched sparring partners.

'So I can go ahead then?' Mel turned to Fabian Williams.

'Well, yes, I suppose so. But please make sure you keep John informed and that he approves the text of any press releases or staff announcements.'

'Of course.' She smiled at MacDonald who was studiously adjusting his cuff-links. 'I'll be happy to.'

'I hope I'm not disturbing you.'

Paul Carter straightened up and pushed a lock of shiny brown hair back from his round pleasant face. He was the image of Richard Crompton's *Just William*, grown up; even his tie was askew. 'You're not disturbing me at all, Mel. I was just packing up.'

'Are you moving offices?'

'No. I'm moving from Cape Wrath. I've resigned.'

'I'm sorry, I didn't know—'

'There's nothing dramatic about it. I just decided it was time to move on. I'm going to a Government research laboratory down south. There's no media angle – sit down, please.'

Mel moved a pile of papers from a chair and and watched him continue to stow things into two orange plastic crates. 'Would you mind if I asked you something?'

'Sure. What do you want to know?'

'Look, I'm just playing devil's advocate, but what would you say if I asked whether Cape Wrath was safe?' The question had been plaguing her ever since the meeting about the spilling of the radioactive effluent. Paul had looked distinctly uneasy about something.

'I'd say it wasn't unsafe.' He gave her a searching look before turning back to his crates.

'I'm not sure you've answered my question. Is "not unsafe" the same as "safe"?'

Paul turned to face her again. 'If you really want to know – and this is off the record – the safety culture here's not right. There are too many commercial pressures, too many contract staff to supervise and that leads to people taking short cuts. The right systems are in place but people don't always do what they're supposed to. That's why we've had so many incidents. They work round the system rather than within it.'

'How about low morale? How does that affect safety?'

'Low morale doesn't help, of course. Most people don't feel they've got a stake in what happens here – and it shows.'

'Does that go for you as well? Is that why you're leaving?'

'Me?' he paused and then said half-defiantly and half-embarrassed, 'I'm getting out while the going's good.'

The long piercing wolf-whistle made her jump. Mel spun around. A group of plant workers in blue overalls were sprawled on the grass. They were too far away for her to be able to read their expressions but she sensed them laughing at her. It was hard not to feel self-conscious as she walked down the tarmac path to the canteen. She made a mental note to ask Jock Maitland whether the plant had an equal opportunities policy; the answer was probably no, if the girlie calendars in the reprocessing plant were anything to go by.

But it wasn't the whistle which annoyed her really. It was the fact that she didn't seem to be able to establish any genuine contact with anyone. Fabian Williams didn't really want to know. John MacDonald merely tolerated her. He wasn't actively hostile anymore, just very dismissive. Docherty was so laid back it was unreal. And the other managers seemed to shy away from her. Jock ought to be an ally and she'd tried to engage Janice Griffiths about developing the site's IT systems. Electronic notice boards would make a big difference to employee communications, but no one seemed interested in doing anything new. Yet, without their help it was impossible to get to the wider workforce – or was it?

She opened the door into the canteen and joined the line at the counter, lost in thought. There might be a way she could get employees interested, if only she could convince them they'd benefit – the good old 'witfm' factor: 'what's in it for me?'

'What would you like my dear?' The kindly-looking woman behind the counter had to ask her twice.

55

'Sorry. Chicken salad sandwich and a Diet Coke, please.'

Mel carried her tray over to a table by the window where a group of people were laughing and talking. As she sat down they fell silent.

'Hello, I'm Mel Rogers, the new PR Manager,' she said brightly, feeling like the Avon lady. They nodded, muttered something polite then began to gather up their plates. It wasn't long before she was alone.

How was it possible to feel so isolated on a site which employed 3,000 people? It must be something she was doing wrong. Was it the way she looked; the way she sounded? Perhaps it was because she worked for the Director? In the short time she'd been there she'd seen enough to know that Cape Wrath wasn't exactly a democracy. If anything, it seemed to belong to the nineteenth century, and a particularly unenlightened part of it at that.

Mel gazed out of the window at the defunct reactors twinkling in the sunlight. So this was where the great dream of unlimited energy had begun. Her father had told her about it. The best scientists in the world had flocked to Cape Wrath to work on the fast reactor programme – the reactors that would be able to breed their own nuclear fuel. No more worries about gas reserves or oil prices or wars in the Middle East, or even rising uranium prices.

Now the fruits of those labours were just sitting there like giant dinosaurs whose day was done. Their innards were being torn out and their spent fuel rods were being sent for processing in the plant. In a few years' time they'd be gone for ever. Maybe that was Cape Wrath's problem. It was still too enmeshed in its past to face up to its future.

'You look miserable. Your sandwich can't be that awful!'

Mel glanced up to find Ishbel pulling out a chair opposite her.

'I'm sorry. I guess I've just hit a bit of a low. I went to another of the Director's management meetings this morning and found it rather hard going.'

'What did you expect? That's not where the real business

gets done. It's just a cosmetic event to make Mr Williams feel he's in charge.'

'And he's not?'

'Of course not!' Ishbel gave a snort of laughter. 'Everyone knows he wouldn't recognize a beta ray if it came out of his backside. The scientists here run rings around him.'

'Why on earth was he put in charge?'

Ishbel shrugged and began attacking a pile of steaming lasagne. 'No one really knows. He used to be a senior civil servant in the Cabinet Office. Maybe he blotted his copybook and they sent him here. It's common knowledge he hates Wrath and he thinks the locals are savages. He only gets agitated if he thinks something's going wrong. Otherwise he takes no real interest. John MacDonald and his team are the ones who really run the plant.'

'And Sean Docherty?'

Ishbel coloured just a little and Mel smiled inwardly. She was getting the impression that Sean Docherty was the local Romeo.

'Sean gets involved when he wants to be.'

'You haven't answered my question.'

'I know!'

Mel couldn't help laughing. 'OK, let's get back to business. I have an idea I want to talk over with you.'

It was already half-past twelve. Where was everyone? Mel paced impatiently to the door and looked up and down the corridor outside. Was this yet another idea that was going to bite the dust? The trays of sandwiches arranged on the table under the window were still covered in clingfilm. Was there any point peeling it off?

She and Ishbel had worked so hard deciding what to say in the notices they'd pinned up around the site, inviting employees to come and talk through their concerns about Cape Wrath's image. Just how apathetic could people get?

Mel didn't know whether to laugh or cry. It was absurd

57

to have been recruited for a job that no one seemed to want her to do.

But she'd been over-pessimistic. They came in dribs and drabs, and by a quarter to one she had a group of about thirty mostly male employees sitting around the room munching sandwiches and crisps in a reserved silence. So, she might as well get started.

'I'm Mel Rogers, your new PR Manager, and I really want to thank you for coming along today. I'm new to everything here and I need to get to understand what you think and feel about so many things.' She swept the room with an encouraging smile which faltered as she took in the hostile expressions and negative body language of the group.

'For instance, I don't know what you think about communications at Cape Wrath. Do you get all the information you want from your managers? Do you think Cape Wrath gets a fair hearing in the outside world, and if not, what can we – all of us – do about it?'

Silence.

'If we can only work together, I think we can make real progress. Outsiders think our industry is dishonest. We need to prove it isn't by showing them that we have an open and honest culture. We need to demystify the science and get the true facts to the public so they can make up their own minds rationally instead of being swayed by prejudice.

'But I can't do this on my own. I must have your help. Without the support of the people who work here I can't achieve anything and I might just as well pack up and go home.'

'If I were you I'd do just that, lassie,' a deep voice cut in.

A large-framed man with straggling dark hair got to his feet. 'I don't know what kind of fairytales you believe in, but don't expect us to swallow them here! I've been a union man all my life, but there was a time when I believed in the management here. Not anymore! They'd sell their own pee if they thought anyone would buy it. We've got nothing left to look forward to but redundancies or being sold off to the highest bidder. So I'm not interested in being an ambassador for you or for Cape Wrath. You can do your own dirty work.'

With that he walked out of the room, leaving an embarrassed silence.

'Is that really how you feel?' Mel couldn't keep her bewilderment from her voice. How naive she'd been, and crass. Paul Carter had warned her what people thought but she'd ignored him, confident in her ability to win people round.

'There's no trust here anymore,' another man spoke up at last. 'What Malcolm said was right: we don't know where we are, so why should we care what the public think? It's all very well for you – you're just an outsider. If you don't like it, you can go back south and get another job. You've probably only come up here to make your CV look better – show what a tough wee girl you are by taking on Cape Wrath. But the rest of us – we belong to the community. We were born in Wrath. Our fathers worked at the plant in the days when it was something to be proud of. Ten thousand people were employed here. It brought prosperity to Wrath – schools, houses, new businesses. Now it's all turned sour. All we're doing is knocking things down and acting as the nuclear dustbin for the rest of the world.' He too got up and walked out.

'That's right,' another broke in. 'This place is just an embarrassment to the Government. They wish we didn't exist. Look at the Director they sent us! But in the meantime they'll milk us for everything they can get before they kick us out. So you tell us why we should give a toss!'

Before Mel could respond there was a general exodus. The notes she'd been going to distribute about setting up communication workshops and asking people to volunteer for media training or to go out into the community to talk about the plant's work fluttered from her hands. She didn't bother to retrieve them.

'You mustn't take it personally.'

A small elderly man in blue overalls with an engaging weather-beaten face was still hovering in the doorway. Surely she'd come across him before? Wasn't he one of the workers she'd met in the reprocessing plant on the day of the incident?

Mel managed a faint smile, grateful for any crumb of comfort. 'But what can I do?'

The man shrugged. 'Take Malcolm's advice. There's nothing for you here.'

'And just go? I've only been here for three weeks.'

'What d'you expect – a long service medal? You'd best leave us to fight our own battles here. You'll never understand what makes this place tick.'

'But I want to learn, I want to understand – so I can help. You're all so defensive.'

'That's because we're used to fighting our own battles.'

'But is there *nobody* in the management that you trust?'

'John MacDonald,' the man said without a moment's hesitation. 'He's the only one who's on our side.'

A stone path fringed with sweet-smelling aubrietia led up to the front door of the low granite house. The door was open and Mel could see into the cool dark interior. She paused on the threshold.

'Hello? Is anyone at home?' No answer. It seemed wrong to just walk in but there was no doorbell. Not even a knocker.

'I'm sorry. I was at the bottom of the garden feeding the rabbits. I didn't hear your car.'

Mel turned to find Sarah Grant with her auburn hair in a tangled cloud and buckets of lettuce leaves in both hands.

'I'm a bit early. I always allow too much time.'

They both hesitated for a moment, then Sarah said, 'I'll make us a cup of tea. Come inside.'

Mel followed her in. The house was small but very neat and tidy. Most of the ground floor had been knocked into one room with the kitchen at one end and the sitting area at the other. A pottery vase with an arrangement of teasels stood in the centre of a scrubbed pine table. Mel noticed other pots and vases dotted around. They were beautifully shaped in rich, dark hues, tempting her to run her hands over them. She reached out a finger to stroke the satin glaze of a plum-coloured dish filled with dried rose petals.

'You like my pottery?'

'Yours?'

'I took it up as a hobby a few years ago, it became my livelihood. It took me a bit of time to afford a kiln but I love it. It's very therapeutic.' Sarah pushed open a white-washed door that led off the kitchen. 'Here's where I work. Take a look.'

Mel wandered in. There was a very particular smell of wet clay that took her straight back to the days of child-hood. She remembered making little pots out of coiled ropes of clay. The room was lined with wooden shelves covered with pieces of pottery waiting to be painted and glazed – candlesticks, butter dishes, great, round fruit bowls. In one corner, high up under the ceiling, Mel noticed a row of little clay figures. Looking closer she saw that they were babies. They reminded her of the tiny statues in a cemetery she'd seen long ago in Japan when she'd accompanied her father to a conference. He'd explained how mothers who'd miscarried lit candles to effigies of their dead children.

Did those little figures have a similar meaning for Sarah? Did they remind her of the baby she'd lost? A shiver of feminine sympathy ran through her.

'Tea's ready. Let's take it into the garden.'

As they went outside again a blackbird burst into full-throated song, eyeing them beadily. 'That's what we call a "blackchock" here.' Sarah smiled gently. 'We're lucky to have them. After Chernobyl the birds turned white.'

Mel was glad to be outside in the sunlight. 'It's nice of you to let me come and see you.'

The other woman shrugged. 'I need to understand what's going on at the plant. That way I can oppose it more effectively.'

'That's what I really wanted to ask you. What *are* your concerns? I know you didn't believe me but I meant it when I said I'd try and give you any information I could.'

Sarah sipped her tea, her fine-boned face thoughtful and a little sad. 'I don't envy you your job,' she said after a while.

'Believe me, I don't envy me either,' Mel said lightly, but she knew the seriousness in her voice wasn't lost on the other woman.

'I have personal reasons for opposing what goes on at Cape Wrath, but that's not why I do it. I believe I have a responsibility to this community – *my* community – to tell them what's going on in their midst. I'm lucky. My livelihood doesn't depend on the plant so I can see things more objectively than many other people. I can speak out without fear of losing my job!'

'And what do you see?'

'I see an old plant with a bad safety record that's being allowed to take foreign fuel from overseas – fuel that no one else wants to deal with, that arrives in our harbour, is transported along our roads and when it's reprocessed produces radioactive discharges into our sea and our air. Do you think for one moment that a decrepit plant like this would be allowed to operate in England?'

Sarah's words reminded her of Hamish's. 'But the discharges are well within the authorized limits.'

'That's not the point. The point is, why should we take any extra risks? Radiation isn't safe. It isn't good for you, even in the smallest doses, whatever the scientists would like us to believe! And we're stuck with the resulting nuclear waste for ever.'

'No, we're not. It's only here for a while. It all goes back to the country it belongs to.'

'When, exactly?'

'The contracts say within twenty-five years at the latest.

62

But Cape Wrath have promised to return the waste as soon as it's practical.'

Sarah gave her a pitying glance. 'That's what they told you, is it? Ask them whether any waste has ever been returned. Ask them whether they even have the necessary facilities to package it properly so it can be sent back. They haven't. All I see is an ever-growing stockpile of nuclear waste that we'll never get rid of. Why should Scotland be the world's nuclear dustbin? Why should our environment suffer? Do you know that over the years Cape Wrath has been so careless with low-level waste that traces of radioactivity are even found in the local seagulls' droppings? And there's so much radioactivity on their feathers and in their bodies that dead birds should be classed as low-level waste themselves? How does all that square with sustainable development? Go and ask them about some of these things, and if you can come back with some convincing answers, maybe I'll listen to you . . .'

'Well, and what can I do for you?' Fabian Williams leaned across his desk and smiled at his PR Manager. His Crusader research was making excellent progress, his tickets for his next research trip to Syria had just arrived, there'd been no major crises at Cape Wrath and Christine was staying with friends for Wimbledon. Overall he was content with life and in a benign frame of mind.

'I need to discuss some issues with you.' Mel paused. It wasn't easy to put this diplomatically.

'From what I've seen so far, morale at Cape Wrath is terrible. I've tried to talk to employees, but when I do manage to make contact, all I hear is that they think that management's trying to sell them down the river. I wanted to be able to use them as ambassadors for the plant, but there's no way until we can get them to see things more positively. They seem to feel that senior management is remote from them and just isn't interested. Perhaps if you could spend more time going around the plant talking to people . . .'

The expression of alarm on his face was unmistakable. Cape Wrath could sink into the sea like Atlantis before Fabian Williams went on walkabout.

'Miss Rogers, if you're concerned about employee morale I suggest you take it up with Jock Maitland and his team. It's their responsibility to get a handle on these things.'

'But if you could only—'

'That's not my role. My job is to represent Cape Wrath in the local community and to deal with our colleagues in Whitehall. Was there anything else?'

His smile was less welcoming now but Mel decided to press on. Sarah Grant's comments had been nagging away inside her and she needed some answers.

'The local environmentalists are particularly concerned about our overseas reprocessing work. They simply don't believe we have either the will or the capability to send nuclear waste back to the country of origin. I need facts and figures about any waste we've already returned, about the state of our waste packaging facilities so that I can—'

'You'll have to talk to John MacDonald and his people about that one, but there's no problem. Our contracts give us twenty-five years to sort it out.'

'Yes, but we have an obligation to get rid of it as soon as we can. What are we actually doing about it?'

'Miss Rogers, please, there's no need to hector me. You're beginning to sound like an environmentalist your-self. I've told you, you need to talk to the technical people about it. Now, I'm glad you've come to see me today. There's something rather important we need to discuss.'

Meaning that what I've raised is unimportant, Mel thought wryly. 'Yes?' She tried to sound interested.

'Down on the foreshore we have a rather delicate and important task. As you know, we are fortunate to have on the western edge of our site the remains of a medieval castle. It dates from the fourteenth century and has one of the best-preserved keeps in the Highlands. Historic

Scotland want to take it over and open it to the public. But first it needs to be decontaminated. It seems that a number of years ago, some caesium and strontium pollution was accidentally caused by discharge experiments. Some of it found its way into the sand under the castle's foundations. It is essential that we devote resources now to cleaning it up and letting people in to discover something of their history.'

'Is that a problem?'

'In a sense, yes. We haven't budgeted for a task of these dimensions in this financial year. Some of our less sophisticated colleagues think it's not worth the effort to decontaminate the castle while keeping it standing. They would prefer simply to bulldoze the site and remove the contaminated soil. And I'm sorry to say that some of my colleagues in the Treasury incline to a similar view. We may have a battle on our hands to preserve the archaeological value of the site.'

'A battle?'

'Yes. I do not intend to let the Philistines win the day, but I will need your help. Get the papers interested in the castle. Give it some "profile" − isn't that what you PR people call it? Then Government will have to find the money to preserve it or face a public outcry. And it will be excellent PR for Cape Wrath. It will make us look caring and responsible custodians of the environment, past and present. Now tell me what you think you can do . . .'

And Fabian Williams leant towards her, his face suddenly alight with enthusiasm. It was depressing to realize that nothing she had said earlier had made the slightest impression on him.

The music was wonderful. It made her want to jump to her feet and dance and dance. She'd surprised herself by deciding to go to the *ceilidh*. But if she spent many more evenings cooped up in her hotel room with its rickety furniture, temperamental shower and faded tartan carpet she'd go crazy! The posters outside Wrath's elegant Victorian town hall had caught her eye earlier in the evening, and now here she was.

The band were playing on a raised platform at the far end of the room. Through the smoky atmosphere she watched the dancers reeling and whooping. The good humour was infectious and she felt her spirits lighten. It was odd, but ever since she'd arrived in Wrath she'd felt oppressed by something. Perhaps 'foreboding' was too strong a word for it, but everything around her had seemed a bit tarnished. She'd had the sensation that she was looking at old photographs whose edges were beginning to darken and curl.

'Can I get you a drink?' Sean Docherty's voice snapped her out of her private thoughts.

'Sean! I didn't see you there. Yes, that would be nice. What do people drink at *ceilidhs*?'

'Whisky or beer maybe. Let me get you one of the local malts to try.'

Without waiting for her answer he shouldered his way to the bar and was back by her side within minutes.

'See what you make of that. The Gaelic name translates as "tears of the clans".'

'That's a sad name.'

'People don't forget the past around here, that's for sure. The guy who founded the distillery – Angus Fraser – was a grandson of a local crofter who was evicted during the Highland clearances, went to America and made his fortune. But he never forgot Scotland and his grandson returned here, bought an estate and started the distillery. They only make about a thousand bottles a year. What do you think?'

Mel sipped the spicy, peaty golden liquid. Its honeyed scent reminded her a little of the Indian whisky she used to drink long ago in Tenango. 'It's delicious,' she said quickly, blotting out pictures that were beginning to take substance inside her head, like a genie coming out of a bottle.

Then: 'What brings you here?' Mel asked curiously.

'Somehow I hadn't imagined that this would be your kind of thing.'

Sean shrugged broad shoulders. 'I could say the same to you.'

'In my case it's easy. I get fed up of hanging around the hotel in the evenings. If I go and sit in the hotel bar, men try to pick me up — particularly oil workers who've just come ashore and haven't seen a woman in months. It's quite sad. In a way, I feel sorry for them.'

'Not too sorry, I hope. Come on, let's dance.'

Before she realized what was happening, Docherty had whirled her into a wild reel. She found herself advancing, retreating, crossing hands and spinning round with the best of them, laughing and gasping for breath. Whenever she was about to take a wrong step Docherty was there to push her in the right direction. She knew he was enjoying watching her have a good time. The room went round like a kaleidoscope until at last the fiddlers stopped.

'Let's sit down for a bit.' Docherty led the way to a small table in the far corner of the room. 'More whisky?'

'No, thanks. Just some water.'

He returned with a large bottle of sparkling Highland mineral water and two glasses. 'Here.' He handed her a brimming tumbler. 'I haven't seen you look so happy since you arrived — it suits you.' His eyes ran approvingly over her neat body in jeans and silk shirt, her flushed face and dishevelled hair.

Mel knew the look so well. A woman's man. But there was nothing threatening about it. Docherty's admiration had a detached quality as if he was looking at a painting or a sculpture, and God knows it was nice to be reminded that she was an attractive woman.

'I really enjoyed that,' she admitted. 'It's the first time I've felt really alive since I got here.'

'Bad as that, is it?' Docherty's deep voice was amused.

'Yes, I think it is.'

Maybe it was the whisky or the unexpected sense of

intimacy between them, but it all came flooding out before she could help herself.

'I don't know why but I don't seem to be able to make any impression on anything. The employees at Cape Wrath don't want to talk to me. The managers don't seem to want me to do anything, except just to be there in case the shit hits the fan. I can't get answers to any of my questions.'

'Like what?'

'Well, like this reprocessing business. Sarah Grant says we've never returned any nuclear waste anywhere and that we don't even have the ability to because we don't have a waste packaging plant. But when I ask John MacDonald, he just bites my head off for talking to the environmentalists. He barks at me that reprocessing is a legitimate part of Cape Wrath's business and that it's done with full Government approval. End of story: i.e. nobody outside the plant has any right to question it!'

'Perhaps he's right.'

'Of course he isn't. At the very least the plant has a responsibility to talk to people in the local community and respond to their concerns. He carries on as if Cape Wrath is in a parallel universe.'

'Do I take it you don't care for John?'

'That's not the point. It doesn't matter a toss what I feel about him. It's just that no one will help me.' Not even you, you sod, she thought, looking at Docherty's handsome, slightly wrecked face.

'What did you expect? You're almost at the end of the universe here.'

'That's what everybody keeps saying, but it's not true. Why does this place have to be so special and so different?'

'Because it just is. Stay here a little longer and you'll understand.'

'You mean I'll get like you – apathetic. Just content to sit on the sidelines and laugh.'

The blue eyes opposite her hardened. She wished the words unsaid as soon as they were out of her mouth.

'So that's what you think of me is it? Cape Wrath's professional cynic? Well, in a way you're right. I don't give a damn about the job. I negotiate reprocessing contracts for the plant with foreign reactor owners, but frankly I find it too boring to even discuss. But that doesn't mean there aren't things in my life I care about. Just that my priorities are different. You should be a bit more subtle in your rather clinical analyses of people and less two-dimensional. Then you mightn't end up so wide of the mark.'

'I'm sorry, I didn't mean to—'

'I know. And with respect that's exactly your problem. Good night.'

He stood up abruptly and vanished into the crowded room. The music began again, lively, beguiling, but it no longer made Mel's feet tap. Oh shit, she thought wearily, Shit, shit, shit.

The coastal path wound along the clifftops. With Cape Wrath behind her the scenery was breathtaking. Mel walked quickly, loving the feel of the sun on her face. Her row with Docherty didn't seem to matter so much now, though she'd spent most of the weekend brooding over it. What had he meant when he called her 'clinical'? She was just trying to be logical about things, to make sense of the situation. Well, it was just too bad if she'd offended him. He'd goaded her to it.

The dense, honeyed smell of gorse hung in the air. Bees were working busily to gather in their harvest of nectar, and for a moment she could picture her father in his large garden in Cambridge, moving slowly and contentedly in his bee-keeper's outfit between the hives. Bees had had an almost mystical quality for him, and she could hear his voice: 'Raw honey is the only food known to man which possesses immortality; all other foods ferment and decay.' And he'd told her something else as well – how bees had sensed the contamination from the Chernobyl nuclear accident before the humans, and had hidden in their hives. How funny that she should remember that now.

The cliff path was skirting a deserted cove. Far below, a lump of driftwood had been washed high up on the very white sand. It lay bleached by sun and pounded by the sea like the bone of some giant animal. And there was another piece, some fifty yards further along, just at the water's edge, half in and half out. It was a less angular shape and there was something soft at one end of it that rose and fell with the swell – fronds of seaweed, perhaps?

Some slabs of rock shelved gently down to the cove. It was tempting to climb down and look at the driftwood and to spend some time poking about in the rockpools for crabs and shrimps as she had on childhood family holidays on Skye before her mother had left. Mel scrambled down onto the sand, grazing hands and elbows. Sitting on a rock she kicked off her shoes, peeled off her socks and walked slowly into the sea. The water was as cold as she remembered and she gasped as she began to splash her way along the shore towards the gently floating object.

She'd been wrong. As she got closer she could see that it wasn't a piece of wood at all. It was something softer-looking. The sail of a boat perhaps, washed overboard during a storm? Or maybe a dead sheep? Yes, it had a bloated look as if it might be some dead animal. To think she'd climbed all the way down to look at a drowned sheep!

Curiosity drew her on, but even while her brain was still analysing the possibilities there was a sickening moment of realization. She knew what it was. The waves gradually coaxed the object over and she saw the body with its swollen face, sightless eyes and grotesquely gaping throat turn as if in slow motion towards her. What she'd mistaken for seaweed was long dark hair mingling with the foam.

Mel fell to her knees in the surf as the awful thing rotated slowly in front of her, and covered her face with her hands.

Chapter Five

The memory of that smell of beer and sweat and marijuana and fresh red blood made her want to throw up. Their dead faces looked at her reproachfully. Their violated throats yawned at her – Daniel and Simon and now this new, unknown victim. She scrambled and clawed her way up the rocks, gasping with fear and effort. Everything she'd tried to forget about that dreadful night in Guatemala eight years ago burst over her like a shell on a battlefield, invading her senses.

Thank goodness, she was back on the coastal path. Sanity returned as she paused a moment to check her bearings. Yes, there it was, that cluster of towers and domes. For the first time since she'd arrived, Cape Wrath spelled security and safety. She began to run, wincing as her bare feet struck sharp stones but not really caring. Her breath tore at her lungs, which felt as if they were on fire. Good God, what was happening to her? It was like a nightmare in which you know you're being pursued, but the faster you run, the more you seem to stand still. The horror was behind her but still so close . . .

Her foot caught in a network of roots and she was flung sprawling to the ground. A verse from *The Ancient Mariner* came into her mind as she lay there stunned, earth in her mouth, her tongue tasting of blood:

> 'Like one that on a lonesome road
> Doth walk in fear and dread,

And having once turned round walks on,
And no more turns his head;
Because he knows, a frightful fiend
Doth close behind him tread.'

Don't let it get me, Daddy, she prayed. Don't let it get me.

'Don't be silly Melissa, there are no such things as ghosts.' Her father's voice was in her ears – cool, assured, logical. 'You're being hysterical, just like your mother.'

Mel struggled to her feet again and a sharp, hot pain pierced her ankle. But she could still hobble and she didn't care what it cost her. The path curved sharply around some gorse bushes and then broadened out. Ahead of her something gleamed blue in the sunlight – her car. Oh God, where were the keys? Frantically she felt in her pockets and her fingers closed over cold metal.

Yes, yes. Almost there. A noise roared in her ears but she ignored it as she staggered towards the MGF. There was a flash of dark green. She dived to avoid it, flinging herself to one side and curling instinctively into a ball, hands cradling her head.

I can't breathe. I can't breathe. She tried to inhale but couldn't. She felt herself being dragged to her feet and then a sharp blow between her shoulder blades. Suddenly her breath was coming again in painful spasms.

'Come on, baby, you're OK. Keep calm and try to take deep breaths.'

'You try!' she wanted to yell back only she couldn't. She knew she was hyper-ventilating and it felt like someone was stabbing her lungs with a needle. Her eyes were closed but her world wasn't black: a mass of stars exploded against her eyelids. 'Just imagine – there are ten billion, billion stars in the universe.' Her father's voice murmured in her ears. Well, it seemed as if she was seeing them all.

Something was being pushed against her dry lips. 'Drink this,' said an authoritative voice. She tried to obey and immediately choked, but a little water managed to get down her throat. Gradually the chaos inside her quietened. Her breathing slowed and cautiously she opened her eyes. A blond man was holding her by the shoulders. His eyes, behind steel-rimmed glasses, searched hers. Instinctively she lowered her gaze to his sunburned throat. It was still intact. The bogeyman hadn't got to him yet. She began to laugh but her jerking, mirthless giggles turned quickly to tears.

The man held her to him and she felt him caress her hair, making soothing noises to her as if she were a child.

'It's OK. It's going to be OK. You're all right.'

And then it dawned on her. He thought she was traumatized because he'd nearly run her over. That was just a detail.

'Please,' she said, grabbing at the lapels of his cotton jacket. 'Down there, on the beach in the waves, there's something awful – *dead* . . .'

Someone had wrapped a blanket around her; even so she was shivering. Police lights flashed; a group of men went past carrying something on a covered stretcher. When Mel thought about what was lying underneath, a bitter fluid filled her mouth.

'Here, drink this. It's tea with a lot of sugar in it. You're in shock.'

'Thank you,' Mel responded numbly, then looked up to see who had handed it to her. It was the blond man. Vaguely she realized he was speaking with an American accent.

'I guess we'd better get you to a doctor,' he said gently, kneeling beside her.

'No, I'm all right, really. It was just the shock.'

'Shock must be taken seriously, believe me – I know. Come on, get in the jeep and I'll take you to Anderson Base. They've got a first-class medical team there.'

"But what about the police? Don't they want a statement?'

'That can wait. I'll tell them where I'm taking you. They can contact you later.'

73

Mel watched him walk over to a police sergeant and explain. The sergeant looked across at Mel and nodded his agreement. A moment later they were heading back down the bumpy track to the main road into Wrath.

'I guess it's a bit late for introductions but my name's Schultz, Commander Tom Schultz, US Navy.'

'I'm Mel Rogers. I work at Cape Wrath.' She winced as she spoke, and putting fingertips to her face felt the outline of a huge bruise that was swelling up on one cheek where she'd caught it as she fell. Great, she thought, just great. A deadly weariness was stealing through her and by the time they drove through the gates of Anderson Base in Tom Schultz's dark green jeep her head was against his shoulder and she was fast asleep.

'If you'd just like to check through your statement and sign it, Miss Rogers, you can go.'

Inspector Murray of the Highland Constabulary handed Mel a piece of paper. As her eyes quickly scanned it she tried to remain detached. What had happened had happened. She must get over it.

'That seems fine,' she said briskly, and wrote her name at the bottom.

'If you'd like to receive counselling it can be arranged. Situations like this are very traumatic. You may believe you're OK but it can take a bit of time to recover.'

Tell me about it, Mel thought involuntarily, but he meant it kindly. 'Thanks, I'll consider it,' she said. 'Just now I want to get back to work.'

'We think we know who the victim was,' Inspector Murray volunteered as she was halfway to the door.

She turned and gazed at him wide-eyed. It was hard to equate that swollen, hideous thing with a human being, and yet once it had lived and breathed, just like her.

'Who was it then?' she whispered.

'A young Pakistani waiter from Khan's Curry House who disappeared a few weeks ago. He was lodging with

74

Mrs McKeague down in the town and didn't come home one Saturday evening. When he didn't turn up for work either, the proprietor of the restaurant reported him missing.'

'But who would want to kill someone like him in a little place like Wrath? Unless I mean, was it a racial attack?'

'We're still waiting for the pathologist's report but it looks to me like a professional job. If I had to put my money on it I'd say it was a drugs-related killing.'

'Drugs – here?' A coldness began to creep through her. She thought she'd left all that behind her in Guatemala, but there seemed to be an awful symmetry at work. 'You're not serious?' she stammered.

Murray shrugged. 'Why not? You can't get much remoter than this stretch of coastline. With all its sea lochs and caves it's a perfect place to land consignments. Just last month we got a tip-off from Interpol and intercepted a fishing vessel carrying two million pounds' worth of cannabis.'

'So you arrested them?'

'No, we only caught a couple of sprats who are too frightened to tell what they know. The big fish got away in a speedboat. We've known for a while that there are at least two rival gangs operating in this area – one Chechen and one from the Middle East.'

'And the man whose body I found?'

'Who can say? Maybe he wanted more than his fair share. Maybe he was killed in revenge for something.'

Murray was in a talkative mood but somehow Mel felt she'd heard enough. There were too many echoes from the past. She closed the door quickly behind her and hurried down the corridor, head bent.

'Thank you for coming to see me.'

'That's no problem, my afternoon's quite clear.' Mel sat down on a hard bleached wood chair. James Everett's office was a peculiarly antiseptic and clinical-looking room. There wasn't a paper out of place. Even his computer mouse was perfectly positioned bang in the middle of the mat. The only picture was a grey-framed painting of two grey fish on a plate against a white background, neatly signed *Scott*. Everett himself was as fastidiously dressed as usual.

'It must have been very traumatic for you, finding a body like that,' he began. 'I thought it might help you to talk about it a bit.'

Mel looked at him in surprise. He was the last person she would have contemplated confiding in about her personal feelings. 'Thanks but I don't think—'

'I know how difficult it can be to cope with this kind of situation,' Everett cut in. 'I am aware of what it's like to go through trauma – real trauma. Perhaps there's something I should explain to you ... then you'll understand.' He looked at her from under straight, fair eyebrows, as if calculating how much to tell her.

'When I first came to Cape Wrath four years ago I was in ...well, I suppose you could say I was in a bit of a mess. I was still suffering from recurring nightmares – "post traumatic stress disorder" the doctors called it – because of something that had happened to me.' He paused to look with expressionless eyes out of the window which faced the reprocessing plant. The building's mirror-glass panels reflected a bank of swollen purple clouds sweeping in from the Orkneys.

'I'm sorry,' he said, 'I'm not being very coherent, am I? I used to be a soldier – a major in the Special Air Service. It was what I'd always wanted, ever since I was a boy. When the Gulf War came it seemed like a godsend. Here was a real opportunity to show I was made of the right stuff.'

'And what happened?' Mel asked quietly.

'I was helicoptered into north-western Iraq with a squad. Our job was to seek out and destroy mobile Scud missile launchers in the desert. Saddam was firing scuds on Tel Aviv and Haifa to provoke Israel into joining the conflict. Of course, it was vital to the stability of the allied coalition and the whole of the Middle East to keep them out of it.'

Everett was speaking rapidly and matter-of-factly as if he were conducting an official briefing,

'Everything went wrong from the start. We overshot our target and landed in a minefield. The others were blown to bits before we realized the danger. I was luckier. I managed to get clear of it but by then they knew we were there – my comrades weren't easy to miss, splattered to kingdom come – and I was captured. They took me back to Baghdad and put me in a cell in a commando camp on my own.'

Everett stood up and turned his back on her. 'It was like descending into hell. I could hear the screams of men I couldn't see. I could only imagine what was happening to them. I waited for them to come for me. The Iraqis haven't signed the Hague and Geneva Conventions on the treatment of prisoners of war and they have a reputation for being inventive. I tried to prepare myself – number, rank, name, date of birth. That's all I was supposed to give them.

'But they didn't come for me. At all hours of the day and night I heard screams and feet going by and waited for them to stop outside my door. I'd been trained how to cope under torture. But I hadn't been trained to cope with this . . . No human contact, nothing. Just a bowl of food and a jug of stinking water pushed through a flap by hands I couldn't see. They let my fear grow greater and greater until they must have been able to smell it.'

After a moment he turned back to her. His face had gone very white.

'They just left me in my cell – my stinking fetid cell – wallowing in my own filth. Turning into shit myself. Just rotting. In a matter of weeks they'd made me into an animal. I'd have done anything to get out of there.'

He shuddered, then: 'In fact, all they wanted of me was to video me holding up a placard denouncing Britain and America. That's why they hadn't beaten me up – so I'd look OK on camera. I'm not proud of myself, but I did it. Anything to keep my sanity and survive. I can remember the studio, and the bright lights in my eyes and how the only thing I could think of was that they had let me have a shower and given me a clean set of clothes. It took me a little time to realize the consequences – I'd blown my cover. I'd also given the SAS a rather public demonstration that I wasn't made of "the right stuff" after all.' Everett gave a twisted smile.

'So what happened to you?'

'I was released when the war ended. The SAS gave me a short stint as a trainer at Hereford while I was being debriefed and to help rehabilitate me. But after six months I was out. A friend got me a job as an adviser to the security forces in Northern Ireland, but it was still too stressful. The nightmares just got worse and worse. So I came here to a nice desk job – checking people's security records and advising on the physical security of the site. But I still get nightmares. When the images in your mind won't go away, it's important to be able to go to someone who understands – so if you ever want to talk . . .'

'That's kind of you. Thank you.'

As she left his office it struck Mel that Everett was the one who really needed to talk, not her . . .

'What do you think, Mel? Should Cape Wrath submit written evidence to the Select Committee Inquiry into the impact of the nuclear industry on the environment?' Everyone's face turned towards her but she was so surprised that the Director had called her by her first name that it was a second or two before she answered. They all seemed to be making special efforts to be kind to her after her discovery of the body.

'I think we should accept the invitation. The Parliamentary Select Committee on the Environment is very influential and it's an honour to be asked. Crudely, the opportunity is greater than the risk.' She looked around the room, glad to see that she was holding their attention.

'If we're confident about our environmental performance, we could do ourselves some good,' she said enthusiastically. 'It's a chance to explain to MPs what we actually do and why. It might even help to reduce the number of hostile Parliamentary Questions about Cape Wrath. Equally, if we don't give evidence our opponents will say it's because we're secretive and we've got something to hide. All the other players in the industry will be getting in on the act. The nuclear power generators will be making a big play of their contribution towards reducing CO_2 emissions. We need to show Cape Wrath's commitment to the environment.'

'John?' Fabian turned to MacDonald who was looking pensive.

'I'm not sure. These House of Commons Committees can turn into a bit of a circus. If we send written evidence they'll probably summon us to attend a hearing to give oral evidence.'

'But we can prepare for that. We can draw up sample questions and answers and put the team through some intensive training.' Mel leant forward, hands clasped on the desk.

MacDonald sighed. 'You're probably right. I'll get one of my people working on a draft submission.' He looked at her. 'We'll need your help to make sure the key messages come through strongly and simply enough. We don't want to blind the Committee with scientific jargon. After all, they're only politicians.' He gave her a wry smile.

Mel sat back and felt a glow of satisfaction. It had taken time but it looked as if they were beginning to accept her at last. Perhaps her vulnerability and shock after finding the body had roused protective instincts, pulling her within their closed ranks. Perhaps the trauma was actually helping her to find acceptance. Would Sean react the same way when he came back from the business trip which had taken him to the Far East? She hoped so.

Her mind was far, far away and she didn't see him until he was right in front of her.

79

'You're a hard lady to get hold of.'

'I'm sorry. I've been pretty busy the last few days.'

'I just wanted to check you were OK.' Tom Schultz pulled out a chair and sat astride it, resting his chin on the back.

Mel coloured and stared into her drink. This was embarrassing. He'd rung her several times and she'd ignored the calls, not even telling Ishbel why. She wasn't sure she knew the reason herself.

'I should explain . . .' she began awkwardly.

'No reason to.'

'I should at least say thank you.'

'For what? Nearly flattening you under my jeep?'

She smiled. 'For calming me down and taking me to Anderson Base. I'm afraid I went a little crazy.'

'Shock has that effect. It shuts down the brain: you can't think rationally.'

'I wasn't thinking at all.'

'You certainly came down that path like a bat out of hell!'

'I was afraid . . .' And I'm still afraid, she thought to herself . . . I don't know why or of what, but it's there all the time . . . She bit her lip and looked down at her half-empty glass of tomato juice. She was clenching it hard with both hands and her knuckles were white.

'It's certainly shocked this sleepy little community,' Schultz said. 'It's the first time they've had a murder in five years. Where I was born we have a homicide every five minutes. I guess we kind of take it for granted.'

'Where are you from?' Mel asked.

'Chicago.'

'How long have you been in Wrath?' She was genuinely interested.

'Nearly three years. I have another nine months to go at Anderson Base on my current assignment. I'm an engineer. Nuclear submarines are my special babies. I always wanted to work with subs, even when I was just a kid.'

'What's the appeal?'

'I guess I just like machines.' His eyes, very blue behind his steel-rimmed spectacles, held hers for a moment. Then: 'I'd like to take you out on a date.'

'No! I mean, I'm really busy right now.'

Why had she said that? Even in the dim light of the hotel bar Mel could see how good-looking he was in a clean-cut all-American way. Short fair hair, a lean, muscular body, very white teeth. His detachment was attractive in her current frame of mind. Commander Tom Schultz didn't seem like a man who carried a lot of emotional baggage around with him.

But it was no good. He reminded her of what she wanted to forget. She wasn't ready. Not yet.

A sixth sense told her they were being watched. She looked up to catch Hamish Cameron's appraising glare. He was over at the bar buying what looked like a bottle of whisky which he rammed carelessly in his jacket pocket. He smiled briefly at her before turning to leave.

She turned back to Tom. How could she explain? But it seemed she didn't need to.

'Maybe another time then. Take care, Mel.' His smile was friendly and open, no resentment. Then he too was gone. Mel drained her tomato juice and smiled ruefully into her empty glass.

'Two, four, six, eight, Wrath says no to nuclear waste!'

What on earth? Mel opened bewildered eyes. For a moment she was disorientated. Surely it wasn't time to get up yet? Then she heard the chanting again.

She looked sleepily out of her hotel window into the pale pre-dawn haze. At this time of year it never seemed to get dark. Even though it was 4 a.m. there was enough light to see clearly down the narrow street below. Fergus Brown, pale dreadlocks bobbing, was running in the direction of the harbour, cameras hanging around his neck like garlands. At the same time he was talking urgently into a mobile phone.

A crescendo of voices rose again, coming from the harbour. It didn't take a genius to work out what was going on. The Malaysian nuclear fuel shipment was coming in for reprocessing.

Mel flung on jeans and a sweatshirt, put in her contact lenses and tugged a brush through her tangled hair as she tried to puzzle it out. Everyone knew the ship had been en route from Malacca for twelve weeks, but the precise arrival time had been kept quiet for security reasons. Even she hadn't known exactly when it was due. Only someone from the plant could have leaked it. But why?

She ran down the road towards the harbour, catching her foot against an empty milk bottle and smashing it to pieces. Although it was summer there was a nip in the early morning air. The chanting was getting on her nerves, making it difficult to think straight. Why couldn't people be a bit more rational about things? Cape Wrath had been reprocessing other countries' nuclear fuel for years.

Yes, there was the ship. The 5,000-tonne *Orchid* was nosing her way into Wrath Harbour and right into the middle of a protest demonstration. The cat-calls and shouts of derision escalated around her. Mel ducked and pushed her way through to get a better view.

The ship was coming in from the east, the sky behind her turning a glorious pale gold as the sun began its slow ascent. She could see a rectangular container covered with yellow and black radioactive symbols secured to the deck. The fuel was inside. Members of the crew were moving busily around it, loosening the steel hawsers so it could be hoisted onto the quayside. They were working frantically, aware of the need to be quick.

But the crowds were growing with every passing minute – people who had simply heard the noise and come out to investigate mingled with local activists. Some of them were still in their nightclothes, giving the scene a surreal quality. Sarah Grant was holding a megaphone, a striking figure with her pale face and flowing red hair. This time it was her demonstration and she didn't have to yield the stage to Earth Alliance. She stood on an upturned crate and began reading a statement out to the crowd. Mel caught the words 'Scotland' and 'nuclear dustbin' and noticed how the people around her had fallen silent.

She turned away to see the transporter lorry from Cape Wrath with its Nuclear Police escort lumbering down to the quayside. It was having difficulty getting through and Mel glimpsed the driver's pale, anxious face. This was such a closed community he probably knew every person pressing around him. The police were ordering people to stay back, but being ignored as the crowd tried to surge forward to see what was going on. At last the transporter managed to nudge its way through and draw up alongside the ship.

It shouldn't be long now. All they had to do was unfasten the container and load it on but the minutes passed and nothing seemed to be happening. Surely they should be lifting the flask off by now? What was wrong? If she could see a problem, so could everyone else. What a gift to the media!

And they were there, of course. The local press must have been among the first to be tipped off. Fergus Brown was in the thick of it now, snapping away with his camera. It wouldn't be long before the national press were on the scene. Bang on cue a helicopter wheeled overhead with a video camera mounted on the side. Welcome to breakfast TV. That was all they needed.

'Excuse me.' She tapped on the window of a Highland Constabulary vehicle which had pulled over, lights flashing, on the verge. A young constable got out.

'I'm Mel Rogers – I'm the PR Manager at Cape Wrath. I need to get down to the ship to find out what's going on.'

'You'd best stay out of the way. We've cordoned off the dock while they unload.'

'But I need to know what's happening – please?' Despising herself, Mel gave him her most winning smile and held out her pass. Reluctantly he forced a way for her through the restless crowds.

She made for a tall, familiar, sandy-haired figure in white overalls bearing the Cape Wrath logo. 'Dougie, what's going on?' Mel gasped, dishevelled and out of breath.

'We've got a hitch, I'm afraid.' Dougie MacBain gave her a strained smile. 'The metal clamps holding the container to the deck have warped and rusted while the vessel was at sea. We can't loosen them at the moment. I've telephoned to the plant for extra assistance. We need an electric hammer.'

'How long do you think it's going to take?' This wasn't exactly making Cape Wrath look like a slick operation, Mel thought wearily but she didn't let her frustration show. This wasn't Dougie's fault.

'It could take some hours.'

'I'll do what I can to keep the media off your back,' she promised.

It wasn't long before radio and TV journalists from Inverness and Glasgow began to arrive. The girl with the shaved head was there again. This time she was wearing a tight *Make Scotland Nuclear-Free* T-shirt, which clearly revealed she was bra-less beneath it, and posing for photographs with the *Orchid* behind her. It would make a powerful image. The fragile but sexy eco-warrior battling the evil czars of the nuclear industry. Mel could see the front pages now.

Hours passed and Mel lost count of the number of interviews she gave. At last, in the late afternoon, the canister was finally unloaded and the transporter rolled on its way up to Cape Wrath flanked by police vehicles. Some of the demonstrators followed in their cars, jeering and heckling, but the worst was over. Mel sat on the harbour wall and closed her eyes. It had been a long day.

'So much for your "open and honest" communications.'

Mel's eyes snapped open again. 'Sarah?'

'When you came to see me I almost started to believe

that you might be going to make a difference. At least that you were honest.'

'I hope I am honest.' Mel felt bewildered.

'In that case, why do you sneak consignments of nuclear fuel into Wrath in the middle of the night? In secret?'

'We don't. And it's *not* a secret. It's just that we don't publicize the detailed arrangements for security reasons. Just as a bank doesn't publicize when it's having cash delivered. We don't want terrorists turning up.'

'That's just playing with words. You know this is a dirty business and that you're turning Scotland into a nuclear dump simply to make money.'

'But it's not like that!' Mel jumped off the wall and faced Sarah Grant. 'We're *not* damaging the environment. The radioactive discharges from the Cape Wrath plant are well below the safety limits, and only a fraction of natural background radiation levels. Please, try to look at it rationally.'

'Tell that to the parents whose children are dying of leukaemia. Why do there have to be any discharges at all? Cape Wrath ought to be closed down now. If you don't agree you're as good as a murderer. Good heavens, you're a woman too. Don't you have feelings? How can you defend something so wrong?'

The older woman's eyes shone with tears. Mel had never seen her in such a highly charged emotional state. Her pain was almost tangible.

'Sarah . . . come away.' A young bearded man came up to her and put his arm around her shoulder. 'This isn't the best way.' He talked to her like an adult to an overwrought child.

Sarah bowed her head, then gave Mel a long, sad look. 'I meant what I said just now. Two years ago my friend's daughter died of leukaemia, here in Wrath. She was only six years old. We watched her turn from a happy healthy little girl into a ghost. And do you know what she loved most – playing on that damned polluted beach next to Cape Wrath! And my son might have lived if it hadn't been for

Cape Wrath. So I don't think I'm the one who should be apologizing, do you?'

Somehow she couldn't face going back to the hotel. At least not for a while. The raw emotion in Sarah Grant's eyes haunted her. So did the taunt: 'You're a woman too. Don't you have feelings?' Of course she did, of course she sympathized, but she tried not to let her emotions rule her.

At the far end of the breakwater she could see a tall figure in jeans and T-shirt. Hamish Cameron again. She was going to turn back before he saw her but she was too late. He glanced around.

'Were you at the demonstration? I didn't see you there,' she asked coolly.

'I was watching from afar. You don't seem to have convinced your public yet.'

'These things take time. But I admit it's our fault people don't understand what happens at the plant. We're just going to have to try harder – OK?'

'If at first you don't succeed try, try and try again, as Robert the Bruce once said.'

'Yes,' Mel said tautly.

'You look washed out. Come back to my house and I'll make you a cup of coffee. Best Colombian beans.'

Without waiting for a reply he turned and Mel found herself following. Her curiosity was roused. Somehow he didn't fit in with the rest of the scene in Wrath.

He wasn't quite the wild man she'd first thought. She could see that the long, thick hair was expertly cut. The T-shirt exposing his powerful arms and neck looked like Calvin Klein. His desert boots were an unusual, expensive-looking design. If Hamish Cameron was a rebel he was a designer one.

The granite house, part fortified dwelling, part castle, made Mel catch her breath. A rambling, romantic jumble of architectural styles, it stood on a piece of rising land west of the town. To one side a peat-coloured river flowed down to the sea. A gleaming navy-blue Range Rover was drawn up on the gravel drive and an elderly wolfhound was slumped beside it. As they approached, it raised its head and gave a welcoming bark.

'Shhhh, Wilf,' Hamish said softly, adding a few words in what Mel guessed was Gaelic. Wilf regarded him for a moment with reproachful eyes then slumped back, resting head on paws.

There was no sound except birdsong and not another house in sight. It was hard to believe they were just ten minutes' walk beyond Wrath.

'Come in.' Hamish pushed open the oak door he hadn't bothered to lock. It swung easily on great metal hinges. 'I'll get you that coffee.' He disappeared down a stone staircase.

The house was chaotic but as mysteriously charismatic as its owner. The ground floor consisted of one great chamber. Deep-hued Persian rugs were scattered over the floor, their dark blues and reds glowing richly against the rough flagstones. Above the fireplace a white marble Buddha reclined gracefully on one elbow, a necklace of old Chinese coins hanging from its neck. Tartan plaids were flung carelessly over old oak chests which gleamed with the dark silken patina of centuries. At the far end, under a stained-glass window, stood a long oak table with two huge pewter candlesticks encrusted with yellowing wax.

Although it had been a warm day, a wood and peat fire smouldering in the grate spiced the air. Mel breathed deeply and fought a temptation just to lie down in front of it and go to sleep. She seemed to have been on her feet for hours. The fragrant smell of coffee beans had never been more welcome.

Stifling a yawn she wandered down to the far end of the room. In one corner, to the side of the dining-room table, was an easel. An almost completed canvas rested on it. The light still streaming through the stained-glass window coloured it afresh but it was already dramatic, disturbing even. A turquoise sea smashed against mustard rocks under lowering purple skies. It was daubed rather than painted.

Mel caught her breath at a sudden noise. A haunting sound – she wasn't sure what it was at first but it sounded like saxophone and bagpipes – stole into the room. The notes seemed to hang in the air and entwine themselves around her like a siren song. The magic grew as a Celtic chant sung sweet and low fused with the melody that seemed to swell and fill the room. Sadness and beauty together. For some reason Sarah Grant's face floated before her once again.

Ringing footsteps announced Hamish's return. 'What do you think of the music?' He gave her a pottery mug brimming with black coffee and didn't ask whether she wanted milk.

'It took me by surprise, but it's beautiful.'

'The sound system is concealed. Hold this. I'm going outside for a pee.' He handed her his own mug. 'But don't worry – there's a toilet upstairs if you want one.' Was he implying that she was bourgeois and inhibited and he wasn't? If he had any idea how she'd once lived! She grinned inwardly.

Mel continued her exploration of the room and was drawn by a picture she hadn't noticed before, carefully hung in the shadows away from the light. It needed cleaning but she could see that it was a portrait of a clan chieftain. He was wearing a bonnet with a feather. In one hand was the traditional metal-studded target and in the other a great claymore. The face that looked back at her across the centuries was strong-featured with a defiant, arrogant expression. Who was it? Someone famous? There was no clue on the frame so she gently pulled it a little way from the wall, peering to see whether there was a label on the back. There wasn't. Instead there was a white sticker announcing that the painting had been lot 101 in a recent fine-art auction at Christie's in Edinburgh.

But what made her gasp with surprise was the fact that there was a safe behind it, carefully cut into the stonework. Why should a man who seemed so casual about his possessions and who left his house unlocked want such a sophisticated security device?

At the sound of footsteps scrunching on gravel she released the picture and hastily stepped back from it.

'Come and sit down.' Hamish arranged his long limbs in a wing armchair by the fireplace, leaving the sofa for Mel. She lay back against a soft Pashmina shawl woven in rich, bright colours. It was so soft she ran her fingertips over it and held it against her face. Then she caught it – that once familiar smell. The gentle aroma of cannabis was unmistakable. She hadn't smoked it since that night by the lake in Tenango. With it came a yearning for those simple days working with Daniel. But she mustn't go down that track. Painfully she pulled herself back to the present.

'What do you do? How do you make a living?' she asked, and watched him over the rim of her coffee mug.

'I don't do anything much.'

'You must do something. Are you an artist?'

'I paint a bit. But I'd rather talk about you.'

'What do you want to know?'

'Why you want to work at Cape Wrath would be a good start.'

'Is this an interrogation?' she asked lightly, but tension began to coil up inside her. She was so tired . . . she couldn't cope with this....

'I'm just curious what brought you here. Tell me to mind my own business if you want to, but somehow you don't quite fit.'

Mel looked at him. How strange. That was exactly what she'd been thinking about him. 'I wanted to work at Cape Wrath because I believe in science and I think it gets a raw deal,' she told him flatly. 'People get emotive and irrational about issues they can't be bothered to try and understand.'

'Like Sarah Grant?'

This was a high price to pay for a cup of coffee. 'No, not like Sarah Grant. I respect Sarah and I'm sorry for her. I suppose you agree with her. You think Cape Wrath should be closed down.'

'I do, but not entirely for the reasons you think. I believe it should be closed for *political* not just environmental reasons. The English have been dumping on the Scots for centuries. Cape Wrath is just another example of English imperialism.'

'That's sentimental, nationalist rubbish.' Mel shook her head.

'Just listen, will you. Isn't that what you're trained to do – listen sympathetically and look caring?' His wry smile had such charm and was so unexpected that she shrugged and let him go on.

'The only reason the plant is at Cape Wrath is that it's about as far away from England as you can get and no one gives a damn about the people who live here. It's only inhabited by Highlanders – and who gives a toss about a few crofters?'

'That's not true,' Mel said steadily. 'Cape Wrath once pumped millions of pounds into the local economy. It still brings money and jobs.'

'The people here have no other option. Just as their ancestors were thrown off their land during the Highland Clearances.'

'That's a silly comparison.'

'Is it? The people here have always been economic pawns. They were cleared off the land when it became more profitable to rent it out to English sheep farmers. Today they pick up the dirty jobs at Cape Wrath that no one from the south wants to do. Yet this was once the domain of the Lords of the Isles. All that pride and passion and history has gone . . . Just look at Dunstan Castle if you want an example. It was wrecked and vandalized by the English after the Jacobite risings and now it's been contaminated with radioactivity by Cape Wrath. Yet it's one of the most significant monuments to – Scottish history. Fabian Williams is trying to get something done. It's the only sensible thing he's done since he arrived. But I doubt he'll succeed.'

Hamish got up and poured a generous amount of whisky from a decanter into two tumblers. 'Try this. It's a malt from a tiny distillery just twenty miles from here. It tastes of peat and heather and Scotland as it once was – and just listen to me . . .'

Mel lay back and as Hamish talked, his words painted vivid pictures in her mind. The aroma of the fire, the poignant Celtic music and the pungent taste of the whisky began to work their spell. She saw the drama and the tragedy, the beauty and the pathos of the history of the Highlands. The siren call of lost causes and heroic failure. His passionate conviction reminded her of Daniel . . . People like him were attractive but dangerous too. She'd learned that lesson only too well. The thought sobered her instantly.

'I must go,' she said abruptly.

'Why?' He came and sat beside her. Slowly he took her face in his hands and held her eyes with his. 'What's the matter?'

'Nothing. I'm just tired.' Why didn't she pull away from him? But the warmth of his hands was seductive . . .

'I didn't mean to upset you. What was it I said?' His deep voice softened and it seemed to hypnotize her.

'It wasn't what you said. It's just that you reminded me of someone a long time ago.' The words were out before she'd realized. She had never talked to anyone about Daniel but now she felt she was teetering on the brink. She mustn't. This man was a stranger. She only felt this way because she was tired and the whisky was making her stupid.

'Who do I remind you of?' he persisted gently.

'Someone I used to know a long time ago. He felt passionately about things as well, but in the end it destroyed him.'

91

'Was he your lover?'

'No, he was much more important than that. He was my friend. Look, I really don't want to talk about it.'

'I don't want to talk either.' Hamish lowered his head and kissed her lips, twining his hands in her hair. Mel felt herself begin to respond, gripping his muscular back, pulling him to her when she should have been pushing him away. All the tensions of the last few weeks seemed to melt away as a deceitful weakness flowed through her. Her lips opened under his.

But the cool logical side of her fought back. She knew nothing about him. He'd only invited her back to get her into bed and she was falling for it naively like a silly, inexperienced girl.

She twisted out of his grasp and without giving him a chance to say anything, got up, grabbed her bag and ran out into the soft evening light.

She half-expected to hear Hamish come after her but there was silence. She slowed down to a walk. The lights of Wrath were a welcome sight. She'd never felt so glad to see the hotel. Slowly she climbed the steps to her room. In the morning, everything would fall back into place.

As she inserted her key in the lock she noticed a piece of paper sticking out under the door and picked it up. It was too dark in the hallway to read it so she pushed open her door and reached for the light switch. It took a couple of moments for her brain to connect with what she was seeing. The message was stark. In obscene, brutal language it told her to leave Cape Wrath. Underneath was a sketch of a pin-figure wearing a T-shirt with *PR* on it. The bubble coming out of its mouth said: '*Whose arse shall I lick today?*'

Mel sank to the floor, door still open and began to cry softly.

Chapter Six

'Sean, I didn't realize you were back. Can we talk? Something's happened.'

Docherty glanced up from the contract he was checking. Jesus, she looked done in. There were great shadows under her eyes and she was pale as ivory.

'Of course we can talk.' He pulled out a chair for her and she slumped down.

'I wasn't sure . . . I thought you might still be angry with me.'

'No, I had no right to react like that and I'd been wanting to apologize. Then I heard about the body on the beach and I wasn't sure what to do. Is that what you want to talk about – finding the body? It must have been one hell of a shock.' He watched her closely but she hardly reacted.

'It was, but it's not that. When I got back to my room last night, after the demonstration had ended, I found this lying under my door.' She pushed the piece of paper across Docherty's desk. 'What kind of twisted creep would do a thing like that?'

'I can think of at least a dozen.'

Mel stared at him. 'You're joking!'

'Not really. Cape Wrath's not a happy place just now and not everybody agrees with your policy of being open and publicly admitting our past mistakes. People are loyal to the past and have a funny way of showing their frustration.'

'So you think it was someone from the plant?' Mel was incredulous.

'Probably.'

'But I thought it must be one of the environmentalists.'

'Why should they target you? You're just a spokes-woman for the plant. Their real grievance is with the management. I wouldn't let it bother you.' He tore the note into small pieces and tossed them in the bin. But in her mind's eye Mel could still see the malicious little parody of herself.

'If it cheers you up, two months ago someone pushed an envelope of dog shit through the Director's front door. Most of us thought it was a pretty appropriate protest about the quality of the canteen food. If you'd tried the Haddock Kiev you'd sympathize.'

A smile lightened Mel's face. 'I must be losing my sense of perspective. It's been much harder settling in than I'd expected.'

'This is a hard place for outsiders to understand. The tensions, the politics, the local loyalties run deep. Look, have dinner with me tonight and I'll try to explain some of the background.'

'That's nice of you.'

'Not really. I've been meaning to invite you for a while. Seven-thirty OK?'

As soon as she'd gone Docherty got up. Stooping swiftly he retrieved the pieces of paper from the bin, arranged them in his ashtray and set fire to them with his lighter. He watched them burn and let out a long, exasperated sigh.

Walking down the corridor Mel wondered what had prompted her to confide in Docherty. Logically she should have gone to the Director or maybe to John MacDonald or James Everett, but Sean was more approachable in spite of their spat. Anyway, it was done now. With a wrench she made herself focus on her work again. What had happened yesterday down at the harbour had been a fiasco and she had the press clippings to prove it. It was time for some frank talking.

There was no one in his outer office so Mel went straight through and tapped on John MacDonald's door before entering. He was on the telephone and his irritation at being interrupted was obvious. He waved her to a chair and terminated his conversation abruptly.

'Do we have an appointment?' He raised surprised eyebrows at her.

'No, we don't. But I thought it was important to discuss what happened yesterday. As you were away in Inverness you may not know all the details yet.'

'Very well.' He linked his small neat hands. 'Fire away.'

'It's various things. First of all, someone from the plant leaked information about the precise timing of the arrival of the fuel shipment. The demonstrators were already in place when the *Orchid* came in.'

'Why are you so sure it was someone from the plant?'

'Who else could it have been?'

'It could have been a crew member from the ship. They have satellite communications. If one of them wanted to sabotage our operations they'd be able to. And there's not a damn thing we can do about it. The ship was hired by the Malaysians, as our customers, not by us.'

'But there'll be an investigation, surely?'

'That's up to James Everett. If he thinks there was any serious breach of security here at Cape Wrath he has full powers to hold an enquiry. But tell me something. I'm a little curious about your attitude.' An ironic smile played across his compact features. 'I would have thought you'd have wanted us to publicize the arrival of the shipment in line with your "open and honest policy". I can't believe that you're an advocate of secrecy, or have your ideas changed? I am aware that PR is built on shifting sands. Has openness gone out of fashion?'

Mel felt her colour rise; his words reminded her of Sarah

Grant's. In a way, of course, he was right.

'It's not up to me to decide how issues with security implications should be handled,' she said reasonably. 'I'm just concerned that when we try to keep information to ourselves we do it properly, otherwise there's no point having fuel arriving in the early hours of the morning. We might as well let the consignments come in in broad daylight.'

'OK, point taken,' he said after a moment's reflection.

'There's something else. It's really an operational issue and I don't know what the answers are, but we looked complete idiots yesterday. The container sat on the deck of that ship for nearly twelve hours before it was finally unloaded. Look at these headlines.'

Mel spread the day's press cuttings across his desk. Photographs of Cape Wrath staff grappling ineffectually with the rusted clamps were spattered across the front page of every Scottish newspaper.

'In the public's mind if we can't even unload a container we shouldn't be in this business.'

'That's another fair point. Was there anything else?'

'No.'

'By the way, while I was in Inverness I watched you being interviewed on the lunchtime news. You came across very well.'

'Thank you. I was doing my best but it wasn't easy in the circumstances.'

Mel almost had to pinch herself as she stood up. John MacDonald had agreed with her; he had even paid her a compliment! It was only as she closed the door behind her that she realized he hadn't promised to do a damned thing.

'Good morning.' Sheena McKeague was back at her desk. 'If I'd known you were in with him I'd have brought you a cup of coffee.'

'That's fine. I've already had some this morning and I'm trying to cut down on the caffeine. It seems to be an occupational hazard in my job.'

'It must have been a terrible shock, finding that poor

young man's body washed up on the beach. Such a shame. He was a nice lad.'

'Did you know him then?' Mel looked at the older woman in surprise.

'He'd been lodging with my mother in the town. She's had the police round about half a dozen times and that hippy journalist from the *Wrath Courier*. But there wasn't much she could tell any of them. He was quiet. Very quiet. Always kept himself to himself and never any trouble to anyone.'

That couldn't be quite true, Mel mused as she went downstairs to her own office. He must have caused trouble to someone . . .

Sean Docherty lived in an apartment on the top floor of what had once been the local library, built at the same time as the town hall. The handsome Victorian building had proved too expensive to maintain. A smaller purpose-built library had been erected to accommodate the needs of the declining population of Wrath and the old library had been converted into apartments.

Mel rang the bell and waited. After a moment leisurely footsteps approached. It was hard to imagine Sean doing anything in a hurry unless he had to.

'So you found the way all right?' He held the door open for her.

'It's pretty hard to get lost in Wrath. Anyway, your directions were excellent. I brought you this.' She gave him the bottle of wine. It was poor stuff but the best the hotel had to offer.

'Come into the kitchen and I'll pour you a glass of some wine I've already opened.'

The apartment looked spacious and airy. The plaster cornices of the high ceilings had a rich moulding of fruit and flowers. Mel followed him down a long corridor into a surprisingly modern kitchen – all granite surfaces and distressed wooden fittings. A bewildering array of herbs and spices was assembled next to a giant wooden chopping board. A Thai cookbook was propped open behind a Perspex screen.

'You shouldn't have gone to so much trouble,' Mel smiled.

'When I cook I do it seriously. You can help me by chopping up this coriander for a start.' He poured her a glass of claret and handed it to her with a mock bow. 'Food first. Then we'll talk properly.'

'Where did you find all these ingredients? Not in Wrath surely?'

Sean grinned. 'I share a supplier with Mushtaq Khan – the guy who owns Khan's Curry House.'

An hour later they were eating an exquisite Thai meal of chicken and lemon grass soup, green beef curry with fried vegetables and a salad of cucumber and lotus roots.

'You are full of surprises, you know.' Mel smiled at him. 'I could have sworn you were a "boil in the bag" man.'

'That's one of the most insulting things anyone's ever said to me.' He poured her some more wine.

'Aren't you having any?'

'No – but I'll tell you about that later. First I promised to try and explain Cape Wrath to you.'

'I wish you would. It's weird but I just feel like I'm floating there. I don't know the context of anything and nothing seems to make sense. And then there's that horrible note someone sent . . .'

'I can't promise it'll make sense even when I've finished but let's try.' He took a long draught of mineral water. 'You'll know some of it already, but as it says in all the best stories, "Let me begin at the beginning . . ."

'The story of Cape Wrath goes back over forty years. After the last war, nuclear power looked like the great white hope that was going to solve the nation's energy problems. Scientists began to experiment with different reactor types but they needed large amounts of uranium to fuel them and it wasn't clear whether uranium would remain readily and cheaply available. People began to believe that the answer was the so-called "fast reactor".'

'The "fast breeder"?' Mel put in.

'That's right – a reactor fuelled by enriched uranium and capable of breeding plutonium in its blanket which could then be turned back into fuel. It promised a limitless source of energy. So in the 1950s they established a research station at Wrath to design and build prototypes like the WFR – the "Wrath Fast Reactor" – and after that the "Wrath Advanced Fast Reactor".'

'But then Government decided to cut the funding?'

'Exactly. The prototypes kept breaking down and there were reactor accidents, first at Three Mile Island in the States and then at Chernobyl in the Ukraine. Public confidence in nuclear energy plummeted. And it looked as if we didn't need it anyway. Suddenly there was a glut of oil, then of gas. Britain's own reserves were larger and easier to get at than anyone had previously thought. The nation didn't want or need to invest in nuclear power, not even the conventional stations let alone the expensive and unproven fast reactor. So in the early 1990s the Government pulled the plug.'

'How did the workforce react?'

'They felt let down. From being a world-renowned centre of scientific excellence Cape Wrath changed almost overnight into a blot on the landscape. The best scientists left. The reactors were shut down and now we're just waiting for the radioactivity to decay so that we can dismantle them, reprocess the spent fuel and dispose of the radioactive waste. Meanwhile we exploit spare capacity in the reprocessing plant by reprocessing reactor fuel from overseas.'

'But the reprocessing plant looks so old inside.' Mel swirled her wine in the bottom of her glass.

'That's because it *is* old. That flashy mirror glass on the outside was just an afterthought one year when a bit of money was going spare in the budget. The plant itself is on its last legs. That's why the workforce are depressed. The real purpose of Cape Wrath went years ago. You can't expect people to be excited about knocking things down and operating some old creaking plant that's well past its sell-by date. They know they're into self-liquidation; teams are being laid off or sold on to contractors and the local economy's declining all the time.'

'Won't anything else be built at Cape Wrath?'

'Like what?' Docherty shrugged. 'I suppose it's possible the oil or gas industries might want to make use of our facilities, maybe site a terminal here, but it's not that likely ... There's a sense of futility and corruption hanging over Cape Wrath that taints everything. That's why I don't get involved anymore. It's too depressing to do anything more than spectate.'

'What do you mean by corruption?' She was finding Docherty's bleak exposé disturbing.

'I mean "corruption" in every sense. But most of all Cape Wrath has become corrupt in spirit, from our Director who hates the place and has only been sent here because he got up someone's nose in Whitehall to our Plant Manager who runs Cape Wrath like a private fiefdom and thinks he can do what he likes. What I see is a huge gap between the senior staff and the workforce, who just feel they're being betrayed and exploited.'

Mel took a sip of wine. This was the second night in a row she'd listened to someone talk about exploitation, but unlike Hamish the passion and commitment weren't there. How had Docherty lost his ability to participate in life?

'What keeps you here, Sean?' she asked curiously.

He smiled a little sadly. 'I don't know. Lack of ambition, or a desire to see how it's all going to end. Would you like some more wine?'

'No, thank you.'

Sean stood up and poured the remainder of the bottle down the sink. 'Out of sight, out of mind. I used to be an alcoholic,' he said casually. 'Giving up drinking was the promise I made to keep this miserable job of mine.' He smiled at her, watching for her reaction.

'Promise to whom?'

'John MacDonald, my so-called boss.'

'Why "so-called"?'

'Because it's impossible to respect someone you know is promoted above his talent. We were at Oxford together. We were both mathematicians and we shared tutorials. I know he's a bull-shitter. The only real talent he's got is for brown-nosing.'

'He doesn't seem very smooth to me.' Mel frowned. This new perspective on MacDonald was intriguing. So were Docherty's motives for feeling this bitter.

'He's not really trying with you, that's why. In his terms you don't matter. Neither does the Director. John knows that Fabian Williams is just a time-server with as much influence as a preacher in a whorehouse. And Williams doesn't give a damn how John runs the plant so long as he can keep his patrician nose clean and preferably tucked in a book about the bloody Crusades.' Sean paused. 'And of course he doesn't know that MacDonald's bisexual. But to be fair I doubt it would worry him. His Crusaders probably screwed each other silly.'

'Bisexual? But I thought John was married with children?'

'He is, but his wife's got a figure like a Boy Scout. I'm sure he's basically gay, it's just that he's too scared about his security clearance to do anything about it.'

'But how do you know all this?'

'Like I said, we go back a long way. He tried to get me into bed with him at Oxford one night when we were both pissed. I was rather a pretty boy in those days. Sometimes I think he's scared I'll rat on him to Everett and he'll lose his security clearance, but on the other hand he knows about my drink problem so I suppose we're all square.'

'How can you go on like this? You sound as if you hate him.'

'Hate's too strong a word. I despise him, as I imagine he

101

despises me. It's a bit like a marriage where we've run out of energy to fight but we're too used to each other to split up. Anyway, where would I get another job? I'm forty-five and my track record's not exactly spectacular. And to be fair, it was John who got me this job in the first place when I was on my uppers.'

'What did you really want to do with your life, Sean?' Mel asked softly. Beneath his flippancy she could detect real pain.

'I don't know why I'm telling you all this.' Docherty clamped a hand defensively across his chest, his eyes half-rueful, half-amused.

'You don't have to if you don't want to.'

'No, I'm an egocentric bastard. The opportunity to bare my soul doesn't come that often in Wrath. What did I want to be? I wanted to be a classical musician. I was a very, very good violinist. But my wife didn't think I'd ever be quite good enough. She didn't fancy being married to the number two violin in some provincial orchestra. Being young and totally obsessed with her and her body I listened. She pushed ahead with a career in the City and I became an academic. I'd got a First and it was all a bit of a doddle. Until I got bored. Sasha was working long hours and travelling the world. We barely saw each other. Everything seemed to lose its point. Even the sex became mechanical. One night I got so pissed I urinated into a decanter during a Vice-Chancellor's dinner – very discreetly, I thought! I stood in the corner of the dais with my back to the room.

'Universities pretend that they're liberal, unshockable places but they're not really. I was out on my ear. Sasha dumped me and married her Head of Corporate Finance and I got a job teaching maths at a grotty little boys' school where I drank in secret and felt sorry for myself. Then one day some spirit of devilry possessed me and I went to a college reunion. There was John, clawing his way up the greasy pole of Civil Service scientists. Perhaps it gave him a kick to be able to offer me a job.' Sean paused and then added softly, 'But

102

perhaps he was genuinely trying to do me a favour.'

Mel looked at the dissolute but still handsome face in front of hers and felt a strong impulse to put her arms around him. What a waste of life and talent. He'd blown it and, what was worse, he knew it and part of him still cared, whatever he said.

'It's not too late, you know. I'm sorry if that sounds trite but it's true. You could change things if you really wanted to.' Like I did, she thought privately.

'That's the trouble. I *don't* want to. Frankly it's too much trouble and there are diversions and compensations. And I'm not sure I could cope if I left Wrath. I'm used to it – institutionalized, you might say. Moving south would be the equivalent of being released into care in the community. That's the trouble with a lot of us up here. Cape Wrath attracts waifs and strays and people looking for somewhere to lie low and lick their wounds.'

A bit like me, Mel thought with a shock. And James Everett.

'I'm sorry. I was supposed to be helping with your problems this evening.' He was smiling now, trying to lighten her mood.

'You have.' Mel got up. 'And thank you for dinner. It was spectacular. You could have a new career as a cook.'

'I'll see you back to the hotel.'

'I'll be fine.'

'No, I'd like to. You've had some nasty shocks since arriving in Wrath.'

Half an hour later Sean Docherty climbed the curving staircase back to his apartment then stopped. The door was open, just slightly ajar. He waited but there was no sound. He began to climb again, this time light and silent on the balls of his feet. He paused on the threshold and looked carefully down the hallway. At the far end the light was on in his bedroom. Then he heard her.

'Docherty . . .'

He closed the door behind him and leaned against it for a moment. What could he do? He wasn't a saint. Slowly he began to loosen his collar.

Mel looked up from her office desk. 'Ishbel, I want you to get me out some files from the archives. 'I've been looking through the lists and I've marked the ones I want.'

'Sure. It'll take a little time because the archives are over on the other side of the site, but I'll go across now.' Ishbel picked up the list. 'These are quite old ones.' She looked enquiringly at Mel.

'I know. I want to read up on the history of Cape Wrath.' While Ishbel was gone Mel stood at the window and stared out across the site. Men in white overalls were streaming into the reprocessing plant. Glancing at her watch she saw it was dead on four o'clock: the afternoon shift. The sun glanced off the dull metallic dome of the Wrath Fast Reactor. You poor old dinosaur, she thought. No one loves you now.

She couldn't get her strange conversation with Docherty out of her head. His bitterness and disillusionment seemed like a terrible warning. Some of the things he'd said could have come from Hamish. They were more similar than she'd realized. But their scepticism only reinforced her determination to make her mark at Cape Wrath. The key was to understand every aspect of the plant's past.

Four hours later, as the sky turned saffron in the setting sun, Mel pushed her chair back from her table and rubbed her forehead. Then she stretched her arms high above her. Her brain was bursting with facts. One stood out above everything else but she could find tantalizingly little extra material about it. Docherty would know. He hadn't been at Cape Wrath when the incident happened, but he must know about it.

She walked slowly down the empty corridor, her footsteps echoing, and tapped on his door. He often worked late and she wasn't surprised when she heard him call out to enter.

'I hope I'm not disturbing you,' Mel said tentatively.

'Of course you're not. I'm hardly busy. I only work late because I start so late. I can't get my brain in gear before ten in the morning.'

Despite what he said, Mel noticed there were papers spread all over his desk. He certainly looked busy. She guessed he was just being polite.

'First of all, thank you for dinner last night.'

'My pleasure.'

'You said a lot of very revealing things.'

'I suppose I did.'

Why was his tone so guarded? Mel coloured. 'I mean about Cape Wrath. Anyway, it set me thinking and I've spent some time reading up about the plant. And there's something that puzzles me.'

'Oh?'

'What's the shaft?'

'That's just old history,' Docherty replied quickly.

'Maybe, but it exploded, didn't it? I found some press cuttings in the archives. According to them, this shaft – whatever it is – blew up one night in 1974. Debris was scattered for hundreds of yards. Some of it even went into the sea. What actually happened?'

'Do you really want to know?' Docherty made a face. 'Like I said, it's water under the bridge.'

'Yes, I *do* really want to know.' Mel pulled up a chair. Why did he seem so reluctant to talk about it? It wasn't like Sean to be reticent – or discreet, for that matter.

'Was it a nuclear explosion?' she asked outright.

'God, no! It wasn't a mini-Chernobyl if that's what you mean. The shaft is – or rather *was* – a disposal facility for nuclear waste. When they were digging up the site to build a discharge pipeline to the sea, they created a bloody great hole about a hundred feet deep in the rock formation close to the edge of the beach. Some bright spark had the idea that it would be a good place to dispose of intermediate-level nuclear waste from the various operations in the plant.

Things weren't as tightly regulated in those days. The authorities didn't object and they began filling this thing up. Then one fine day someone dumped some fuel shavings in it contaminated with sodium from the coolant of the fast reactor. The sodium reacted with the water in the shaft, and as any child with a chemistry set would know, this caused a hydrogen explosion so powerful that it blew the fifteen-tonne concrete plug off the top. It landed a hundred yards away.'

'That's an appalling story.'

'Yes, but like I said, it happened nearly twenty-five years ago. The climate was different then. You weren't considered a "real man" unless you'd had the maximum radiation dose allowed under the law.'

'All the same, it can't have done much for the reputation of this place!'

'Remember what I told you last night. Those were the days when Cape Wrath could do no wrong. Of course they hushed it up as best they could and the site management closed ranks. But frankly the press weren't that interested. There was no Earth Alliance to make a fuss. I expect all it merited was a couple of paragraphs in the *Wrath Courier*.'

'Yes,' Mel said thoughtfully. 'It wasn't even the lead story. The big news that day was something about the Wrath Sports and Social Club. There was just a brief paragraph on an inside page reporting that there had been a small explosion in one of Cape Wrath's waste disposal pits and a short quote from the site management that the incident shouldn't be exaggerated and that there was "no effect on staff or the public because of the extreme safety precautions taken". You'd never get away with it like that today – and rightly so.'

Docherty gave her a quizzical look from under his dark brows. 'Allow me to shock you a little bit more.'

'I'm not sure you could.'

'Try me. When the shaft began to fill up, what do you think they did to make more space?'

'I've no idea.'

'At weekends, the plant shift managers used to wander down there with shotguns and fire at the contents to make them settle by releasing air pockets and so on.'

'You're joking!'

'No, it's the truth. Honest injun.'

'Well, I just hope and pray everyone's forgotten all about it.' What an extraordinary story! It was so farcical she could almost laugh out loud.

'If I were you, I'd hope and pray for something else.' The tautening in Docherty's voice made her stare. His expression was suddenly stark and deadly serious. Stripped of irony and sarcasm he was like a stranger.

'Sean, what is it?' Her voice was a whisper. In the silence that followed she felt the hairs on the nape of her neck begin to stir.

'I'm sorry. I shouldn't have said that. Forget it.' His tone was lighter but forced and the blue eyes were watchful.

'Please – what were you going to say? You can trust me.'

He rose and went over to the window, keeping his back to her. 'John's begun using the shaft again. Over the past two years he's been putting nuclear waste down it.'

'But why?' Mel could scarcely believe her ears. 'It can't be safe. Supposing it blows up again?'

'He claims he's very careful about what he puts down there and how he packages it, and that there are now plenty of hydrogen monitors to detect gas build-up. His argument is that it saves on the costs of storage and reprocessing and that he can keep the plant's profits up so that the managers get paid their bonuses and the employees keep their jobs. He says there's no risk.'

'Is he right?'

'I honestly don't know.'

'Do the regulatory agencies know what's going on?'

'No, of course not. As far as he's concerned, the regulatory bodies are outsiders, enemies even, pandering to public prejudices and ill-founded perceptions. He thinks

107

that because of public pressure they're only concerned with potential hazard – i.e. what could happen – and don't give enough attention to assessing risk – i.e. the actual *likelihood* of an accident occurring. Let me give you an example. The risk of a serious accident in a nuclear power plant in the UK is about one in a hundred million or about the same probability as a large meteor landing on London. The consequences may be huge but the risk is minute. Do you understand what I'm saying?'

Mel nodded. She could just about appreciate the argument but it didn't excuse John MacDonald's actions. 'Who else knows about this at Cape Wrath?'

'Very few people. Of course a couple of the shiftworkers are in on it because he needs their help, but they're not going to talk. He's tried to defend their jobs against privatization and they're loyal to him. But the reality is that he's intellectually corrupt and is bending the facts to suit his version of the truth. He's convinced it's no problem and won't listen to argument. Almost unconsciously he alters his recollection of events and conversations to suit his own purposes. And he's so arrogant he believes everything he does is right. Anyway, even if someone did blow the whistle on him there's so much stuff down the shaft already it would be hard to identify what's new and what isn't. They didn't keep very good records of what they put down there in the first place. They're not even sure there isn't the odd bit of high-level waste in there too.'

'Doesn't the Director suspect anything?' Docherty's laugh made her wince at her own naivety. Of course he didn't!

'Fabian knows bugger all about what's happening here. He's not a scientist and John can run rings around him. He was only made Director because he was born in Stirling. The powers that be in Whitehall are thick as pig-shit about Scottish history. They think any old Scot will go down OK with the locals. They might as well have picked someone from Surrey as the Lowlands. As long as Cape Wrath seems to be working efficiently and keeping to its cost targets he's not going to ask too many questions. And the Ministry and the Treasury aren't going to ask too many questions of him either. The only site project he gives a damn about is that mouldering castle because it once belonged to Colin the Catatonic or Malcolm the Moron or one of those bloody Celtic kings he's always boring on about.'

Sean was right, Mel thought bleakly and unamused. The only time she had seen Fabian show real passion was over the decontamination of the castle. It would be only too easy to deceive him.

She stood up and went towards Sean. He must have heard her but he still didn't turn round. She put out her hand and touched his shoulder. 'What are you going to do about this?'

'Why should I do anything? Anyway, who'd believe the word of an erstwhile piss artist who's been pushed into a dead-end job, against that of the hyper-efficient Plant Manager? That's why John told me in the first place. Anyway, we already share secrets. He knew it was safe to boast.'

'Well, why not surprise him?'

Docherty turned to face her at last. 'Show him I've still got balls, is that what you mean?'

'Yes, if you put it like that.'

He reached out and swept a stray piece of hair behind her ear. 'The sad truth is that I simply can't be bothered.'

Mel jerked away from him; a mixture of disenchantment, anger and despair was rising within her and she couldn't find the words.

'I've disappointed you. That's what I usually do to people in the end. I'm sorry.'

'No, you're not. You've forgotten how to give a damn!' She walked quickly out of the room and heard the door, caught by a sudden draught, slam shut behind her.

Chapter Seven

It was hardly surprising she couldn't sleep. Her frustration with Sean was mingled with shock at his bizarre story. She leant on her window-sill, face cradled in her hands, and gazed out, seeking solace in the perfect night. The light of the waxing moon softened the outlines of the houses in the street below, mellowing the harsh greys of granite and slate.

Rapid footsteps approached but for some reason she thought of Hamish not Sean. Hamish had a habit of appearing at unexpected times and in shadowy places. Craning out she saw it was only Mushtaq Khan hurrying home from his Curry House, whistling quietly under his breath.

Mel felt a pang of disappointment. But what could Hamish ever be to her? He represented the life she'd so consciously rejected. That weakness she'd experienced as he kissed her was just a betrayal of the woman she'd become.

With an effort she turned her mind back to what Sean had told her. She had a responsibility to do something, but what? There was nothing concrete to go on, just a conversation with a man who, by his own admission, despised MacDonald. And could she even be sure he'd been telling her the unvarnished truth?

She must be realistic. Without firm evidence Fabian Williams would never listen to her —and why should he? MacDonald made sure that the plant hit its targets and that the top managers got their bonuses. He also allowed

Williams to keep any operational responsibilities at arm's length. It was a cosy arrangement for the Director. All she could do was watch and wait and ask questions. At least she was in the right kind of job. As PR Manager she could virtually ask what she liked without arousing suspicion.

Her father's favourite saying came back to her: 'Hypotheses need proof to be worth anything.' Mel smiled as she remembered how earnestly he'd expounded his views. Her old stargazer obsessed with solving the mysteries of the universe and perpetually perplexed by people's illogicality. It was only eighteen months since he'd died and she still missed him so much.

The tension began to ebb from her and she wished she'd left those parting words to Sean unsaid. There were aspects of his relationship with John MacDonald that she couldn't begin to guess at. She of all people ought to appreciate that things were seldom what they seemed. Padding back to her bed, she slid under the duvet and at last fell into a dreamless sleep.

'Dougie?' He was standing by the coffee machine in the canteen waiting for it to churn out what was laughingly described as a cappuccino. 'I want to ask a favour.' Her tone was casual.

'What is it?'

'Will you take me to have a look at the shaft?' She watched his reaction carefully. Dougie MacBain had been a young apprentice on the site when the explosion happened. She'd checked his file that morning.

'Why? There's nothing to see. It's just a hole in the ground with a concrete plug in the top and a crane to hoist the plug out.' He looked genuinely puzzled.

'Call it professional interest. I was reading some old press clippings and I came across some references. It's possible some of the media might ask me about it and the Director told me how keen he was that I familiarize myself with all aspects of the site.' She smiled sweetly at him. They'd got

111

on well since that first time he'd taken her around the plant and now she was capitalizing on it in a way that made her feel quite guilty, but this was too important for any scruples.

Dougie sprinkled some granules of cocoa from a sachet onto the top of his cappuccino then glanced at his watch. 'I'll take you over there when the afternoon shift finishes, but don't be disappointed. It's nothing special.'

And it wasn't. It was just as Dougie had described. It took them a brisk twenty minutes' walk along the foreshore to reach it. Navy-blue waves pounded the beach and Mel could taste the salt in the air. A neat row of steps was cut into the rocks that shelved down to the beach and she would easily have walked on by if Dougie hadn't been there. They crunched over piles of shale to reach the steps which climbed some fifteen feet above the beach and there it was. Low metal barriers enclosed a circular metal lid painted with large yellow and black radiation roundels. It was set into the rock with a phalanx of monitors positioned around it like robot sentinels. A heavy, old-fashioned industrial crane stood to one side.

'What are those monitors for?' Mel asked.

'The shaft's about a hundred feet deep, and two-thirds of that is filled with water and nuclear waste – everything from nuclear fuel rods and fuel sleeves to operators' overalls. Some of the monitors are there to check there's no hydrogen build-up which might cause another large bang. Others are there to check there's no radiation leaking out. Look . . .' He pointed to one of the dials. 'You can see the reading is within the marked range. That means radiation levels here are within normal background levels.'

'What do you mean by "normal"?' Mel looked closely at the instruments.

'There's natural background radiation all around us. The levels vary across the country depending on the geology. If you were in Aberdeen or Cornwall, or other parts of the country with lots of granite rocks or buildings, you'd be receiving a higher dose than standing here. People don't realize that you can't get away from radiation. Our bodies are naturally radioactive and it's got nothing to do with the nuclear industry.'

'What would happen if the lid was raised?'

'The lid is made of lead-lined reinforced concrete. The lead acts as a shield against radioactivity. But if you raised it and stood directly over the shaft for more than a few minutes you'd receive a pretty heavy dose. That's why the safety and environment inspectors who check the integrity of the shaft, the level of the water and the settlement of the contents wear protective clothing. Some people say they even wear lead-lined underpants!'

'How often do inspections happen?'

'Once a year, that's all. The shaft's an old facility and it's not used anymore, but the monitors are checked once a day.'

Which means that MacDonald could have a field day, Mel thought to herself. The remote location, the casual way it was relegated to the past, would all play into his hands if he was doing what Docherty had accused him of. But what about the monitors? Wouldn't they give the game away? She looked at them more closely. The configuration of dials was confusing. Some were for alpha, some for beta and some for gamma radiation.

'Can those things be switched off?' she asked.

'Yes — in theory.' Dougie looked puzzled. 'But who'd want to do that?'

Who indeed? Mel wondered, back in her office. She pulled out the files again and found what she was looking for. The old black and white photographs were cracked but they still showed a shocking picture: huge lumps of reinforced concrete strewn around as if there'd been a giant earthquake, twisted pieces of metal which had been flung into the air like spears. It must have been one hell of an explosion and one hell of a clean-up job. It was surprising nobody had been injured. Radioactivity must have scattered all around the mouth of the shaft and some of it must have fallen onto the beach – even into the sea.

What was the risk of it happening again and with worse consequences? She thought of Sarah Grant and all the people she represented. Didn't she have an obligation to them? Sarah's pale face haunted her like a ghost seeking restitution from the living. Yet, she must be careful. If she overreacted or made a mistake she wouldn't be helping anyone, however much she sympathized with them.

The light tap on the door shook her out of her private thoughts. 'Come in.'

'I'm not disturbing you, am I?' It was John MacDonald, spruce as ever in a lightweight grey suit and immaculately starched pink shirt with silver-and-black striped silk tie. 'I wasn't sure whether you had visitors.'

'We do – a group of sixth-form physics students from Wrath College asked for a site tour but Ishbel's looking after them.' Mel was surprised – he didn't often come to her. Instinctively she pushed the file with the photographs to one side behind her in-tray where he couldn't see it so easily.

He sat down in the chair opposite. 'I want to ask you a favour. My wife is involved with this Fair Trade project. They set up craft projects in local communities in under-developed countries and import the goods at a fair price, cutting out the middle-man. They're holding a fund-raising event next month in Wrath and she wondered whether you could cover it in the site journal. Also – and I know it's not strictly Cape Wrath business – the project needs some publicity to get it off the ground. Amelia's not very experienced at that kind of thing and she's unsure how best to approach the media. I just wondered whether you could possibly give her some advice.' He flashed her a winning smile and she caught the golden lights in his eyes. Sean was right. MacDonald *did* have the ability to charm when he wanted something.

'No problem,' she answered pleasantly. 'We can easily do

114

a feature in the next issue of the site journal and I'll talk to some of the local journalists I know. I'll suggest it would make a nice feature for them – perhaps in the weekend supplements or for the local radio stations. It will help project a caring image for the site anyway.' A sudden warmth in her face and a faraway look in her eye would have betrayed to anyone in the know that she was back with her clothing cooperative in Guatemala.

But John MacDonald wasn't in the know. 'Good. Thank you. I'll tell her to give you a ring to discuss it.' His hand was already on the door handle when, coming back to the present, it occurred to her that this was too good an opportunity to be lost.

'John, could I ask you something?'

'Yes, of course.'

'I've been drawing up a list of issues which could pose a threat to Cape Wrath's reputation if the media got hold of them. I want us to be prepared so they don't wrong-foot us.'

'And?'

'I've been reading up about the shaft and in particular about the explosion.'

'That's history.' He shrugged. 'No one's interested.'

Wasn't that almost exactly what Sean had said? 'They might be if they thought there was a risk an explosion might happen again,' she said carefully.

'It couldn't. The shaft's been closed for years, we know exactly what's down there and it's carefully monitored.' His voice was perfectly level and seemingly relaxed. He was even smiling slightly. 'If I were a journalist I'd be much more interested in pressing Cape Wrath about these radioactive particles which turn up from time to time on the beach. The fact that we can't identify where they're coming from is a much bigger issue than the shaft. If you want to know the background, talk to the safety and environment team. Anything else I can do for you?' He turned that newly discovered winning smile on her again.

115

'No, nothing. Thanks, John.'

Mel sat back in her chair deep in thought as his footsteps died away down the corridor. She was more than puzzled, she was confused. Her questions about the shaft hadn't seemed to worry John one little bit; in fact he'd tried to be positively helpful. Was Sean's story just fantasy – the result of a jealous and unhealthy obsession with MacDonald going back to their student days? Had he been trying to manipulate her for some game of his own? He was certainly clever and possibly bitter enough to do so. It was an uncomfortable thought, because deep down she'd liked Sean from day one – and trusted him. If she was wrong about him, what else might she be deluding herself about?

'Mel Rogers?'

'Yes?' The voice was young, male and familiar but she couldn't quite place it.

'It's Fergus Brown. We ... er ... met at the demos.'

'Yes, I remember. What can I do for you?' Mel pulled a sheet with the latest, not very impressive site safety statistics towards her. They'd been released to the media earlier that afternoon. That must be what he wanted to discuss.

'I'd like to interview you.'

'Very well. Go ahead,' she invited him.

'No. I'd like us to meet up in Wrath. I want to do a profile on you for the local press. We don't get many newcomers to Wrath and you're an important person in the local community.'

'Am I?'

'Of course. Everyone here's affected by what goes on at Cape Wrath and you're the plant's public voice. They want to know what brought you here and what you're trying to achieve.'

Mel smiled. She could see what was coming a mile off. Fergus would do a hatchet job if he could but she didn't really have any option. It was her job to keep on the right

116

side of the press, even sensation-seekers like Fergus. 'OK,' she sighed. 'When and where shall we meet?'

'Come to my house for a drink around eight o'clock. It's in the main street. Number fourteen.'

The little fisherman's cottage was about thirty yards beyond her hotel on the opposite side of the road. It was white-washed with a very plain front door made of bright green planking. Whoever had painted it hadn't made a very good job. It was covered with runs and the brush had caught the white paintwork. She knocked and waited.

Fergus opened the door almost at once. His dreadlocks were caught back with a rubber band revealing the lines of his thin, rather predatory face. His legs were encased in tight black jeans and his Fruits of the Loom T-shirt empha-sized the bony narrowness of his chest.

'Drink?' he offered, showing her into the cluttered living room that led in off the street. Books and cushions were piled carelessly against the once white walls.

'A beer please.'

He plucked a can from a small fridge standing in the far corner of the room and tossed it over. She pulled the ring with an expert movement which clearly surprised him and took a pull. He'd expected her to ask for a glass. Round one to her. She sat down in a shabby dark blue armchair by the window with the evening light stream-ing in over her shoulder.

'If I tell you what you want to know, will you do me a favour?' Mel asked.

'I'll try. What is it?' He was fiddling with a tape recorder and notebook.

'Come and visit Cape Wrath. You hardly write about anything else but you never come on site.'

'I need to keep my distance from the plant,' he said. 'I can't afford for people to think I'm in your pocket.'

'No one who's seen what you write would ever think that. Talk about biting the hand that feeds you!'

117

'Come on. You know the game. I don't want to be up here for ever and I've got a name to make for myself. But to do that I need to stick to the environmentalists' agenda. They're the underdogs and they have the public's sympathy. I can't consort with the faceless scientific enemy. Anyway, Good News stories are No News stories.'

'That's a cynical view of investigative journalism. Can I have another of these?' She tossed her empty can into the brimming wastepaper basket. 'Now, what did you want to ask me about?'

He clicked a switch on the tape recorder and a faint whine filled the room. 'What were your first thoughts when you found the body on the beach?'

'I thought this was supposed to be a feature about me?' Mel stiffened.

'Everyone knows it was you who found it.'

'I'm not sure I want to go into all that again.'

'I'd really appreciate it,' Fergus badgered. 'It's the biggest story to hit this community in years.'

'There's not a great deal I can tell you.'

'Just give it to me like it happened.'

Mel sighed. It was easier to give him what he wanted than to argue, but she felt herself beginning to shiver inside. 'I was walking along the coastal path away from Cape Wrath. It was a fantastic day, really beautiful. I could see pieces of driftwood washed up along the beach . . . all kinds of shapes, like sculptures. And then I saw something pale floating in with the tide. I thought it was another piece of wood and climbed down to take a look. Then I saw that it wasn't a piece of wood at all but a dead body.' Her voice was more matter-of-fact than she felt.

'So what did you do?'

'I ran back along the path to get help. Someone from the US base was just parking his jeep and he phoned the police on his mobile.' That hardly described her panic-stricken headlong flight but it was all she was going to give Fergus.

'Did you see anybody else about?'

'No.'

'The police say that the corpse's throat was cut.'

'Yes.'

'Did you realize that at the time? I mean could you see it?'

'Yes, I could.' She swallowed.

'What exactly did you see? What else did you notice?' He paused. 'Like it's not every day you find a body that's been razored; according to the pathologist's report the cut was so deep the spinal cord was nearly severed.' Fergus came to an awkward halt.

Without warning nausea rose from the pit of Mel's stomach. No, it wasn't every day you found a body with its throat cut. And it wasn't every day that you got to see it actually happen in front of you. The memory of Daniel's death returned so vividly it was like a physical pain. She closed her eyes for a moment, fighting it.

'I'm sorry. I find it very difficult to talk about this . . . call it post-traumatic stress if you like. If I'd realized what you really wanted to interview me about I wouldn't have come.' Mel stood up but with an effort. More than anything she wanted to get back to the hotel and be alone. She moved towards the door but a sixth sense stopped her in her tracks as she was about to open it. She stepped back as the girl with the shaved head came flying through it. She fished a brown paper bag out of her pocket with a whoop and tossed it across to Fergus.

'Hamish has given us a big enough stash for the entire weekend.' Fergus's wary expression must have alerted her and she became aware of Mel standing in the shadows. The lynx eyes flickered.

'What's she doing here?' The girl slung herself onto a huge cushion in the corner of the room and began to roll herself a joint, crumbling the resin with quick aggressive gestures and mixing it with tobacco, mouth in a sulky line.

'I invited her. She was helping me with a story.' Fergus sounded embarrassed, defensive even.

119

'Want a puff of this?' the girl asked Mel. 'Or we've got a beer can with holes you can use as a hookah if you like.' There was a malicious edge to her voice.

'No. I was just going.'

'I suppose you think smoking dope is morally wrong,' the girl challenged and was rewarded by Mel's heightened colour. 'Well, it isn't as immoral as forcing cigarettes on Third World countries or what you're doing at Cape Wrath. You're just a hypocrite, like all of them.'

'Leave her,' said Fergus. 'I've upset her. I'm sorry.'

But before he could finish Mel stepped out into the street and hurried towards the hotel, barely holding back the tears. In a way the girl might be right. She *was* becoming conventional, even hypocritical. In Guatemala she hadn't been so conventional, but that was before Daniel was murdered and – as she'd already been reminded once that evening, his death had changed everything . . .

'Buenas tardes, señorita.'

'Buenas tardes, señores.' Mel smiled at the neatly dressed Mexican with the briefcase and his two Spanish colleagues. It was nice to be able to practise her Spanish again, and after a few minutes she was talking quite fluently. Across the table Fabian Williams relaxed. It was rare for inspectors from the International Atomic Energy Agency in Vienna to arrive unannounced, but when they did it was important to roll out the red carpet.

As he carried on with the niceties Mel translated them into Spanish. The inspectors could speak quite good English but it was a courtesy to them to speak in their own language and she was glad she'd suggested it to Fabian. It had certainly calmed him down. His first reaction when he'd discovered that John MacDonald and most of the senior team were offsite at a conference had been to panic.

As the inspectors outlined why they had come and what they wanted Mel struggled a little to understand the nuclear terminology but she grasped enough. The Agency, which belonged to the United Nations, had the right under the International Non-Proliferation Treaty to tour nuclear plants at random to make sure nuclear material was not being diverted for weapons purposes. The nuclear weapons powers like Britain and America were obliged by the Treaty to keep their weapons material separate from the material used for civil purposes.

'Did you know,' one of the inspectors was explaining, 'that according to Britain's own Royal Society there are fifty-four tonnes of plutonium at civil reprocessing plants in England alone? That is enough to make a thousand large nuclear bombs or many more smaller terrorist devices. And there are hundreds more tonnes of plutonium in nuclear weapons stockpiles.'

As her mind slipped into Spanish and out again she remembered something she'd read in the files during her very first days at Cape Wrath. There had been some sort of problem about two years earlier with the IAEA's inspectors. If she was right, the plant had been criticized for the amount of 'material unaccounted for' or 'MUF' as the experts called it – nuclear material which according to calculations had been lost during reprocessing.

Cape Wrath's scientists claimed that the loss was notional and that material inevitably disappeared during the complex chemical process because it was impossible to measure what went in and what came out with absolute precision. There was always a one per cent margin of uncertainty. But over a period of time losses and gains would balance themselves out. The inspectors had been less sure and had nearly shut the plant down. Only assurances from Whitehall and concessions from the Foreign Office on United Nations funding had prevented a very embarrassing incident. Was that question mark still there in the inspectors' minds? It was hard to tell. Their manner was courteous but they were making it very clear that they were here to police Cape Wrath.

The preliminaries over, the Director turned to her. 'Miss Rogers, I would like you to escort our visitors over the

121

next couple of days as they go over the plant. You have my authority to give them access to anything they wish to see.' He stood up, shook hands with the visitors and left. She was on her own.

'Señor Valdes—,' she turned to the senior inspector, 'perhaps you can tell me what you would like to see and I'll make the necessary arrangements.'

'Thank you. As I'm sure you will appreciate, we never give advance warning of our intentions but I and my team have drawn up a list of the facilities which we wish to inspect. None of us have been to Cape Wrath before.' He fished a neatly typed piece of paper out of his pocket and pushed it towards her.

No surprises really. They wanted to see the entire reprocessing plant and the nuclear waste stores. While they poured cups of the horrible coffee sent up by the Cape Wrath canteen Mel made some swift telephone calls to arrange security passes.

She returned to find them standing, clipboards ready, coffee barely touched, and made a mental note to buy a decent coffee machine. 'Very well, gentlemen. Please come with me.'

'Please sign your names in the book.' She saw them exchange surprised glances about the register with the curling pages used to record visitors to the reprocessing plant. They were presumably more used to computerized systems with complex voice, fingerprint or iris recognition checks. She remembered her own first visit to the plant; like her they must have been struck by the contrast between the high-tech shell of the complex and the dismally old-fashioned interior that now greeted them. It was embarrassing to see everything through their eyes, but there was nothing she could do about that. She only hoped they'd be satisfied with the technical efficiency of the processes carried out in the plant.

'Mr Campbell here will show you where the changing

rooms are and issue you with protective clothing. I will meet you on the other side of the barrier.' She nodded at the shiftworker who had been detailed to look after the team.

Fifteen minutes later the inspectors were kitted out with white coats, protective overshoes and film badges, and were given the all-clear by the radiation monitors before entering the restricted area.

'Where would you like to begin, Señor Valdes?'

He consulted his notes. 'First we wish to see the head end of Plant number 8. I believe that is where you reprocess the spent fuel from your own research reactors and where you also reprocess fuel for your commercial customers. Is that correct?'

Mel nodded. It was a good job she'd spent some time over recent weeks with Dougie MacBain. He'd been able to give her a good understanding of the main principles of what went on. Her guess was that the inspectors would want to know exactly what records were kept of the spent nuclear fuel and its isotopic content as it was fed into the plant at the start of reprocessing. After all, if there was no accurate record of the amount and purity of the uranium and plutonium, how would Cape Wrath's management know for sure that none of it had been stolen or substituted with lower-grade material to allow someone to construct a bomb? The inspectors would want to talk to the technical experts about that. By now they should all be in position at the key points in the plant.

They walked down the long corridor to Plant 8, their feet in the baggy white overshoes gliding over the lino.

Señor Valdes was looking around, noting the old pipework and flaky paint. 'How old is this complex, Miss Rogers?'

'It was built in the late 1950s at the same time as the first of our research reactors was being built. The idea was that it would both fabricate fuel for use in the reactors and reprocess it afterwards.'

'Interesting. It's rare to find a plant of this age still in operation. Are there plans to upgrade any parts of it?'

'There's an on-going maintenance programme and components are replaced as they wear out. The dissolver in Plant 8 was replaced last year.' She was pleased to be able to tell him that. The dissolver was one of the most critical parts of the plant – a great vessel filled with acid where the spent nuclear fuel was dissolved so the process could begin of recovering the plutonium and uranium from the waste products.

Señor Valdes nodded but his faint frown grew more pronounced. 'You still seem to rely on mechanical systems to protect your material, but most other plants have replaced hand-operated door wheels with coded electronic bolts. You have no plans to replace the manual security systems in the plant with electronic ones?'

'Not as far as I am aware, but the technical managers will be able to advise you on that.'

They had reached the security gate leading into Plant 8 and Mel punched in a code on the large key-pad next to it. There was a series of clicks as the locks released. One by one the inspectors pushed through the rotating metal grille to the other side. Again they exchanged glances.

'Who issues the access code?' asked Señor Santos, the youngest of the inspectors.

'The Security Department.'

'Biological recognition systems are more secure. Anyone can steal a code.'

'I suppose so.' They were right, it was hardly state of the art, but did it need to be? With relief, Mel saw Dougie MacBain come towards them. He could take charge while she acted as interpreter.

But the questions went on, relentless and persistent. Why not have more electronic surveillance? Why were there so few closed-circuit TV cameras positioned at strategic points around the plant? What was done to prevent someone tampering with them? Why were so many of the accounting

124

systems analogue and not digital? Why was so much manual intervention required? How did Cape Wrath cope with the ergonomic risk – the human factor? What were the security vetting arrangements? Was there random drink and drugs testing?

Dougie was clearly anxious and it was making him sound over-defensive. Leaving the group for a moment, Mel made a hasty call to the Security Department. She prayed that James Everett was on site and felt relief flood through her at the sound of his voice.

'James? We've got some IAEA inspectors on site. They turned up this morning without warning.'

'Yes, I know. Dagos, aren't they?'

'They're Spanish and Latin American, if that's what you mean.' She bit back a sharper reply. This wasn't the moment to tackle James on his obsessive xenophobia. 'Look, they're asking a lot of questions about security vetting as well as about the physical security of the plant. They don't seem very happy. It would be a real help if you could join us and explain how our systems operate.'

'Getting in a twist, are they? I'll be with you in a few minutes. Where exactly are you?'

'Plant 8, just by the head end.'

'I'll be there with you in fifteen minutes.'

The inspectors were conducting an animated conversation amongst themselves, and the two junior ones were making ominous numbers of notes.

'I've asked a colleague from the Security Department to join us,' Mel announced to the group. 'He will be able to explain our security systems to you in more detail. In the meantime, perhaps you would like to come into Plant 8's central control room?'

As she led them in, a shiftworker put down his book and swung his feet off the 1960s gunmetal-coloured desk. In front of him was a grey-painted metal console with a row of black and white TV screens showing the various parts of the plant which he should have been monitoring. His whole attitude suggested that Colonel Gadaffi could be in there stocking up for World War Three and he still wouldn't notice. Two of his colleagues stood in a corner chatting, one of them propped casually against a control panel. They glanced round at the group and one said something Mel couldn't quite catch about 'garlic' which set them both sniggering exaggeratedly.

Dougie cursed under his breath. 'They're doing it on purpose,' he muttered. 'It's their way of getting back at the management.'

'We would like to inspect the records for reprocessing operations over the last three months.' Señor Valdes's tone was getting dourer by the minute. Dougie whispered something to the shiftworkers and one of them went slowly to a cupboard and produced an armful of index-card boxes which he dumped on the table with an insolent smile. This was dreadful, and Mel had no idea how to retrieve the situation.

'Good afternoon, gentlemen,' came a voice from behind her. James Everett, fastidiously neat, even in white overalls, stood in the doorway, pale eyes flickering over the scene. His presence had an immediate effect on the shiftworkers who began to bustle about checking dials and instruments. Mel relaxed again.

'What's all this? Why on earth wasn't I informed?'

John MacDonald had come into her room so suddenly that Mel jumped. He was holding a copy of the IAEA report in his hand. The inspectors had returned to Vienna three days ago but had only just faxed their conclusions through. The report's arrival had coincided almost to the hour with John MacDonald's return to Cape Wrath from the conference.

'I'm sorry?' Mel said, confused.

'Why was I not told that IAEA inspectors were on site! I should have been here! I would have returned from the conference at once!'

'I expect the Director didn't want to bother you,' Mel hazarded. It was hardly a matter for *her* to summon the Plant Manager back to Cape Wrath.

MacDonald seemed to take the point but slumped to a chair and thwacked the report with a frustrated hand. 'Look at these criticisms – inadequate manual records, poorly protected waste storage facilities, old-fashioned unautomated surveillance equipment. The improvement programme they're suggesting will cost hundreds of thousands of pounds – millions even.'

'It could have been worse. They might have ordered us to cease operations. But James Everett showed them the inner electric fences around the site and explained how they were activated during the Earth Alliance demonstration. He also described our plans for dealing with terrorist incursions and how his SAS experience meant he could give them categoric assurances on that score. They were satisfied about those aspects, even though they have misgivings about what happens inside the plant.'

'I suppose you're right – it could have been worse.' He looked very weary, with deep shadows under his eyes. 'Did they want to inspect the shaft?' he asked after a moment.

'No, they didn't.'

'You're sure of that?'

'I was with them the whole time.' Mel's heart started to beat a little faster. What had made him bring that up?

A high-pitched electronic whine cut through the air. MacDonald detached his pager from the clip on his belt and swiftly read the message.

'I need to phone the plant.'

Mel pushed her phone across to him and watched as he tapped in the number.

'Hello? John MacDonald here. Get me the Shift Manager now!' His voice was tense, exasperated. 'Dougie? What is it? ... No, not under any circumstances. I want the plant kept running and ready to start the new batch of fuel tonight. Maintenance will just have to wait ... It's too

127

expensive to shut down now. Have you got that?' His voice began to rise in anger. 'I said *have you got that!*'

He replaced the receiver and looked at her, face now drained of expression. 'I'm sorry, I'm tired. We've got a major run going on but we've been having some small reliability problems. I was worried in case the inspectors had slowed us up.' He sat down wearily. 'I can't for the life of me see what good they do anyway. It's not even clear to me why some countries should have a God-given right to own nuclear weapons while others don't. Isn't it just a bit hypocritical and superior, the nuclear "haves" telling the nuclear "have nots" that we're allowed to have nuclear weapons because of our supposed moral virtue, but that they're not to be trusted. Do we really have any right to impose sanctions on India and Pakistan for detonating their own devices?'

He had a point, but Mel was more struck by the way he looked than by what he was saying. The man was showing clear signs of stress. A pulse twitched in his temple and his fingers were drumming restlessly on the desktop. For the first time since they'd met she was actually feeling sorry for him.

Chapter Eight

The invitation said 'Black Tie'. Mel opened the door of the narrow wardrobe with its fake wood veneer and looked doubtfully at the row of clothes hanging inside. Did she have anything formal enough for a dinner party at the Director's house? Then she had an idea. Fishing under the bed she found the white cardboard box lined with tissue paper which she'd stored there the day she'd arrived in Wrath. It was the one relic she'd kept from those days in Tenango because it held such happy memories.

Smiling gently she shook out the purple cotton dress and ran her fingers over the delicate tracery of birds and butterflies worked in a deeper shade around the neckline and the hem. The dress was such a simple shape, straight and sleeveless, but it followed the contours of her body perfectly. Or at least it had. How long was it since she'd last worn it?

Mel slipped it over her head and fastened the short zip which ran from hip to midriff on the right-hand side. Then she walked over to the mirror and took a good long look. The woman who gazed back with such a serious expression in her eyes wasn't so different from the girl who'd first worn the dress. Her face was thinner, her breasts and hips perhaps a little fuller, but that was all.

She carefully slipped the dress off again, put it on a hanger and because, it was too long for the wardrobe, managed to hook the hanger to the top of the curtain rail. The light summer breeze wafting through the open window rippled through the light fabric and made the exotic embroideries seem like living things. Mel lay back on the bed and watched and remembered . . .

It was a spectacular drive up to the Director's house on the headland. The early evening light was falling in bright shafts through a crown of clouds, turning the sea pale silver. Glancing in her rearview mirror Mel could see another car coming up behind her, travelling fast. It looked familiar. Unwilling to be hurried, especially when she was early, she slowed, pulling over just before a bend. As the car flashed by she saw Docherty at the wheel. He must have known it was her – the blue MGF was unmistakable – and yet he hadn't even bothered to slow down . . .

'I'm so glad you could come. We hold these dinners from time to time – the local community expect it.' The woman standing in the wide black and white flagged hall had a handsome leonine look. Her expensively tinted blonde hair was held back by a black velvet alice band revealing a strong wide-boned face, with a rather leathery complexion. She looked like a woman who spent her time on healthy outdoor pursuits like gardening and riding.

'It was kind of you to invite me,' Mel said politely.

Judging by the number of coats in the cloakroom with its bowls of pot pourri and prints of hunting scenes, Mel was far from the first to arrive. She followed Christine Williams in the direction of the buzz of conversation.

About a dozen people were already gathered in the drawing room. John MacDonald and James Everett were listening to a small red-faced man whose wing collar looked too tight for him and who was talking animatedly about something.

Fabian Williams was deep in conversation with two women – one a lean, smartly dressed redhead and the other a short, slight woman with neatly cropped hair. Instinctively

130

Mel scanned the room for Docherty but he wasn't there. Where had he got to?

A girl in a neat black dress and white apron approached with a tray of drinks – red, white and sparkling wine, and mineral water. Her pretty freckled face was familiar and Mel recognized one of the sixth formers who had recently toured the site. She took a glass of sparkling wine but before she could say anything, she was propelled by Christine's gentle but insistent hand in the small of her back towards the Director.

In his black velvet dinner jacket Fabian looked like a character in an old-fashioned advertisement for cigars. He was sounding unusually animated, holding up a glass of red wine and twirling it in his thin hands as he inspected the colour.

'I'm glad you like the wine,' he was saying approvingly. 'It's Château Musar from the Lebanon, just at the top of the Bekaa Valley. The conditions are perfect – at three hundred feet above sea level it's not too hot for the grapes. Of course, it's the combination of Cabernet Sauvignon, Cinsaut and Syrah that gives it that smoky, spicy taste. It's made by the Hockar family – I met them during a research trip to the region. They told me they'd managed to produce a vintage every year throughout the troubles with the exception of 1984. That year the wine trucks bringing the grapes down from the hills were hijacked and the grapes were spoiled . . .'

He registered Mel's presence at last and broke off his monologue to introduce her to the two women by his side.

The small short-haired woman was Amelia MacDonald. She nodded at Mel with a brisk, friendly smile. The elegant red-haired woman turned out to be James Everett's wife Charlotte, who murmured a greeting. She was as scrupulously turned out as her husband. Mel wondered whether she shared her spouse's obsession with hygiene.

After a few minutes the Director led Charlotte away to meet a new arrival, leaving Mel with Amelia. After everything Docherty had said she was curious to meet John's wife, yet at the same time she was uncertain what to say. She felt as if she already knew an indecent amount about her and her marriage.

Amelia filled the gap. 'There's something I've wanted to ask you from the moment you came into the room. That wonderful dress – where is it from?'

'Guatemala. It was made in one of the villages near Tenango in the highlands.'

'I thought it was Guatemalan from the style of embroidery. It's exquisite work. I think John may have mentioned that I'm involved with a charity called "Fair Trade". We import goods from developing countries around the world, including Guatemala.'

'Yes, he did mention it. He said you might like some help with publicity. I'll certainly do whatever I can.'

'Thank you. I'd be very grateful, as I don't know where to begin. That embroidery really is spectacular! The birds and butterflies look as if they might fly off at any moment.'

'Every village has its own particular designs; none of these are real creatures, they're mythical,' Mel said softly, glancing down at her neckline. 'On feast days and holidays the men wear short, striped trousers with deep embroidery like this around the bottom of the legs – it's a tradition.'

'You sound very knowledgeable.'

'I was working out there. We started up a women's cooperative making clothes which could be exported direct to the States for dollars.'

'That's exactly our philosophy with Fair Trade – getting a fair price. These people have been exploited for too long by middle-men who pay them a pittance and take all the profit.' Amelia spoke with real passion.

'You must lead a very hectic life. I think Sean Docherty told me you were a JP too?' The noise in the room was rising and Mel moved a little closer. Amelia was quite short and she had to lower her head to catch her voice.

'Yes, it does keep me pretty busy but that's how I like it, especially with John working so hard and our boys away for most of the year. John insisted they went to boarding school; he didn't think the local school was good enough and that going away would make them more self-reliant.' She glanced across the room to her husband and although her expression was fond, it seemed to Mel that her eyes clouded for a moment.

But if it was a shadow it was a fleeting one. She turned back to Mel and said brightly: 'John's been very impressed with your work since you arrived. He worries such a lot about what happens at Cape Wrath – those recent demonstrations really upset him! He takes such pride in his job . . .'

There was a sudden stir at the other end of the room as a large, silver-haired man was ushered into the drawing room by a radiant Christine. There was a respectful hush as Fabian came forward to shake him by the hand.

'Who's that?' Mel asked curiously. The handsome, well-fed face looked familiar. Had she seen it in the press, or perhaps on TV?

'It's Sir Angus Prothero, our local MP. He's an ardent Scottish Nationalist and he owns a large estate to the west of Wrath. He and John have had a number of disagreements. John wanted to purchase fishing rights on one of his rivers for corporate entertaining. Sir Angus said he wasn't having English bankers and journalists and "other scum" – I think that's what he called them – on his land. The irony is he's half English himself. His mother comes from Lancashire like me.'

'What does he feel about Cape Wrath in general?' Mel looked curiously at the bluff figure who was now downing a large whisky and clapping the Director on the back.

'John says he's quite supportive of Cape Wrath really. He knows that the plant provides jobs for local people so he stands up for it in public. In private he can sometimes be a little difficult.'

'I hadn't realized until I came to Wrath what a complicated place this is.' Mel watched Sir Angus working the room like a true politician, a smile and a greeting for everyone but not waiting long enough to catch their reply.

133

'It *is* complex.' Amelia's voice was serious, sombre even. 'Wrath is a goldfish bowl where everyone knows everybody else's business. That's what puts John under such a strain as Plant Manager. And of course, on top of that he has his mother to worry about.'

'His mother?'

'Yes, he's devoted to her but she has Altzheimers now. He goes to see her every other weekend and I know how much it distresses him that she doesn't recognize him anymore.'

'How old is she?'

'Seventy-five.'

'And is she a widow?'

'I'm not sure. That sounds absurd, I know, but the truth is that John's father – he was a draughtsman in a small engineering company – walked out on them when John was only three. John remembers nothing about him but that doesn't stop him being bitter. He left them with no money and no forwarding address. John's mother had to struggle to bring him up. She moved into a council flat in Aberdeen which she found very demeaning – she didn't approve of taking anything which looked like charity; she thought it was beneath her. Anyway she took whatever work she could get – mostly cleaning – and worked day and night to give her son the best start in life she could. Sometimes I wonder whether she was right.' Amelia paused, frowning slightly.

'Why?' Mel asked, 'I mean, what more could she have done?'

'I think she was too preoccupied with keeping up appearances. She brought John up to believe that they were superior to the people around them and that they should keep themselves to themselves. When he was growing up he had very few friends because she didn't think any of the boys John met at school or on the estate were good enough. And somewhere along the line, with all this striving, she lost the capacity to show him much real affection. Nothing he could do ever really seemed to please her, outwardly at least. She became as hard as her native granite hills, but I

134

don't suppose it was her fault, poor woman.'

'It certainly doesn't sound as if she's had an easy life,' Mel said sympathetically.

'No, but who does?' Amelia smiled a little sadly. 'I'd better get back to John: he finds these events a big strain. Fabian may be Cape Wrath's figurehead, but John is the one the locals complain to – as you can see!'

'Who's that he's talking to?' The small red-faced man Mel had noticed when she'd first arrived seemed to have cornered MacDonald. James Everett had made his escape and was standing by the open French windows.

'That's Jimmie Macduff. He owns one of the local salmon farms. He moved up here from Glasgow three years ago.' She lowered her voice. 'To be honest, the locals don't like him much. It's hard enough for strangers to get accepted here and he doesn't help by throwing his weight around.'

'He looks angry about something,' Mel noted.

'Yes, you're right. He's trying to sue Cape Wrath for damages. He thinks the radioactive particles which have been turning up on the beaches are damaging his sales. I really must go to John's aid. It's been very nice meeting you at last.' And Amelia hurried across to her husband who acknowledged her with a grateful smile.

'Hi! You look great!' Tom Schultz, immaculate in a white tuxedo, a scarlet cummerbund around his lean waist, was at her elbow.

'Tom! I didn't realize you were here.'

'How are you?' He scanned her face.

'I'm fine, really! It's taken a bit of time but I'm perfectly OK now. I even go for walks along the coastal path again.' She'd hardly given Tom a thought since their last meeting, she realized guiltily.

'I only came this evening because I hoped you'd be here. You look as if you don't believe me. Listen . . .' He lowered his voice. 'Do you think I'd come to something like this under any other circumstances? Every time I see that

135

woman . . .' he nodded towards Christine who was holding court in the centre of the room '. . . it reminds me why we Americans fought the War of Independence.'

'That's mean,' Mel laughed.

'No it's not, it's honest. Now what about that date?' His voice softened. 'I didn't want to call you at work or at your hotel in case you thought I was hustling you . . . that's why I waited.'

'OK. I'd like to go out with you.' She meant it. After the disturbing events of the last few days there was something refreshingly open and straightforward about Tom. And above all he had nothing to do with Cape Wrath. The thought reminded her of Sean Docherty but there was still no sign of him. She bit her lip as a horrible thought struck her. Could he have had an accident? The road went on beyond the Director's house to a viewpoint. He might have driven up there for some reason before coming to the dinner party. Maybe she ought to mention it to someone. It would be awful if he was lying in a ditch somewhere.

A gong sounded and she glanced round, uncertain what to do. Christine was marshalling her guests, ready to go through to the dining room. It was on the tip of Mel's tongue to say something to Tom when the door opened and Docherty entered.

He advanced slowly into the room, as if unaware that all eyes were upon him. Christine was standing in the centre, an expression of frozen hauteur on her scarlet lips, taking in his ruffled hair and ill-tied bow-tie.

'So sorry I'm late,' he smiled. 'I got held up.'

'That's perfectly all right.' Christine responded with a faint smile, but an angry little jerk of her head as she caught the Director's eye showed that Docherty was far from forgiven. 'Well, if we're all ready, shall we go in?' Sir Angus took her arm and they led the way through the double doors at the far end of the room into the dining room beyond.

The other guests followed in their wake. Mel tried to

catch Docherty's eye but he looked strangely distracted, like a man who was just going through the motions of something and whose mind was elsewhere.

'I'm not a poor man – not a poor man at all – but I don't see why I should suffer!' Jimmie Macduff had gone on and on like a stuck record since the beginning of dinner.

Mel glanced surreptitiously at her watch. She'd certainly had to sing for her supper. Any thoughts of sitting next to Tom or Docherty had vanished when she'd seen the place-cards.

At least her companion to her right was undemanding – a dour Mancunian businessman who was chairman of the company which had scooped some of the privatization contracts from Cape Wrath. He had made it very plain before he'd even finished his soup that he loathed Wrath and would be away down south as soon as his business was concluded. Again Mel had listened and nodded understandingly. She achieved a couple of minutes of almost animated conversation with him by raising Manchester United's chances of coming top of the Premier League again, but it hadn't lasted and she'd left him to his own gloomy thoughts.

She glanced down to the far end of the table where Sean was sitting. Jimmie Macduff's wife was next to him, prattling away with the same vigour as her husband, impervious to his abstracted expression. But was it just boredom or something more? There was a look close to despair on his face, which looked pale in the candlelight. She saw deep shadows under his eyes and watched as his fingers tapped nervously on a wine glass. She could see it was unused and that he'd stuck to drinking water.

She wished she could have the opportunity to talk to him but it looked as if that would have to wait for another time.

A decanter was circulating. Would Christine rise now and lead the women back to the drawing room, leaving the gentlemen to cigars and port? Everything had been so extremely formal that it wouldn't be any surprise. But she had to concede that Christine had tried very hard. The food had been excellent, including the poached salmon tactfully purchased from Jimmie Macduff's fisheries. Good wine had flowed, and the long polished table with its sparkling silver and glassware and colourful flower arrangements had looked spectacular. If anything, the setting had outshone the guests.

'Excuse me – Oh, damn and blast it!' Jimmie Macduff was lunging for the port. Somehow he lost his grip and the crystal decanter went spinning across the smooth, polished surface, collided with a vase and tipped on its side. Mel managed to stop it falling off the table but was not in time to prevent some of its contents tipping onto her dress, staining the delicate colour.

Mel sprang up. 'It's all right. Please, don't worry – it doesn't matter.' She made the standard responses but inside she was anguished – *not this dress!* Jimmie Macduff was making pawing motions with his napkin, meaning to be helpful. She stepped back from him hastily and left the room. Maybe if she splashed some salt and cold water on quickly, that might help. She ran down a corridor that was more like a labyrinth. Where on earth was the kitchen? Perhaps it was through that door at the end.

She pushed it open and stopped dead. The girl with the shaved head was sitting at the kitchen table calmly buttering herself some pieces of toast. Her long eyes widened as they took in Mel and her dishevelled appearance but the expression in them was as hostile as ever.

They stared at each other for a moment. The last time Mel had seen the girl she'd been dancing around Fergus Brown's living room with a bagful of cannabis in her hands. What was she doing here of all places? The only logical answer was that she'd been hired for the evening like the girl who'd handed around the drinks, but instinct told her that wasn't right. Mel felt stupid – like someone faced with a puzzle they can't fit together.

138

The girl lowered her contemptuous stare and began to eat, taking big chunks out of the toast and wiping buttery hands on her baggy cotton trousers.

Mel glanced around, half-expecting Fergus to pop out with his camera from behind the fridge. She thought of the two of them as a package.

'Laura, darling – I thought you were out.' Christine Williams was standing in the doorway, a dark red flushing her cheekbones. There was an awkward silence while she advanced into the room. Her poise seemed to have deserted her and she began speaking rapidly, not even pausing to draw breath.

'This is our daughter. She's been studying music at sixth-form college but she's come home for a few months. It's very stressful when you're as talented as Laura – they have such high expectations of her, you see. She'll probably be concert standard. We've got a lot of talented classical musicians in the family . . .'

As Christine Williams prattled nervously, it struck Mel that she was actually scared of her own daughter.

There was a soft thud as a piece of toast hit the wall and slid greasily downwards. The girl got up off her chair. 'Why don't you just shut up and leave me alone. Classical music's crap. Anyway, I'm not good enough. Don't pressurize me!'

'Laura,' Christine said helplessly.

'Why can't you just shut up, shut up, shut up!' Laura's voice rose to such a pitch that it hurt Mel's ears. She went closer and closer to her mother until she was virtually screaming in her face.

Christine Williams crumpled up under the onslaught, her face twisting with a pain that was beyond embarrassment. Mel slipped quietly from the room and closed the door behind her. Her dress was probably ruined but it didn't seem to matter anymore. She felt painfully sorry for both of them.

The dinner party was breaking up, which was just as well. Fabian Williams was looking around in a helpless way for his wife who came hurrying into the hall a few moments later, smoothing stray blonde locks back under the alice band. Mel marvelled at her self-control.

The guests were saying their farewells and making their way out to the row of cars parked along the drive in the shadow of a line of stunted trees. Tom was beside her as they stepped out into the cool night air and he kissed her once, but lingeringly, on the lips. Mel felt too confused by the scene she'd just witnessed to respond, but he didn't seem to mind.

After he'd gone she sat quietly for a few moments before inserting the key in the ignition. Her MGF was almost the last car left, although she could see that Docherty's was still there. She waited a moment, hoping he'd come outside. They really did need to talk. He'd obviously been avoiding her since that afternoon when he'd told her about MacDonald and the shaft. When he didn't appear, she turned the key, kicked the engine into life and drove slowly down the drive, deep in thought.

He sensed she was there before he felt her slender arms entwine themselves around his neck. Her face, damp with tears, was against his cheek, filling his nostrils with the scent of her.

'Christ Almighty – don't do that!' He hit the brake and brought the car to a halt in the nick of time before ending up in a ditch.

'I thought you liked it when I put my tongue in your ear ...'

'I do, but not when I'm driving. How long had you been hiding in my car anyway?'

Laura detached her arms from around his neck and slumped back on the rear seat like a beautiful but sulky child. He watched the pale outline of her face in the rearview mirror.

'I heard the dinner party breaking up and slipped out by the back door. I know you never lock your car ...'

'Laura, *please.*' There was an edge to his voice as he turned to look at her.

'Please what?'

'Think about what I was saying to you earlier this evening.'

'You mean before or after we fucked?'

Sean didn't answer. The knowledge that this was all his own fault only added to his regrets. He'd always been weak – indulgent – and this was the result.

'Wasn't it funny to think that my parents' precious dinner guests were standing around sipping sherry and making polite conversation just a few feet below us while we were screwing away doggie fashion.'

'Laura . . . you know what I think.'

'I know that you want me.'

'Of course I want you. What man in his right mind wouldn't! But it's no good – it's got to stop.'

'Why?'

'I'm old enough to be your father – a cliché, but sadly true. And there's no future in it. You've got your own life to lead and you're wasting it.'

'It's my choice, I know what I'm doing.'

'Do you?' His voice was bitter but the bitterness wasn't directed against her.

'I ran into Miss Goebbels in the kitchen this evening. Someone had spilled something red on her. She looked like Lady Macbeth.'

'I take it you mean Mel?'

'Yes.' Laura put her hands to her face and laughed delightedly to herself. 'I sent her an obscene note a few nights ago . . . I'd love to have seen her face.'

'I know. Well, I *did* see her face. She was hurt and upset.'

'So?' There was a stubborn twist to the girl's mouth.

'You'll get yourself into trouble. I destroyed the note.'

'I don't care if everyone knows it was me. Or that it was me who tipped off the demonstrators about when the fuel shipment was coming in. I saw all the details in a fax which came through at home for Daddy.'

'Sometimes I think you don't care about anything. In fact, I think you *want* your parents to find out what you've been up to. It's a way of getting back at them. Isn't that the real reason why you sleep with me?'

'No, that's not true – at least about sleeping with you.'

'Isn't it? Are you sure?'

'My father's only interested in his field trips to the Middle East and the designs on Crusaders' shields, and my mother wants to get back to "our set" in the Home Counties. They don't give a toss about me and it's mutual.'

'You sound very cynical and unforgiving. You're too young for that.'

'Don't patronize me, Sean.'

'I'm sorry.' He looked down. He knew he should just walk away from this.

The next sound he heard was the click of the door as Laura slid out of the back of the car. Then she was close to him, half in his lap, running her fingertips over the contours of his chest, nipping the skin of his throat with her teeth.

'Make love to me again – *now*. I want you to.'

'Laura, please try to understand!'

'No, I won't. I need you. You're my big, strong, protector – my *real* daddy.' Her hands moved between his legs. He seized them in his much stronger hands and tried to hold her away from him.

'Please, Daddy, please,' she whispered. She wrenched free of him only to put her arms around him and pull him towards her. His resistance crumbled as she ran her tongue cat-like over his closed eyelids and he groaned as he felt his deceitful body respond wantonly and thoughtlessly to hers.

What the hell was he going to do? Sean Docherty felt like a man poised on top of a cliff with a pack of ravening wolves behind him and a row of sharpened stakes below. Everything was going wrong. He used to be so sure of himself, so cool – the clever, cynical observer of other men's follies who didn't bother to get involved because, frankly, it was beneath him.

Well, that was a laugh. He'd cocked everything up good and proper, Sean thought furiously as he ran water for a shower. He wanted to wash all traces of lovemaking from him so he could think straight. He needed his wits about him just now. And he needed a drink, just one, to help him.

Naked and dripping he walked down the hall to the drinks cupboard which he kept locked to make it easier to resist temptation. The key was Sellotaped to the underside. Kneeling down he fished it out with a grunt of satisfaction. His hands were steady as he unlocked the door and took out a bottle of whisky. He poured two inches into a tumbler and downed it in one gulp. It shot through his body. He closed his eyes and took a series of deep breaths. God, that was good . . . He began to relax just a little.

But there was no point in deluding himself that he was going to get any sleep. Too many things were going on his mind. If it were only a question of Laura . . . but life was a great deal more complicated than that. As he filled his glass again, Mel's wistful oval face slid into focus in his mind. He'd seen her looking at him during that God-awful dinner party, wondering and doubting. He'd been a fool to tell her anything.

Draining the glass for a second time he put it down reluctantly and made for his bedroom. It didn't take him long to put on jeans and a sweatshirt and to grab his car keys. He was way over the limit but who was going to spot him on the road to Cape Wrath at this time of night?

He was right. At 3 a.m. the streets were deserted. Not a single light shone in the Old Library as he swung the heavy communal front door closed behind him. The high Victorian sash-windows gazed like blind eyes out into the night.

At twenty-past three he was driving up to the main gate, rock music belting out on the car stereo at a pitch to blot out unwelcome thoughts. The night-duty constable raised

143

the barrier and let him through, barely bothering to look at his pass. The police were used to Dr Docherty's nocturnal visits.

Over in the reprocessing plant lights shone as the night shift went about their work. Sean drove past it and on past the nuclear waste stores. His head was aching and he switched the cassette off abruptly. That was better. Silence.

But there shouldn't *be* silence – the realization burst upon him. The waste store was an 'active' building. The criticality and radiation monitors positioned around it should be bleeping to confirm that no radioactivity was escaping. The absolute quiet was unnatural.

Docherty got out of the car and walked across to the nearest monitor. Was he seeing straight or was the whisky playing tricks with him? He looked more closely and swore out loud. There was no mistake: the monitor had been switched off. Running round the perimeter of the building he found that the others were off as well. What in God's name was going on?

He turned to go back to his car and then he saw them – two lights down on the foreshore, moving backwards and forwards. But nothing was supposed to be happening down there tonight ... He broke into a run. Soon his feet were scrambling over the sand and shale of the beach. To his right the sea was inky. Bright moonlight illuminated the steps cut into the rock and he made for them, half-slipping on piles of rotting seaweed. As he reached the top of the steps he could see the outline of the crane, gallows-high, above the shaft ...

Chapter Nine

'You'll have to speak to him. This sort of thing really won't do!'

'How can I ? No one's seen the man for three days.' The sharp edge to MacDonald's voice made the Director glance up angrily.

'You know very well what I mean. When he turns up – as I have no doubt he will – you must tell him if it happens just one more time he'll be out. I can sack him for misconduct – the rules are quite clear.' Fabian Williams leaned towards MacDonald and his expression relaxed a little. 'Look, you've done your best to protect him in the past and I've turned a blind eye, but we both know it can't go on. He's had his chances. I can't have a senior manager, however capable, behaving in such an irresponsible way, can I?'

MacDonald sighed. 'No, of course not.' He dragged an exasperated hand across his forehead. 'We're in real problems already with the Venezuelan contract. Sean was the only one who knew the details of the terms we'd offered them, and now they're screaming blue murder that we won't go firm on the deal. Of course we can piece it all together, tracking back through Sean's e-mails, but it's taking time. It makes us look stupid and incompetent. The Venezuelans will take their fuel elsewhere if we don't get our act together.'

'Isn't anyone worried that something might have happened to Sean?' Mel asked.

The two men glanced round at her as if they'd forgotten she was still in the room.

'The only thing that's happened to Sean is a massive hangover. He's gone on a bender and will eventually crawl out from whichever stone he's hiding under,' MacDonald said bluntly.

'But you can't be sure,' she argued. 'He could have had an accident or been taken ill. Perhaps we should ask the police to check with the hospitals? He could have had a crash after the dinner party.'

'This is such a small community that we would have heard immediately if anything like that had happened. Anyway, he was seen on the site later that night. According to the police log book, he drove in around 3.20 a.m. and left again two hours later. If we report Sean missing it will set all sorts of rumours going which will only be harmful to Cape Wrath,' the Director explained patiently. 'It's not as if this is unprecedented either. This has happened at least twice before. He will turn up, believe me.'

It was on the tip of Mel's tongue to say that Docherty had been making a real effort to give up drinking. Why should he have chosen just now to lapse – it didn't make sense – but she bit her lip. Why should she know any better than them how Sean might suddenly take it into his head to behave?

'Well, if you're sure there's nothing to worry about . . .' She began gathering up the papers she'd spread in front of her at the meeting.

'I *am* sure,' MacDonald said quietly. 'In a few days' time everything will be back to normal.'

But things didn't return to normal. Two more days passed and there was still no sign of Sean. The weekend came and went with no news. But on the Monday morning – over a week since Sean had disappeared – something happened at last. A Highland Constabulary squad car drove slowly onto the site and parked just beneath Mel's window. She watched two officers get out and walk towards the entrance.

146

Something in their expressions warned Mel that this was no routine visit: they'd come about Docherty. She sat at her desk but her eyes wouldn't focus on her paperwork. Instead she saw Docherty's cynical, detached face; that lazy, knowing smile hovered in front of her. The way he had of looking at her from under his brows. She'd missed him these last few days. Even though there'd been moments of tension, their relationship had at least been something human and real to take hold of.

That didn't come so naturally at Cape Wrath. There was a constraint and a formality superimposed on everything, and suspicion hung in the air. Everyone watched their back every minute. There was no one she could talk to as she and Docherty had talked. And there'd been so much else she'd needed him to tell her . . .

Although it was a warm day, Mel shivered a little and pulled her pink linen jacket more tightly around her. Then she sat and waited for her phone to ring. Ten minutes later it did.

'The police have been to see me.' Fabian Williams was looking paler than usual, his angular face pinched and anxious.

'I saw them arrive. Was it about Sean?'

'Yes.' He seemed to be turning things over in his mind. 'It seems his boat has been washed up on the beach a few miles west of here.'

'His boat? I didn't know he owned one.'

'It's a dinghy with an outboard motor, but there's no sign of the motor. The police think it probably broke down and Sean fell overboard while he was trying to dismount and repair it.'

'You mean Sean's drowned?' She was horrified.

'It seems a likely explanation. Especially if he'd been drinking – he could easily have overbalanced. The police have been to his apartment and they found a half-empty whisky bottle and a glass.'

'But they haven't found a body?' Mel's voice was almost a whisper.

'No – not yet. The police said that he could have been swept out to sea. If so, the body will probably turn up somewhere on the Irish coast.'

Tears were suddenly running down her cheeks. Mel sat down and turned her face away from the Director. Ashamed of this sudden, uncontrolled outburst of emotion; she needed a moment's privacy.

To her surprise she felt her shoulder being gently patted. Looking up through matted eyelashes she was touched by the look of concern on Fabian Williams' face.

'It's a shock for all of us, God knows,' he said bleakly. 'Perhaps I should have taken your advice and contacted the police earlier but I'm not sure it would have made any difference.' The appeal was unmistakable.

'No, it wouldn't have made any difference,' she reassured him gently. She wiped her face clean of salty tears and smudged mascara and breathed deeply, forcing herself to focus on the present. 'Now, what are we going to say about this to the staff and the press?'

'What do you suggest?' He was looking his age now, the colourless skin on his bony jawline sagging slackly.

'I'll put out a short general announcement to our staff reporting what the Highland Constabulary have told us. But you or John ought to talk to the people in the Contracts Department direct. They'll be hardest hit by the news. They'll also need to know how you intend to run things without Sean. There are so many deals in the offing you'll have to appoint someone else to take charge temporarily until we get news one way or the other. Leave the press to me. I'll brief them in a low-key way. If they want more they'll have to ring the Highland Constabulary.'

The Director nodded his agreement but she had the feeling he wasn't really listening to her. He seemed bowed down by the news, which surprised and touched her. He had never given the impression of even liking Sean, but maybe that was it. Now that it was too late, he must be feeling guilty that he hadn't taken a greater interest in him.

'You think he's dead, don't you?' she asked quietly.

Fabian Williams met her gaze dully. 'Yes. I don't think there's much doubt of that, do you?'

It was strange to think that a church had been standing on this very spot for a thousand years. Perched on a tongue of rock, high above the sea between Cape Wrath and the town, it had been refuge and fortress in its time. St Aidan's had seen the terrifying era of the Viking raids when the dragon-prowed longboats stole southwards across the seas to raid this stretch of coastline. Destroyed and rebuilt many times, St Aidan's had nevertheless survived – a simple stone building with a square tower standing serene in the sunlight.

Mel parked in one of the few remaining spaces in the gravelled area beneath the path that led up to the church. The Director's sleekly elegant Bentley was already drawn up on one side and MacDonald's maroon Rover was nearby. Yet her watch told her there were still twenty minutes before the service was due to start. She began to walk slowly up the path, her black shoes crunching on the gravel.

The explosive sound of a motorbike bit into the tranquillity. Glancing over her shoulder she saw Fergus Brown arriving on his red BMW, and looked away again. The next hour or so was private. If he wanted to speak to her he could do it later.

She quickened her pace. The brim of her black straw hat was wide, shading her face. It felt comfortingly protective, like hiding behind sunglasses. She paused outside the church. The granite stonework, softened by a covering of yellow lichen, looked mellow in the afternoon sunshine. Around her, Celtic crosses marked well-tended graves. Bunches of late summer flowers – chrysanthemums, roses, delphiniums – gave off a sweet scent. On other graves small shrubs, capable of surviving the harsh winter winds, were growing sturdily.

As she stepped into the simple white-washed entrance, Mel's mind slid involuntarily backwards in time to the lakeside church in Guatemala where Daniel had preached. The dark interior had been filled with images of the Madonna, festooned with so many little pieces of jewellery donated by the Indian women that the features of the tiny statues had barely been visible. For a moment she could smell the spicily pungent incense that had seemed to cling to the very fabric of the building. Daniel had hated all that. He would have preferred the austere lines of this little church lit by shafts of sunlight pouring through plain leaded windows.

The verger handed her an order of service and Mel snapped back to the present. She sat at the end of one of the pews in the back row. Would any members of Sean's family be here? What about his former wife? She looked around her, but as far as she could tell nearly everyone seemed to be from the Cape Wrath plant or from the town. She wasn't really surprised to see so many people. There'd been something fundamentally likeable and appealing about Sean Docherty. She'd felt it herself and she'd only known him a few weeks.

As the remaining minutes ticked by, the church filled up completely. By the time the Reverend Stuart Mackenzie mounted the small oak pulpit, there were no pews left and people were clustered at the back.

'We are here today to pray for Sean Docherty who disappeared three weeks ago. As the size of this congregation shows, he was a popular member of our small community in Wrath. He wasn't born and bred here but he became one of us. Nor was he a religious man. I say with all honesty that he seldom came to St Aidan's but I can also say that I thought of him as a friend. Over the years I have been the chaplain to the Cape Wrath plant, I came to know him well and to value his intelligence and humour. Sean Docherty was no saint. Like all of us he had some very human failings which he would have been the first to acknowledge – and even to exaggerate . . .'

150

As the Minister painted an accurate but compassionate word portrait of Sean, Mel thought back through all the conversations they'd had. There had always been something elusive about him. Maybe if she'd had the chance to know him for longer, all the loose ends would have been tied up and she would have understood him more completely. She might have been able to make some sense of everything, including his strange stories about the plant and John MacDonald ... But just now none of it really seemed to matter against the feeling of grief and loss.

The Minister had finished and Fabian Williams was rising to his feet to take his place at the lectern and read a passage from the Bible. With his silvery hair brushed back from his face in two perfect wings, and his stern fine-boned features, he looked like an elderly archangel.

'The reading today is taken from—' His deep tones rang out impressively but a sudden noise at the back of the church made him pause and look up. His expression lost its calm assurance. 'Laura?'

Mel turned. The girl had pushed her way through the people standing at the rear and was clinging, white-knuckled, to the back of the pew where Mel was sitting. Her face was so pink and swollen with tears it was almost unrecognizable. Her mascara was in thick streaks, giving her the grotesque look of a distressed clown. She struck an alien, discordant note, but her grief was so real that Mel could feel it almost physically. She half-rose, wanting to offer some word or act of comfort.

But at that very moment there was the sound of high heels clacking briskly over flagstones. Then Christine Williams was by her daughter's side, taking her firmly by the elbow and steering her through the curious onlookers and out of the church. Mel saw Fergus Brown glance round at what was happening, brows raised and curious, but he turned quickly back to the notes he was taking.

Nasty, heartless little shit, Mel thought and was surprised by the violence of her reaction. But hard on its heels came

151

another thought. Why should Laura have been quite so upset?

'The reading today is taken from . . .'

Mel turned her attention back to the Director who had resumed his task at the lectern, but now his tones didn't have quite the same resonance.

'Hi there!' Tom Schultz seemed to have materialized out of nowhere, very formal in his naval uniform.

'Tom, I didn't see you in the church.' Mel smiled up at him and took a sip of the weak tea which had been handed out to everyone in the church hall. 'And I didn't know you knew Sean.'

'I didn't. I met him a few times but I didn't really know the guy at all. I'm here because your Director sent us an invitation and our chief thought Anderson Base should be represented.' He drew a little closer and lowered his voice. 'What actually happened?'

'No one really knows. That's the horrible thing,' Mel said slowly, reviewing it again in her mind. 'He suddenly disappeared after the night of that dinner party. Then a few days later his boat was found west of Wrath minus its engine. The most likely explanation is that he fell over-board trying to fix it, got washed out to sea and drowned.'

'Poor bastard,' Tom said softly.

'Yes.' Mel focused on her tea cup. 'I suppose it's only a matter of time before his body turns up somewhere.'

Before she realized, Tom had taken her chin in his strong hand and was tilting her face up to the light.

'That's better. I couldn't see you properly under that hat. You look pale and there are circles under your eyes.'

Mel felt herself colour under that searching, intimate look. 'I was fond of Sean. He was a friend. And I can't quite believe this has happened.'

'Sure, I know. I lost friends in Vietnam and in the Gulf War. You keep expecting them to just walk in. It doesn't seem real.'

152

'Do you remember how Sean seemed that night at the dinner party?'

Tom shrugged. 'Nope.'

'He arrived late and he looked preoccupied, worried almost.'

'*I'd* be worried if I was late for one of Christine Williams' dinner parties. Don't read too much into things. It probably had nothing to do with whatever happened. Anyway, you'll never know so what's the point in speculating?'

'I suppose you're right.'

Tom paused and his eyes looked lightly but directly into hers. 'Perhaps this isn't really the place to ask, but come out to dinner with me and let me convince you some more . . .You promised me a date, remember?'

'I remember.' It would be good to be with someone who had nothing to do with Cape Wrath. But before she could say any more, John MacDonald joined them.

'Well, that went off OK apart from the little outburst of histrionics halfway through.' MacDonald looked cheerful, perhaps forcedly so, Mel thought, remembering his ambiguous relationship with Docherty. At once he began talking quickly to Tom about Anderson Base, barely leaving time for the American to respond.

After a few minutes he paused in mid-sentence. 'Listen. I've been meaning to ask you this for some time. How about coming out on my boat, Tom? What do you say? The weather's perfect just now. Another couple of weeks and we'll be into autumn squalls.'

'Fine,' Tom agreed easily. 'That would be great.'

'And you'll come along as well, Mel?'

'Sure she will,' Tom replied for her.

'OK. We'll fix a date.' MacDonald wandered away to join another group. He seemed defiantly jaunty. But funerals, particularly funerals of the relatively young, had that effect on some people, Mel reflected. They reminded you that you were still alive and should exploit life to the full before arbitrary extinction cut your plans short too. And

153

this was pretty much like a funeral. All the same, a boat trip was a tactless thing to suggest when it was a boat trip which had probably killed Sean.

'Look, I've got to go. But I'll call you to fix up about dinner. Take care now.' Tom kissed her cheek. As she watched his tall figure weave through the packed hall, Mel's mind was far away from him.

She felt furtive, like a burglar, but it was stupid, she wasn't doing anything illegal. Inserting the key in the lock she stepped inside Sean's apartment and closed the door behind her. She stood for a moment, just listening. The silence seemed immense, overwhelming, and she couldn't shake off the feeling of trespass. She should have brought Ishbel with her then everything would have seemed more normal.

Still, the sooner she found what she'd come for the sooner she could leave. Sean's secretary had described the report to her – a twelve-page document called *A Layman's Guide to Risk and Radiation* in dark blue covers with spiral binding. Sean had taken it home to give it a final proofing before publication. It wasn't anything directly to do with his contracts work but one of the tasks he liked doing to keep his scientific hand in. She'd been delighted when he'd offered to write it for her.

If she remembered correctly, the study was down the long corridor next to Sean's bedroom. The heavy Victorian door creaked a little as she pushed it open and she noticed a film of dust on the glossy ivory paintwork. But then no one had been here since the police had made their cursory examination after finding Sean's boat.

Sean's study was exactly what she would have expected – an organized mess. There were piles of papers relating to different topics all over the floor – some of them so high they'd toppled over. She began searching carefully through them, putting any papers relating to Cape Wrath to one side.

Two hours later there was still no sign of the report. Mel sat back on her heels and wiped grimy hands on the legs of her jeans. Maybe she was looking in the wrong place? The room was shelved on two sides from floor to ceiling. Standing up she began to read the titles on the bookspines. Mostly academic books and books about music. But on the second shelf from the top, towards the corner, she noticed an uneven gap between two large volumes. Automatically and without thinking, she reached up to straighten them but something was in the way. Inserting her hand she felt something – a small chunky book – pushed right to the back and next to it a package wrapped in something stiff and metallic.

The book had dark red covers and some loose papers were tucked inside. The whole thing was secured with a thick rubber band. Mel glanced at it and was about to push it back when curiosity got the better of her. She sat down at Sean's desk and pulled the rubber band off. The thick cardboard covers fell slackly open.

It looked like some kind of diary. The paper was covered with Sean's flowing but erratic handwriting. As she turned the pages a blank brown envelope dropped out and fell plumply to the floor at her feet. Picking it up she could feel the thickness of its contents. Again she succumbed to the seductive power of curiosity and her fingers gently opened the flap and pulled out the contents.

Mel gasped. She was holding a wad of fifty-pound banknotes so fresh and clean she could almost smell the ink drying on them. There must be at least five thousand pounds here, maybe more. But there was something else as well. A neatly folded glossy piece of paper was tucked inside the envelope. Opening it out, Mel saw it was a page of advertisements torn out of a yachting magazine, dated several weeks before Sean vanished. One of the ads – for a second-hand oceangoing yacht – had been ringed in biro.

A piece of foolscap was stapled to it, containing a list of dates and what looked like co-ordinates at sea – some kind of navigational log? Again it was in Sean's handwriting but it made no real sense to her. She turned it over, seeking an explanation. On the back was a sketch of the coastline around Wrath with several points circled. Mel stared at the dots and crosses marked on it in thick felt-tip pen. What did it mean? It could be the location of the local fishermen's lobster pots for all she knew. Yet why try and conceal it? The diary and the envelope hadn't been very well hidden, but they had been put where the casual observer wouldn't see them. And Sean clearly hadn't expected anyone to come prowling around his apartment as she was doing.

In fact, what *was* she doing? She had come to look for an official report. She had no business searching through Sean's personal possessions, but now she had started, the compulsion to carry on was irresistible. There might be some clue here to what had actually happened to him.

Whatever the case, she wanted nothing to do with the money. She crammed the notes back in their envelope and replaced it the shelf. As she did so, her fingers came in contact again with the small parcel. She gently pulled it out and laid it on the desktop. It was about six inches square. Suddenly she knew exactly what she was going to find inside.

How familiar it felt as she opened the paper, noting the careful way the foil had been pleated to allow a little air to circulate around the contents. Her hands were trembling as she slowly pulled the shining covering back to reveal the oily crumbling brown contents. At the same time a faint herbal smell spiralled into the air. Cannabis resin and enough to keep a small village high for a week!

Mel stared at it, pictures beginning to form in her mind as she made connections. Blurred at first, they came into sharper focus with every passing moment. Sean Docherty hadn't been what she had thought. The money, the map, the ad for the boat, the cannabis – all pointed to one thing. He had been involved in some way with drug smuggling. Which also meant he might have known something about the waiter's murder. Mel hastily closed her eyes but that didn't stop her seeing that white bloated thing rising and falling in the surf with its gaping, mutilated throat.

156

And suddenly she was travelling back in time to that other life in Tenango. Daniel and Simon's bloodsoaked bodies were slumped over the café table while the army jeeps churned the gravel. In her brain the two incidents were one and she was the helpless onlooker again. The sense of betrayal and past guilt overwhelmed her once more. She should have guessed then what was going on: that her clothing cooperative was being used as a front to smuggle drugs into the United States by her lover. But naive and in love, she'd never suspected a thing. John's interest in the project had seemed so natural . . .and she'd trusted him unquestioningly. And because of her blind trust Daniel and Simon had died.

Now it felt like it was all beginning again. God, she was cold. Suddenly she was shaking so violently she was gripping the edge of the desk for support. The walls seemed to be pressing in on her, threatening to crush her under their weight of books.

She must get out of this place. *Now!* Instinct also told her to cover her tracks. Somehow she managed to rewrap the resin, squashing the foil around it and ramming it to the back of the shelf where she had found it. What else? She looked around the room in a panic. Her brown suede bag was hanging on the back of a chair. She grabbed it, slung it over her shoulder and made for the door. But then she stopped.

The sound of approaching footsteps – heavy and deliberate – resonated in the stillness. Where? Outside the apartment, but close, so close. She tensed, straining every nerve like a hunted animal, but all was bewilderingly silent again. A sick feeling gripped the pit of her stomach as she remembered that Sean's apartment was on the top floor. There was nowhere else to go. Whoever it was must be standing outside – waiting!

For one crazy moment an image of Sean swept before her, returning home at last from full fathom five to gaze around him with dead, drowned eyes. It was almost a relief to hear the solid human sound of a key turning in a lock and it brought her back to her senses a little.

Mel snatched the diary and the other papers still lying on the top of the desk and crammed them into her bag. Peering through the crack in the door, she could see the heavy, handsome front door beginning to open. For a second or two it would prevent whoever was entering from seeing down the corridor to the right.

Taking her chance, Mel dived out of the study and darted silently into the adjacent bedroom. Surely it was a better place to hide? But the only refuge seemed to be under the big Victorian iron bedstead or perhaps in the wardrobe. She stood in the middle of the room wracked with indecision, her breath coming in ragged gasps. If she wasn't careful, whoever it was would hear her.

She forced herself to take some deep breaths, then listened again intently. By the sound of it the intruder had gone into the sitting room. If she ran for it, could she get to the front door and through it in time? Her brain seemed to have turned to jelly, robbing her of the ability to be decisive. She could hear the sound of someone opening and shutting drawers and cupboards. Looking for something, but carefully. Not like a burglar wantonly throwing things around.

And then it struck her. Was she being a complete fool? It could be someone from the plant on a similar quest to her own. Sean had left several sets of his keys in his desk. His secretary could easily have given them to someone else. It might even be Ishbel! She was so sure she was right that she went close to the bedroom door and looked through the crack.

And froze. Her sense of relief had been premature, for Hamish Cameron was walking towards her down the corridor, his giant physique seeming to dwarf everything, casting shadows on the walls. His eyes looked cold and focused. This was a man she'd drunk whisky with in front of a fragrant fire – a man who had roused desire in her. But now she felt her skin prickle with fear. No way did she want him to find her there.

She backed away from the door, sensing a very real danger. Hamish must be involved with the drug smuggling as well. What was it Laura had said that day in Fergus's house? Something like, 'I've got enough dope from Hamish to last the whole weekend ...' It all fitted. Hamish's bohemian but affluent lifestyle, his frequent absences from Wrath, the lack of any visible means of support ...

She heard him go into the study next door and the rustle of papers as he searched. I could spare him the trouble, Mel thought bitterly. I could tell him exactly where the money and the resin are! But if Hamish was absorbed by his search in the study then maybe she had a chance to just slip quietly past ...

Mel moved lightly up to the bedroom door. From the sound of it, Hamish was going through Sean's desk, which faced away from the door. With luck his back would be turned. Holding her breath she slid through the door and paused. She was right. Glancing into the study she could see Hamish's head bent over a pile of papers he was rifling through. Slowly, slowly she tiptoed past the study and down the corridor. Just a few more yards and she'd be there. All she had to do was ease the Yale lock open and she'd be free ...

And then her bag slipped from her shoulder, the metal buckle scraping on the parquet floor. Hamish moved with the speed of a powerful cat. She hadn't even reached the door when she felt him grab her, lifting her off her feet and swinging her around to face him.

'What the hell are you doing here?' His grip was so tight that it hurt, his expression chilling.

'I . . . was looking for something,' she gasped.

'Snooping, I suppose. Making sure Docherty didn't leave any embarrassing papers around about the plant. And just what have you found?' His eyes went to her bag. He released her but planted an arm either side of her against the wall, trapping her.

159

'I wasn't "snooping". I was looking for a paper Sean had written for me. His secretary gave me keys so I could come and search. And I didn't find it.' Mel tried to put indignation in place of her fear. 'What are you doing here anyway? And how did *you* get in?'

'I could tell you it's none of your business,' he said slowly, then stepped back, arms falling to his sides but watching her.

Mel took several paces away from him and waited. He was still between her and the door. He read her look.

'Go if you want to. I'm not going to stop you.'

'You frightened me. I didn't know who it was.'

'Evidently. Well, now you do. Mystery solved.'

Oh no it isn't, Mel thought, not by a long way. She edged past him towards the door, half-expecting him to grab her but he'd turned away from her and gone into the sitting room. Her hand was on the latch but some impulse stopped her. In spite of her fear she had to know.

'Hamish, what exactly is going on?'

'What do you mean?'

'Why are you here? What is it you want?'

He looked at her coldly. 'If you really want to know, Laura sent me.'

'*Laura*?' Mel looked at him in astonishment.

'She and Docherty were lovers. She wants her letters back. And more important, she wants back a naked photograph she gave him. Satisfied?'

'But Laura's half Sean's age . . .'

Amusement flickered in his amber eyes. 'Don't be so naive, please. Since when has that ever been a problem? Now if you don't mind I'd like to carry on looking. Unless of course you can give me any clues?'

'No,' Mel whispered. 'No, I can't.'

Slowly she let herself out of the apartment. As she walked down the wide staircase she found she was shaking.

Chapter Ten

It was getting late – nearly ten o'clock – but Mel wasn't ready to go back to the hotel. Instead she walked down to the breakwater and sat on the wall. The moon, luminous and golden, signalling the approach of autumn, was rising, casting a gilded ladder over the dark sea, but the beauty of it passed her by. She glanced nervously into the shadows, remembering how Hamish had seemed to materialize here out of nowhere.

She must think logically about what had happened. Had her reactions to everything been too emotional? Had she been leapfrogging to the wrong conclusions? She thought again about the cannabis in Sean's flat, the money and the map and the advertisement for a yacht. But what else could it mean except that Sean had been caught up in some drug syndicate?

That would explain his sudden disappearance. Or at least why he had chosen to go out in a boat alone and at night. But had he really had an accident? Perhaps his body would be washed up one day, throat cut, irony banished at last from eyes chewed by fish. Nausea rose from the pit of her stomach. For a moment she thought she was going to be sick and although the evening was cool she was sweating.

Restlessly she got up and began to walk along in the shelter of the wall, going over and over what Hamish had said about Sean and Laura. Why had it disturbed her so much? Because it reminded her of things in her own life she'd rather forget? Because it was yet another facet of Sean she'd known nothing about? Or because it seemed too incredible to be true – something Hamish had invented to justify his presence in Sean's apartment?

If so, what had his true motive been? To find the money and the cannabis before anyone else did and started asking dangerous questions? And was it just a precaution or because Hamish knew for sure Docherty wasn't coming back? Mel shook her head in despair. And Laura – how did she fit into this macabre jigsaw puzzle? Mel remembered her white face grotesquely marked with rivulets of mascara.

Maybe she should just resign, Mel thought. She really didn't need all this. She'd tried to begin a new life and yet everything was full of echoes from the past. On the other hand, why should she run? She was a different person from the frightened girl who'd sat impassive as a piece of wood on the shores of the lake that night. She was capable of taking control of her life.

Mel put her face in her hands and closed her eyes. The careful, orderly world she'd constructed around herself was disintegrating like the sandcastles the local children built on the beach at Wrath as the tide came in. She felt like a fly caught in a web – but who was the spider?

The missing report had turned up in Sean's office after all. She could have saved herself the trauma of visiting his apartment if she'd only known. The pages were neatly typed and well set out and the title leapt crisply from the first page: *A Layman's Guide to Risk and Radiation*.

It was strange, and touching, too, to think of Sean diligently working away on this report for her. Glancing at her watch, Mel saw it was nearly seven o'clock in the evening. She should be getting back to the hotel but her interest was roused. It was very quiet; the only sound came from a pair of curlews swooping out to sea as she bent her head over the dense text and started to read.

162

Radiation is all around you in the natural world. Did you know that you are radioactive? And so is your home and everything you eat? And that some foods like Brazil nuts, tea, coffee and bread are more radioactive than others? Did you know that Cornwall has the highest natural radiation levels in the UK? Or that a week's holiday there would in theory give you a chance of dying from radiation-related disease of 1 in 250,000? That may sound alarming, but look how this compares with other risks of death per year in the UK –

1 in 200 from heart disease or from smoking 10 cigarettes a day
1 in 850 from all natural causes if you're aged 40
1 in 5,000 from influenza
1 in 7000 if you're a coal miner
1 in 10,000 from a road accident
1 in 26,000 from an accident in the home,
1 in 100,000 from murder
1 in 500,000 from a railway accident
1 in 2.5 million from radiation in 135 grams of Brazil nuts
1 in 5 million from a bite from a venomous creature in the UK
1 in 10 million from living about one mile away from a nuclear power station operating normally
1 in 50 million from being hit by a falling aircraft

Mel smiled to herself. Not bad. He'd avoided some obvious traps but it wasn't easy for ordinary people to think in terms of millions or billions. Also, the risks he'd listed weren't strictly comparable. Some were statistically derived, where death was delayed, like risks from radiation. Others, like road deaths, were immediate and could be recorded more accurately. And he'd overlooked the importance to people of choice. People could choose to eat Brazil nuts or smoke cigarettes. They couldn't always choose how much radiation they were exposed to.

Also, you couldn't assume that because people were prepared to accept one type of risk they must be prepared to accept another. That was where the dread factor came in: most people were far more frightened of dying from

163

radiation-induced cancer than of a quick death from a car accident or lightning. Mel got up and walked over to the window. It was sad to think she'd probably never have the chance to discuss the paper with him. Whatever the truth about Sean, she missed him.

Outside, the sky was slowly changing colour. Fingers of pale coral light were stealing along the horizon and tinting the sea. It was unbelievably pretty and Mel stood there for a while, spellbound by the quality of the dying light ... Then, without any warning, a face appeared, pale eyes protruding from a black balaclava, pink lips pressing obscenely against the glass. As she reeled backwards she heard her door being kicked open and then a voice barking: 'Freeze − *now*!'

She spun round to see two other figures in the door, dressed in black, also wearing balaclavas. One had a pistol trained on her. The other was toting a submachine gun.

The man with the pistol leapt forward and pushed her up against the wall. 'Spread your arms and legs ...' He held her spreadeagled against the flaking paintwork and began frisking her. She tried to say something but her throat was too dry. She saw the other man go to the window and help his colleague climb inside, pulling his rope and grappling hook in beside him. She closed her eyes, trying to think, but her brain was in chaos. Her face felt bruised where she'd caught it against the wall in her panic.

'OK. She's clean. Let her go.' The man who'd been searching her stepped back but she stayed where she was. 'It's all right, Miss Rogers, you can relax now. Miss Rogers? It's OK. It's over.' She felt a hand gently touch her shoulder and slowly turned round to face them.

The three men had taken off their headgear and were grinning at her cheerfully. They were all members of the Nuclear Police. She recognized one of them − Constable Calum Fraser − and the two others looked familiar.

'Thank you for taking part in "Operation Magnum Force", Miss Rogers. It makes these exercises much more realistic when employees volunteer . . .' Calum began, but his voice tailed off as he saw her expression. 'You *did* volunteer, didn't you, Miss Rogers?'

'No, I bloody well didn't. I didn't know anything about it.'

'But we were told there were volunteers in Room 162 this evening.'

'This isn't Room 162 – that's around the other side. This is Room 102.'

The men exchanged worried glances. 'You were supposed to be simulating a disaffected employee using a shortwave radio to guide a terrorist attack. We were supposed to overpower you before you succeeded in getting the message away,' Calum mumbled lamely. The sight of her pale, incredulous face was making him feel even more upset than she was. 'Something must have gone wrong. I mean with our communications . . .'

'You could say that,' Mel said wryly, feeling her pulses return to normal as the farce unfolded in front of her. 'You ought to give anybody else likely to be in the area some kind of warning. You can't assume no one will be about just because it's out of normal hours.'

'Sorry, Miss Rogers. You won't be saying anything about this to anyone, will you?'

'No, I won't complain, but just imagine if I'd been an elderly employee with a heart condition or if I'd had a group of journalists in here. Think what great copy they'd have made out of being spreadeagled against the wall by masked men! And meanwhile, what do you think's going on in Room 162. They must have got their message away while you've been wasting your time here.' She couldn't help smiling at their stricken faces. What a shambles.

The three men looked at each other, horrified. Then they were leaping for the door and tearing away down the corridor. She could hear their boots pounding on the linoleum and the sound of swearing. Mel felt her lips twitch and she started to laugh. Cock-up not conspiracy was usually the best theory.

165

*

January 21st

I don't know why I've started this. Self-preservation perhaps or conceit that no one can fool me? But it's too intriguing to stop now. Anyway, I need to know the answers. Consider the facts:

FACT ONE – Cape Wrath's recorded throughput for October, November and December was 20 tonnes of irradiated fuel – mostly made up of enriched uranium but small quantities of plutonium, americium, neptunium, technicium. Other elements present as well. No surprises there. A dead ringer for the previous three months' throughput.

FACT TWO – According to the raw health physics data, i.e. the total detected radioactivity levels in the operators' film badges, there was a higher throughput than 20 tonnes. Yet the level of radioactive dose received by individual operators remained within authorized limits. How is that possible? Are the data wrong? They must be unless the explanation is that more plant operators are being used than usual? But shift patterns haven't been altered. Perhaps 'Neptune' can help me.

February 8th

Christ, I can't believe I used to call myself a mathematician! I've been trying to rewrite 'Neptune' for over a week to do what I want. If I could ask the IT specialists for help, life would be easier but they don't even know the 'Neptune' computer programme exists. My invention. My problem. Anyway, I don't want anyone else to know about this. I'll just keep on burning the midnight oil. Lucky that they're used to me working at night. It stops the questions.

February 12th

Still no success – or luck.

February 14th

She came to see me tonight. Bringing me my personalized

Valentine's Day present, she said. I'm relaxed, exhausted and on a real high. Why do I bother with 'Neptune' or to keep this bloody diary? Vanity, I suppose. If I am being clever I want it on the record.

February 18th
Bingo! 'Neptune's' up and running. I've fed in all the data from health physics and I'm plotting it against the throughput figures day by day.

February 28th
Spots in front of the eyes, but I'm getting there. Interesting – *very*. There must be a logical explanation. Why can't I work it out?

March 3rd
I don't believe what I'm seeing. And I don't *dare* to believe it. I must have made an error somewhere along the line. There's only one thing for it. I'm going to download everything I've done and start again from scratch. No cheating. Then we'll see.

March 12th
I nearly hit the whisky tonight. I was on my hands and knees reaching beneath the drinks cupboard for the key but somehow I stopped myself. I feel virtuous but a drink would have helped. I'm scaring the shit out of myself.
Time to review the facts again.
FACT ONE – According to my calculations the recorded radiation levels indicate a throughput nearly 20% higher than the official records.
FACT TWO – This means so much fissile material is being put through the plant that even a partial blockage in the pipework could cause a criticality incident – a small nuclear explosion even – very quickly. The plant operators would need to be on maximum alert.
FACT THREE – The IAEA Safeguards Inspectors

haven't noticed anything wrong. The only explanation is that the records supplied to them have been tampered with. But by whom? And why?

March 15th
The evidence looks conclusive but I'm still not sure. There's a little voice nagging away inside my head, telling me to make absolutely certain. Have I really covered all the angles, done enough sensitivity studies? Solution. Cross-check the figures for January and February. Question? Will the pattern be the same as for October, November and December?

March 24th
I've not written anything in this diary for over a week because I don't know how to express what I'm feeling. I've done the calculations for January and February and they're showing a similar pattern. Why and what next? Aren't those always the big questions in science and in life?

Mel put Sean's diary face down. Her curiosity had been rewarded with a vengeance. It was funny how she'd forgotten all about the diary for two whole days. Almost as if she'd made a subconscious decision. It wasn't until she'd come back from Wrath tonight that she'd found it at the bottom of her bag. Searching for her room key her hand had come in contact with the hard covers. And then it had come back to her in a wave of panic: the memory of standing in Sean's study. Her terror of that unseen intruder. The desperate instinct to hide any trace that she'd been there, causing her to sweep the diary into her bag.

She removed it almost gingerly, guilty at having it in her possession in the first place, doubly guilty that she knew she was going to read it. But she *had* to know what was going on. Ever since she'd arrived in Wrath she'd sensed she was being excluded from something. She'd tried to put it down to the insularity of a remote community, the reticence of a Government plant engaged in a controversial activity, and suspicion of her sex and profession. But all the strange things that had happened – the murdered waiter, Sean's disappearance, her disturbing encounter with Hamish – were telling her it was something bigger, less personal and more menacing than she could imagine.

The phone rang on the bedside table and she jumped. She must get a grip on herself.

'Miss Rogers? It's Moira on reception. Will you be down for dinner tonight? The dining room's due to close in half an hour.'

Mel glanced at the clock on the ugly Formica-topped table. 'Thanks, Moira. I'll be down in a couple of minutes.'

She hadn't even changed out of her work suit. Quickly she swapped her navy linen skirt and jacket for a cream cotton shift dress. Then she paused. What should she do with the diary? Instinct told her not to leave it out, but where could she hide it? It would be better to keep it with her.

Mel ran down the stairs into the now empty dining room and sat at her usual table under a wooden case containing a stuffed salmon of immense proportions. It was a standing joke that it had been caught near the Cape Wrath effluent outfall and that it glowed in the dark. She smiled wryly and laid the diary face down on the table in front of her.

How seductive it was. She could barely keep herself from reading on as she sat eating the Tuesday night special – venison casserole, boil-in-the-bag version. There were many more pages to go through, all written in Sean's slanting hand, the turquoise-coloured ink leaping out from the page. Flicking through, she'd seen detailed scientific notes, mathematical formulae, columns of data. She'd never be able to understand some of it in a million years. But what she could understand was Docherty's growing excitement and apprehension about something.

As the diary went on, the entries became more and more

frequent and cryptic. Whatever Sean thought he'd found out seemed to have become an obsession as the weeks passed.

'Coffee?'

'No thanks, not this evening.' Mel smiled automatically at the waitress but her mind was a million miles away. She rose from the table.

'Hello, there.'

Mel glanced up. Dougie MacBain was in the doorway. At once her hand shot out to retrieve the diary. She snatched it up and put it in her bag.

'I was just on my way through to the bar for a late-night drink with some of the lads when I saw you sitting in here on your own. You're worse than my radioactive isotopes. At least they have half a life! Will you not join us?'

She smiled at the weak joke and accepted. There was nothing she'd rather do less, just at this moment, but what could she say without appearing rude?

'Thanks. I will, just for a little. That would be nice.'

She followed Dougie into the lounge bar with its tartan wallpaper, recognizing the two Deputy Shift Managers who worked for him. Jamie Forsyth was a red-faced red-haired man in his early thirties. Alex Brodie was slightly older with eyebrows that bushed out over dark, deep-set eyes.

She smiled at them as she sat down by the open unlit fireplace. They responded politely, but she sensed they didn't really want her there.

'What will you have? One of the local whiskies?' Dougie made up for their lack of warmth with a wide smile that transformed his rather tired face.

'Sounds great,' Mel smiled back. When he returned from the bar she raised the tumbler to her lips, feeling the warm spicy liquor tingle in her mouth. As much to break the silence as anything else she said forcedly, 'To Cape Wrath.'

'That's a joke,' Alex Brodie said dourly.

'What do you mean?'

'There's rumours today that another fifty men are to be

made redundant. Where's the point in drinking to a plant that's annihilating itself. With all this laying off and contracting out there'll be no real employees left. Except maybe yourself and the Director.' He watched her face closely for a reaction, for any involuntary confirmation of the story.

Mel felt a great tide of weariness sweep through her. It probably hadn't been a particularly sensitive toast but she'd meant no harm. She decided to ignore the jibe.

'I've not heard anything. Honestly.'

'It's just a rumour,' Dougie said after a further moment's embarrassed silence. 'But that's the way everything is these days. And rumours round here have an unfortunate habit of turning out to be true.'

'But then you'd know about that, wouldn't you, Mel?' There was an aggressive edge to Jamie Forsyth's voice as he joined in.

'I'm not sure I understand you . . .' Mel put her whisky down and sweeping her dark hair back from her brow cupped her face in her hands.

'Isn't that your job, running the rumour machine?' Forsyth sneered. 'In the old days they used to tell it to you straight at four o'clock on a Friday afternoon so you'd have the weekend to get over it. If we were lucky they might even consult the unions and let them have some influence over what happened. Now they hire someone like you to manage the communication and leave it to you to decide whether it's better to let something leak out. Get the poor silly sods used to the idea before you make the formal announcements. Get them suspecting the very worst so they'll be grateful when they find out it's only the second worst that's going to happen . . . Isn't that the technique?' His voice was more resigned than bitter.

'Jamie, I don't think you should—' Dougie began

'It's OK, Dougie,' Mel interrupted gently. 'I'm sorry you feel that way, Jamie, really I am. All I can tell you is that that's not the way I work. I try my best – that's all I can do. Now if you'll excuse me I have some work to do this evening. Thank you for the whisky, Dougie.' She managed a smile and made for the stairs, very aware of three pairs of eyes following her, and of the telling silence.

She pulled a small table in front of the window. Then she unplugged the bedside light and carried it over. The flex was just long enough to reach to the socket by the wardrobe. She pressed the switch, casting an arc of light, and sat down. It was quiet outside now that the two bars in the main street had closed. For a moment or two she just sat looking at the glorious night sky. Wrath was so small there was no competition for the stars which shone out diamond bright; her father could have named every constellation as easily as old friends which, in a sense, they were.

Opening the diary Mel began reading where she'd left off, frowning a little as she tried to make sense of the increasingly erratic handwriting. There was more and more scientific data, but fewer comments from Sean, as if he'd begun to focus right down. From late April there was an entry almost every day. It looked as if from then onwards he had been keeping a complete record of the throughput into the plant and the radioactivity readings.

Every day that the plant was in operation, Sean had noted: the country of origin of the nuclear material being processed, the exact isotopic content, the amount of plutonium and uranium that had been recovered, the level of enrichment of the uranium, and finally the radioactivity of the waste products which had been separated out during the process, broken down into low-level, intermediate-level and high-level waste. What had been the point of all this? Mel put the diary down and tried to recall her conversations with Sean, searching for a clue, but drawing a blank.

It was one in the morning and her eyes were hurting but she couldn't stop now. She stood up and stretched, then splashed some cold water on her face and changed her contact lenses for glasses. From the street below came the sound of a motorbike. Glancing out she saw Fergus Brown parking his red BMW and securing it carefully before going into his cottage. That was a point. Where did Fergus fit into the picture? He was a friend of Laura's. He was also one of the happy little band of Wrath cannabis smokers. She remembered how Fergus had questioned her about finding the body of the waiter. Had he had an ulterior motive for wanting to find out how much she knew?

The thought was a stimulus. Mel sat down again and reopened the diary. At first it was just more of the same. But then something changed. Mel sat up and began to read more closely.

May 5th
Of course, the shaft is just the place! Why didn't I think of it earlier? No one would ever look in there. After all, what is it? Just a hole in the ground with a lot of nuclear detritus thrown down it by people who should have known better. They let it blow up. Now it's an embarrassment they'd rather forget about which means it has distinct possibilities . . .

Possibilities for what? Mel stared at the page, trying to build something coherent out of the words. It was typical of Sean to have written in such a cryptic way.

May 8th
I've been doing my homework into the shaft and it's been a revelation. A thirty-metre vertical drop bored through solid granite rock. At the base the shaft kinks round at an angle of forty-five degrees and drives for another eight metres through the rock to the sea. It's sealed with a concrete plug identical to the one at the top of the shaft. Seawater is pumped in to make sure that the radioactivity is contained and can't leach out. So the pressure of the seawater on both sides holds the lower plug in position.

The diameter is three metres. That means a cubic

173

capacity of around 250 cubic metres. But according to the inventory the shaft is only about two-thirds full. That means there's plenty of room. It's so obvious now. I've been an idiot, worrying and worrying, and the solution's been staring me in the face all the time.

It was beginning to make sense in a grim kind of way. Mel pushed her chair back from the window. What would her father have said? 'Check the facts. Don't jump to conclusions; always validate them. Be logical. Be thorough.' She smiled to herself. Too late. She'd made the links intuitively but she could track back and check out the conclusion.

If she was right and Sean *had* been involved in an operation to smuggle drugs into the country, perhaps with Hamish, it was also logical that he would have needed somewhere to conceal them. If they were being landed along the Cape Wrath foreshore what could be more convenient than the shaft? A remote place, inspected regularly at known times and seldom randomly. And wouldn't it appeal to Sean's anti-Establishment sense of humour to stash drugs on a Government nuclear site right under the noses of the Director and John MacDonald and the Nuclear Police? And who would ever suspect that that was what was going on?

That would also explain why Sean was so interested in the workings of the plant. He would need to have precise information about the reprocessing work and to calculate when MacDonald might be likely to want to dispose of nuclear waste into the shaft himself. Again, it would have amused Sean to think that both he and MacDonald were using the shaft for their own, very different ends.

And yet, Mel still couldn't quite see her way through the miasma, for if Sean and Hamish were using the shaft as a temporary hiding place when shipments came in, why had Sean told her what MacDonald was up to? Perhaps to cover himself? If she had subsequently discovered that the shaft was being used for drugs drops she would naturally have suspected MacDonald and not Sean. She would have been a very convenient witness, able to recall that Docherty had volunteered that strange things were going on at the shaft.

MacDonald would have been suspected of having lied about disposing of waste down the shaft as a cover for what he was really doing – drug dealing. And Sean would have had a neat revenge on a man whose intellect and ambition he despised and have gone scot-free himself. Sean was shrewd enough to have planned something this complex.

But if she was right, it meant that Sean had been using her detachedly and deliberately. Once again she'd been an unwitting, trusting pawn. And it also meant that Sean could well have had something to do with the death of the waiter. That was harder to believe. Yet into her mind came a sudden picture of Sean's razor-sharp reaction as he had pushed her out of the way of the flying paint can at that first demonstration. A different man to the indolent, lazy non-conformist and capable of . . . well who knew . . .? As for Hamish, his raw physical power was more obvious – but could he too be capable of murder if someone got in his way?

When you have eliminated the impossible, whatever remains, however improbable, must be the truth. Sherlock Holmes had said something like that, hadn't he? Well, she wasn't Sherlock Holmes and she wasn't sure she had the staying power for this. She snapped the diary shut and hid it on top of the wardrobe, pushing it right to the back, out of sight. The amount of dust which came off on her hand suggested it was likely to be safe in that spot. She wished she could climb up there with it. For the third time that evening, Mel checked her door was locked and resisted the temptation to put a chair under the handle.

'After the technical briefing we'll take you around the site and show you the facilities. For example, we have a new intermediate-level waste store which has just opened with a capacity of ten thousand, five-hundred-litre drums. Also our cementation facility for encapsulating the intermediate-level waste in concrete prior to storage is currently on line, and I'm sure you'll find that process interesting.'

The journalists were consulting their press packs. Frank O'Farrell of the *Daily Gazette,* balding and cadaverous, was whispering in the ear of Lisa Duffy of *The Sunday Voice.* Whatever he was saying had nothing to do with Cape Wrath, that was for sure, Mel thought, noticing Lisa's disgusted expression. But she knew Frank's reputation of old from her own days in journalism. The man regarded any assignment as a chance to get someone into bed.

Mel rose, preparing to lead them through to the small lecture theatre where some of the plant staff were waiting to give a series of short presentations on Cape Wrath. She was pleased to have got the visit off the ground. God knows, it hadn't been easy. The journalists had been hard to woo. Cape Wrath had such a reputation for secrecy they'd immediately suspected the motive. She'd had to work hard to convince them there was no hidden agenda, no disinformation campaign.

She'd had to work even harder to persuade the Director to allow her to invite a group of environmental correspondents from the national media on site. 'We'll only be giving them the ammunition to shoot us with,' had been his immediate reaction. 'They'll shoot at us anyway,' she'd retorted. 'If we get closer to them and understand their angles, at least we'll know better which bit of us they're aiming at. And you never know – they might even be less hostile if they understand us better.' To give Fabian Williams his due, he had listened and he had supported her when she had raised it at the management meeting and asked for staff to be made available to meet the journalists. John MacDonald had seemed indifferent, but that too was something to be grateful for.

The lecture theatre belonged to the early days of Cape Wrath. Rows of seats were banked up in semi-circles around a dais. A frieze of very 1960s art – all pink and black squiggles – ran around the walls and the colours were picked out in the carpet squares and the synthetic covers on the seats. Well, at least no one can accuse us of wasting public money on state-of-the-art facilities, Mel smiled to herself.

The eight journalists sat together in the front row, notebooks and tape recorders ready, looking around at the time-warp décor and making amused observations to each other. O'Farrell was sniggering openly. But the mirth stopped as the presentations got underway. David Tregonning, the amply built, bearded Cornishman who was Project Manager for the site's decommissioning work took them through the stages of decommissioning. He was one of the few managers at Cape Wrath whom Mel trusted to give a presentation clearly in layman's language and to keep cool when the flak began to fly . . . which it would.

'The point of the work is eventually to return nuclear sites like Cape Wrath back into green-field sites. In a hundred years, no one will know we'd ever been here,' David was explaining in his soft accent.

'Why does it take so long? Why can't you clean up the mess quicker?'

'I don't think I'd agree with you that it's a "mess". What we're talking about are research facilities that made a major contribution to the UK's civil nuclear programme.'

'But the fast reactor – which was the reason Cape Wrath was built – turned out to be a dodo. You couldn't get your prototype reactors to work properly – the heat exchangers leaked. Sodium got into the coolant systems and caught fire.'

'True, but that's why we carry out research and build experimental reactors and prototypes – to make mistakes and learn from them. If we claimed to know all the answers you'd accuse us of being arrogant,' David pointed out reasonably. 'And I don't believe the fast-reactor work was valueless. One day as fossil fuels run out and people realize the limitations of wind, wave and solar power, Britain will need fast-reactor technology. It is the only fission system which can deliver limitless power because it can manufacture its own fuel. And

177

like all nuclear power it doesn't contribute to the greenhouse effect. Since 1973 the use of nuclear power in the UK has saved two and a half billion tonnes of coal. Each ten million tonnes of coal saved reduces the country's CO_2 emissions by six per cent.'

'As far as I'm concerned, the only safe fast breeder's a rabbit.' Frank smirked round at his colleagues but the old chestnut was embarrassing them. They were from serious broadsheets and Frank's tabloid antics had run their course.

David gauged the mood, quickly returning to the facts. 'You questioned our decommissioning timescales; you have a point – we *could* go quicker. The reason for phasing the programme is to allow time for the radioactivity in the facilities to decay. Each material has a half life, which is the time it takes for it to reach half its previous level of radioactivity. So in two half lives it would be a quarter of its original level. Half lives can vary from milliseconds to billions of years. Just to give you an idea, the half life of caesium 137 which we often encounter in decommissioning is about thirty years. What that means in practical terms is that if we put a facility into a regime of safe care and maintenance for a few decades – what we call "stage two" decommissioning – it becomes less "hot". There's less radioactivity to deal with so there's less risk to the workers who have to go in.'

'*And* less cost?' Lisa Duffy asked sharply. 'That has to be a factor, surely?'

'Of course. We're spending the taxpayer's money so we have to be responsible. If we can cut the costs of decommissioning, that means more money for the Government to spend on schools and hospitals. But safety – the safety of the public and of our own workforce – is paramount.'

'Well, that all sounds hunky dory,' Frank O'Farrell said. 'But what about this shaft thing of yours? If you're so safety conscious, how come you let that thing blow up and scatter its contents around like a school chemistry lesson that's gone wrong?'

'That incident happened before my time. I've only been

at Cape Wrath for three years so I can't give you the details.' David looked towards Mel for support.

Damn, damn, damn, she was thinking inwardly. Why did we have to get onto this? There was so much more ground she'd wanted to cover – the commercial reprocessing programme, the wider site remediation work, the worthy if as yet unsuccessful attempts to diversify into some non-nuclear areas to secure employment for the local community. And, if she were honest, there were all kinds of other reasons why she didn't want to even think about the shaft, but eight pairs of eyes were looking at her expectantly. She gave them her best professional smile.

'The explosion occurred over twenty years ago and it shouldn't have. But things were done differently in those days. The shaft was fully licensed but standards were different. It couldn't happen today. You can visit the shaft during your tour around the site – not that there's much to see – and I'll arrange for one of our managers who knows the full background to accompany us. He can explain the history of the shaft and the current monitoring regime and answer your questions. But let's finish the presentations, shall we?'

As David Tregonning carried on his explanation of decommissioning, Mel went outside into the lobby and paged Dougie MacBain. Poor old Dougie, she thought to herself, it's the short straw for you again.

The wind was blowing hard as the party struggled up the beach towards the shaft. Lisa Duffy had taken off her Manolo Blahnik sandals and was plodding along in a pair of wellies that were about four sizes too big. It was only late August but already autumn was in the air and with it the hint of harsh weather to come. The sand whipped into her eyes, causing Mel to gasp with pain, and pause for a moment, blinking furiously to let the tears wash away the grit that had got under her contact lenses.

She hurried to catch up with the others but they were

already standing in a semi-circle around the shaft by the time she reached them. Dougie was pointing out the radiation and hydrogen monitors and explaining how nothing had been disposed of into the shaft since the explosion.

His voice faded in her ears as Mel stared at the lid to the shaft. Last time she had seen it, the yellow and black roundels warning that radioactivity was present had been positioned on the same side as the sea. She remembered it so clearly. Yet now they were on the inland side. She looked again more closely. Were her sore eyes deceiving her? No. Since her last visit, somebody had definitely opened the shaft . . .

Chapter Eleven

'I'll pick you up around two o'clock tomorrow afternoon.'

'That's a little early for dinner, isn't it?'

'No, not considering where we're going. And bring an overnight bag.'

'Tom?'

'Relax. Trust me. Look, I have to go right now. I'll see you tomorrow.'

The line went dead and Mel slowly replaced the receiver. Tom Schultz was taking a lot for granted, but somehow she didn't resent it. In the circumstances, the thought of getting away with an open, uncomplicated man like Tom was very attractive.

The last few days had been pretty lonely and stressful. Everything – exercise 'Magnum Force', Sean's diary, the shaft, Hamish's strange behaviour – had been preying on her mind but there'd been no one she could really talk to. Not the Director. Fabian Williams was completely caught up with his plans for decontaminating the castle. Not James Everett with his own preoccupations. And certainly not John MacDonald, for even if what Sean had told her was just lies or fantasy, he was buttoned down too tight, not the type of man she could ever confide in. Unlike Sean, ironic though that now seemed.

Any empathy she'd ever felt with Hamish had gone right out of the window. It was a relief he'd left Wrath. She'd seen the navy-blue Range Rover sweeping out of town,

Wilf slumped in the back, while she was queuing at the cashpoint outside the bank. If Hamish had seen her he hadn't acknowledged her.

Yes, the big Scotsman was at the heart of whatever was going on – of that she was sure. The thought both disappointed and frightened her in some indefinable way, casting long shadows over everything. Since their meeting she had tried to put him out of her mind, but failed. The more distance there was between them the better.

Mel glanced at her watch, forcing herself to forget the whole disturbing business for a while. Two-thirty. At least it had been a quiet day. No national media coverage and the only piece of interest in the local paper was about a cow called Christine shown at the local show and named by a 'friendly' farmer as a courtesy to the Director's wife. Some courtesy! Or did irony survive this far north?

It was good to have time to catch up with some reading on the internet. She was engrossed in the Greenpeace website and didn't hear him come in.

'I don't know how you have the patience with all that stuff.'

Mel swivelled round to find John MacDonald staring critically at her computer screen.

'You get used to it,' she answered, a little flustered. 'And there's so much information on the web that in my job you can't afford to ignore it.'

'I suppose not.'

'Have you looked at our own website since I had it redesigned? We've received something like five hundred hits already this week. That's way up on what we used to get.'

'No, I haven't seen it. Show me.'

MacDonald pulled up a chair and sat down next to her, carefully lifting his suit jacket and hitching up his trouser-legs to avoid bagging the knife-edge creases. Mel glanced at him curiously. In the last few weeks he'd definitely mellowed towards her but this was the first time he'd shown any real interest in what she was doing. She caught the clean, sharp tang of his aftershave as he leaned towards the screen, the deep violet of his irises almost black as he focused.

'Our website has a very simple address and once you're in, it can take you down to whatever level of information you want.' Mel's fingers moved lightly over the keyboard to call up the Cape Wrath pages. A graphic showing the outline of the site – towers and domes – came up in dark blue against a pale blue background. A menu was superimposed.

'Take the mouse and click on whatever interests you.' Mel passed him the mouse and watched as he selected *Reprocessing*.

'See – now you can choose a specific aspect. Suppose you wanted to find out about the technical process itself, you'd click on the third box. That takes you into a general explanation in which key words like *uranium*, *plutonium* and *waste products* are highlighted. Click on them and you get a detailed description. If that's still not enough, you can go in even deeper and access a list of the key scientific papers on those subjects published over the past three years.'

'Very impressive. You've done a good job.' MacDonald interrogated the various menus with practised ease. He might not have much patience with the Information Superhighway, but he certainly knew all about computers. 'Did you write all this material yourself?'

'Oh no,' Mel laughed, shaking her dark head. 'I asked various people to help me, like Dougie MacBain and David Tregonning – and of course Sean. He was writing me a layman's guide to risk and radiation that I was going to put on the website.'

MacDonald shrugged and stood up. 'Poor old Sean . . . he was his own worst enemy.'

'How do you mean?'

'He was too rash and impulsive. Taking his boat out like that when he'd had too much to drink. It was typical of the kind of thing he'd do. He was always reckless . . . When we were students together he climbed up some scaffolding after our final exams, fell off and nearly killed himself.'

'It must be strange for you without him,' she said gently. 'You'd known each other so many years.' She couldn't help remembering Sean's revelations about their student days together. *He tried to get me into bed with him at Oxford one night.* Had MacDonald once desired him, and if so, when had that passion ended? It was hard to connect this dapper, fastidious man with sex of any kind, and yet he'd been married for over twenty years and had two sons.

'Sean and I were used to each other. We didn't always see eye to eye and to be honest I was becoming tired of having to cover up his indiscretions. But yes, it *is* strange without him.' MacDonald's voice was colourless and he fell silent for a moment, expression bleak. Then he rallied. 'Actually, the reason I looked in was to ask whether you were doing anything this weekend. Amelia and I would like you to come to dinner tomorrow. She's very grateful to you for the publicity you managed to get for her charity event and wants a chance to thank you.'

'That's really kind, but I'm afraid I'm busy.'

MacDonald gave her a sceptical look. He must think she was just making excuses. He knew the quiet life she usually led at weekends.

'I'm going out to dinner with Tom Schultz,' she explained.

'Tom? I see. Well, another time then.'

'That would be nice.'

'Good.' He walked briskly out of her office and away down the corridor, whistling lightly under his breath.

Alone again Mel suddenly felt she couldn't stand it a moment longer. She had to talk to someone about the shaft. Reaching for the phone she tapped in Dougie MacBain's extension number, thinking rapidly. She needn't reveal what Sean had told her, or tell him what was in Sean's diary, or about her suspicions that drugs were being hidden there. But at least she could tell Dougie that someone had opened the shaft and see how he reacted.

'Hello, Dougie MacBain, Shift Manager speaking. Hello?'

184

But at the last moment some deep-seated instinct over-ruled the impulse, hauling her back from the edge. *Trust no one and don't give anyone any reason not to trust you.* Since she had arrived in Wrath, one man had died and another had disappeared in mysterious circumstances. And Cape Wrath itself might be a part of the story. It was better to say nothing to anyone at the plant. Safer for her. Safer for them. Just wait, and watch and hope that two and two would eventually add up to four.

'It's Mel. Dougie, I'm sorry, I dialled the wrong extension.'

'No problem.'

Mel hung up slowly. Had she made the right decision, or was she going to regret keeping all this to herself?

It was still there. Mel's fingers made contact with the diary and she pulled it towards her. The contents both fascinated and repelled her. She didn't want to get involved; reading the diary made her an accomplice in whatever Sean might have been doing. And the whole question of drugs – smuggling drugs, concealing drugs – was too emotional an issue for her to react rationally. But on the other hand she couldn't draw back now.

Her heart was beating fast as she sat in her usual seat at the window and opened the scruffy little red book. There were still some twenty or thirty pages to go. Some were only half-filled, with just a few notes or sums. Others were blank. Interestingly, Sean seemed to have given up his obsession about what was happening in the plant, why the data didn't tally and the risk of an explosion. Perhaps he'd got bored.

But as she turned the final pages, a section leapt out. It was written in black ink, not turquoise, and the writing was more than erratic. It was wild, as if Sean's hand had been shaking badly as he wrote. It was dated in early June and was so difficult to decipher that she trained the lamp on it and began to try and transcribe it. Half an hour later she was staring at what she'd written on the piece of paper before her.

185

June 6th

What is he up to? He's playing God and loving every minute of it. Holding all of us in the palm of his hand to be manipulated, crushed or rewarded as the mood takes him. Fuck him and all his works. I suppose I should stop him if I can. But that's just it. Can I?

And even if I could, is it worth the risk? He seems to have a sixth sense. That's what's kept him safe up till now. If I blow this I could end up making matters even more dangerous. There's nothing I can do. Nothing. Nothing. *NOTHING.*

June 7th

When I read what I wrote yesterday I'm ashamed. I'd been drinking when I wrote it and I'm still drinking — but I see myself more clearly now. Spiritually impotent and practically useless. But what did I expect? I shouldn't be disappointed by what I already know.

I've never been very good at this thing called 'responsibility'. That's why my fellowship went down the tubes and why my marriage failed. But now I have an opportunity to make a difference. Shouldn't I take it? If I don't, others could be hurt — people I care about. Could I bear to have that on my conscience? Do I *have* a conscience? I'd like to think so but I'm not sure.

June 8th

I'm soberer now, sitting here with the pale light streaming in. And I'm thinking. Deciding what to do. I've never cared enough about anything to commit myself totally. And at the same time I've expected everything to be offered to me on a plate. 'Sean Docherty, academic, musician, piss artist, this is your life. And for the record, you've failed. In fact, your failure has gone platinum.'

But perhaps I've been given a last chance to redeem myself.

186

What on earth was he talking about? Who was playing God? Hamish? And what had they been doing? Who were the others he cared about and who might be hurt? Or was it all intellectual masturbation – scientific and psychological wanking, compensating for tedium, disillusionment and disappointment? Or was he just pissed? Mel felt her brain was in a fog. Where were those cool deductive powers she prided herself on?

Glancing down, she noticed that a dried flower had drifted from the pages of the diary and floated to the floor. The edges of the petals had turned brown but it was still unmistakably a bluebell. She could even catch the ghost of its once-sweet scent. Picking it up carefully she laid it on the table. Then she looked to see where it had come from.

It was towards the very end of the book that she found it. Two pages must have become stuck together when the flower was pressed between them. She could see the stains left by the dark blue fluid. Her frequent handling of the diary must have loosened them, releasing the flower.

Written in the faintest pencil was a simple heading *Laura*.

It was no good: she couldn't sleep. Not after what she'd read. Life had still had some focus for Sean. Mel sat up, switched on the bedside light and tucked her duvet tightly around her. The autumn nights were getting chilly now and she nestled down into the comforting warmth. Then she picked up Sean's diary and read the passage again.

It was still as moving. A lyrical outpouring of his love for Laura, his hopes that other men wouldn't exploit her vulnerability, his passionate conviction that she mustn't throw away her life as he had done. Any shock or disgust melted away in the face of the reality. It was so unlike the cynical, detached man she remembered that Mel found herself close to tears.

Her eyes were so full she could hardly focus on the last paragraph:

187

Laura gives me back my youth. She intoxicates me and feeds my senses. She says she loves me and that she wants no one but me. But for once I *have* to be strong. She mustn't waste her talent, compromise her future. She's just a child at the very beginning of her life and she doesn't really know what she wants from me – father figure or potential father? A child – now that's a responsibility neither of us could handle. I mustn't be one of the mistakes or bad bargains she makes. I must force her to see that we can't go on, but it's so hard. She loves me as I am, not for what I was, or even for what I could still be. When she comes to me I'm powerless – the taste of her, the scent of her . . . She came to me tonight, out of the darkness, soft and warm as a kitten. Oh, Laura . . .

So Sean and Laura had really been lovers; Hamish had been speaking the truth. She felt no sense of revulsion. Quite the reverse in fact, but she didn't bother to ask herself why. Instead she gazed out of her window at the night sky beyond and just before dawn fell into a deep sleep at last.

'Hi, you look great!' Tom's eyes swept appreciatively over Mel's soft green chinos and yellow cashmere sweater. He took her bag and tossed it into the back of the jeep.

'You haven't said where we're going.'

'I know. It's a surprise.'

'Maybe I don't like surprises.'

'You'll like this one – I promise.' He smiled at her, blue eyes very bright and she smiled back. 'I need to stop for some petrol,' he went on. 'I forgot to fuel up at Anderson. Then we can hit the road.'

Tom turned into a garage on the outskirts of Wrath. While he was unlocking the petrol cap Mel saw a dark blue Range Rover reflected in the jeep's wing mirror. *Hamish.* She watched as he drew up behind them, waiting for Tom to finish using the diesel pump. His long hair was tied back with a navy ribbon and he was wearing shades.

Her hand was on the door handle but then she paused. This was hardly the place to try and rebuild bridges. And anyway, what could she say? Hamish didn't even know she had Sean's diary. It was all too complicated. And this weekend she was determined to push everything to do with Wrath right out of her mind. It was about time she had some simple, uncomplicated fun.

Getting back in beside her, Tom saw the look of indecision on her face.

'Anything you want?' he asked.

'No, I'm fine.'

The jeep shot forward and as Tom turned onto the highway Mel resisted the temptation to look back.

It was one of the most romantically beautiful places she'd ever seen – a small castle with a square, turretted keep, standing on an island in the middle of a loch. The waters of the loch were dark emerald-green, paling towards the edges which were fringed with clumps of gently swaying reeds.

'I knew you'd like it.'

'It's wonderful!' Delight lit up her face. It was like something from a poem.

'There's a story that Mary Queen of Scots was imprisoned here for a short while and that she bribed a boatman to row her to freedom – but he betrayed her trust.'

'Is it true?'

'I doubt it – but it's a good story for the brochure. Let's hope our boatman is more reliable.' Tom pointed across the loch to a landing stage at the foot of the castle. A man in a tweed hat was untying a rope and stepping into a rowing boat.

'You mean this is where we're staying?' she asked, amazed. 'It's a hotel?'

'Yup.'

Tom pulled their bags from the jeep, locked up and set off down a short grassy path to the water's edge. There, concealed among the tall reeds was another landing stage.

As they waited, dragonflies hovered in the air around them and there was a sweet honeyed smell from the last of the year's wild flowers.

Mel was completely captivated. Nothing had moved her so much since those days by the lake in Guatemala when she'd watched the never-ending patterns of light on water.

'Good afternoon,' called the man from the rowing boat as he manoeuvred it close up against the landing stage. 'Welcome to Inverross Castle. You'll be having it to your-selves tonight.'

'You mean we're the only people staying here?' Mel asked.

'That's right.' He smiled at her as he stood up and Tom passed him their cases to stow in the bows. 'We did have a block booking from a whisky company's headquarters in Glasgow. They wanted to bring some Japanese clients here and give them some golf, but it seems they missed their flight and won't be arriving until tomorrow.'

He pushed off from the shore and began to row smoothly and rhythmically. Tom put his arm around Mel's shoulders.

'I knew I could get you to look like that,' he said softly.

'What do you mean?' She looked up at him curiously.

'Happy. You usually look kind of anxious − like you've got the cares of the world on your shoulders. I think they work you too hard at Cape Wrath. Hey, I didn't mean anything.' He caught a fugitive, wistful look on her face.

'No, you're right. I sometimes take life much too seri-ously . . . but not today.' She could feel the warmth of his body against hers. How long since she had wanted to make love to anyone? It seemed too much an abandon-ment of self − too risky. But now she felt desire stir deep inside her.

She leant against Tom and closed her eyes, listening to the dip and rise of the oars and the sound of a curlew as it swooped high above them. This was about as good as it gets. Wrath and all its problems were far, far away.

190

The boatman moored in the shadow of the castle and they followed him up the steep path and then up a flight of stone steps into the keep.

'As you're the only two guests we've given you the suites in the turrets,' the receptionist explained, pushing a registration card over to Tom to complete. 'They're the best rooms we have.'

'That's great.' Tom swiftly filled in the details.

So he wasn't taking her quite for granted; he had booked two rooms. Somehow that was what Mel would have expected of Tom. He had a kind of old-fashioned chivalry that didn't lend itself to crude assumptions. But all the same, this wasn't quite the kind of place she would have associated with him.

Mel followed one of the staff up the beautiful Georgian staircase. He was explaining how it had been installed in the 1780s by one of the castle's owners, a wealthy man with sugar plantations in the West Indies. But Mel's mind was far away. She was wondering how Hamish would have handled a situation like this. A picture of him took substance in her mind but she resolutely pushed it out again.

Her bedroom was exquisite, with windows on three sides with views to the mountains and woods beyond. Opening one, she leant out and found herself looking straight down to the stone buttresses at the base of the castle wall. It made her feel like Rapunzel. A pity she didn't have long golden hair to cascade down . . .

She quickly unpacked, putting the few things she had brought into a shining mahogany chest of drawers lined with scented tissue paper and hanging her dress in the wardrobe. It was the same one she had worn to the dinner party at Fabian Williams' house the night Sean had disappeared. Contrary to her fears the local cleaner had managed to get the port stain out. She shook out the delicate fabric with its embroideries of birds and butterflies. This time she had brought the matching shawl. The centrepiece was a single butterfly held in place by hundreds of strands of

191

coloured silk. As she held it to the light it seemed to dance in her hands.

'What made you come to a place like Wrath? I mean for me there was no choice. I just got posted. But you – you could have gone anywhere you wanted.' Tom's eyes held hers in the candlelight.

'You mean, why didn't I take an ordinary PR job with a company which makes biscuits or toothpaste or soap?'

'Yeah, why not?'

She sipped the glass of brandy; its fumes, mingling with the scent of the pinecones burning in the grate, made her feel lightheaded and very young again. She was on a kind of high, like she'd just been let out of prison. That was how good it felt to get away from Wrath.

'I wanted a challenge, I suppose. My father was a scientist – an astrophysicist. He believed that science gets badly misunderstood. I want to be a part of trying to bridge the gap between the scientist and the man or woman in the street.'

'And are you succeeding?'

'Not yet. It takes time. Sometimes I feel nobody's on my side. The scientists are suspicious of me. The public don't trust me either.'

'At least on a military base we don't get into those kind of problems. What happens is confidential for security reasons and that's that.'

'That's not completely true, surely? Look what happened at Greenham Common and the peace camps. You can't get away with saying that what happens on a base is classified. The public do have some rights.'

'Maybe, but it can go too far.' Tom's face tautened a little. 'Look at the Gulf War. You couldn't bend down to tie up your boot-laces without falling over some journalist with his camera-man. Who gave them the right to get in the way? Or to have instant access to information?'

'It's a question of balance. The military recognized that. That's why they laid on regular press briefings, wasn't it?'

192

'Yeah, but at the same time the world was tuning into CNN in Baghdad who were getting in first all the time. It was crazy.'

'But that's why you have to learn how to play the communication game and get in there. It's not an option anymore. Wasn't that one of the lessons of the Vietnam War? You lost the war for PR reasons a long time before you stopped fighting.'

Tom gave her a sharp look. She'd caught him on a raw nerve. He was certainly no liberal but he wasn't stupid either. In some ways he reminded her of her father – the way his mind sifted and reviewed facts and tested propositions.

'I guess you're right,' he said after a moment. 'You have to accept things the way they are rather than the way you want them to be.'

'You mean compromise?' Mel smiled. 'Of course, we all have to do that. That's what makes things tick. It's the people who refuse to compromise on principle who cause the trouble. Like in Northern Ireland or the Middle East.'

'Look, I didn't bring you here to talk about the world's problems,' Tom said softly. 'I want to find out about *you*. I never met a woman less eager to talk about herself.'

'All right – what do you want to know?'

'Well, let's try this for starters. How come a woman as beautiful and clever and sexy as you doesn't have a boyfriend? I hope I'm not offending you but I've been curious a long time.'

'I did have a boyfriend. It was serious – at least I thought it was, but things . . . didn't work out. After that I changed. I decided to concentrate on building my career as a journalist and then in PR. I didn't have room for a permanent relationship with anyone.' Mel looked at him steadily. It was the truth. An edited version, missing out the odd one-night stand, but the truth.

'And now?'

'I'm not sure.'

'But you're willing to try and find out?'

193

Her eyes met Tom's. 'Yes . . . definitely.'

Reaching across the table he stroked the outline of her cheekbone and felt the responsive tremor which ran through her soft skin.

'You're sure this is what you want?' he said, a little huskily. 'I don't want to rush you.'

'You're not. I want you to make love to me tonight. I decided that hours ago.'

'I see.' He grinned. 'So you were planning to seduce me?'

'If necessary, yes.' Her voice was humorous but something in her expression made him catch his breath.

'You're an extraordinary woman, Mel Rogers. I only hope I'm equal to the challenge.'

'So do I.'

The sunlight woke her, playing over the mellow stonework. Mel stretched luxuriously. Tom was still asleep, arm outflung, his body lean and tanned against the white sheets. She smiled to herself. What had come over her last night? The wine and the brandy? The gloriously romantic setting?

It wasn't as simple as that. Her need of Tom had been absolute. As he'd slid her clothes from her, the sharpness of her desire had overwhelmed her, driving out any doubt. She'd behaved like an animal in the wild, free to satisfy its instincts.

She stroked Tom's short fair hair, enjoying the feel of it, half-silky, half-bristly, against her fingertips. There was a bite mark on his neck which she didn't even remember making.

Tom represented something strong and clean, simple and good while Cape Wrath was wreathed in shadow and complexity. Making love with him had been an act of liberation – a physical affirmation of life and independence. At the thought of it and the fact that she'd be back in Wrath tonight her happiness sagged a little. If only she could confide in Tom, if only he would agree to help her then things would be different. But it was still too soon. Good sex was no substitute for trust . . . but maybe in time?

As she watched him, Tom stirred beside her and opened his eyes. Very gently he pulled her towards him and lowered his head to her breasts. In a moment her mind was plunged back into oblivion.

She knew she shouldn't be doing this. She could get herself sacked, but she had to take a look before suspicion and curiosity drove her insane. Through the Perspex window of her protective helmet she could see the two shiftworkers walking along the shore a few paces ahead of her. It was a cloudy night and she needed her torch to guide her. Even so she kept slipping on rubbery bands of seaweed. It was diffi-cult enough to walk in radiation suits anyway. They looked like a party of penguins waddling along. Mel's sudden laugh, locked inside her helmet, sounded odd in her ears.

They were almost at the stairs now. They began to climb and the outline of the crane came into view. The shiftworkers turned to look at her and she nodded. As she watched they went towards the shaft and positioned themselves on either side of the lid. It was in exactly the same position as the last time she'd seen it. Then they took out a set of tools and began to unfasten the clamps, two on either side. It was slow work and Mel couldn't help glancing over her shoulder. Every moment she expected to hear the voice of the Shift Managers asking her what the hell she thought she was doing.

But she had chosen her time well. John MacDonald, Dougie MacBain, Alex Brodie and Jaimie Forsyth were all away at a safety seminar in Glasgow. There had been no one in the plant who would think of challenging the right of the PR Manager to have the shaft opened. Her excuse had been that Cape Wrath and Anderson Base were plan-ning a joint emergency exercise based on a hypothetical release of radioactivity from the shaft caused by another night-time explosion. To write a realistic scenario she needed to take a closer look at it at night when there weren't too many observers around.

They were ready to lift the lid now. After taking readings

195

from the monitors around the shaft, one of the shiftworkers fastened the metal chain embedded in the shaft lid to the hook suspended from the crane. Then the other man began to operate the crane's hydraulic winch. There was a rasping, grating noise as the concrete plug sealing the shaft was slowly hauled up. Mel stepped forward eagerly. What did she expect to see? Cannabis resin neatly stacked inside like goods on a supermarket shelf? Feeling a little foolish she peered into the dark depths.

At first she could see little except the faint sheen of oily water far below and some odd shapes protruding through it. Bits of metal and old kit. It was like peering into a dirty old canal. She wouldn't have been surprised to see some pram wheels sticking out of the water or a rusting supermarket trolley.

She was about to turn away when something else caught her eye and she stiffened.

'Let me have your torch, will you? It's got a stronger beam,' Mel called to one of the shiftworkers. The man handed her the torch and stepped back. She trained it down to the soft, indistinguishable shape she'd noticed caught against the side of the shaft.

No, it was no good. She still couldn't see. Stepping closer to the brink she peered down, trying to accustom her eyes to the gloom. Slowly her eyes made out bundles of old fuel casings and twisted pieces of metal and what looked like the arm of a remote control manipulator, sticking up like the limb of some great insect. The softer object was quite small and seemed to be partially wrapped in something like a tarpaulin.

But as she stood there, the pattern of clouds in the sky shifted and in the sudden moonlight Mel saw something which made her stomach turn over. She fell to her knees, her hands tearing off her helmet in a panic. She must take it off so she could see properly.

The two men looked round surprised and hurried over to her. 'What is it, Miss Rogers?' one of them asked.

196

She gazed at him dumbly for a moment, forcing him to repeat the question. Seconds passed but still she couldn't bring herself to say it, to describe that disgusting, decomposing thing down there in the darkness. The shiftworkers were now looking into the shaft themselves, shining their torches down into the murk. They exchanged glances and one of them turned aside and began speaking rapidly into his mobile telephone. Mel stood up and and backed away, feeling as if her legs were about to buckle under her but staying upright through sheer willpower.

Within minutes a police vehicle was tearing down the beach, its flashing blue lights piercing the darkness.

Chapter Twelve

Mel walked slowly down the steps to the beach and waited. The lights from the approaching Nuclear Police vehicle were dazzling her and she put up her hands to shield her eyes. She was sobbing under her breath but as footsteps approached, crunching on the sand, she knew she must pull herself together. There were going to be questions and she must stick clearly to her story.

The vehicle stopped and two police officers got out. She stepped forward. 'I'm Mel Rogers, the Cape Wrath PR Manager.' The cool night air, salty and fresh, was bringing her back to her senses. She must be very careful . . . for all kinds of reasons.

The two shiftworkers were coming down the steps from the shaft behind her and she swiftly took the initiative. 'Thank you for coming so quickly.' She forced herself to sound brisk. 'We thought you should be alerted at once.'

Now that she could see the police officers properly she recognized one of them – a distinctively grizzled man in his late fifties with bushy eyebrows who attended the Director's site security meetings. The flashings on his uniform reminded her he was an inspector but she couldn't recall his name. She could see that the younger sandy-haired man was a sergeant.

'I'm Inspector Ross and this is Sergeant Dundas. We received a message from the police control room to get

198

down there, but I'm not clear what the problem is.' Ross's tone was curt.

'The problem is that ... well, there seems to be a body down the shaft.' It sounded so absurd. Unreal. In a moment she'd wake up.

She waited for the reaction, expecting them to tell her she must have made a mistake. But instead a look passed between the two men and Ross cleared his throat.

'If I could just have a word with you, Miss Rogers?' He took her by the elbow and steered her towards the vehicle.

'You don't understand. It's up there on the cliff,' she protested, hanging back.

'If you wouldn't mind just stepping into the car, Miss Rogers.' He held the door and she slid into the back seat. It felt like she was being arrested.

'I don't think you realize—' she began but he cut her short.

'Just a moment, please.' He got into the driver's seat and flicked a switch on the dashboard. 'Control? Ross here. I'm at the scene of the incident. It looks like Charlie's been showing his face again. Yes, OK ... Understood. Over and out.'

'What do you mean? Who's Charlie?' She was completely bewildered now.

Ross took out a packet of cigarettes and offered them to her.

'I don't smoke.'

'Mind if I do?'

Mel shook her head and waited. Ross lit up and took a couple of long satisfied drags then he shook his head.

'It's been a while since Charlie's given anybody a surprise. But you weren't to know about him, of course.' His rather grim face relaxed and he chuckled as if at some private joke.

'Inspector, could you please tell me what's going on,' Mel asked in desperation. 'I've had a shock and I don't appreciate being kept in the dark like this.'

199

'I'm sorry, I can understand that. He's not a very pretty sight, but what could you expect after twenty-five years.'

'*Twenty-five years*? Are you telling me there's been a body in the shaft for all that time?' Mel could hardly believe she was asking such a question or that Ross was nodding.

'That's right. It all goes back to the time of the explosion. But mind you what I'm telling you now is classified. You understand that?'

'Yes.' She was completely at sea.

'I remember pretty well what happened because I was the duty sergeant that night. The first sign we had that there was a problem with the shaft was when a police patrol spotted white smoke pouring out of the top of it.'

That must have been when the sodium reacted with the water, Mel thought, remembering her conversation with Sean.

'The site's fire brigade was called out to deal with it. Dealing with fires in radioactively contaminated facilities is a specialist job – it's not the kind of thing the town fire brigade could handle. Anyway, they put on their radiation suits and went down the beach to the shaft. After an hour or so they thought they'd dealt with it and were packing up their equipment so the technical chaps could come and assess the damage.' Ross paused. He wasn't smiling now. 'They were wrong. They *hadn't* dealt with it.'

'The others were already away down the steps when one of the men – his name was Charles Clark – went back. He must have forgotten something. No one really knows. But it seems that just as he reached the shaft the explosion occurred. The concrete lid blew into the air and killed him.'

'But why wasn't his body taken away?' It was inhuman that he'd just been dumped in the shaft.

'Well now, that's a good question.' Ross scrubbed out the remains of his cigarette. 'It wasn't easy for them to know what to do. The body was highly contaminated. And on top of that, he had no immediate family or close relations. He'd come up to Wrath from Manchester after

200

getting divorced and his ex-wife had emigrated – to Australia I think it was – to make a new start. The authorities tried to contact her but she couldn't be traced. In the circumstances, disposing of the body down the shaft seemed the best solution.'

Mel thought of that poor decomposed thing down there and shivered with a mixture of pity and disgust.

Ross seemed to read her thoughts. 'It was done decently, mind you, and the body was treated with respect. The site chaplain read prayers for the dead. It was like a burial at sea. But of course it was all kept very quiet. You can imagine the sensationalist rubbish the journalists would've written even in those days if the papers had got hold of it.'

And they would probably have been right. What kind of place was this where an employee who'd been killed because of management incompetence could be tossed down a shaft like a piece of nuclear waste! It was shocking and obscene.

'And now he's just "Charlie"?' Mel asked in a low voice.

'It was a long time ago. I'm one of the very few people who was here when it happened. And yes, he's become "Charlie" to us. Call it a term of affection.'

'But I don't understand. If the body has been down there all this time why hasn't it just sunk out of sight?'

'Originally the body was weighted down but it must have worked free as it began to decompose. What was left was spotted about ten years ago during a routine check. As I recall, it was reweighted so it sank down beneath the water level. I'll say this for Charlie, he's persistent. I certainly never expected to see him again. Something must have disturbed him.'

Ross reached for another cigarette. Through the car window she could see Sergeant Dundas talking and laughing with the shiftworkers. She hardly knew what to think about all of this. It seemed so incredible and yet it must be true.

Again Ross seemed to read her mind. 'I must remind you that you are bound by the terms of the Official Secrets

201

Act and are not at liberty to disclose anything that I have just told you. And now we'd better get you down to Health Physics. They'll be wanting to check you over for contamination and this car too, I expect. We've broken all the rules tonight.'

But Mel was hardly listening. Through her brain, again and again, she heard Ross's words: *Something must have disturbed him.* But what? There had been no drugs down the shaft, but maybe someone had just removed a consignment? That would explain why the shaft had been opened . . .

But if she'd hoped this evening would begin to unravel some of the mystery she couldn't have been more wrong.

'I need a statement from you to put on file.' James Everett's voice was colourless. If he was irritated at being called out in the early hours of the morning he didn't let it show.

'I don't understand.' Mel was dismayed. 'I told Inspector Ross everything.'

'This is a security rather than a police matter.'

'I don't see why.' Mel flicked back a strand of wet hair. After being checked by Health Physics and pronounced clear of radioactive contamination she had taken a hot shower. But just as she was leaving, Everett had arrived on the scene.

'This evening's events are rather unorthodox, to say the least,' Everett said carefully. Her wet hair was dripping on the edge of his highly polished desk and a flicker of irritation passed over his face. He didn't look like a man prepared to talk caringly about trauma this time.

'Putting dead employees secretly down a shaft is certainly unorthodox. In fact, I'd call it pretty unique.' Mel couldn't help the sarcasm. She was so tired. All she wanted was to go home and crawl into bed.

'This needn't take very long.' Everett wrote on, ignoring her comments, 'but I do need to know a few things.'

'OK.' There was no point arguing; it would only make things worse. Mel straightened up in her chair and sat waiting. She must be calm and matter-of-fact.

'What exactly were you doing at the shaft tonight?'

'I wanted to take a close look at it. As I agreed with the Director when I first came to Cape Wrath, I'm working out scenarios for site emergencies so we can test our ability to respond to the media in a crisis. I wanted to see whether the shaft would be a suitable element to include in the story.'

'But why did you need to go there after dark?'

'Because I'm writing a night-time scenario. In fact, I'm basing it on the events of the shaft explosion, and that happened at night.' She was quite pleased at her inventiveness.

'Why didn't you seek formal permission to have the shaft opened?'

'For two reasons. First of all, nearly everyone I could sensibly ask is away at a conference. The Plant Manager, the Shift Manager, several of the Deputy Shift Managers. But secondly – and this is much more important – when we hold the exercise I want the details to be a secret. It won't work properly if everyone knows it's based on an incident in the shaft. There was to be an element of surprise.'

Everett made a few notes with his elegant stainless-steel fountain pen. 'I understand the exercise is intended to be a joint one with Anderson Base?'

'Yes. If there were a serious release of radioactivity from Cape Wrath the base could be affected – depending on which way the wind was blowing.' She smiled at Everett. 'And I thought it would be a good way of cementing relations with them. You know how much importance the Director attaches to enhancing Cape Wrath's standing in the community. He always invites the senior officers like Commander Schultz to official receptions.'

'And is Commander Schultz the contact with whom you've been discussing this at Anderson Base?'

'Yes,' she said without hesitation. It was unlikely Everett could have already got to Tom, and why should he anyway? He had no reason to disbelieve her story.

'Formally you should have checked with security before

203

discussing a site exercise with anyone from outside, but in Commander Schultz's case there's no problem at all. Quite the reverse in fact.' Everett's face relaxed. 'Well, that all seems satisfactory. I'm sorry I had to delay you further but those are the rules. Any unforeseen incident out of normal working hours must be investigated immediately.'

'So you have no further questions?'

'None. From my point of view the incident is closed. I'm perfectly satisfied with your explanation and all I intend to do is place this short note recording our discussion on file. May I just ask you to read it and sign it at the bottom.'

Mel scanned it swiftly, wrote her signature and passed it back to him. As she did so something struck her.

'James, can I just ask you something?'

'Of course.'

'What did you mean just now about Tom? When you said there was no security problem with him, in fact "quite the reverse?".'

Everett's face was bland. 'Did I say that? All I meant was that the military personnel at Anderson Base are cleared to the highest levels. By analogy, as the Americans are our allies, we regard US security clearances as equal to British ones. That's a long-winded way of saying we regard Tom Schultz as "one of us".'

'I see.'

'I must ask you to say nothing about what you saw to anyone who isn't cleared. You do understand the position, don't you?'

'I do. Inspector Ross mentioned it as well – the Official Secrets Act.'

Everett nodded. 'Exactly so. The Official Secrets Act.'

'You're sure you don't think I'm crazy?' Mel was sitting naked on the end of Tom's bed, knees drawn up under her chin. She liked watching Tom shave. He did it like he did everything, with a concentrated precision. He caught her face reflected in the shaving mirror.

'Of course not.' His lips brushed her throat. 'I'm glad you told me. I only wish you'd confided in me earlier.' His eyes looked into hers. 'I'd have been there for you, you know that . . . And I'll back your story about the exercise if anyone mentions it.'

How would Tom feel if he knew she hadn't confided quite everything? But it would be unfair to tell him MacDonald was the man she suspected of using the shaft. She had no proof, only Sean's allegations and those strange entries in his diary. And Schultz and MacDonald knew each other; it would put Tom in an intolerable position.

'I may be completely wrong about everything. I'm only going on things Sean hinted about, and on what I found in his apartment – the map, the money, the cannabis, the weird diary . . .'

'And the murder of that Pakistani and what you noticed when you took the journalists to the shaft. It's perfectly logical to think it might all add up to something even if it doesn't in the end.' He shrugged. 'Anyway, what do you have to lose?'

'Only my job – and my sanity, I suppose.' she smiled. 'But I'm not the only one to be curious. Fergus Brown from the *Wrath Courier* has been asking a lot of questions about the waiter. He's quizzed me and he's also been questioning the man's landlady.'

'He's the guy with hair like a raggedy man, right?' Tom looked at his smooth-shaven face with approval and splashed on some Calvin Klein aftershave.

'That's right,' A shadow crossed Mel's face. 'I wonder what Fergus would make of poor "Charlie"? If it wasn't for the Official Secrets Act I'd tell him. It all seems so wrong. Why should the fact that some poor man got thrown down the shaft instead of being given a decent burial be classed as an official secret and hushed up?

'You're getting uptight again.'

'I'm sorry. I was thinking about James Everett.'

'There's no need to be so hard on the guy. He's only doing his job. And anyway he bought your story, didn't he?'

'Yes.'

'And that wasn't exactly the unvarnished truth, was it?'

'It was only a few white lies, and I wasn't doing any harm. Whereas Cape Wrath have been secretive about something serious which really happened.'

Tom turned round, razor in hand. 'You're being naive about this, honey. Responsible organizations have to protect themselves. Democracy has its limits and sometimes those in authority have to take decisions which may look autocratic, for the common good.'

He turned away but not before she'd seen a look she couldn't quite interpret. Exasperation? No, not quite that. More a kind of wariness. But she couldn't leave it alone.

'Look, nothing would happen if I told the press. It would be a one-day wonder and maybe that poor man would be given a decent burial instead of being left to fester down the shaft. I know I can't do that but joining in this conspiracy of silence goes right against my instincts. How can I try to be more honest with the public and the media when we've literally got a skeleton in the closet?'

'You really don't understand, do you? Maybe if you were my generation you would.' Tom's blue eyes behind the steel-rimmed spectacles looked remote now. 'If you knew the number of lives that were lost in Vietnam because people couldn't keep their mouths shut. And the media were the worst offenders. You said the other night that the PR battle in Vietnam was lost long before the fighting was over. Well, some of those media guys had blood on their hands. Their obsession with "the truth" – whatever that is – helped betray our secrets and demoralize our men. So don't talk to me about the public's right to know.'

'Tom.' She hadn't realized how deeply he felt and it shocked her. Mutely she held out her arms to him. There mustn't be any barriers between them. It was a moment before she saw his face relax again.

He came towards her. 'I really don't have time for this,' he murmured into her ear, but already he was nuzzling her stiffening nipples and she could feel his mounting heartbeat.

'Yes, you do,' she said softly. She arched her neck as he kissed the hollow at the base of her throat and began rhythmically to make love to her.

'Are you sure you'll be all right here on your own?'

'I'll be fine. Thanks for showing me where everything is.'

Irene Maclean shook her head at the rows of dusty files. 'It's high time most of these were sent down to the Public Record Office. But I'm the only archivist at Cape Wrath now. There used to be three of us so it's no wonder I'm behind.' She indicated the tattered card index on the table with a grimace. 'All that needs to be computerized.'

'I'm sure I'll be able to find what I want. Please don't worry.'

'Well, I'll be away for my lunch then. Make yourself some tea or coffee if you want. Everything's there.' She pointed to a battered old tray with a picture of kittens on it. Then Irene put on a navy Barbour worn through at the elbows, jammed a yellow beret on her greying hair and plunged out into the needle-sharp rain that had been driving in across the sea all morning.

The room was dusty with the unmistakable smell of old files. Perhaps it was something they'd used in the ink in those days. Mel sat down at the table and began to look through the index she'd requested covering personnel at Wrath in the 1970s. The sound of the rain pattering on the tin roof of the shack which served as the archive was soothing. She worked through the index swiftly.

It was sorted under organizational units. There, that was what she wanted – Cape Wrath Fire Brigade. There were files about its grading structure, shift arrangements, special exercises, efficiency reviews etc. The cards went on and on, relics of a bureaucratic past which made her smile. But yes, this was more like it!

She came to a series of cards listing all the members of the fire service each year by grade. What was she after? The explosion happened in 1974, but Charles Clark had come to Wrath several years earlier. 1969? No, there was no Clark in the fire service that year.

She also drew a blank in 1970. But the records for 1971 showed a C. Clark recruited in July. Next to his name was a file number and the details of the archive box where it was stored. She noted the row of letters and numbers carefully and stood up.

Where would she find it? She wasn't even quite sure why she was doing this. Except that she wanted to put a face to that thing they called 'Charlie' and make some kind of amends by taking an interest in him.

A row of boxes on the top shelf over by the window caught her eye. Climbing on the kick-step she was just able to reach them. How short little Irene ever managed to retrieve anything was a mystery. The box was heavy and she needed to hold it with two hands but it looked like the right one.

No one had touched it in years. A frosting of thick grey dust covered the top. She took some tissues from her pocket and wiped it clean. The red clothboard underneath had long since faded to a dull coral. Settling herself at the table again she opened the box and began to sift through the buff folders, each secured with a black ribbon.

There it was, with *C. Clark – Fire Officer Grade 1* in spidery handwriting. Across the top someone had written *died in service* in red biro and underlined it twice. She opened it and stared at the faded passport-sized black and white photograph inside. The face that looked back at her across a quarter of a century was young, with the long hair of the time. The lapels of his jacket were wide, so was the kipper tie. The expression was startled, the way people always look in cheap pictures taken in photo-booths.

After a moment she began to turn the pages. They were

mostly flimsy carbon copies recording his recruitment interview and potential assessment, his training records and annual performance markings. If ever someone was Mister Average it had been Charles Clark. Pleasant, likeable, conscientious . . . fundamentally ordinary.

She turned back to the photograph and studied the face for a final few moments. It moved her almost unbearably to think of the bizarre twist of fate that had led to his death. Again she felt a wave of revulsion that he had just been thrown in the shaft like a lump of nuclear waste. At least she had seen his face. That was what she would remember, not the disgusting shapeless thing that had leered up at her in the wavering torchlight.

'RIP, Charlie,' Mel whispered, 'Rest in peace.' Outside the rain grew heavier, ricocheting off the metal roof like bullets.

'I'm not sure I'm looking forward to this. I don't mind him in the office anymore but I don't want to spend the whole day with him.'

'Why not? It could be fun.'

'I doubt it, but he's been so persistent that in the end I couldn't refuse – and he was really keen you should come as well.'

'I'm flattered.' Tom manoeuvred the jeep with practised ease around the sharp bend up John MacDonald's drive. Amelia was brushing up the tumbling autumn leaves, short hair confined behind her ears by an alice band. 'John's just attaching the trailer to the car.' She smiled at them.

'Aren't you coming with us?' Mel asked, noting her long flowered skirt and open-toed sandals.

'No, I'm not keen on sailing. I get sea-sick. But it's nice for John to have some company today. I know he's been looking forward to it. He wants to show you some of the coastline around Wrath. It really is very pretty.'

'Good morning!' MacDonald came around the side of the house, spruce in jeans and a navy sweater. 'It looks like we have a good day for it. Give me a hand with the tarpaulin, will you, Tom?'

'Sure.' As Tom followed MacDonald, Mel looked up at the sky. Battalions of fluffy white clouds were sailing by, driven by a brisk easterly breeze. It was a wonderful, invigorating kind of day.

'John's delighted you're both going out with him. He seems to get on really well with Tom.' Amelia paused and leant on her long-handled brush. 'It was so sad about Sean. He and John used to be quite close.'

'I know,' Mel said softly. 'You must have known him a long time.'

'Ever since he came to Wrath. Of course, John knew him at university.'

'It'll be hard not to think of him while we're out in the boat today. Was he a good sailor?'

'Not very. He'd only recently taken it up . . . I suppose it was his lack of experience that was to blame for the accident.' Amelia's expression was sombre but she brightened as her husband sounded the Rover's horn. 'I've packed plenty of sandwiches for you all and there are two flasks of hot tea. Have a nice time and don't let John keep you out too late. He can get carried away!'

'She's a little beauty, isn't she?' MacDonald said. 'Climb aboard.'

It had been a matter of minutes to get the boat off the trailer and into the water at Lochiel Bay, a lonely cove with a white strand. Shaggy Highland cattle grazed in the ruins of an abandoned croft, but otherwise it was deserted.

The bay was five miles east of the Cape Wrath plant – well beyond the spot where she had found the body of the young waiter, Mel thought gratefully. In some ways it seemed so long ago now. Other things had come along to preoccupy her, but the horror of it remained.

Tom ran an experienced eye over the red and white paintwork. The name *Endeavour* was painted in black

210

letters and an outboard motor was concealed under a cover.

'How long have you had her?' he asked MacDonald.

'About three years. I've had a boat ever since I came to Wrath, but the problem is finding time for sailing. I try to take my boys out in the school holidays. Here, you'd better put these on.' MacDonald dished out some phosphorescent yellow life-jackets that fastened with velcro strips across the chest and neat straps that fastened around the waist.

Like everything John MacDonald did he'd organized the trip meticulously. Soon they were clipping through the swell and Mel could taste the salt on her lips. It was exhilarating and she closed her eyes for a moment.

She'd always loved the water. Into her head came a picture of a little girl with shiny red boots on a long-ago beach in Skye. She was running towards the sea, drawn by foaming waves and the sound of seagulls in her ears.

'Melissa, stop!' Too late. She was in the water and it was over the top of her boots, the sand sucking and hissing beneath her feet. Just as she began to cry her father's strong arms lifted her to safety. Her mother pulled off her boots, tipping out the water and spreading her socks out to dry. They'd both laughed and she'd laughed too . . .

They took a wave sideways on. Jolted back to the present Mel saw that they were rounding a rocky point with some kind of ruin clinging to its spine. It was very overgrown. The trunks of gnarled and stunted trees had fused and become one with the fallen stone walls.

'What's that place?' she asked curiously.

'St Malcolm's Priory. It was abandoned centuries ago. There's nothing there now but a few bats. Of course, our Director thinks it's wonderful.' MacDonald's tone was scornful.

But as they sailed closer she could see that the Priory must have been beautiful once. Roof and stained glass were long-gone, but the stone walls and arches remained like the skeleton of a once-graceful animal, along with the delicate

211

stone tracery of a rose window. It was easy to imagine rows of cowled monks walking its cloisters and the sound of religious chanting rising above the wind and the crashing of the waves below.

'Looks like something out of Dracula to me.' Tom stared at it, teeth very white as he chewed gum. 'But it's certainly atmospheric.'

'Speaking of atmospheric I gather you took a look at the shaft the other night,' MacDonald said, altering course as they rounded the point.

Mel glanced at him sharply. She'd wondered whether he was going to bring that up. He hadn't said a word to her about it in the office since he'd got back. She'd begun to wonder whether he even knew. He must have been talking to James Everett or to the Nuclear Police.

'That's right. I'm writing a scenario for an emergency exercise based on another incident in the shaft—'

'And you found more than you bargained for.' There was an ironical smile on his lips.

He knows about Charlie, Mel thought to herself, but he would, wouldn't he? He had been on the site as a young graduate when the explosion happened and he had been at Cape Wrath the last time poor Charlie had appeared.

But he didn't seem to expect an answer. 'I gather it's to be a joint exercise to test how Cape Wrath and Anderson Base would react?'

'That's right. We've talked theoretically about co-ordination but we've never put it to the test. That's why I suggested it to Mel,' Tom said easily. 'She thought the shaft might make a good focal point.'

'Good idea. The more realistic these exercises are the better.' MacDonald was steering them further out to sea and they were going at a cracking pace. 'Are you still going to use the shaft in your scenario?'

'I'm not sure. Maybe,' Mel said casually. 'It was only an idea. Perhaps you could suggest something different?'

'Perhaps.' He seemed to have lost interest and was

checking the direction of the wind. 'But I don't suppose it matters either way.'

Mel was surprised and at the same time relieved. The more she thought about it, the more certain she now was that Sean had told her a farrago of lies about MacDonald and the shaft. Perhaps the whole story was just fantasy. Perhaps even the diary was fantasy. *He's playing God.* The words went round and round in her brain – mad, meaningless. But the diary hadn't lied about Laura . . . She thought of the empty space where the bluebell had been . . .

They sailed on, but after a while Mel noticed the wind was shifting and beginning to blow really hard. Darkening clouds were bowling across the sky and the *Endeavour* began to buck up and down in the swell. A cold, stinging rain caught her in the face and she shivered. MacDonald deftly angled the sail but the boat still heaved.

'We'll have to go back,' he shouted. 'It's getting too rough. Tom, can you give me a hand?'

Mel watched the two men work quickly and efficiently together, turning the *Endeavour* for home. They seemed to have no need of her.

'Isn't there anything I can do?' She pulled up the hood of her anorak and tugged some woollen gloves from her pocket.

'No, you sit tight. I'll tell you if I need you,' MacDonald instructed. Stepping to the back of the *Endeavour* he unzipped the cover on the outboard motor. As he pulled the cord a throaty roar cut through the air and the *Endeavour*'s bows rose in the water.

Chapter Thirteen

She was back at the shaft but this time she wasn't wearing the clumsy radiation suit. Instead she was in some soft, floating garment and her whole body felt free and light. The great cumbersome crane and winch had gone, and instead the shaft lid was standing open.

Although it was blackest night, without stars or moon, a light was coming from deep inside and its radiance lit her steps as she walked slowly forwards. It was inviting her, luring her within. Everything she wanted was waiting for her there. The promise was almost unbearable but at the same time she wanted to make it last.

As she approached the edge she closed her eyes and breathed deeply, spreading her arms wide and tossing back her head. Her bare feet were poised on the very rim of the shaft; the purifying touch of cold metal on naked flesh went through her like an electric shock.

Now. She opened her eyes and gazed down into the very heart of the shaft. The water inside was golden-bright like the sun. The light reflecting from it hurt her eyes and she closed them in sudden agony, eyelids burning. She rubbed them with her hands but they were hurting her too. Forcing her eyes open again she saw lumps and blisters beginning to form as the skin of her hands, her arms, her whole body started to burn.

She tried to step back but couldn't. The golden light held her in its destructive radiance. Desperately she stared down into the shaft as if help might come from there. And then she saw him. His face was half-eaten away and his naked body was rotting. Suddenly it went dark and she was falling down ... down ... through diseased and fetid air.

It was Sean and he was waiting for her.

'No, please no!' She was clawing wildly but there was nothing to grip. In a moment she'd collide with the corpse, their arms and legs would intertwine, they'd become one ... The stench in her nostrils was overpowering. What would it feel like to touch soft, decomposing flesh?

'Mel!' Tom's voice recalled her from the darkness. Then the light snapped on. 'What is it? What's the matter?'

'It was him − I saw him at the bottom of the shaft.' She was rubbing her hands together compulsively as if she needed to cleanse herself of something. To force herself to stop she sat up and pulled her knees under her chin.

'Who did you see? I don't understand what you mean.' Tom was slowly coming awake.

'It was Sean,' she sobbed.

'It was just a bad dream. Come on, Mel, wake up. It's over now.'

His warm hands reached out and she felt him unlock her tensed fingers. Then he lifted her hands and put them around his neck, and holding her tight in his arms, he began to rock her gently. The faint, familiar tang of his aftershave comforted her.

'Hey, now, that's better. You're still a little girl, aren't you? I bet you were scared of lightning and storms.' He stroked her hair and she lay passive against him. She heard his words but her mind couldn't quite connect yet.

'I thought ... I thought it was ...'

'Sure you did, but it wasn't real. This is reality, now.'

Gradually her breathing slowed and she came back to the present. The chrome furniture of Tom's apartment looked back at her. The plain white walls, the brushed-steel rack of well-polished shoes, the single limed oak chest of drawers

215

and the expensive multigym were aggressively real and down to earth.

She began to be ashamed. These days, she was becoming more and more emotional.

'Are you OK?' Tom raised her chin. Without his glasses his eyes looked ice-blue, the pupils dark pinpricks. 'I'll get you a drink if you like.'

'No, I'm fine. I'm sorry for waking you, Tom.'

'No problem. What exactly did you dream?'

'It doesn't matter. I'm not even sure now. It was confusing.'

'Just put it out of your mind and try to get some proper sleep.'

Tom lay her back against the pillows and tucked the duvet around her. Then he kissed her cheek, checked the alarm clock and switched off the light, turning his lean back to her.

Mel lay for a long time in the darkness, eyes open, staring into nothing, but her mind was full of images. Should she confide in him more? Maybe even show him Sean's diary? Being with Tom had made her feel safe again. Maybe she should trust her instincts

'Tom?' she whispered after a few moments, but his regular breathing told her he was asleep.

Mel glanced at her watch. Thank goodness she wasn't late. Tom had said eight o'clock and it was only five past. A rush of warm fragrant air greeted her as she walked into Khan's Curry House. It was quite crowded but she couldn't see Tom at any of the tables. Maybe his friends were already here?

'Mel?' She turned to find a smiling red-headed woman at her elbow. 'Hi! I'm Bella Connor. We've got a table over there in the corner.'

'How did you know it was me?' Mel smiled back.

'Easy! You know how precise Tom is about everything. He described you in detail.'

A great big bear of a man stood up as they approached and held out his hand. 'Chris Connor – glad to know you. I've ordered us some beers and a few poppadums while we wait for Tom.'

'Sounds good. Tom said you all work together at the base?'

'Sure. I'm an engineer like Tom, and Bella's a computer programmer. And you work over at Cape Wrath, Tom was telling us,' Chris said.

'That's right. I'm the Public Relations Manager.'

'That sounds pretty exhausting. You guys are never out of the news. What was that I was reading about the other day? Radioactive seagulls or something like that?'

'You're right, it was about radioactive seagulls. There was a scare that they were eating radioactive particles off the Cape Wrath site.'

'And shitting mini-atomic bombs all over town?' The big man laughed uproariously.

'Chris! For goodness' sake,' Bella remonstrated, but she was grinning.

Mel laughed too. 'You shouldn't believe everything you read in the papers.'

'I don't. But I believe the evidence of my own eyes—'

The wail of police sirens made him pause. Out of the window Mel saw two police cars, blue lights flashing, tearing down the street. Probably on their way to the first of Wrath's Friday-night brawls. She turned back to Chris. 'I'm sorry, what were you saying?'

'I've been seeing some pretty weird radiation readings from one of our submarines. Are you sure you guys haven't discharged something you shouldn't?'

'Where was the submarine?'

'Within about ten kilometres of Cape Wrath.'

'Do they always take radiation readings in those waters?'

'Yes, it's routine to keep testing at regular intervals all through any manoeuvre. If it came to a real conflict with nuclear submarines attacking each other, it would be crucial to know what the radiation levels were outside.'

'Is everything all right? You do not wish to order yet?'

They hadn't noticed Mushtaq Khan. His fine dark eyes looked anxious.

'Everything's fine. We're just waiting for a friend,' Chris said.

The restaurant owner smiled and moved on to the next table. Mel waited until he was out of range.

'When did you find this out?' She dipped a golden piece of poppadam into a dish of mango chutney and nibbled it.

'Yesterday. I looked at the submarine's log for a report I'm writing.' Chris looked at her, frowning slightly. 'Seriously, have there been any problems at the plant recently?'

'How do you mean?'

'I mean problems with radioactive discharges into the sea. That might account for the radiation levels picked up by the sub.'

'I don't think so. Not that I know of anyway. If there had been any serious unplanned discharges we would have had to report them to our regulators. And I would have been writing press releases about them.'

'Some of the data goes back to the beginning of the year, to January and February – before you came to Cape Wrath. Anyway, it doesn't have to be connected with radioactive discharges. Something else could have happened.'

'Such as?'

Chris shrugged. 'Someone might have dumped something radioactive in the sea. Pieces of obsolete equipment, perhaps?'

'Who'd want to do that?'

'I don't know, but people get lazy.'

'It's very, very unlikely.'

'If you say so. But there has to be a logical explanation.'

'I could take it up officially with the plant management?'

'No, don't do that. It might not be anything to do with Cape Wrath. It might be that *we've* got a problem at

218

Anderson Base, in which case I wouldn't want to broadcast it. But if you could ask a few discreet questions . . .'

'OK, but can you give me something more specific to go on?'

'Sure. I'll send you a list of the radiation readings and the dates.'

'What readings?'

'Tom! We'd nearly given you up.' Chris thumped Tom on the back and pulled out a chair for him. Tom kissed Bella on the cheek and Mel on the mouth before sitting down.

'I'm sorry, guys. I got delayed at the base and then there was a hold-up on the road into Wrath. Some kind of accident, I think. Anyway, what were you talking about? You were all looking pretty damned serious.'

'Chris has been giving poor Mel the third degree about Cape Wrath.' Bella looked at her husband affectionately. 'You know what he's like when he gets an idea in his head.'

'Oh?' Tom took a long pull at a can of Budweiser. 'Tell me something I don't know about the guy! And I promised Mel she was going to like my friends . . .'

'Chris was telling me about some unusual radiation readings picked up by one of your submarines. He wanted to know whether there'd been any incidents at the plant,' Mel said.

A frown crossed Tom's face and he pulled his chair forward. 'But, Chris, they weren't very high and there could be any number of explanations. You can't blame Mel. Anyway, that information's classified. We shouldn't really be discussing it somewhere like this. Now let's order – I'm starving!'

Tom grinned at Mel and she smiled back. But Chris's questions disturbed her. Unexpected radiation readings, hints that something odd might be going on at the plant . . . Could there be any connection with the comments and data in Sean's diary? She felt that familiar cold shadow creeping slowly over her like a cloud blotting out the sun.

★

'I need to look at the site incident reports for the last six months.'

The clerk in the Site Safety Registry looked for a moment as if she wanted to argue.

'I'm writing a report for the Director about the correlation between the site's safety performance and press coverage about our operations,' Mel explained. There was no reason she shouldn't have access to the files, but this was a bureaucratic and hierarchical culture. Mentioning Fabian would make things move more quickly.

The clerk consulted a list then pressed a button on a console. The files in the giant racks behind her began to move around on a conveyor belt like clothes in a dry cleaner's. After a moment she pressed another button and retrieved a chunky folder of papers in a buff cover.

'Please sign here. You must not take them off site and you must return them within forty-eight hours.'

'No problem. Thank you.'

Mel hurried towards the staircase leading to her own floor. With luck she'd be able to study the file before it was time to go to the Director's office for his interview down the line with BBC Scotland. She had at least two hours until then. Ishbel was with some technical journalists down at the nuclear waste storage area so she'd have the office to herself.

She closed her door and sat down at her desk. Taking Chris's notes out of her top pocket she unfolded the two pages carefully and spread them out. They'd arrived that morning by courier; it was good of him to have sent her the information so quickly.

The detail was bewildering at first, but as she read through the lines of dates and scientific hieroglyphics they began to make some sense to her. She flicked her computer on and tapped in her access code. The best way of handling this would be to try and tabulate all the information.

An hour later she sat back and looked at the information

on the screen. Then, taking the mouse, she went through and highlighted some of the information in bold face. The message stared back at her. If she'd interpreted Chris's notes correctly, on at least four occasions during January and February the submarine's monitors had picked up radiation levels treble the normal levels. All those readings had been taken within a ten-kilometre radius of the Cape Wrath plant.

Mel frowned. If that was right, why hadn't the plant's own environmental monitoring programme picked this up? Or perhaps it had but for some reason the information hadn't been published. If the radiation levels were still below the limits set by the regulators there might be no need to report the increases formally. All the same, there must be a reason why the radiation levels had risen and someone should surely be investigating.

Mel opened the buff folder and began to leaf through the incident reports. The first category covered every kind of unforeseen event from a foreman failing to wear protective goggles and getting cement dust in his eye as a result, to a fight between employees of two rival local scaffolding firms which had started with a tussle about ownership of some poles and ended with one man in hospital and another charged with causing grievous bodily harm.

Mel sighed. However, towards the back of the folder she found what she was looking for – the incidents classified as radiologically significant. Each was recorded on a separate sheet with the date, a brief explanation of what had happened, an analysis of the radiological consequences and an assessment of any remedial action. There was also a classification at the bottom rating the incident on the international nuclear incident scale and a note of when the relevant regulator had been informed. Each report was signed by the Plant Shift Manager of the day.

Mel smiled as she read the report of the spillage of radioactive liquor during her first visit to the plant with Dougie MacBain. She'd had to battle hard to be allowed to release information about it, but since then she'd been informed about nearly all the incidents in the folder. Now she flicked through them carefully. Was there something she'd missed at the time?

She wasn't quite sure what she was expecting or hoping to find, but she was drawing a blank. The reports were all routine and there was nothing to account for increased levels of radioactive discharges into the sea from the plant. Perhaps they were barking up the wrong tree and the problem was over at Anderson Base. She checked her watch. Another quarter of an hour and she'd have to call it a day. Then she turned the next page. At the very back of the file was a sheaf of papers held together with a metal tag. The top page was an incident report in the standard format headed *External Radiation Monitor Malfunctions – Restricted – Named Distribution Only.*

The distribution list at the bottom of the page was surprisingly short. Fabian Williams, John MacDonald and Dougie MacBain. No one from the Site Safety Department or from Security had apparently been informed, never mind anyone from the press office. Whatever had happened had been kept tight by the senior management. And there was no indication of whether it had been reported to the regulators.

Her interest sharpened, Mel turned the pages with impatient hands. According to the report, the Cape Wrath radiation monitors around the reprocessing plant had unexpectedly failed while nuclear material was being transferred between the reprocessing plant and the storage area. Not just once or twice. It had happened four times within a period of nine weeks in the first three months of the year, and on each occasion the failure had lasted only a few minutes.

What could have caused something like that to go wrong? Scanning the notes, she came across the report of an investigation which Fabian Williams had chaired himself. It had concluded that the instruments had malfunctioned because of their age. MacDonald had been asked to conduct a feasibility study into their replacement but there was no

222

clue about the timing of the study. Perhaps the feasibility study was still going on, in which case the plant was still running with faulty radiation monitors?

Glancing up, her eyes fell on the figures on her computer screen, in particular the dates she'd highlighted. Did they tie up? She picked up a pencil and lightly circled the dates in the incident report. Each of the four cases when the monitors had failed had occurred no more than twenty-four hours after the submarine had taken its measurements. There *had* to be a connection!

Mel stood up, feeling like shouting and cheering, though she wasn't quite sure why. Although she'd established a link she still didn't understand the significance – and maybe there wasn't any. She frowned at the folder, trying to puzzle it out, and noticed there was a final page at the very back which she hadn't read. It was a further incident report and what it told her was that there had been a later and fifth occasion when the radiation monitors had failed. The date and time made her catch her breath. Three-fifteen a.m. on Sunday 15 June. Just two hours before Sean Docherty was last seen alive as he drove out through the gates of the Cape Wrath site.

'We'll be coming through to you in about five minutes, Mr Williams, OK? You'll hear some music and then the presenter, Kirsty Macbride, will introduce you. We expect the item to last about fifteen minutes with one short break in the middle.' The phone went dead again as the production assistant in Glasgow put the line on hold.

Mel pushed the triangular-shaped microphone a bit closer to the Director. 'Keep the telephone on the "hands free" setting then we can both hear what the presenter is asking you. It also means you don't have the distraction of holding a receiver in your hand. But you must lean in towards the microphone while you're speaking so it picks up your voice properly.'

Mel tested the connection between the microphone and

the telephone one last time. Fabian was well-briefed and knew exactly what he wanted to say. He'd been surprisingly receptive to the media training she'd given him, rehearsing sound bites, learning how to parry questions and turn them to his advantage.

'I've asked your secretary to switch off all phones in the outer office and not to let anyone in during the interview. We want to avoid any "noises off".' Just as she spoke, two RAF Tornadoes from the base fifty miles south came screaming in from across the sea and peeled off on either side of the Cape Wrath plant. Fabian Williams glanced out of the window and tutted in irritation.

'That's their last flight of the day. We checked with the base this morning,' Mel said reassuringly. 'Here's a glass of water for you, just in case . . . And by the way, I'm taping this for you so you can have a copy afterwards.'

'Thank you.' The Director glanced at some notes he'd made and began shuffling them around.

'I really don't think you need those. You know the message you want to get over, and we don't want the sound of rustling paper going down the line.' Mel gently moved them out of his reach. Before he could say anything the sound of the Spice Girls flooded the room.

Fabian was staring at the microphone in astonishment. He'd probably never heard of the Spice Girls. Mel had to struggle hard not to laugh. But if he wanted to publicize his cause on popular radio he was going to have to get used to this sort of thing.

'Thirty seconds to go, Mr Williams,' said a disembodied voice from the studio in Glasgow. He took a quick sip of water and Mel gave him an encouraging smile.

'This afternoon we're delighted to have the Director of the Cape Wrath Nuclear Reprocessing Plant on *Round Up Scotland*. Fabian Williams is joining us down the line from Cape Wrath, but he's not here to talk about nuclear repro-cessing. What he really, really wants is to succeed in his campaign for the preservation of one of Scotland's oldest castles which happens to be on the Cape Wrath site. Now, Fabian, why does Dunstan Castle matter?'

The Director's nervousness soon disappeared as he got into his stride. Mel was glad she'd been able to get him on this programme. She could trust Kirsty to give him an easy time. Other presenters might not have been able to resist having a dig at Cape Wrath and asking how come the castle had become contaminated in the first place. Which was a fair enough question, she thought wryly, though it had nothing to do with Fabian's time as Director.

The longer the interview went on the more clearly his knowledge, passion and commitment came across. It was an impressive performance. If only he could sound like that when he was talking about the operations at Cape Wrath . . .

Her mind began to drift back to the strange set of data on her screen. How would Fabian explain that? With the same assurance with which he was making the case for a public campaign to decontaminate Dunstan Castle and open it to the public?

'And there we must leave it,' Kirsty Macbride wound up the interview. 'Fabian Williams, thank you for being our guest this afternoon. We wish you every success with your campaign to preserve such an important part of Scotland's heritage.'

There was a click on the line. 'Hello? This is Allie Stewart the producer speaking. Thanks very much for taking part. We'll forward any letters from the public to you. Bye . . .'

Mel disconnected the microphone from the telephone and cancelled the 'hands free' facility. 'That was great. No problems.'

'I wish it was as easy to persuade the Government to give us the funding we need for the environmental remediation work. But if we can get a big groundswell of public opinion, that should help – particularly when the new Scottish

Assembly begins flexing its muscles. They'll be keen on this type of project and won't want to see it blocked by a lot of Englishmen in Whitehall or Westminster.'

'I suppose not.'

'And that reminds me. I want to call a meeting to discuss how we're going to handle this autumn's political conferences.'

'I thought that as a Government organization we had to take a low profile?' Mel frowned. 'I mean, we mustn't get involved in anything political or be seen to be lobbying.'

'But we have a responsibility to make sure our activities are well understood,' the Director fussed. 'We have enemies in all the main political parties. I want to host a reception at each of the major conferences and use it as a platform—'

'For talking about the castle?' Mel ended shrewdly.

'Why not?' Reaching across the table, Fabian gathered up the notes he'd made and put them carefully into a plastic folder. 'There are occasions in life when one must be ruthless. Have you ever heard of the Crusader Reynald of Châtillon? I visited one of his castles on the Jordan/Iraq border a couple of years ago.'

Mel shook her head. She was beginning to wonder whether the Director was going quietly insane. His interest in the Crusades and castles and medieval warfare was becoming an obsession.

'Well, he had a trick for dealing with his enemies. He used to drop them over the castle wall or down a deep *oubliette*. And just to make sure that they had a few seconds to reflect on their stupidity in crossing him, he invented a special box. This was fitted on their heads before they were flung over the edge to stop them losing consciousness before they hit the ground.'

The Director coughed. 'The man was clearly a psychopath, of course, but there is something admirable about the clarity with which he viewed the world. One of his sayings roughly translates from the Norman French as

"If you're not with me, you're against me." Sometimes I wish I could adopt his tactics.'

Fabian Williams adjusted his cuffs and gazed absently out of the window. It was half-past four and the workforce – apart from those on the evening shift – were beginning to leave the site. A queue of orange double-decker buses was waiting on the other side of the gates ready to ferry them back to Wrath and the outlying crofts and villages. But she doubted he was thinking about the workforce.

'Fabian?' She had to say his name twice to get a reaction.

'Yes?'

'I was reading some incident reports today. One of them mentioned that our external radiation monitors had failed earlier in the year.'

'Oh?' He smiled at her absently.

'You chaired an enquiry into what happened which recommended that there should be a feasibility study into their replacement. No one told me about it. There could be some very negative PR implications if the story got out.'

'I'm sorry, but I simply don't remember the circumstances. You should talk to John MacDonald if you want to know more.'

'What about the feasibility study? Has that been completed?'

'As I said you'll really have to talk to John . . .'

The door opened and the Director's secretary came in with a cup of tea for him in a white china cup and saucer.

As Mel left the room she caught the fragrant scent of lapsang souchong. Sometimes, she thought to herself, just sometimes, she could feel a certain sympathy with Christine and Laura Williams in their search for a response – *any* response.

Ishbel was rewinding the tape as Mel walked back into the office.

'He was OK, wasn't he?' Mel flung herself down in a chair. 'A bit nervous at first but he settled down once the interview

227

got going. I thought he was quite convincing. I wish he'd go on air and talk about Cape Wrath's future like that.'

'I guess the problem is that he's more interested in the castle . . .' Ishbel paused. 'But listen, Mel, someone's just told me something dreadful. There was an accident along the coast road. Fergus Brown went over the edge on his motorbike and, well – he's dead.'

'Fergus?' Mel blinked in shock. 'When did it happen?'

'Last night apparently but they've only just released the details because they've been trying to contact his next-of-kin.'

'Have they any idea what happened?'

'It looks like he misjudged a bend. It's a treacherous stretch of road, particularly in the dark.'

'I saw some police vehicles tearing out of Wrath last night with their sirens going. That must have been what it was. I didn't much like him, but all the same . . .' And poor Laura, she thought. First Sean and now this.

That evening when Ishbel had left and Mel had the office to herself it took her a while to gather her thoughts. Fergus and that red motorbike of his had been such a feature of Wrath life. She gazed out of the window, remembering her first meeting with him. It seemed an age ago. And now she'd probably never know whether he'd had any connection with drug smuggling.

The thought reminded her what she was supposed to be doing. It should be safe to begin as most of the administrative staff left at five o'clock. Sean had been one of the very few to work late. In a funny kind of way she'd stepped into his shoes, she thought, as she re-booted her computer. Working late, collating figures, making notes, harbouring suspicions. Had Sean had any more idea what he was doing than she had?

But intuition was still telling her there must be a connection between the incidents on the site with the radiation monitors and Sean's disappearance. After all, he had been on site the last time the monitors failed. Perhaps he had even had something to do with it? Could he have sabotaged them for reasons of his own?

She thought back to the cannabis and the map and the money. He might have damaged the monitors to create a diversion while a consignment of drugs was being landed. Then maybe he'd taken his boat out to take delivery. Maybe he'd even marked the drop points with radioactive tracers. That would have appealed to his quirky sense of humour. And maybe he'd prepared the shaft ready to take delivery. That would explain why the lid had been moved and why the contents had apparently been disturbed, bringing poor Charlie to the surface.

Perhaps if she shared some more of this with Tom it would help her. But then she hesitated. She needed to be surer of her facts. In Guatemala after Daniel's death the officials in the British Embassy had tried to make her believe she'd imagined his murder, that the warm blood which had spurted over her and dripped down her body had existed only in her imagination. That the whole thing was a fantasy brought on by drugs.

Tom was going to Washington for a Pentagon briefing. By the time he returned to Wrath she should have more of the facts.

She opened the folder with the incident reports again and continued the task of checking and cross-checking. But would it help her solve the riddle? That was the question.

It was a perfect September evening. A luscious harvest moon hung low on the horizon and the air was still soft and warm. She wasn't sure what impulse led her to drive along the coast to the rocky spit of land where St Malcolm's Priory sat in all its beautiful desolation, but it had caught her imagination. She wanted to walk through the ruins in all the luxury of solitude.

Tom would think she was mad. What had he called the

ruin? "Something out of *Dracula*." His cool practical mind had no time for her more fanciful thoughts.

A mile or two beyond Wrath she had the road to herself and put the MGF through its paces. It was high tide and the surf was foaming over the rocky shoreline. Briefly she glimpsed tail-lights ahead of her but they were receding fast.

Mel pushed a button and music from one of her favourite cassettes flooded the car. Latin-American salsa. She loved the sheer passion and vibrancy, and found herself tapping her fingers to the rhythm on the small steering wheel.

She was still singing the tune under her breath as she locked the MGF and set off along the track down to St Malcolm's. She felt for the torch in her pocket for the return trip, but right now it was still light enough to see where she was going. The ground beneath her feet felt springy and dry. She passed an old stone bothy, abandoned long ago. It looked forlorn, but once it must have been full of life.

There was no one around, just a few sheep who looked at her without interest. The track began to climb steeply. As she neared the top of the headland she stopped to catch her breath and take in the amazing views. The land fell away below her and a path led down to the narrow promontory. She could see St Malcolm's at the far end, silhouetted against the sunset, and beyond it, dark blue waves surging against darker rocks.

She caught the distant sound of a car door being slammed shut: probably a farmer coming to check on his livestock for the night. She walked the last few yards to the summit and then she saw them. The navy-blue Range Rover was drawn up a few hundred yards away where the land sloped down to a small cove, its headlights casting twin pools of light. The tailgate was up and Hamish and Laura were standing beside it, talking. Instinctively Mel ducked behind a crumbling stone wall, feeling the sudden thudding of her heart.

When she looked again, Hamish was reaching inside the Range Rover and pulling something heavy towards him. It looked like a large rectangular package wrapped in tarpaulin. He carried it carefully down to the shore, bracing his powerful frame against the weight. Laura followed carrying something which looked like an aerial but Mel couldn't be sure. She moved a little closer in the shadow of the wall.

They were right down on the beach now, just a few yards from the water's edge. Laura was on her knees, unwrapping whatever was in the package and laying the contents out on the tarpaulin. In the gathering dusk the pair began setting up what looked like a battery of electronic equipment, working with silent concentration. What were they? Transmitters? She could see a flashy array of aerials and now they seemed to be testing something, each of them holding a handset. Laura began walking along the cove talking to Hamish who had put on a set of headphones and was adjusting his receiver. The moon was rising, silvering Laura's ash-blonde hair.

Mel felt a sick feeling deep inside. She could guess what they were doing. The equipment set up on the beach was nothing less than a sophisticated radio system. They were signalling to someone out at sea and there was only one reason why they would need to do that. Drugs. They were signalling that it was safe for a shipment to come in.

So Hamish was the one behind it all. And he was using Laura to help him – an emotionally damaged youngster whose life he was ruining before it had begun. It was all falling into place at last. He and Sean must have been in this together, and somehow they had drawn Laura in. No wonder Hamish had been in Sean's flat. He was looking for the cannabis before the police found it and began to investigate Sean's disappearance seriously. That story about a naked photo of Laura, even if it existed, had just been a blind.

Rising slowly to her feet again she saw Hamish take a collapsible bike out of the Range Rover and assemble it. Then he kissed Laura casually on the cheek and they exchanged a few words before she pedalled away across the sand towards the road. Within seconds she had disappeared from view, leaving Hamish alone on the beach.

The light was fading fast but the headlights of the Range Rover guided Mel. She didn't want to use her own torch in case it gave her away. Her emotions were almost choking her as she half-ran across the tussocky grass and down towards the cove. She felt no fear, just pure unadulterated anger – anger for what he was doing to Laura, anger for the way he had tried to pull the wool over her own eyes. Her mind was a jumble of macabre images – Daniel butchered in front of her, the dead waiter floating in the sea like so much flotsam and jetsam, the sweet seductive smell of cannabis masking the stink of corrupting flesh, Charlie's decaying body rising reproachfully to the surface in the shaft. Exploitation of the innocent. That was what this was all about ...

His back was towards her as she stumbled onto the sand. He was reloading the equipment into the Range Rover and didn't hear her until she was just a few feet away. Then he turned.

'Mel?' He took a step towards her.

'Don't come any closer.' Her breathing was ragged.

'What are you doing here?' He took another step.

'I know what you've been doing. At long last I know what's really going on, you bastard.' Her voice, her whole body, were vibrating with emotion.

'Do you now.' His eyes shone golden as a cat's as he came forward and caught her by the wrists. 'Now suppose you tell me what you think that is.'

The physical contact, the sense of his tremendous strength brought her back to her senses. She was alone on a remote beach with a man who was a drug smuggler and very probably a murderer, and she'd offered herself to him like a lamb to the slaughter.

Chapter Fourteen

'You must have followed us.' Hamish released her. 'Why?'

'I didn't follow you. I saw you by accident. I was walking up on the headland.'

'That's rather a coincidence, isn't it?'

'Like you turning up at Sean's apartment while I was there.'

'What precisely is it you're accusing me of? I take it you *are* accusing me of something?'

'I saw you setting up your equipment on the beach. I know exactly what you're doing. Somewhere out there is a boat waiting, isn't there? You were setting coordinates . . . telling it when and where to make the drop. And now I suppose some other dupe is going to go and pick it up for you. Laura Williams maybe? You don't seem too scrupulous about using her. What does she do it for – a couple of ounces of cannabis resin and a quick screw to make her feel wanted? Now that Sean's gone have you taken over manipulating and controlling her? At least he thought he loved her. You haven't even got that excuse.'

Hamish's face tautened. He looked very pale. 'And just how exactly did you manage to work all this out?'

'Ever since I met you something's puzzled me. Like how you make your money. It's certainly not from your painting, which is crap. But now I know. You make it from smuggling drugs. You're behind the ring which has been operating around here.'

She just couldn't stop herself now she'd started. 'I've been such a fool not to see it more clearly. I had my suspicions when you were searching Sean's apartment but somehow I didn't want to believe it.'

'Why not? You seem to think you know me very well.'

'I didn't understand you at all till tonight. How you must have been laughing. There you were sniping at Cape Wrath, pretending to agree with poor, sincere Sarah Grant, masquerading as a Highland eco-warrior and lecturing me about the need for "open and honest" public relations – accusing *me* of hypocrisy! And all the time you were orchestrating this – pulling the strings like a puppet master. Is that what Sean got fed up with in the end? Is that why you got rid of him?'

'*What* did you say?'

Mel swallowed. 'I want to know why you killed Sean.'

It was beginning to rain, the drops falling in a fine mist. As she looked up at Hamish she could feel it running down her face, mingling with droplets of sweat. He was staring at her with a mixture of bafflement and anger in his eyes, but now she'd started she didn't care. She had to know the truth. But he just shook his head in what looked like disbelief and turned away from her.

'I think we should continue this conversation in the car.'

Mel stood motionless. 'You must be joking.'

'Please yourself. I'm going to pack up my gear before it gets soaked.'

As she watched he quickly wrapped the pieces of equipment up in the tarpaulin and put them back in the Range Rover. She began to feel a little foolish just standing there.

Hamish slammed the tailgate shut. 'Well? Are you getting in or not?'

She hesitated. Hamish shrugged and got into the driver's seat. Warily she climbed in beside him. He took a hip flask out of his pocket, twisted the top open and held it out to her. She shook her head but he took a long pull then sat in silence, gazing out at the wet night.

234

She was wondering now whether she'd made a terrible, stupid mistake. 'Hamish?'

'Let's get a couple of things straight, shall we?' His voice was very low. 'I'm not a murderer or a drug smuggler or an exploiter of teenage girls or any of the other imaginative things you accused me of tonight.'

'But what were you doing on the beach with all that equipment?'

'I could tell you it's none of your business.'

'I only want to understand. I don't feel I've understood anything since I arrived in Wrath. The whole place is so odd and dislocated I think it's sending me deranged.'

'Laura and I went down to the beach to record the sounds of the sea to lay over some tracks we've put down in the studio. I thought it might take her mind off what happened to Fergus. The equipment you saw was simply a Sony digital audio tape machine, an amplifier, some speakers and some fairly sophisticated Sennheiser directional microphones. We'd intended to play some songs with the sea as background to test how it sounded. If it was any good we were going to make some recordings of waves breaking at high tide to take back to the studio. I didn't want to use a synthesizer if we could avoid it. But it wasn't any good. We'd forgotten to bring the right tapes so we decided to try again another evening. Laura went off home and I stayed behind to pack up the gear.'

'I – I had no idea. I didn't understand.'

His expression softened a little. 'Evidently. Were you really here just by chance?'

'Yes. I wanted to walk down to St Malcolm's Priory in the moonlight. I thought I was all alone and then I heard you.'

'And you thought Laura and I were setting up a signalling system.'

'Yes. That's what it looked like.' She felt so embarrassed. He must think she was mad.

'You wouldn't have jumped to that conclusion unless

235

you already had some suspicions. I think it's time you were honest with me, don't you?'

Mel looked down. He was right. If she'd trusted him a little bit more, none of tonight would have happened. But on the other hand, how was she supposed to know whom to trust? 'It's difficult,' she said slowly. 'Ever since I came to Wrath I've had the feeling of being in the middle of something I couldn't understand. Even before I found the body on the beach . . .'

'Well, let's try this for a start. Why were you so afraid of me in Sean's apartment?'

'You took me by surprise. I didn't know who it was.'

'It was more than that.' Hamish looked her directly in the eyes. 'What were you really doing in the apartment yourself?'

'Like I told you, I was looking for a report.' Mel decided to let him know everything. 'While I was there I found some other things, too. There was a map – a large-scale nautical chart, really, and fairly well-thumbed – with various navigational bearings plotted on it, and a boating magazine with an advertisement for an expensive seagoing yacht ringed in biro. There was also an envelope containing thousands of pounds in cash, and a large packet of cannabis resin.'

'And you assumed Sean was involved in drug smuggling?'

'I wasn't sure what to think, but that seemed the obvious conclusion. When you arrived I thought you were looking for the same things, and that you and Sean had been in it together. It even crossed my mind that you'd killed him or that you knew what had happened to him. After all, his body's never been found. For all we really know he might not even be dead.'

'What did you do with all those things?' Hamish asked quietly.

'I put the money and the cannabis back where I found them. As far as I know, they're still there. I kept the map and the navigational notes.'

'Why?'

'I thought they might help explain Sean's disappearance.' Mel paused and thought carefully for a moment... 'And I kept something else as well,' she said finally. 'Sean's diary.'

Hamish looked at her sharply. 'A diary?'

'Yes.' She was shivering now with delayed shock and her teeth began to chatter uncontrollably. 'Hamish, please take me home.' She was close to the end of her tether.

Mel lay back against the wide leather seat as Hamish slid into gear and began to drive slowly back to the road and along the coast to Wrath. She'd have to pick the MGF up in the morning. At the moment she just didn't care. The warmth from the Range Rover's powerful heater cocooned her and in a few moments she was drifting into sleep.

She woke again as Hamish brought the car to a halt. As he opened his door the cool night air rushed in. She looked around a little dazed, expecting to see the hotel in front of her. Instead Wilf was leaping up against her window, pink tongue lolling. They were at Hamish's house. She wasn't sure if she was glad or sorry.

He lit candles all around the room and the flames danced, casting their long, flickering shadows. Then he left her alone for a few minutes. When he returned he was holding a thick white towelling bathrobe in his arms.

'Here you are. There's a hot bath running for you upstairs.'

Mel felt too tired to resist and went up to a luxurious bathroom with expensive Victorian-style fittings. He'd thrown some heady essence into the running water and its sweet perfume filled the room.

An hour or so ago, she'd thought this man could be a murderer. Now he had run her a bath. She laughed a little raggedly then stopped herself before it got out of control. To reassure herself she looked at her reflection in the huge mirror with its beaten copper frame. The face that was gazing back was pale and wary – apprehensive even. The

237

evening had been full of surprises. It would be wrong to assume they were over.

She let her clothes fall to the floor and stepped into the steaming water. It was wonderful. For a while the trauma of the last few hours evaporated as she surrendered to the warmth and let her mind relax at last.

Half an hour later she came barefoot down the stone stairs, a towel, three times as thick as anything her hotel could offer, twisted around her wet hair. A peat fire was burning in the wide hearth and she sank onto the sofa in front of it, digging her toes into the rich Oriental rugs that covered the flagstoned floor. There was no sign of Hamish.

She listened to the hissing of the peat and closed her eyes. Then a haunting, enchanting tune began to steal around the room, so faint that at first she thought she was imagining it. Over it came a sweet, fey voice singing in Gaelic. Laura. She didn't need to ask. And it was a song to twine itself around your heart and break it — a soft, yearning strain that dipped and soared.

'Do you like it? It's called *Remembrance*.' Hamish had bathed as well. His wet hair was hanging over his shoulders. It was the colour of copper.

Mel nodded.

'Are you hungry?'

'Yes.' Surprisingly she was ravenous.

'I'll see what I can find in the kitchen.'

He returned with a wooden tray which he set down in front of the fire. There was a loaf of soda bread on it and some cheese. She cut herself a hunk of each while Hamish poured two glasses of red wine.

'Here.'

She took one from him and held it between both hands.

'Don't look like that.'

'What do you mean?' she asked.

'I mean that you still look terrified out of your wits.'

'I've given up trying to make sense of anything,' she said wearily. 'Things seem to happen around me and I have no

238

control of them. It's small wonder I'm scared.' She looked into her glass at the rich, red fluid glinting jewel-like in the candlelight and then up at Hamish. His face tautened and he stepped back from her a little.

'There are aspects of my past I'm not proud of, but I'm not what you seemed to think,' he said, gruffly. 'Will you let me explain? Then, perhaps, you'll believe me.'

She nodded and lay back passively against the cushions. The room, the music, the soft light were giving everything a dream-like quality. She had neither the power nor the will to intervene or take control.

Hamish sat down in a deep armchair to the right of the hearth. Wilf came ambling in, toes scratching on the stone floor and slumped at his feet. Hamish began to fondle his ears and the animal gave a grunt of satisfaction.

'You think I make my money out of drugs – well, I don't. I do however believe that cannabis should be legalized – after all, what was good enough for Queen Victoria is good enough for me – but I've nothing but contempt for commercial smugglers. They're just in it for profit and they don't care what methods they use. In fact, that's one of the bonuses if cannabis were made legal, these people would go out of business overnight.'

'But I don't believe in hard drugs – and I know what I'm talking about. I used to be in the music business. At the end of the eighties I was a session musician and a good one – I played sax for some of the big names here in the UK and over in the States. I also co-wrote several successful numbers. I made one hell of a lot of money and it's still coming in. One of the things you learn quickly is to go for royalties rather than up-front fees, however tempting.' He smiled wryly. 'Did you know that the saxophonist on Gerry Rafferty's *Baker Street* took a flat fee of twenty-eight pounds and that's all he ever made out of it? Or that you can hire an entire orchestra from Eastern Europe for three thousand pounds a session?

'I enjoyed being on the road but it's a tough kind of a

life. I got into the drugs scene and developed quite a habit – cocaine mostly but I wasn't fussy. For a while it was great. I was on a permanent high. My music had never been better and I felt like I was untouchable. But I didn't realize what was happening to me. I was parting company with reality. The rock business can be artificial enough but I tipped over into a kind of paranoid fantasy world where I didn't know what was real anymore. I suppose you'd call it a type of schizophrenia.

'Then one evening I was doing a gig with a band in Edinburgh. I took a cocktail of God knows what, but including quite a lot of LSD . . . They found me naked on the castle battlements. I was screaming that I was a Highlander who had fought at Culloden alongside my kinsman Cameron of Lochiel and that I had escaped from the lice-ridden prison hulks in Tilbury. I'd stripped naked to avoid the stench of death which still clung to me. I wanted to be Flora Macdonald's lover and much more nonsense like that. Apparently I tried to kill the policeman who arrested me. I thought he was the Duke of Cumberland – the Butcher of the Highlands . . .' Hamish grinned sheepishly.

'It sounds ridiculous, I know. But I was very lucky. I had a complete breakdown and I was sent to a drugs rehabilitation clinic for six months. When I came out they told me to take things very quietly – to try to restore the roots and connections in my life . . . to cool my imagination so I could distinguish fantasy from reality again. While I was in the clinic I did a lot of reading – about Scottish history, about the Highland Clearances and the area my family originally came from in the far north before they were turned off the land.

'So I came here and bought this house. A friend gave me Wilf. For a while I turned my back on my music because I was afraid of what it had done to me and because I was afraid I mightn't be any good anymore without the stimulus of drugs. Instead I spent time thinking and getting back to my roots and coming to terms with the mess I'd made of my life . . . I began to paint as a kind of therapy – though as you observed, I'm no Picasso.'

'Why didn't you tell me any of this before?' she whispered.

'I don't find it very easy to talk about my past. I don't enjoy looking back on the mess I made of things.'

'But Laura knows . . .?'

'Yes. She and I are similar in many ways. We're both creative and we both resent other people trying to channel us in a particular direction. Perhaps that's why I let her help me.'

'What do you mean?'

'Like I said, at first I gave up music completely. I didn't want to know anymore. But after a while I began to listen to Celtic music – the old traditional songs – and I became interested in how it could be worked in with rock influences. But it was only when I met Laura a couple of years ago that I began to take it seriously and to feel the motivation again.'

Hamish looked at her. 'Do you know what it's like to feel you've lost the most important thing in your life? The fear that you're never going to get it back again?'

Mel lowered her head but said nothing.

'Well, that's what it was like for me but Laura helped me over that hurdle and I gave her something in return. We began to record some songs in the studio that I've had built in the basement. Her voice has got an ethereal quality that's perfect.'

The song came to an end as he was speaking, the last notes dying away. For some reason Mel felt her eyes fill with tears. She unwrapped the towel from around her head and began to rub her hair dry, face averted from Hamish.

'I'm going to send the tapes to some of the record companies I used to work with. I've still got a few friends in the business I might be able to interest. She really needs something to hold onto after Sean disappearing and then Fergus dying. . .'

241

Hamish stood up and refilled Mel's glass, then his own.

'So I haven't been exploiting her ... And when I told you I was looking for a photograph in Sean's apartment, it was the truth.'

'I'm sorry,' Mel stammered. 'I just didn't understand.'

'How could you? The problem for Laura just now is coming to terms with losing Sean. It was a very complicated relationship. I think she really loved him, but she's so insecure. When he was with her she believed he cared. Now she's torturing herself over whether she meant anything to him or not. Deep down she thinks she needed him more than he needed her.'

'Why do you say that?'

Hamish sat down again and stared into the fire. 'You've seen her parents. They mean well enough but neither of them really understand Laura or have ever taken any real interest. I think she was looking for some kind of father figure and she found it in Sean Docherty. It was a way of getting back at them as well.' He smiled a little sadly. 'Like the stud she wears in her nose on "formal" occasions, or splashing graffiti around the town or joining anti-nuclear demonstrations.

'As for Sean, he knew he'd wasted his life. His marriage hadn't worked out. He'd abandoned his musical career. All he had was a job he needed for the money but didn't like. Having Laura gave him someone to care about again. At least, that's what he told her. He wanted her to persevere, succeed and be happy where he'd compromised and failed. But at the same time he wanted to end their relationship.'

'But Laura wouldn't let him?'

'No. It was all she had ... She was the one who began it and she didn't want to let go. That money you found – it was hers, she told me about it. A legacy from some relation. She'd drawn it out and given it to Sean to keep for her. She was obsessed with going away with him. But I think he knew it couldn't go on. What he really felt for her, I'm not sure.'

'He did love her – I know that he did.'

242

'Did he tell you that?'

'No, he never talked to me about Laura. I didn't know they were lovers until after he disappeared. But there's a passage in his diary all about Laura . . . He was really scared he was screwing up her life and that someone else would come along in the future and exploit her. He understood how vulnerable she is. Hamish, have you any idea what happened to Sean? Is he really dead?' Her voice was a whisper. Talking about him had brought him back to her so vividly.

'If he's not dead, where is he?' Hamish shrugged. 'I think it's only a matter of time before his body gets washed up somewhere.'

'Laura was lucky in a way.'

'What do you mean?'

'Girls of that age . . . it's so easy for them to be exploited – used. At least Sean had some scruples.' She couldn't keep the bitterness from her voice.

'Mel – what is it?' He cupped her face in his hands, forcing her to meet his eye.

'It's nothing.'

'I thought tonight we were being honest with each other.'

I can't, she thought, I just can't. I've never talked about it to anyone. As she sat huddled on the sofa her mind plunged back in time, scenes flying past like a film being rewound. Some of it a blur, other parts standing out starkly for a split-second before they rushed by. Scenes she'd never wanted to think about again and that she had hoped were buried deeply and irretrievably within her mind.

She was a child again, putting her key in the lock of her parents' suburban house on the outskirts of Cambridge, sensing that something was wrong. Through the strange stillness of the house came a noise she couldn't interpret. It was coming from the kitchen. Her father – her quiet, logical, matter-of-fact father – was sitting at the kitchen table, head in his hands, crying.

She'd understood at once and rushed into the street, not

243

sure where she was going or why. She'd ended up at the railway station pushing among the crowds of strangers before finally sitting down on a Speak Your Weight machine and staring sightlessly at the blur of bodies around her.

Then she was a teenager, sixteen years old, coming home to a different house in a different city. There was another man waiting for her. Dark-haired, good-looking, always ready to understand her adolescent fears and dreams until that evening when his comforting, enveloping hug had become something different. One of his warm hands had begun to explore the silken skin of her breast, the other caressing her thigh, moving upwards, questing and urgent . . . He'd gripped her more tightly as she tried to push him away but somehow she'd managed to break free, running out into the hot night, terrified and bitterly ashamed. Even now, just thinking about it, she could smell the pungent fragrance of his Paco Rabanne aftershave as he held her against him, and it sickened her.

'Mel?'

Hamish pulled her towards him gently, as if she were a child. She pressed her face against his chest and closed her eyes, fighting wave after wave of panic as they closed in on her. He felt her shudders and tightened his grip.

'You don't have to tell me if you don't want to.' His voice was softer than she'd ever heard it. Was this how he sounded when he comforted Laura?

She pulled away from him, but couldn't meet his eyes because of the shame and the guilt. 'I'm an only child,' she said in a low voice. 'My father was forty-five when he met my mother at an astrophysics conference in San Diego. She was a Canadian journalist fifteen years younger than him. They married within a year, and within another I was born. But it didn't last. My mother left my father when I was ten. I came home from school one day and she just wasn't there . . . my father told me she had gone abroad to Argentina with another man – a rich businessman from Buenos Aires. My parents divorced and she married Felipe.'

She was trying to tell the story economically and factually, driving the emotion out of her voice. But this had been a long night of drama and surprises and she just wasn't sure she could keep it up. She took a deep breath.

'My mother wanted me to come and spend the summer vacations with her. They had a beautiful house in Recoleta – a smart district of Buenos Aires – and a ranch outside in the Pampas. She was really proud of it. But we had nothing to talk about anymore. She had changed into a smart society woman and I couldn't forgive her for leaving my father. I felt protective towards him and hostile to her. She tried to tell me that she couldn't help herself – that she loved Felipe in a way she could never have loved my father but it took me a long time to come to terms with it. In the end it was Felipe who helped me – not her.

'He always seemed ready to listen and understand what I felt. My dislike melted away and I began to trust him. But neither my mother nor I realized what Felipe was really like. He thought he could have any woman he wanted, including his stepdaughter. One day he tried to seduce me ... It was very difficult to get him to stop, but I did.'

'What did you do then?'

'I was afraid. I didn't want to tell anyone what had happened in case they thought I'd led him on. In particular I didn't want to tell my mother. She was crazy about him and she'd never have believed me.'

'And your father?'

'It would only have made things worse for him. He never got over my mother leaving him like that. He just turned in on himself and his work and his bee-keeping and cut himself off from his feelings. But his one consolation was that at least she was happy – he was a generous man like that; he didn't bear a grudge. But if I'd told him what had happened to me, it would have destroyed his peace of mind. And anyway I felt too embarrassed. We could never really talk about the things that mattered. Like emotions and feelings. That's why I still find it so hard.

'So instead I ran away. At least, that's what it amounted to. I wrote to both my parents that I was going travelling for a while. I had a few dollars with me and I took a bus north, first to Iguassu Falls and then on through the Andes to Peru. I eventually ended up on the border between Belize and Guatemala. I wasn't really sure where I was going. I had some vague idea I might be able to teach English in Mexico – and then I met Daniel.'

'Daniel? Who was he?'

'He was an American priest from Manchester, Massachusetts. He was running a mission in the Guatemalan highlands. When I met him he'd just returned from America and he had all these bundles of clothes and blankets.'

A soft smile covered her face as she remembered her first sight of him. A farmer had dropped him off at that flyblown little bus station. The back of the pick-up truck had been full of packages and she'd watched, fascinated, as Daniel had unloaded them one by one until he was almost hidden by them. She'd been sitting at a table outside a bar drinking a Coke and he'd called over to her, face alive with laughter and energy. And that was how it began . . .

'I offered to help him get his gear on the bus and I helped him argue with the customs officials on the border. My Spanish was better than his. He invited me to come to the Mission and I had no reason to refuse. I wasn't leaving anything behind that mattered to me then.'

'Did he become your lover?'

Her eyes met his unflinchingly now. Hamish understood something of what she'd felt for Daniel. It must be so obvious even after all this time.

'No – he wasn't my lover, but I loved him. Perhaps more than I've ever loved any human being.'

'You talk about him in the past tense.'

'He . . . died . . . And I left the Mission and came back to England and my father. I finished my education and became a journalist. Then I went into PR and came to Cape Wrath and the rest, as they say, is history.' Mel looked into the fire, exhausted by the memory of past emotions. Of how she'd tried to make up to her father for leaving him like that by becoming like him.

'So we've both had our crises – in different ways.' Hamish's strong face was sad and reflective.

'I suppose so. And we both chose Wrath. Isn't life stupid sometimes?'

'Would you object if I rolled a joint? I feel like I need it.'

'No, go ahead.' She watched him go to a carved wooden box – it looked like an old writing slope – and take out some hash and some Rizla papers.

'Where do you get it from if you're not smuggling it?'

Hamish laughed. 'From a retired rock musician who has a castle outside Inverness. The cellar's fitted with a greenhouse system artificially lit and heated by solar power and he grows his own supply. An environmentally friendly cottage industry in a castle. And he's generous to his friends.'

He sat down and began to make a roach. He was surprisingly bad at it.

'Here, let me. You're packing it much too loose.'

He watched, startled, as Mel rolled an expert joint and handed it to him. He lit it and the room filled with that fragrant autumnal smell she'd noticed the first time she came here.

'One day I'll tell you how I learned to do that.'

He offered it to her but she shook her head. 'I'm tired. I must go.'

They looked at each other in the flickering warm glow of the fire. It was dying low now.

'I wish you'd stay.'

'I can't.'

'I'd be much better for you than that aluminium Nazi you're running around with from the US base.'

'You mean Tom Schultz, I suppose.'

Hamish said nothing but reached out and pulled her gently towards him. She surrendered her mouth to his without a moment's hesitation. To make love with him

247

now, here by the fire, would be the most natural thing in the world. She knew how much she wanted him. He was pushing her bathrobe open and caressing her breasts, his long hair falling against her.

For once in her life she should follow her instincts and let the consequences go hang. But she wasn't there yet, however much she wanted to be – and there was nothing she could do. Making love with Tom was different, she felt in control and detached. With Hamish it wouldn't be like that. The commitment, the surrender would be total.

She pushed him gently away and stood up. 'I want to,' she told him, 'but I can't.' She expected anger but instead she felt him kiss the hollow of her throat.

'One day you will,' he murmured. 'Go now and put your clothes on and I'll drive you back to Wrath ... I'll wait for you outside.'

Five minutes later they were driving back to town. The sky was clear again and the moon was even more brilliant. Mel leant her head against Hamish's shoulder as he drove in silence, and realized that for the first time in weeks she felt completely at peace. *Safe.*

Chapter Fifteen

The hotel was in darkness. Not surprising considering that it was 2 a.m. Mel glanced at her watch, feeling utter weariness engulf her, then reached in her pocket for the keys. She let herself in and felt for the light switch on the wall. It was on a timer and she had ten seconds to make it up to her room.

She ran up the stairs knowing that the third one would creak. Then she remembered she had a torch. Taking it out she followed its pool of yellow light to her door. Moving through the silent building made her feel like an intruder. She could see a note sticking out from underneath the door and her heart began to pound.

Picking it up she quickly closed the door behind her and locked it. After a moment's hesitation she tore the note open. It was a telephone message taken by Reception. *Tried to call you tonight. Will try again tomorrow. Tom.* She sat down on the edge of the bed and looked at it. She should have been relieved. No, she should have been delighted that he'd rung. So why didn't she feel like that?

The whole bizarre evening had somehow changed her perspective on everything. Without warning a mass of pent-up emotion welled inside her and suddenly she was crying – for Hamish, for Laura, for Sean and still – after all these years – for Daniel. And just a little for herself. If she could turn the clock back to that evening when Hamish had first asked her to stay and make love, would she want to? She didn't know. She'd played safe. She glanced at the crumpled piece of paper in her hand. She'd made her choice and taken Tom and maybe that was for the best.

'I need to see you urgently. Are you free?'
'Yes. Shall I come along to your office?'
'That would be best.'
What could Everett want? The only thing she could think of was the shaft. Was she in for another warning about keeping quiet about Charlie? Whatever her personal feelings she wasn't likely to broadcast anything so macabre or controversial from the rooftops.

He was waiting for her, sitting very upright behind his desk. He looked grey and bloodless, like the fish in the Scott painting behind him. She'd hardly sat down before he began.

'Everything I'm about to tell you is in strict confidence. There are implications for national security. Please remember you are bound by the Official Secrets Act. You understand what I'm saying?'

She nodded.

'That young man whose body you found on the beach . . .'
'Yes, the waiter?'

Everett studied his immaculate nails. 'He wasn't really a waiter. And he wasn't a Pakistani either, as we first thought. It turns out he was an Iraqi.'

She was gazing at Everett in astonishment now. 'How did you find that out?'

He paused. 'I must remind you that this is in the strictest confidence; however, it was Commander Schultz who told me . . . The American Security Services believe he may have been an Iraqi Government agent. For some reason he was spying on Anderson Base when someone killed him and dumped his body as a warning. We've no idea who or why. According to the autopsy he was dead long before his body was put in the water. He certainly hadn't been in the sea for long – the corpse wasn't battered enough. Anyway, that's why there's been no formal inquest. This needs to be kept very quiet for the moment. And of course it means you won't be called as a witness.'

'It'll be a relief not to have to give evidence. But I don't understand . . . what do you think is really going on? Could it involve Cape Wrath as well?'

'We have no idea as yet. But we will. I know how their minds work.' His tone was bitter and his eyes looked hunted. 'As I told you, I had plenty of opportunity to find out. It's odd, isn't it? I came here because I wanted to be somewhere quiet and remote – out of the mainstream. But life has a habit of playing unpleasant little tricks. You think you can cut yourself off from the past but it's not always possible. There are echoes you can't escape – like this. It's as if they've followed me. As if they can still smell me.' A neurotic, hysterical note had crept into his voice. 'But I can smell them, too. Whatever they're up to, I intend to be ready.'

Silence fell. He was locked in his own world.

Mel got up. 'Thank you, James.' She hesitated, but for a moment her words didn't seem to register. Telling her all this had drained him. He might think he was over his post-traumatic stress, but he wasn't.

Her hand was on the door handle when she heard him speak.

'You mustn't tell anyone else what I've said. You realize that?'

Mel nodded. 'I understand.'

He came towards her and, formal as ever, held out his hand. It was clammy with sweat; her own was trembling slightly.

It was a long time since she'd been for a stroll around the site but she needed fresh air and space. The dome of one of the defunct research reactors loomed up at her, an immense white elephant waiting for its long and complicated journey to the scrap heap. She walked on down to the sea. The tide was going out, revealing long, sharp slivers of black rock. Ropes of seaweed twisted and turned in the foam, trapped in the fissures.

251

The more she thought about it, the more fantastic Everett's story seemed. Yet a man had been murdered and she was the one who had found the body. It made her feel threatened. She hadn't seen anything except a sodden dead body, but Everett had somehow got to her. Just like Cape Wrath had got to her. She'd been seeing conspiracy and subterfuge in every corner ever since she'd arrived. The shrill ringing of her mobile cut into her thoughts.

'Mel? Hi. I'm back. Will I be seeing you tonight?'

'Yes, OK.'

'Come over about seven. Some friends of mine at the base are giving a party for Bella and Chris. They've just heard they've been posted back to the States.'

'I'd love to. I really liked them.'

'And Mel?'

'Yes?'

'I missed you.'

She hesitated.

'Mel? I said I missed you.'

'I missed you too, Tom.'

As she slid the phone back into her pocket and turned her back on the bleak shoreline it wasn't Tom's face she was seeing in her imagination but Hamish's. And that was another complication as well.

'Mel!' Chris Connor wove his way towards her through the throng of people, holding two glasses of white wine high above his head. 'Go away, Tom,' he grinned at his friend. 'It's my turn to talk to the lady.'

'OK, OK,' Tom said good-naturedly and wandered away to join a group on the far side of the room.

'I didn't realize you and Bella would be leaving Wrath so soon.'

'Neither did we. I only got the news this morning.'

'Where are they sending you?'

'To the nuclear submarine base at New London on the east coast. They've offered me a great job there and Bella

252

will be able to do the same work she's doing at Anderson.'

'I'll be really sorry to see you go – just as I was getting to know you! And Chris – thank you for that data you sent me. I'm going to check it against the site records.'

The big man shrugged. 'I'm glad to help. The sub readings puzzled me but now I guess I may never know the answer – unless you send me a postcard.'

'I will, I promise,' she laughed, 'and in my best joined-up writing.'

'But seriously,' Chris lowered his voice, 'you've got one hell of a PR problem on that site. Please don't get me wrong but it's clear to anyone that the local community doesn't trust you. The wider community would like to see you get closed down. You don't have to be a genius to know that. All you have to do is read the papers. Why?'

Mel shrugged. 'It's all kinds of things – standards were different in the past but we have to live with the consequences today. Most of the current environmental problems go back decades. And then there's the fact that the plant wasn't open about its activities in the past and people have lost faith in it. The way they see it, why should they believe us now when we didn't tell them the truth in years gone by?'

'I saw that environmentalist in town today. You must know who I mean – a tall lady with long kind-of-reddish hair.'

'Yes. Sarah Grant.'

'She was outside the library with a petition. Something about foreign reprocessing . . .'

'She believes it should be stopped.'

'And should it?'

'It's a question of balance. It's good business and the profit goes back to the taxpayer and helps pay for the things society needs, like schools and hospitals. But Cape Wrath has an obligation to show that it can do the work safely and that it will send the nuclear waste back to the customer.'

'You don't sound like you're too sure Cape Wrath can deliver.'

253

Mel was silent. He was right – she wasn't sure anymore. There were too many careless incidents occurring in the plant. Workers who received higher radioactive doses than they should. The confidence she had felt when she first arrived had slowly evaporated. And yet she was still spinning the party line to the media, the public, the workforce. Was she becoming dishonest herself?

'I have to question whether Cape Wrath can deliver all the time. In a way I have to be the public's spokesperson and ask the questions before they do. And I have to encourage the plant management to be open. No, sometimes I'm not as confident as I'd like to be.'

'Everybody has doubts sometimes,' Chris said slowly. 'But you have to come to terms with them. If you believe something is right, you have to get on with it regardless of the consequences.'

They were both silent for a moment.

'Come and get something to eat. There's some great chilli next door.' Tom's voice broke into their thoughts.

Chris led the way. As Tom followed behind her he bent and kissed the nape of Mel's neck but she didn't look round.

For the first time she didn't climax during their lovemaking. Had Tom realized, or had she been convincing enough? He was asleep now, one arm outflung towards her.

Why had she begun her affair with Tom? If she was honest, it was partly because of a desire for simple, uncomplicated sex with an attractive older man far removed from her problems at Cape Wrath, and partly because she'd admired his cool, dispassionate way of looking at the world.

I'd be better for you than that aluminium Nazi you're running around with . . . Hamish's words came unbidden into her mind. Maybe he was right, even though he belonged to the kind of world she'd tried to escape from – emotional, erratic, unpredictable. It was curious to think she'd told Hamish things about herself she'd never confided to Tom.

But then Tom hadn't been entirely open with her. Why hadn't he told her about the Iraqi, she wondered again. And why hadn't she mentioned her conversation with Everett? Perhaps *that* was the real question.

She turned her back on Tom and pressed her face into the pillow, but when sleep came at last it was fitful; in her dreams she saw nothing but faces – Sean Docherty smiling, Fergus Brown's enquiring, ferrety features, James Everett with haunted, fanatical eyes, Laura with her face swollen and running with mascara, the dead Iraqi on the beach and Charlie looking up at her reproachfully from the shaft.

'OK, Dougie, that's fine. I really appreciate it.' Mel replaced the receiver and made a note in her diary. In three days' time the plant was going to shut down for routine maintenance. It would be a good opportunity to let in a film crew who were making a science documentary for the Open University about the nuclear fuel cycle. She could rely on Dougie MacBain to take them around and give them a lucid explanation.

It was lunchtime now. Outside she could see groups of employees walking over to the canteen, some of them in the white overalls of shiftworkers from the plant. As she watched, Fabian Williams swept past in his grey Bentley. She'd forgotten: he was going to London to argue with officials from the Ministry for funds to clean up the castle. It really was an obsession.

'There he goes. Our inspirational leader, off to fight the good fight with the mandarins of Whitehall.'

Mel looked round. John MacDonald's eyes were fixed on the Bentley as well. 'At least he doesn't interfere with the day-to-day operations, thank God.'

Mel said nothing.

'Look, I want a piece of advice,' MacDonald went on. 'This talk I'm supposed to be giving tonight in the town hall – how formal should I make it?'

'That's up to you, really. The main thing is to get the

255

messages over very clearly in layman's language. Don't blind people with technical jargon. And leave plenty of time for questions.'

He sighed. 'I'm not sure I should have let myself be talked into doing this. I'm just setting myself up as a target for every anti in the area.'

'I don't think so. Not everyone in the community is hostile. They just want to hear that the operations are safe and well managed. They want to be told that Scotland's not being turned into the world's nuclear dustbin. You're the Plant Manager and you're well known in the community. They'll listen to you.'

She was saying all the right things, but just like last night the doubts were there, niggling away at the back of her brain. Theoretically everything was OK at Cape Wrath. There were rules and regulations, quality assurance instructions galore, but they were so much paper and could so easily be breached. What if something really serious went wrong? Or if someone decided they weren't going to play by the rules. That was how Chernobyl had started . . .

MacDonald was looking quite relaxed. She'd never have thought when she first arrived at Cape Wrath that she'd be able to persuade him to do something like this. But he'd mellowed. In fact, during the last few weeks he'd seemed positively cheerful.

'There's something else,' she told him, deciding to seize this favourable moment. 'If you agree I'd like to let a film crew into the plant. It's for an Open University programme. They need access for a couple of days to get some footage. I've lined up Dougie MacBain as the main contact.'

'OK. I don't see any problem,' MacDonald responded. 'Except of course they can't go in while the plant's operational. It's just too much hassle for a load of camera equipment to be taken across the barrier and checked out again.'

'Dougie says the plant's shutting down in a few days for maintenance. I thought that would be a good opportunity . . .'

'What did you say?' All of a sudden he was frowning. He didn't wait for an answer but grabbed her phone and quickly tapped in some numbers. 'Dougie? What's this I hear about a shut-down for maintenance? . . . No, definitely not. I want the plant kept running at full capacity until all the Malaysian fuel's gone through. Why stop halfway through a campaign?'

'I sometimes think that common sense is a commodity in short supply at Cape Wrath,' he said, replacing the receiver and shaking his head in exasperation. 'I'll see you at the town hall tonight. Don't be late.' He made for the door.

'I won't.' She could hear his footsteps retreating down the corridor, rapid and purposeful.

The applause was polite and respectful as MacDonald finished his formal presentation and asked for questions.

A tall man in a tweed jacket stood up. 'People don't want to buy my salmon because it's been farmed close to a nuclear establishment. If I don't receive adequate compensation I intend to sue,' he said belligerently.

'So how is it you've been able to afford that new Range Rover?' shouted a small weatherbeaten man, to a ripple of laughter. The salmon farmer sat down again, glowering.

'My lobster pots have been damaged by your divers,' said another man.

'We use divers as part of our environmental monitoring programme, but if that's the case I'm sorry and you will certainly be compensated. Please write to me with the details and I'll see that it is dealt with as a matter of urgency.' MacDonald looked genuinely concerned and people around the room nodded approvingly. Ishbel flashed Mel a smile of quiet satisfaction. It was different for her as a local, Mel thought. Cape Wrath's reputation meant so much to her personally.

Sarah Grant's low voice interrupted her thoughts and she looked round to see her in the back row. She must have come in at the last moment.

'How can you justify the continued import of foreign fuel for reprocessing at Cape Wrath in the light of the plant's age and its appalling safety record?' she asked. Her spectacular hair was tied back with a printed Indian scarf, her face looked drawn.

MacDonald began to go through the arguments, spelling out the scientific and economic benefits of reprocessing, defending the plant's record. The room had gone very quiet and all eyes were on him. Except Mel's . . .

As she'd been looking at Sarah the heavy mahogany door of the assembly room opened and she saw Hamish come in. He didn't sit down but leant against the wall, arms crossed, quietly watching the proceedings. Mel looked away, confused by a range of emotions.

'How much longer must Scotland accept the unacceptable? How much longer can Cape Wrath defend the indefensible?' Sarah was demanding, tossing sound bites to the local media.

Mel forced herself to focus her mind and she looked up at MacDonald on the stage in front of her. He was doing well, making reasoned comments in a low-key voice, acknowledging Sarah's concerns and her right to have them, but also refuting them.

'If you would like to pay us a visit at Cape Wrath, Mrs Grant, we'd be delighted. Then you can see the facilities for yourself instead of relying on hearsay or the imaginative reports in our local newspapers. But as I understand it, for some reason you haven't felt able to accept any of our previous invitations,' MacDonald went on.

'That's because I don't believe the plant is safe, Mr MacDonald, and nothing you've said this evening has convinced me otherwise. I've talked to your people often enough officially and unofficially. There is nothing you could show me during a superficial visit that would change your safety record or the age of the plant.'

'I'm sorry that's how you feel,' MacDonald said gravely. Sarah sat down again, shaking her head.

'Well, if there are no more questions for the present perhaps you would like to stay for a cup of coffee in the adjoining room. There are other members of the Cape Wrath staff here tonight who would also be happy to do their best to deal with any points.'

'Didn't John do well?' Amelia MacDonald's gentle face was flushed with pride at her husband's performance. 'He wouldn't want me to tell you this but he was really quite nervous.'

'He was excellent.' Mel smiled as they shuffled forward in the queue for coffee. But her whole mind was on Hamish. She'd tried not to think about him since that evening on the shore. She'd tried to tell herself that she mustn't get involved with his damaged, charismatic personality. But now she knew how dismally she'd failed.

As they were given their milky coffee in thick white china cups, a local councillor's wife pounced on Amelia, wanting to talk to her about a donation to a Christmas charity event. Mel immediately scanned the room for him. Was he still here? She couldn't see him. Or Sarah Grant.

She carried her cup back into the room where the presentation had taken place, but there was no sign of him here either. What was she doing, anyway? Why did it matter so much? But maybe for once in her life she shouldn't ask questions, just accept things for what they were. It did matter to her. She *did* care.

She should be mingling with the crowd, supporting John MacDonald and giving Cape Wrath an acceptable face, but not just now. She put her coffee, untouched, on the edge of the stage and made for the door. She badly needed a breath of fresh air.

'I was hoping you'd come out before long.' He was standing in the shadows. 'Mel, I need to talk to you.'

'About what happened the other night?'

'Yes.'

It was a cold damp evening with a strong promise of rain. In fact, the first drops were already beginning to fall.

259

'We'd better go to the hotel.' She looked at him and he nodded.

They walked side by side and silently down the main street. There was a blast of raucous music from an upstairs window as they passed the Caledonian Bar.

'They're having a country and western evening.' Hamish smiled down at her. 'God knows why!'

'Not your sort of music, I suppose?'

'No.'

They were outside the hotel now. She'd never felt more awkward or at a loss for words.

'We can't talk in the bar. There'll be too many people,' Hamish said.

'Come up to my room then.' She led the way along the thinly carpeted corridor past the bar to the stairs. Hamish was right. Through the open door she could see the usual sprinkling of Cape Wrath employees grouped around the fire.

She opened the door of her room and Hamish followed her inside. He looked around him critically. 'Why don't you get your own place?'

'I want to, but I haven't found anywhere quite right. I haven't really tried properly, I have to admit. I seem to have been so busy. Anyway, it's very convenient here.'

He pulled out a plastic chair from against the wall and sat down, long legs outstretched. 'You're not thinking of moving in with the bionic man, then?'

'Tom?' She felt her colour rise. 'No.'

'Good.'

'Hamish, what do you want?'

'I wanted to see you again. That was the first thing.'

'And the second?'

'Sean's diary – the pages about Laura. It's a lot to ask but if you were prepared to trust me with them I'd be very grateful. Unless she sees them she won't believe me. It's important she knows the truth – that she has something to hang onto.'

Mel hesitated for a moment. She hadn't shown the diary

to anyone until now, not even Tom, and she felt a strange reluctance. As if everything that it contained was private and personal to her, which was rubbish, of course.

'I put it up there.' She nodded towards the top of the wardrobe. 'You can reach it easily.'

Hamish stood up and felt for it. After a moment his hand closed on the book and he held it out to her. 'Here. You know which are the right pages – could you find them?'

Mel took it and turned to the back. Then very carefully she tore out the two pencil-written pages under the heading *Laura* and handed them to him. He glanced at them, smiled a little sadly then put them in his wallet.

'There's something else as well. It may mean something to Laura.' She put the diary on the table and carefully tipped the dried bluebell onto it. Then she took a piece of tissue paper from her dressing-table drawer and wrapped it round the fragile, faded flower.

Hamish took it from her and they looked at one another in silence. There was so much she wanted to say to him but the words just wouldn't come.

'Mel . . .' He stepped towards her and kissed her, long and softly. She felt herself respond. She felt she needed him as much as he wanted her, but something was stopping her. It had nothing to do with Tom. It was something deeper, more primal. A terror of becoming involved again. Of losing control. And she was right on the brink . . .

She closed her mouth under his and twisted her head away. 'No, Hamish! I'm sorry.'

'But why not?'

'I don't know.' She turned away. 'I really don't know.'

'It's all right, Mel.' His voice became gentle. 'It's all right, I understand, or at least I can guess and I can wait.'

She couldn't say anything. Couldn't even turn her face to look at him. He kissed the top of her head. Then he left, quietly closing the door behind him.

She ought to be glad she'd had the strength to stop, but there was no satisfaction in it. Instead she had the feeling

261

she'd just made one of the bigger mistakes of her life – and God knows, she had made a few.

It was still early, not even ten o'clock. Tom was at an official dinner for a visiting Congressman. The politician's intensive programme meant she hadn't seen Tom since the night Hamish had come to her room. She was glad. She needed time to sort out her feelings. However, there was one thing she couldn't put off any longer. If she could only convince herself her suspicions were groundless, she could at least regain some peace of mind about the plant.

Mel spread all the papers out on the table – Chris Connor's notes about the submarine readings, printouts from her computer with the details about the radiation monitors which had failed, and Sean's diary. It was odd to think that she must be the only one who had all the data. No one else had seen Sean's meticulous records or shared those strange conversations with him.

She opened the diary first and began to check through Sean's notes again, cross-referencing the dates he mentioned with the other material. It was a long process and difficult without a computer. She should have brought her laptop home. But she had all night . . .

There were two main sets of data in Sean's diary – the plant throughput figures and Health Physics data for October, November and December of the previous year, and then again for this January and February. Chris's figures only began in January, but if she looked at the precise dates . . .

As she began to work she became totally absorbed. By 2 a.m. excitement was beginning to grip her in the pit of her stomach. She pushed her chair back and looked down at the table she'd drawn.

There was a pattern: over the first two months of the year there had been four specific occasions when the recorded plant throughput was far below the level suggested by the Health Physics readings inside the plant – 6–9 January,

17–19 January, 1–2 February and 13–15 February. During each of those periods, US submarines from Anderson Base had detected unusual levels of activity off the Wrath coastline. And – the final piece of evidence – the incident report she'd found on the file showed that the external radiation monitors had failed during each of those times. She must check and re-check to be certain. It all depended on her ability to decipher and interpret Sean's complex lists of scientific data, but if she was right . . .

Dawn was rising by the time she finally finished. God, she felt stiff. She got up from the hard chair, yawned and decided to make herself a cup of coffee. She opened a sachet of powdery instant coffee and flicked the switch on the kettle. While it was coming to the boil she leant her elbows on the table and closed her eyes. The radioactivity levels recorded at sea, the site incident reports, Sean's notes about the discrepancies between the throughput in the plant and the levels of recorded radiation all correlated. They covered the same groups of days . . . there was no longer any doubt in her mind.

The kettle wasn't automatic and the room was disappearing in a cloud of white vapour before Mel came to. She'd lost interest in coffee anyway. Her mind was starting to leap from point to point. There was even a link between some of the dates and the day she'd visited the shaft with the journalists and noticed that something had happened to the lid. The shaft was somehow a part of the story.

But why? What was going on and how could it be happening right under everyone's noses? For some reason, Everett's words came back into her head. *They can still smell me – but I can smell them, too.* The Iraqi agent must fit into the picture somewhere. Could he be the missing link?

The more she thought about it, the more certain she became.

Chapter Sixteen

'You're not serious?' Tom was standing barefoot in his tidy kitchen, clad only in pale blue pyjama bottoms. There was a half-eaten bowl of cereal on the table and the smell of strong filter coffee. She had been so hyped up she'd come straight over.

'But it all makes sense,' she said excitedly. 'Look at the dates, the measurements Sean recorded in his diary, the submarine data – they all tie in. The only possible explanation is that material was secretly being put through the plant. And the submarine data suggests it's still happening. It's staring us in the face! Somebody's tampering with the radiation monitors while it's going on – and d'you know what I think? I believe the waste is being dumped into the shaft. Maybe the fuel's even being stored in the shaft before it goes for reprocessing. It would be a good place to hide it.'

'But just a few weeks ago you thought some deadly drugs syndicate was using the shaft to store illicit cannabis. Isn't it much more likely that Cape Wrath has discharged more radioactivity than they intended into the sea because of some error they've kept quiet about, and that everything else is coincidence?'

Mel bit her lip. 'I know I got it all wrong last time – but that doesn't mean I'm not right now. I've just been barking up the wrong tree. Ever since I came to Cape Wrath I've felt there was something going on I couldn't understand.'

Tom was still looking sceptical. The faint smile on his

lips didn't escape her. She had come to him instinctively, relying on him to help her as he'd helped her before. But maybe she had chosen the wrong man. She considered for a moment, then: 'There's something I need to tell you.'

'What's that?'

'Several days ago, James Everett asked me to come and see him. He told me that the man whose body I found on the beach was an Iraqi – possibly a spy – and that he was murdered by someone as a warning. He said the body hadn't been in the sea all that long but had probably been deliberately planted where I found it. He also said *you* were the one who told him.'

Tom's expression was suddenly very serious, almost mask-like. 'Who else knows about this?'

'I've told no one else. Tom, why didn't you tell me? Why did you go to Everett?'

'I had no authority to tell you – it was highly sensitive information. I've no idea what level your security clearance is, but Everett obviously decided you needed to know.' Tom shrugged. His tone was non-committal.

'I'm glad he did because it's made me wonder . . . Tom, suppose that the Iraqis wanted to use Cape Wrath to handle their nuclear material in defiance of the United Nations embargo? We have the technology to extract bomb-grade, highly enriched uranium from spent nuclear reactor fuel during reprocessing . . . I know it seems fantastic, but Cape Wrath is so remote it wouldn't be so difficult to ship fuel in without attracting attention. And if someone on the inside was prepared to help . . .'

As she was speaking, a picture slid into her mind – those coordinates Sean had plotted on a piece of paper. They could be points where a fast boat could come out to meet the mother ship to pick up a consignment of fuel. Had he begun to suspect the real truth as well? Was that why he had disappeared? Or maybe he wasn't dead? Maybe he was involved and just wanted people to think he was dead because it was safer that way?

265

Real fear began to grip her.

'Tom,' she said haltingly, 'what do you think I should do? Who should I go to?

He was silent for a moment, deep in thought. 'Did Everett also tell you I'm in the CIA?' He raised his head to look at her.

Mel stared at him. 'No.' But somehow she wasn't surprised. Another comment of Everett's came back into her head. He'd told her there was no security problem with Tom. *Quite the reverse, in fact.*

'Well, I am. I still think your theories are pretty far-fetched but I'm going to check a few things out with some contacts. I'll call you when I can, but this may take a little time. In the meantime just carry on as usual but keep your eyes open. And don't tell Everett that you've been talking to me about this, or anyone else, OK? We need to keep this tight.'

Mel nodded. 'Tom, I'm scared.'

'No need to be. Don't worry.'

That was easier said than done, Mel reflected, getting back into her MGF. She was tempted for a moment to get out again and look underneath for a bomb, but managed to stop herself. There was no need to be melodramatic – not yet, anyway.

She looked at the fax again. All it said was *Returning Thursday. Meet me at apartment at 8 p.m. Tom.*

The day had never passed more slowly. She could have screamed with impatience at all the trivial things which happened and had to stop herself from snapping at Ishbel when she asked about some small detail to do with the employee newspaper. What was the matter with her? She only had to wait another three or four hours and then she'd know whether Tom had found anything out.

Mel reached his apartment early, as she knew she would, running lightly up the stairs to the second floor of the purpose-built block at Anderson Base. She could see the light on under the door. Just as she was about to press the bell she heard the low murmur of voices. Tom had someone with him. She hesitated then rang.

Tom opened the door, very formal in a dark suit and college tie. His expression was almost grim.

'Hi. Come in.' He didn't kiss her or even smile. 'There's someone here I'd like you to meet.'

Tom's visitor was a small man with greying hair and moustache and very penetrating dark brown eyes. 'I'm Harry. Glad to know you, Miss Rogers.' He held out his hand to her.

'How do you do,' she responded a little awkwardly, looking at Tom for help. It hadn't escaped her that Harry hadn't told her his second name.

'Harry is from the United States Embassy in London. That's where I've spent the past few days.'

She sat down and waited, looking from one to the other. Tom sat down as well but Harry remained standing, facing her. 'Tom here told me about your suspicions. I have to say that we take them very seriously. We've had Intelligence reports from a number of sources that the Iraqis are trying to get their hands on enough material to make a nuclear bomb. They certainly have the technology to do it. All this stuff about chemical weapons – anthrax, plague – that's just a sideline. What our friend Saddam wants is to be able to create a nuclear apocalypse.'

'So you think I'm right?'

'We think you may be,' Harry said cautiously. 'We've profiled the radioactivity readings detected by our submarines off Cape Wrath against known Iraqi holdings of nuclear material. Our scientists in the Pentagon tell me it matches up with nuclear fuel from the Iraqi materials testing reactor Osirak. If you remember, the Israelis bombed Osirak in the 1970s because they were afraid it was being used to produce plutonium. Eight F16s came screaming in and dived at an angle of about thirty to forty degrees. They aimed at the power part of the dome to make the 2,000

267

pound bombs penetrate exactly to the heart of the reactor
. . . it was beautiful.'

The small man smiled reminiscently. 'Those guys from
Mossad really knew their stuff. Their Intelligence was so
good, Osirak was taken out just one hour after construction
was completed, so there was no risk of radiation fall-out.
Anyway, later on during the Gulf War some of the unirra-
diated fuel was shipped out of Iraq and taken back to the
States. That's how we know there's a match.'

'In that case I *must* be right, surely?'

Harry exchanged a glance with Tom. 'Yes, ma'am. I
guess you may well be. But I must ask you not to reveal any
of this information to another party. Not under any
circumstances.'

'But surely I must tell our Head of Security at Cape
Wrath, James Everett?'

'Don't you worry about that, ma'am. I'll make sure he's
briefed. But this *must* be left to the security services to
handle. You do understand, don't you?'

'Yes, I understand.'

'And Sean Docherty's diary – you'll give that to
Commander Schultz here as soon as possible? It may give us
a lead.'

'Yes, of course.'

Mel got up and went over to the window. It was a dark
night full of shadows. She should have been delighted that
they were on the right track at last, but she couldn't relax –
not until she knew whether it was really true and how it
was all going to end.

'Is this it?' They were back in her hotel room; the man
called Harry had left to fulfil business of his own. Tom
handled the small chunky notebook in its faded covers with
a smile of contempt and twanged the rubber band holding it
together. 'I was expecting something a bit more formal-
looking.'

'I think it's very typical of Sean.' Mel's smile was fond. In

268

a way Sean himself had been like that – a little frayed around the edges.

'And this is everything? There aren't any more notes or anything?'

'No. That's all.' She didn't want to tell him about the missing pages with their passionate outpourings about Laura. They had nothing to do with any of this and it wouldn't be fair to the girl.

'Tom,' Mel said hesitantly, 'I can't help wondering whether Sean is still alive. Supposing he just decided that it would be expedient for him to "disappear"? Someone at the plant might even have helped him.'

'It's possible.' Tom put the diary in his aluminium briefcase and spun three little dials on the combination lock. 'Everett told me that Special Branch are looking for him across the UK and that Interpol have also been alerted.'

'It's just that I feel that whatever happened to Sean is key to the whole thing – and I was fond of him. I'd like to think that he was still around.' Her voice tailed off.

'Sure,' Tom's voice was brisk and businesslike. He hadn't really been listening. 'I'm leaving tonight for Washington. They want me to brief them on the situation here.'

'You do think this is serious, then – I mean *really* serious?'

'Yes, potentially. The evidence is mostly circumstantial but anything to do with Iraq is given the highest priority. It's a pity we didn't finish the job when we had the chance.'

'What do you mean?'

'I mean we should have taken out Saddam Hussein while we had the opportunity. We should have gone all the way to Baghdad in the Gulf War and sorted the bastard out for good.' Tom's eyes shone very blue and true behind his steel frames and his lean face was deadly serious. Mel felt a coldness run through her at this glimpse into his psyche.

'Will you be all right while I'm gone?' He was smiling down at her warmly now. 'You could move into Bella and Chris's quarters, they're leaving any day now. Or you can move into my apartment. You'd be safer there.' He glanced around the faded little room. 'I'm not that happy about you being here. I mean, it's a hotel. It's too easy for people to wander in and out.' He ran a finger along her cheekbone but she felt remote from him. Stranger rather than lover.

'I'm fine. Really. Like I said before, it's best that everything should stay as normal as possible. Anyway, I like it here.' In a funny way it was true. She'd grown quite fond of this crusty, eccentric little place and of her room with its table and chair facing the street. Literally her window on Wrath. 'When will you be back?' she asked.

'Difficult to say. They may want me around for a few days to talk to some of the Intelligence guys about information coming in from other sources. Anyway, I'd better get back to the apartment and pack up my gear. Take care – I mean it.' He kissed her swiftly on the lips and was gone.

Mel heard him running down the stairs two at a time and out into the street, then she sat on the bed and took a deep breath. Once again she was out in the cold. She'd set in hand the train of events that were happening around her but she wasn't being allowed to take any part. Everett, Tom . . . their attitudes were curiously similar. *Don't bother your pretty little head. Leave it to the big guys . . .*

She got up and went over to her chair by the window. Dusk was falling and there was a delicious autumn smell of burning peat and wood. Puffs of smoke were snaking from the chimneys of the neat little houses along the High Street, and downstairs in the bar they'd be banking up the giant fire in the inglenook.

As she gazed into the night, fireworks exploded over the sea – starbursts of silver and gold. It was Wrath's annual fireworks display night and she'd forgotten all about it. The sky became a mass of glittering, extravagant colours. Rockets roared and screamed and she could hear the appreciative roar of the crowds down by the breakwater.

The Indians used to let off fireworks over the lake on religious festivals and throw crackers that danced and

270

fizzed along dusty streets and frightened the dogs. As she watched her mind began to drift back to another time, another life . . .

'It was a complete waste of time. I might as well have been talking to a brick wall.' Fabian Williams sounded bitter.

'So they wouldn't make any commitment at all?' Mel had been summoned to the Director's office first thing the next morning.

'No. They said the castle will just have to remain in its current condition – contaminated and fenced off from the public because there are more pressing calls on the public purse. And then they gave me all that bleeding-heart stuff about schools and hospitals taking precedence.' He gave an irritated sigh.

'Don't they have a point?' Mel asked gently.

'No! That's just a let-out. In the first place you can't put a price on historical legacies like Dunstan Castle. They're price*less*. They make sense of the past. The present is mean-ingless without them. Secondly, all it would cost would be twenty or thirty thousand pounds for the limited amount of nuclear decontamination required. The other restoration work could be carried out by volunteers from the commu-nity. Of course, as far as *they're* concerned, they'd be happy to see the site bulldozed.'

'But it's not up to them, surely? What about Historic Scotland?'

'You're perfectly right. They can't actually destroy the castle. Instead it will just be allowed to moulder away until it's past the point where anything meaningful can be done with it. That's the real plan of those Whitehall whingers – masterly inactivity until it's too late.'

Mel had never heard the Director sound more passionate or more resentful. She'd thought when he asked her to come and see him that it would be about the Iraqi situation, but he hadn't even mentioned it. Instead he'd launched into his favourite bugbear. Was it possible that Everett hadn't told him? Was Fabian under suspicion like everyone else? After all, he had close links with the Middle East.

'Mel?'

'I'm sorry, I was just thinking about something. What did you say?'

'I was asking your advice. What else can I do?'

Mel frowned. 'Well, if they won't listen to you as the Director, you need other people to argue the case for you – third-party advocates. What about Sir Angus Prothero or businessmen like Jimmie Macduff? They might be prepared to get involved. Or else you could organize a petition starting with the Cape Wrath workforce, and your wife could get signatures from people in the wider community.'

'Christine doesn't believe in fighting to save the castle as much as I do. She's made her feelings very clear,' Fabian Williams said shortly, and got to his feet. 'I'll consider your suggestions and, in the meantime, if any further thoughts occur, let me know.'

'I will. There's just one other thing. That Select Committee Evidence – have you had a chance to read it yet? It needs to be finalized and—'

'No,' he responded, running his hands irritably through the silvery wings of his hair and looking at her bleakly. 'I've been too busy . . .'

'Can you give me any idea when—'

'*No*. As I said, I've had other matters to deal with,' he snapped at her and turned away. She was dismissed.

Back at the hotel that same evening, she took a hand-delivered note from the receptionist. She knew instinctively who it was from. That jagged writing in black ink on the envelope had to be Hamish's. Inside was a single sheet of very expensive-looking recycled paper and she smiled as she unfolded it.

Thank you for giving me those pages from Sean's diary about Laura. It has made a real difference to her, as you can imagine.

We talked about it until well into the early hours but now I think she understands . . . Hamish.

Mel read the note several times. She should be pleased. She'd wanted Laura to be able to take comfort from the diary. But at the same time she realized she was almost jealous! If Hamish was devoting himself to comforting Laura, how long would it be before she turned to him? He was a virile, attractive man – and creative, like her. It would be only natural if they were drawn to each other. Mel walked slowly upstairs in the gathering gloom of the November afternoon.

Her mind was still locked in thought as she opened her door and reached for the light switch. It took her a few moments to believe what she was seeing.

The table by the window had been ransacked. The cheap wooden drawers with their plywood sides were hanging out drunkenly. But the contents – bills, bank statements, miscellaneous pieces of paper – were neatly piled on top of the table. Whoever it was hadn't just tipped the contents randomly onto the floor. They had read them carefully, one at a time.

Not an ordinary burglary then. She felt a tightening of the scalp as the hairs began to rise. She stood stock-still and looked slowly around what had been her room. The bedclothes were off the bed and the quilted mattress cover had been slashed with a sharp knife. Unseen hands had rummaged inside to see whether she had concealed anything there.

Her clothes were piled on the bed. Again she knew instinctively that someone had gone through all her pockets. The chair next to the bedside cabinet lay on its side, as if someone sitting on it had been disturbed and jumped up abruptly.

Now she came to look around more closely, she could see that the intruder hadn't finished the job. Her bedside cabinet with its pile of books looked neat and untouched.

273

So did a pile of reports from work that she had put down in an empty corner.

Her eyes followed the path the intruder must have taken. They'd begun over by the window and then gone to the wardrobe to take out her clothes and lay them on the bed. Next they'd sat down on the chair ready to go through the contents of the cabinet but then they'd heard a noise . . .

As her brain told her the next move in the sequence her throat went dry. Her eyes moved from the chair to the door of the bathroom, which was ajar, and the horror grew. The room was very quiet, so quiet that Mel knew with utter certainty that while she was standing there on one side of the door, *someone else* was waiting on the other – perhaps hidden behind the thin curtain of plastic in the shower. Tensed, straining to catch any sounds, planning what to do next.

She took a step towards the bathroom as if compelled by a force beyond her control, but suddenly something seemed to release itself inside her head. She moved again, but this time it was towards the door into the corridor. Heart thumping, she propelled herself through it and almost tumbled down the stairs and out into the gathering darkness.

The shapes of the hedgerows with their stunted trees looked grotesque in the car headlamps, like drawings from a Grimm's fairytale. Some impulse had made her get into her car and drive out of Wrath. As the lane twisted and turned she suddenly realized where she was making for. Some instinct deeper than logical thought had told her where she would be safe.

As she roared up the drive, pieces of gravel flew up around the car, ricocheting off the paintwork. She slammed to a halt behind the Range Rover and jumped out, the cold night air nipping at her face and the wind whipping her hair into her eyes.

Please let him be there. Light shone from the house through the thin narrow slits of the ancient windows. She ran up the stone steps and hammered on the door. From deep inside the house she could hear Wilf's excited barking and then the sound of paws scrabbling over stone floors.

She knocked again, frantic, and looked back over her shoulder, terrified there was something coming at her out of the blackness. Then the door opened and she fell forwards into the void.

'Mel? What the hell's the matter?' Hamish put his arm around her to support her and pulled her inside, slamming the heavy door shut behind them. Then he looked down at her with a mixture of surprise and concern.

'There was something – someone – in my room at the hotel!' she managed to gasp. She was already feeling ashamed of her blind panic but she didn't try to move away from him.

'What do you mean?' His voice sharpened. 'A burglar?'

'Yes – no – I'm not sure.'

'What did they look like?'

'I didn't see them.' She put her hands over her eyes for a moment as she relived those awful few seconds when she'd realized she wasn't alone in the room.

'Come and sit by the fire.' He led her by the hand, gently as you'd take a child, into the huge sitting room and the warmth of the fire. In spite of the heat she was shaking with the coldness of fear.

Then Hamish went to a side table and pulling out a drawer, began to roll a joint. He lit it and passed it to her without a word. She drew on it deeply, feeling the smoke coil itself around inside her, relaxing her, drawing out the tension. The tip glowed redly and she gazed at it, trying to focus her mind again.

'Don't try to talk. Take all the time you need.' He stood by the fire and waited for her. Wilf came and sat at his feet and he fondled his ears absently.

Her breathing was slowing down and that terrible feeling of being pursued – hunted, was beginning to ebb from her. She looked up at Hamish.

'I'm sorry . . .' she said.

'There's nothing to be sorry for. Just try and tell me what all this is about.'

'I went back to the hotel early tonight. I was feeling tired and there wasn't anything much going on at Cape Wrath. But someone was in my room. They'd been going through my things systematically as if they were looking for something.'

'Money?'

'No, I don't think so. They'd been reading all my papers, one by one. They were neatly piled up.' Mel twisted her fingers together. 'I didn't see anyone but I knew they were still there, hiding in the bathroom. I just knew. I could sense them as clearly as if they'd been standing in front of me. They must have heard me coming along the corridor and hidden just as I opened the door. I only stayed in the doorway for thirty seconds or so.'

'You said you were early this evening. How early?'

'About an hour, I suppose.'

'So, whoever it was must have known what your usual movements were but they chose the wrong evening.'

Their eyes met as they both realized the implications of what Hamish had said.

'Have you any idea what they might have been looking for?'

Mel hesitated. Should she tell him about the Iraqi spy and what she believed was happening at Cape Wrath? It wasn't that she didn't trust him; it was more a fear of drawing him into something he didn't need to be involved in. Whatever was happening was very ugly. Ugly enough for a man to have had his throat cut.

'Perhaps it was someone looking for material about Cape Wrath. Some investigative journalists will go to any lengths,' she said hurriedly.

Hamish was watching her face very closely and she flinched under his scrutiny.

'Is that what you really believe, Mel?'

'No,' she said quietly. 'It isn't. But I can't tell you what I think it might be about . . . at least, not yet . . . I'm sorry. I'll go. It wasn't fair of me to come here in the first place.' She stood up a little shakily and stubbed out the joint in a heavy brass ashtray.

'Where are you going?'

'I . . . I don't know.' She couldn't go back to the hotel. Not on her own.

He came towards her and she put her arms around him and held on tight. Hamish said slowly, 'You'll stay here with me until this is sorted out.'

The tears were running down her face now, dampening his shirt, but they were tears of relief. This ancient house seemed to be wrapping its arms around her too.

Chapter Seventeen

'I don't understand.' It was real yet unreal. The next morning her hotel room looked exactly as it should have done. Not a thing out of place. The papers were back inside the table drawers which were primly closed. Her clothes were hanging in a neat row inside the wardrobe. The over-turned chair was upright again and in its usual position next to the bedside cabinet. The bed had been remade. If she pulled back the clothes she knew she'd find an undamaged mattress cover.

The only clue that anyone had been there was a look of almost unnatural neatness. It was all too precise. Everything set at exactly the right angle.

And something else. The room was usually a little dusty in the more out-of-the-way places. Not now though. She ran an experimental finger along one of the shelves where she kept her books. Nothing. Spotless. The clear, cold morning light displayed none of the usual defects in the cleaning. She pulled a chair over to the wardrobe and climbed up.

'What are you doing?' Hamish was watching with aston-ishment.

'Just give me a minute and I'll explain.' It must look like she was going through some kind of secret ritual.

Standing on tiptoes she managed to reach to the very back of the top of the wardrobe to where she'd hidden Sean's diary. Taking out a handkerchief she ran it over the rough wood surface and examined it. It should have been thick with grey dust and fluff but it was clean.

She jumped down again. 'Thank God for that. I thought I was going crazy.' She smiled a little shakily.

'What do you mean?'

'When I first saw the room I honestly began to wonder whether I'd imagined the whole thing. But now I know I didn't. Whoever was here wanted to make sure they didn't leave any fingerprints. I thought it all looked too squeaky-clean – for this hotel anyway. And they wouldn't normally have made up the room this early in the day.'

'What will you tell the police?'

Mel frowned, thinking quickly. This wasn't a matter for the police; it was a matter for Everett. 'I'm not sure I'll report it to them. They might not believe me in the circumstances. And it could lead to complications.'

Hamish shrugged. 'Only you can be the judge of that. After all, only you know what's going on.'

It was a simple statement of fact, not a jibe and she felt profoundly grateful to him for not pressuring her.

'You should just check out whether there's anything missing. Then pack up a few things and let's get out of here.'

It didn't look as if anything had been taken but it was hard to be sure. After a few minutes Mel gave up and began throwing clothes into a holdall. She hoped she was doing the right thing, but she couldn't stay here. What had happened once could happen again and she couldn't face the thought of lying in bed listening for any sound which didn't seem quite right. Wondering, like James Everett in his Iraqi prison, every time she heard footsteps, whether they would stop outside her door. Looking towards the bathroom and wondering who it was who had waited there so silently.

Even now she could hardly bring herself to go in there. Telling herself not to be ridiculous she pushed the door open, but her hands were shaking as she swept her make-up and toiletries into a sponge bag. She knew she had some shower gel on a shelf inside the curtained shower cubicle but decided to leave it there.

'I think I'm ready,' she told Hamish gratefully. 'Thank you for coming with me. I really appreciate it.'

'No problem. What will you tell them at Reception?'

'I'll just say I'll be away for a few days but that I want to keep the room.'

'They'll soon know where you are. Wrath's like a gold-fish bowl.'

'So long as I pay my bills I don't suppose they'll give a damn.'

'You'd be surprised,' Hamish said with a knowing grin.

'So I have been forced to the reluctant conclusion that I can no longer remain as Director of the Cape Wrath Nuclear Reprocessing Plant. I would like to thank you all for the support you have given me during my time here.' Fabian Williams glanced at the row of astonished faces around the table. Jock Maitland, the Head of Personnel, was gazing at him open-mouthed. So were Janice Griffiths, the Head of Information Technology, and Mike Gordon, the Senior Site Engineer. Other managers had turned to each other and were exchanging hurried comments.

Even John MacDonald looked momentarily taken aback. Their Director's resignation really had come as a complete bombshell, Mel thought. Whoever would have believed that Fabian would feel so strongly about the castle that he'd resign over it? Was it a case of act at speed, repent at leisure? The fact that he'd had a blazing row with the Permanent Secretary at the Department was no reason to resign. After all, who would fight for the castle after he had gone?

But she could tell there was no way he was going to change his mind. And there was something oddly impressive about this tall, thin figure with the ascetic face and silvered wings of hair standing before them like some kind of sage or prophet, his mind bent on higher things.

'When will you actually leave Cape Wrath?' she asked, mentally planning the statement she would have to issue

280

and wondering how the press were going to react to this strange development.

'I will leave at the end of the year. John MacDonald will be Acting Director until a successor has been identified and appointed by the Secretary of State. I am sure that I can rely on you all to give him your full support.'

Mel glanced across the table at MacDonald. What was he feeling? Maybe this was going to be his big opportunity. But his face was impassive again as he surveyed the table in front of him.

'We'll be sorry to see you go, Mr Williams,' said Dougie MacBain after a moment's embarrassed silence, recognizing that the occasion called for some kind of polite remark, whatever they actually thought about Fabian Williams.

'Thank you, Dougie.' The Director nodded at him then gathered up his papers and walked out of the room. After a couple of seconds, excited talk broke out among the managers. Looking through the open door Mel could see his tall figure stride away down the corridor, head erect but still a poignant and pathetic figure.

'I can't believe what I've just heard!' Christine Williams was almost shouting. 'You mean we've been stuck in this dreadful place for nothing? You'll never get your knighthood if you throw in the towel in this childish way. You won't even get a CBE, and all for some nonsensical project . . . Look, I'm sure it's not too late.'

'It is.'

'But have you actually resigned in writing?'

'No, not yet. But I have done it orally and that, as far as I am concerned, is that.'

Christine Williams' face turned an unattractive shade of dark red. 'Don't be silly, darling. Let me give Sir Francis a call and see whether there's anything he can do. I'll say that you just lost your temper and that you've been regretting your hasty words.'

'For God's sake, woman! Don't you understand plain

281

English?' He stood up and faced her across the desk, quivering with exasperation. 'Now, if you don't mind, perhaps you would allow Miss Rogers and myself some peace and quiet so we can draft a press release!'

'You've gone too far this time, Fabian. I wouldn't have believed it possible but you have.' She grabbed her ostrich-skin Gucci bag and walked tight-lipped from the office, acknowledging Mel with the barest of nods.

Fabian had gone very pale. He was obviously fighting to regain his self-control. Mel looked tactfully down at her notebook and said nothing.

'I'm sorry – now where were we?' He looked at her for help.

'We'd agreed to say that you had decided to retire early because of a disagreement with our sponsoring Government Department over the priority to be given to the decontamination of Dunstan Castle. Do you want to say anything about your time as Director?'

'No – except to thank my colleagues at Cape Wrath for all their hard work during my period here and to wish them well for the future. And you'd better mention something about the interim arrangement with John MacDonald stepping into my shoes. Is that enough for you? Have you got what you need?'

'That's fine. I'll draft something and then I'll bring it back to you so you can check it through. If you agree, we'll issue it at three p.m. The rumour machine's already at work and I'm surprised we haven't heard anything from the press yet. The sooner we can get it out, the better. Will you want to do any interviews, or shall Ishbel and I field the media enquiries?'

'I certainly want to speak to the press. I have a number of messages I intend to get over about the crassness of Government policy when our national heritage is at stake.' His pale eyes blinked and he looked very tired and old, as if all the drama and aggravation had sucked him dry. It wasn't as if he was going to have a peaceful time of it when he got home . . .

'Dad!' The door burst open. It was Laura looking like Mel had never seen her. Her eyes were shining. 'Is it true?' she demanded.

'You mean that I've resigned?'

'Yes – you've resigned over the castle?'

'That's right. Who told you?'

'It's all over the town already. It's really cool. I'm so proud of you.'

'Thank you.' The Director and his daughter looked at each other in silence as if surprised and a little embarrassed by what had just happened. Mel picked up her notebook and quietly left the room, pulling the door closed behind her. Her spirits lightened as she walked slowly down the corridor towards James Everett's office. Perhaps something good had happened at Cape Wrath at last.

'James, there's something I ought to tell you. Have you got a few minutes?'

'Yes, of course.' Everett closed the buff folder he'd been reading and gestured to her to sit down.

'Something odd happened last night at the hotel. When I went back to my room after work I found that someone had been going through my possessions. I mean *really* going through them – my papers, my clothes were all laid out. It wasn't just a casual burglary. That's what frightened me.' She looked at Everett to see what his reaction was but his expression was non-committal.

'Go on.'

'I panicked and ran out into the street; I didn't return to the hotel until early this morning. But when I did go into my room, everything was back in its place and everything had been cleaned and dusted. I don't think you'd find a single fingerprint anywhere in the room.'

'Are you sure that it wasn't the hotel? I mean, they might have decided to do some spring cleaning.'

Mel stared at him. She'd expected to be taken seriously. 'Firstly it's not that kind of hotel – I doubt they've ever

283

heard of spring cleaning. Secondly it's the middle of November.'

'I'm sorry. I didn't mean to offend you. It's just that we have to eliminate all the other likely possibilities before we launch an investigation.' Everett reached for a notebook, opened it on a crisp new page and began to make notes. 'This happened yesterday evening, you say?'

'Yes. I got back to the hotel at about five o'clock – much earlier than usual. Whoever it was knew about my movements.' It was on the tip of her tongue to mention Sean's diary. The more she thought about it the more likely it seemed that *that* was what they'd been looking for. But she'd promised Harry she wouldn't talk about it to anyone, not even Everett. Leave everything to the security services, he'd said. Harry must have briefed Everett by now but he was betraying nothing, not even by the flick of an eyebrow.

'I've written down the core of what you told me. Will you just check that the details are correct?' He pushed his notebook towards her and she scanned the neat, closely written lines.

'Yes, that's accurate. You've got all the main points down.'

'And you don't think anything was actually taken?'

'No. Not as far as I can tell at the moment.'

Everett regarded her for a moment, thinking. 'In view of this perhaps you should move out of the hotel?'

'I already have. I'm staying with Hamish Cameron.'

'Ah.' One of his eyebrows arched a little. 'Commander Schultz is away at the moment, isn't he?'

Mel coloured. What was Everett getting at? 'Yes. He's in the States.' Until now she hadn't even thought about it. It was surprising that Tom hadn't called her, but maybe he was trying to reach her at the hotel.

'If he contacts me I'll tell him where you're staying, shall I?'

Mel nodded. There wasn't any alternative but she wondered how Hamish would react to calls from the States

284

from 'the aluminium Nazi'. And how would Tom feel about her living in Hamish's house? But these were problems for later.

'Is there anything else you need from me?' She glanced at her watch. 'Only I've got an urgent press release to prepare.'

'No, that's fine. Thank you for reporting this.'

As she walked back to her own office she was aware of a curious sense of dissatisfaction. Everett hadn't really engaged with her at all. He certainly hadn't seemed interested in the burglary. Still, what did she expect? Sympathy? Empathy? James Everett just wasn't the type.

The restaurant was very simple. A white-washed room on the first floor of an old warehouse overlooking the harbour where the fishing boats were anchored. The wind was getting up, making them buck and sway. A stubby little candle flickered in a pottery holder on the scrubbed pine table. Mel watched a late trawler cutting through the dark water towards its mooring.

'I thought this would make a change. It's great so long as you like steak. I expect you've had enough of my cooking the last couple of nights.'

'What cooking? All you did was heat up a couple of pizzas one night and microwave some spaghetti on the other.' She smiled.

'That's more than I usually do.'

'You should let me cook tomorrow.'

'OK. *Can* you cook?'

'Not very well.'

'Oh.'

They looked at each other and began to laugh. Hamish poured them each another glass of red wine.

'Thank you for everything. I mean it,' Mel said.

He shrugged. 'I've done very little.'

'That's not true.' It was difficult to put into words what she felt, but he'd been wonderful the past three days. He'd just been there as a friend, giving her the space she needed.

285

'I could do more if you'd tell me what's really going on.'

'I will when I can. I promise.'

'I still think you should have told the police.'

'It wouldn't have done any good.' A shadow crossed her face.

Their steaks arrived, huge and sizzling, with a pile of chips and fried onion rings. Hamish attacked his at once, hacking into it with gusto. 'The best grass-fed Aberdeen Angus – no BSE here.'

They ate in silence for a while then Hamish looked across at her. 'You still don't quite trust me, do you?' he asked quietly.

'I wouldn't have come to you in the first place if I didn't.'

'But why do I always get this feeling there's a part of you that you keep under lock and key – that you won't let anybody see? It's nothing to do with all this recent business, whatever it is. I sensed it the very first time we met.'

Mel looked down at her plate. She didn't seem to have made any impression on the mountain of food.

'If you really trust me you could prove it, Mel.'

Mel looked up at him. His strong face looked concerned and his eyes held hers in a way she couldn't avoid.

'Prove it by telling me about Daniel,' he went on. 'He's the key, isn't he?'

'How did you know that?' Her voice was a whisper. She'd thought he was going to press her about the burglary.

'It was obvious that time we talked – really talked – by the fire. You told me a story about what happened to you in Buenos Aires and how you went on the road and met Daniel. When I asked you what happened to him, the shutters came down.'

'Like I told you, Daniel . . . died.'

'End of story?'

'Yes.'

'Come on, Mel. Who are you kidding?'

He was right, who was she kidding? And what good was

it doing keeping it all locked away inside her? She owed it to Hamish to tell him.

'Let's go back to the house,' she said in a low voice. 'I can't talk about it here. Not with all these people.'

She sat with her face in the shadows. Outside the wind was blowing strongly now, roaring around the solid old walls of the house.

'I told you that I loved Daniel. It was true. He meant more to me than anyone else in my life. I never knew anyone who could care so much for other people and so little for himself. That's why I stayed at the Mission – to help him. The Indians in that region of Guatemala have a hard life, particularly the women.

'I worked with Daniel to set up a women's cooperative making clothing. They do fantastic weaving and embroidery in their villages but they had no way of exploiting it and getting a decent price for it. There were plenty of people from America and Europe who used to drive round the villages buying up what they could get, but they only paid peanuts. The villagers had no idea what their work was really worth. They'd sell something for five dollars which would be turned into "ethnic" chic that would sell for several thousand dollars on Fifth Avenue.

'So what we did was to organize the women into groups, not just to weave and embroider, but to actually manufacture whole garments. That meant we had to start to train some of them as designers so they understood what people in the States wanted. In the end we were intending to train a group to handle the marketing and commercial side. Of course, we needed people with the right skills to come and work with us, so we contacted organizations like VSO.'

'And it was a success?'

'It was well on the way to becoming one. It took time to get it all started, of course, and to get the women to trust us. But the fact that Daniel was a priest helped. After about two years we'd built up quite a flourishing enterprise, exporting our goods via Miami. For the first time in their lives the women had financial independence. They could pay for food and medicines and to send their children to school. Our idea was that they would take the business over entirely and the volunteers would leave. We were so nearly, nearly there when . . . well, when it happened.'

Mel could feel her stomach tensing up. Hamish sat in silence, waiting for her to feel ready to go on and she drew strength from his patience.

'Plenty of foreigners came to work with us in Tenango. Two of them in particular became very close friends. There was Simon. He was a newly qualified doctor from Leeds. He set up a clinic for the villagers and introduced vaccinations for the children. And then . . . then there was John, an American from Rhode Island. He said he was a writer but that he had contacts in high places in Guatemala. He wanted to help us, he said. Sometimes it could be difficult to get export licences without paying large bribes. He knew which strings to pull.

'I admired him for wanting to help us, and I trusted him. After a time we became lovers. I told him everything about the business. I never suspected for a moment that he was just using me.'

Mel fell silent. The pain of betrayal was still acute even after all this time. If only she'd guessed what was going on she might have been able to save Daniel and Simon. When would she stop feeling guilty at her blindness? Looking back, it all seemed so obvious. But she'd just been living in a fool's paradise.

'How was he using you, Mel?' Hamish's voice cut into her thoughts, urging her on through the anguish.

'What I didn't know was that he wasn't a writer at all. That was just a convenient cover. He was part of a cocaine-smuggling syndicate that also involved people high up in the Guatemalan military and in the Government. The one thing he hadn't lied about was his connections.

'Of course, when he came across our little cooperative it

288

was a godsend to him. Here was a perfect cover for smuggling cocaine into the States via Miami. He knew the details of all our consignments because I told him. I was so proud of our success I told him everything he needed to know. He didn't even have to ask. All he had to do was to tip off the right people to intercept our consignments and conceal the drugs. And his contacts made sure there was no problem with customs at the Guatemala City airport, from where we freighted our parcels to Miami. It was a whole lot easier than the drug smugglers' usual methods with old Dakotas and jungle air strips.'

'How did you find out what was really going on?'

'I didn't. At least, not until it was too late.' Her eyes filled with tears so that for a moment she couldn't focus. Hamish and everything around her seemed very distant.

'You see, something went wrong. I was never able to find out what exactly, but I've thought about it over and over, and though I could never prove it I'm sure I'm right. I think that someone high up found out what was going on and threatened to blow the whistle. John and his colleagues needed to cover their traces and make sure that someone else took the blame.'

'Daniel?'

'Yes, Daniel and Simon. John's friends in the Army set it all up.' She lifted her head and gazed straight ahead of her into the fire. 'I'll never forget that night. We were sitting by the lake. I was watching the sun set behind the volcano. It was so beautiful – the most beautiful thing you can imagine. We were all there – me, Daniel, Simon and John. There was some important football match. I remember the bar owner had switched on his radio and all the men were gathered around it.'

She could still remember that ear-splitting scream of 'GOAL!!!' and smiled at that last, lost moment of innocence. 'I wandered outside and then I heard it: the sound of vehicles coming down the road. After that, everything happened so fast. I remember the blinding light from the

289

headlamps of a convoy of Army jeeps. John tried to drag me to one side but I broke away from him and ran into the café. Somehow I knew something dreadful was going to happen. I was terrified for Daniel. The Army hate the priests who minister to the Indians; they think they're all revolutionaries. They made us sit down at a table, all of us except John, and they kicked all the local men out.'

Closing her eyes she saw it all again. Miguel the bar owner running terrified out into the night and the sound of stray dogs barking and snapping at his heels. And inside the bar the tenseness and the silence and then that look between John and the Army officer. The casual way John had just nodded his head. Authorizing the executions.

'I saw John give a signal and two of the soldiers stepped up behind Daniel and Simon and cut their throats. The blood was everywhere. I could feel it on my face, taste it on my lips. I thought I was going to be next. I was terrified but in a way I wanted to die as well. But for some reason they left me. They bundled Daniel and Simon's bodies up in a tarpaulin and drove away again into the night. The whole thing probably only took a few minutes.' She tried to sound matter-of-fact but she was shuddering with the horror and the waste of it all. And the anger. The time which had gone by had done nothing to alter that.

'What happened to you?'

'I'm not sure. I remember the jeeps driving away and how quiet it was in the café. And how I looked at the splashes of blood on the tiled floor which were already starting to turn brown. And then I remember an old lady with a donkey who found me down by the water's edge. She took my cold face in her warm hands and I remember how I started to cry.'

'And John?'

'I think he was the one who led me down to the water to wash, but I never saw or heard from him again after that night. I don't suppose John was even his real name. He just vanished away.'

'So what did you do?'

'At first I was in such a state of shock I couldn't do anything. I just got into bed and turned my face to the wall. Some of the women from the cooperative brought me food – they were braver than their husbands. When I eventually pulled myself together and started to go out again I found I'd become a kind of pariah. No one was prepared to talk about what had happened. But they all knew Daniel and Simon had been killed that night.

'I don't blame them for being scared,' Mel went on. 'After all, what could they do? And then about two weeks after the murder someone turned up from the British Embassy in Guatemala City. His name was Arthur James and he was the Second Consul. He said he'd been told there was a British national in Tenango who had got into some trouble and he'd come to "investigate". I think that was the word he used.

'Anyway, he insisted I pack my things and go with him to the City. I didn't argue. It was too painful to stay on in Tenango and there wasn't any point. Everything was just falling apart. I couldn't work there anymore because everyone was afraid of being associated with me. And I thought the British Embassy would want to help me expose the truth and get some justice. Again I was being naive. John and his associates were much too clever and influential for that. The official reply which came back from the Guatemalans was that Daniel and Simon had been engaged in drug smuggling and revolutionary activities and had been gunned down while "resisting arrest". As you can imagine I didn't stand a chance. I had no witnesses. John seemed to have vanished off the face of the earth. The real clincher was that the British Embassy didn't believe my story; the Guatemalan version was too plausible.

'They made me have a check-up and the doctor could tell from a kidney function urine test that I smoked cannabis. They began to say my recollections were confused because of drugs . . . that I'd become paranoid and had had a breakdown. In other words, that my version of events was fantasy.'

'So you left Guatemala?'

'Yes. I came home to England, to my father. In a way he was a kind of antidote to all the drama and emotion of my relationship with my mother and stepfather and to what happened to me in Tenango. It's difficult to explain ...' She paused, trying to find the right words. In a way she was seeing it clearly for the first time, explaining to herself as well as to Hamish.

'There was something very comforting about his rational, scientific, dispassionate approach to life. I began to feel that if only I could be more like him I'd have been able to avoid or at least cope better with all that cheating and betrayal. I'd been, well ... too emotional ... letting my feelings run away with me all the time and losing my judgement. Letting myself be dominated by my senses, not my mind.'

'Don't you think you were being too hard on yourself?'

'Maybe. I think what I was trying to do was protect myself from ever being hurt like that again. And protect those I love. If only I'd seen things more clearly I might have been able to warn Daniel.'

'How could you have known?' Hamish said gently. 'There's no point tearing yourself apart over something you couldn't help.'

'But that's not the way I saw it then. I just wanted to turn my back on the woman I'd been and become a hard-working, hard-skinned, conventional career woman with a well-ordered, respectable life like everyone else. I'd become afraid of what the unconventional could do – afraid of people who had other ways of looking at things. Afraid of people like you and of admitting that part of me was like them.' She smiled a little as she said it, but it was true. She had been wary of Hamish ... wary and suspicious at the beginning of their relationship.

But now her feelings couldn't be more different. She understood what had drawn her to Tom and why their relationship couldn't go on; there was an emotional side to her which Tom would never understand.

'I've never told anyone all this before.' Did Hamish have any idea how vulnerable she felt? She found she was standing up and holding out her arms to him in mute appeal.

Chapter Eighteen

'Is James free for a few minutes, Alice? I need a word with him.' Mel smiled at his secretary, trying to mask her unease.

'He's got a visitor with him at the moment but I'm sure he won't be very long. Would you like a coffee while you wait?'

'Thanks.' Mel sat down and began skimming the day's press cuttings. She heard the door to Everett's office open and looking up was surprised to see Chris Connor.

'Take care now,' he was calling to Everett over his shoulder.

'Chris! I thought you'd already left?'

For a second he looked a little taken aback but then his face broke into his customary broad grin. 'Mel. My favourite PR lady.' He kissed her cheek. 'We're leaving this afternoon. I was just returning some books about climbing to James. I'm afraid Bella and I didn't polish off as many Munros as we would have liked.' He glanced at his watch. 'I must get off or Bella will kill me. Look after yourself.'

Mel turned away and went into Everett's office. A spasm of irritation crossed his face. 'I'm sorry. Alice didn't tell me you were waiting.'

'She's just gone to get me a coffee.'

'Come and sit down.' He managed a faint smile. 'Now, what can I do for you?'

'I wondered whether you had any news yet about what happened at the hotel?'

'No, I'm afraid not.'

'But it is being investigated?'

'Yes, of course.'

Mel fell silent as Alice brought her coffee in, placing it carefully on a mat. She waited until the door closed behind her then tried another tack. 'Have you found out any more about that murdered Iraqi?'

'Investigations are continuing but I'm afraid I'm not at liberty to discuss them with you. The information is very highly classified.'

She could tell he couldn't wait to get rid of her. 'But I'm involved. I found the body.' It was on the tip of her tongue to ask him what he thought about her theory that Cape Wrath was being used to reprocess Iraqi fuel, but stopped herself. Harry might not have briefed him yet. He might still be waiting for more information from Tom in Washington.

Everett interpreted the indecision on her face as disappointment. 'I'm sorry. The rules are quite clear. I must operate on a need-to-know basis.'

'What does that mean?'

'It means that in circumstances like these, Intelligence is restricted to those who need to be aware of it for operational reasons.'

She got to her feet, leaving her coffee untouched.

'And Mel – about what happened at the hotel. You can be assured we're doing our best to get to the bottom of it. The whole room's been checked for prints and the slashed mattress cover has been found in a dustbin just a few yards from the hotel. We have no reason, however, to believe that you are in any personal danger.'

'I see.' She closed James's door behind her but then a thought, rapid and surprising as a bolt of electricity, ran through her and she felt the blood drain from her face.

'Are you all right?' Alice's kindly face swam before her for a moment.

'Yes, thanks, I'm fine.' She managed a smile as she went

out into the corridor and kept on going, walking over the scuffed linoleum. She'd never told Everett about the slashed mattress cover. She'd forgotten all about it when she'd reported the incident. So how had he known?

'Will you be all right here on your own?'

Mel nodded. 'I'll be fine. Really.'

'You could come with me if you want.' Hamish looked concerned. 'Saul wouldn't mind at all. His recording studio's usually like Piccadilly Circus.'

She shook her head. 'I can't go away from Cape Wrath just now. It's the Director's last few days and it wouldn't be fair of me.'

'I'm leaving Wilf with you.' The wolfhound seemed to know he was being discussed and looked soulfully from one of them to the other. 'This is the number and address of where I'll be staying. Remember, it's only on the Black Isle. I can get back to Wrath in three hours if you need me.'

'Just bring me back a tape of what you record.'

He kissed her briefly and she watched the Range Rover vanish down the drive, lights shining in the winter evening light. Wilf gave a whimper of concern and looked at her with accusing eyes.

'I'm sorry, boy. It's just you and me for the next few days.'

She walked slowly back into the house. Already it felt so familiar she'd be sorry to leave. But if she was right about Everett there was no reason why she shouldn't move back into the hotel ... no reason at all. Except that she didn't want to.

If she was quick she'd be able to buy some bread and some milk and some dog biscuits for Wilf from the one shop in Wrath that didn't close at five o'clock. She pulled the MGF up at the kerb a few yards away and peered out through the side window. Yes, the Open sign was still hanging there. She grabbed her purse from the passenger seat and climbed out.

She didn't see it until she was coming back out of the shop, purchases carefully balanced in her arms and car keys in her mouth. At first she wasn't sure. It was a dark, wet night with a cold sea mist beginning to build. But it was definitely Everett's car – a white stylish Alfa Romeo coupé of a very new design. She hadn't seen another like it in Wrath. It was parked up a side street immediately opposite the shop and she could make out two people sitting in the front seat.

Damn. She'd dropped the keys onto the wet pavement. She quickly retrieved them and hurried to where her car was parked. Putting the shopping on the canvas roof she opened the door so she could stow her things inside. Then, drawn by simple curiosity, she walked back along the street in the shadows until she was opposite the side turning again. She still couldn't make out their faces. The one in the driver's seat must be Everett. Whoever was next to him was taller.

But at that very moment another car came along the High Street and turned up the road where Everett was parked. Its headlights were full on and in the yellow glare she could see James Everett and Tom Schultz deep in conversation inside the Alfa. So Tom was back in Wrath. Why hadn't he called her? And why hadn't he rung her from the States? She'd been expecting him to contact her every day for the past week.

She walked slowly back to her car and got in. In a way she'd been dreading hearing from Tom again because she knew she must tell him their relationship was over. She couldn't hide from it any longer. But once more events seemed to be moving on without her. She turned the key in the ignition and drove slowly out of Wrath, her mind full of shadows. What was going on?

'We've put down two tracks already – somewhere between Jimi Hendrix and Enya.' Hamish's voice was faint against a

297

background of drums and rock guitar. 'What did you say?'

'I said I can't imagine it.'

'You will. But everything's OK, is it?' The noise had dropped and she could hear him properly. It was wonderful to listen to his voice and to know that outside Wrath with all its tensions and mysteries, life – normal, cheerful, pulsating life – was rolling on.

'Everything's fine except that Wilf has gone into a decline. He blames me for the fact you've gone away and spends his time slumped on the floor impersonating a huge, hairy, grey rug.' Mel forced herself to sound cheerful and unconcerned. There was nothing Hamish could do about the sense of foreboding that was enveloping her like an impenetrable cloud. It was best to keep him out of things and safe.

Hamish chuckled. 'I'll make it up to him. Listen, I'll call you again tomorrow.'

Mel was smiling as she replaced the receiver. She'd hardly taken two steps before it rang again. Hamish must have forgotten to tell her something.

'Hello – Hamish?'

'No. It's Tom.' The voice on the other end of the line was cold. 'We need to talk. Where can we meet?'

She couldn't get her mind in gear for a moment. 'Anywhere you want. You could come here.'

'No, I don't think so. Why don't you come to my apartment? It's quiet and it's private. There are a number of things I need to say to you.'

'Tom – are you OK? How long have you been back from Washington?'

There was a silence. Then: 'Two days.'

'Why didn't you call me earlier?'

'I wasn't ready to. I'll see you in about a half an hour then. Be here.'

Mel ran a brush through her hair and pulled on a thick jersey. Tom had sounded remote, like a stranger. Was it because she'd moved in with Hamish? Her reflection looked back at her from the mirror – apprehensive and guilty as hell. It wasn't Tom's fault that her feelings had changed.

'Come in.' Tom stood aside for her and she walked slowly into his small sitting room and sat down. Glancing round she saw a half-empty whisky bottle and a glass next to it. It was unusual for him to drink like that. His pupils behind the steel-framed glasses were dilated and his face was flushed.

'Let me tell you a story,' he began.

'Tom – what's all this about? I really don't understand.' Mel was beginning to wish she hadn't come. She looked uneasily at the door.

'Shut up and listen. Like I said, I'm going to tell you a story. It's a morality tale if you like. I had a friend in Vietnam – let's call him Sam. He was the same age as me – just nineteen in the last year of the war. Like me he hadn't even gotten to go to college yet, but he could speak Vietnamese. His father had been a US diplomat in Vietnam and he'd grown up there. So they gave him a job in Intelligence.

'The only problem was, he fell in love with a Vietnamese girl – one of those cute little whores who used to wheedle information out of US soldiers with their cunts so their friends could be murdered. Well, she went one better than that: she got Sam ambushed and captured. Because he was in Intelligence they were particularly – shall we say – "demanding". We got his body back in the last few weeks before the Fall of Saigon. But the only problem was, it was in pieces.'

Tom took a few steps towards her, grabbed her wrists and jerked her to her feet. 'And all because he'd trusted some little bitch like you. Am I beginning to make sense now?'

'No, you're not.' She tried to twist herself free and after a moment he released her. The bitter contempt on his face

299

wounded as well as frightened her. What on earth was he talking about? Was this about Hamish?

'You're good, I'll say that for you. You certainly had *me* fooled. I thought you were just a little innocent who'd got out of her depth. I even thought I cared about you.'

'You're not making any sense to me at all. Please, Tom.'

'How long are you going to keep this up?'

'I'd better go.'

'Where to? Not to the hotel, that's for sure. When I rang them they explained that you'd moved out. It was Everett who told me where you were living and gave me the number.'

'Someone broke into my hotel room. I got scared so I moved out.'

'To Hamish Cameron's house.'

'Yes. He offered.'

'*I* also offered before I went to Washington, God help me.'

'I know and I appreciated it, but there didn't seem any need then. Things changed while you were away.'

'You bet they did. Are you screwing him now?'

She felt her colour rise. 'No, but that's none of your business.'

'Isn't it? I thought we had something going, but I guess that was all part of the fun for you. When you were fucking me you thought you were fucking the Establishment. But Hamish Cameron's right up your street, I guess. What do you do, write protest songs together?'

'You're crazy. I don't understand any of this.'

'When I was in Washington I checked you out. It was quite a surprise to find a file all about your little drug-running enterprise and revolutionary antics in Guatemala. You never told me about any of that, did you? And it turns out you never told Everett either. I can't think how the British Security Service missed it during their clearance checks when you were recruited. But I guess you're all through at Cape Wrath.'

300

'Tom, it wasn't like that!'

He had gone very pale. She thought he was actually going to hit her and she braced herself.

'Wasn't it? And what have you really been up to here in Wrath? If I were you I'd clear out pretty damn fast.'

She picked up her bag and looked towards the door. For a moment she thought Tom was going to stop her, but instead he just ran an angry hand through his cropped fair hair and watched her go without a word.

'James, what the hell is going on?'

'What do you mean?'

'I saw Tom Schultz last night. He said he'd been talking to you about me. What has he been saying?' She was leaning on his desk with both arms, her voice trembling with emotion.

'That was a private conversation. I'm sorry.'

'He told you some things about my past, didn't he?'

Everett looked down at his nails.

'But he's got it all wrong! He doesn't understand. I want to know what he said, what I'm being suspected of.'

'"Suspect" is too emotive a word. Let me just say that in the past few days we've become aware of certain facts associated with your past that mean that your security clearance has had to be rescinded. We will of course carry out a thorough investigation of the facts and hope to reinstate you. But in the meantime I'm sure you can appreciate my position. I must ask you to leave the site immediately and hand in your pass to a member of the Nuclear Police at the gate.'

'Just tell me one thing, James. Did you have my room searched?'

'You may care to think so. I couldn't possibly comment.'

'I see.'

'If you'll take my advice,' Everett said smoothly, 'you should go away for a few weeks – take a complete break from Cape Wrath.'

301

Mel straightened up and walked out of his office. She didn't know whether to laugh or cry.

'John, I've come to ask a favour.' The sense of frustration was boiling over inside her and she was fighting to stay calm.

He was hard at work checking over what looked like a pile of contracts. Since Sean's disappearance no formal replacement had been appointed. John had simply absorbed the Contracts Department into his own team and seemed to thrive on the hard work.

'What is it?' He closed his eyes for a moment and put his hand on the bridge of his nose as if the concentration had given him a headache.

'There seem to be some questions over my security clearance. James is rescinding it and wants me off the site until it's cleared up. Is there anything you can do?'

MacDonald considered for a moment, his remarkable violet irises fixed on her face. Then he shook his head. 'I'm sorry. Security are an independent outfit. I've no control over what they do. If I interfere it will only make things worse. You'll just have to be patient!'

Mel shook her head in disbelief. She'd never expected to be lectured by John MacDonald about patience.

'By the way, how's Tom?' he asked. 'I haven't seen him since that day we went out in the boat.'

'We've split up.'

'I'm sorry to hear that.' MacDonald looked genuinely concerned. 'Tom's a good man and a good friend to Cape Wrath.'

'These things happen.' She smiled thinly. 'Is there anything particular going on in the next few days that I should brief Ishbel on? She's going to have to take over from me until this ridiculous situation has been sorted.'

MacDonald considered for a moment. 'No. I don't think so. At least, nothing out of the ordinary.'

That will be the day where Cape Wrath is concerned, she

thought ironically, heading towards her car. That will be the day . . .

There was no bell, just a massive iron door knocker in the shape of a lion's head. She swung it with more energy than she intended and heard the sound reverberate through the house.

'Oh, it's you.' The door opened to reveal Laura.

'I'm sorry to turn up out of the blue. I just wanted a quick word with your father if he's got a moment.'

'Sure – come in. You're bunking up with Hamish, aren't you?' Laura said casually as she led the way down the corridor.

'I'm staying in his house for a few days. He's away just now.'

'I know. I've only just got back from playing on a couple of the tracks.' Laura paused for a moment in front of some heavy double doors. 'About Sean's diary . . . I just wanted to say . . . well . . . you know . . . thanks.' She shrugged, embarrassed.

'No problem. I was glad to help.'

Laura pushed one of the doors open. 'Dad, Mel's here to see you.'

Fabian Williams was standing in the middle of a group of crates packing up books. There were already great voids in the shelves which ran from wall to wall.

'As you can see, I'm preparing for departure,' he said quietly. 'Christine has already gone back to London to open up our flat. I'll be joining her there in due course.'

Mel recalled that awful scene in his office with Christine shouting at him. She couldn't imagine how they could ever live together amicably after this.

'In the New Year I intend to travel to Syria and the Lebanon to pursue my research into the Crusades more extensively than I've been able to on short visits. Laura may come with me.'

His daughter was on her knees, head bent, diligently

303

wrapping books in bubble wrap. 'I will – that's a definite.'

What a funny combination they were becoming, Mel thought somewhere between affection and surprise. The academic Whitehall mandarin with his head in the clouds and this elfin, ash-blonde tomboy.

'Fabian, I . . .' She was about to launch into the story of her security clearance, but why bother? There was nothing he could do, even if she could gain his attention. 'I just wanted to wish you all the best. When are you actually leaving?'

Laura looked up at him. 'You're not really going to stay another three weeks, are you, Dad? What's the point? We might as well move south before Christmas.'

'No, my notice runs until thirty-first December and that's exactly how long I shall stay in the area, even if I don't go into the office every day. I have some unfinished tasks to see to here.'

Laura shrugged and continued packing, gripping her lower lip between her teeth. She looked very young, more like a child playing with a toy than Sean Docherty's mistress, and Mel was touched.

Fabian looked up from the two volumes he was holding. He was gazing at Laura absently. 'I don't see any problem at all.' He turned away and, bending his long back, began to pile the books Laura had wrapped into one of the cases. Mel left them each absorbed in their task and their thoughts.

At least they had plans. But what was she supposed to do? She'd been frozen out of everything now. She'd never know what Tom had learned in Washington about an Iraqi conspiracy. She couldn't even go on site and do her job. And there was no Hamish. She thought of him with deep longing as she slowly drove back to his house in the gathering dusk.

She slammed the car door and looked round for Wilf.

'Wilf? Where are you, boy?' Her feet crunched noisily on the gravel as she walked towards the house, making her acutely aware of the silence around her. She peered into the shadows, expecting to see a pair of bright eyes. He must have gone off after rabbits.

Mel let herself in. The wind was rising, she could hear it, but the sound was blunted by the house's thick walls. Goodness, she was tired. She could lie down on the sofa and crash straight out if she let herself. A cup of coffee should do the trick.

On her way to the kitchen, she glanced at the answer-phone. Two messages. She pressed the Play button and waited.

'Mel? It's Hamish. We're almost through. I'll be back late tonight.'

There was a click and then: 'John MacDonald here. I was a bit preoccupied when you came to see me today. I just wanted to say I'm sorry about you and Tom – and about the other business. But I hope you have a good rest. Take care now!'

She smiled softly. It would be wonderful to see Hamish. It felt like she'd had everything thrown at her during the past few days. She didn't even seem to have a job just now. Although she couldn't tell him everything, it would make such a difference simply to be with him. And it was nice of MacDonald to call. He must have been feeling guilty that he hadn't shown more interest, she thought as she made her coffee and carried it back to the sitting room.

Now she knew Hamish was coming home it would be worth laying a fire. She arranged chunks of peat carefully in the hearth, deciding to light it later. Then she sat down and gazed into nothingness, just letting her mind blank out. In a few minutes she felt herself begin to drift into sleep and put her half-finished coffee down on the floor. What the hell, she was so tired. It was such a luxury just to close her eyes . . .

The chiming of the clock woke her. How long had she been sleeping? she wondered drowsily. Then she saw it was only eight o'clock. In another hour she'd light the fire. She

305

stood up and stretched and then she remembered Wilf. Where could he be? It was so unlike him. She listened for a moment, but there was nothing. Just the sound of wind in the trees.

Putting on her waxed jacket, Mel collected a torch that Hamish kept by the back door and stepped outside. The wind was so strong that it whipped her hair into her eyes. If she wasn't careful she'd lose a contact lens.

'Wilf? *Wilf!*' she shouted as loud as she could, shining her torch into the clumps of trees. Hamish would be distraught. She must find him. And if she didn't, she would call the police to see if anyone had reported running over a dog. 'Wilf,' she whispered, more to herself than anything. 'Where are you, boy? Please come home.'

She walked towards the outbuildings, wondering if he had gone into the barn and the door had slammed shut. But surely he'd bark? More in hope than expectation she pulled the tall, heavy double doors back and shone her torch inside. There was nothing to see but a jumble of old agricultural machinery covered in cobwebs. She was about to turn and walk out when she heard something.

Was it just the wind rushing in through the open doors? No, it was a kind of rhythmic creaking. She took a few steps towards where it seemed to be coming from, then stopped and listened again. It was somewhere above her in the rafters. She raised her face and felt something warm drip onto it. At the same moment, the beam of her torch showed her what it was. . . a long, grey body swinging slowly from a beam, backwards and forwards, backwards and forwards.

'Wilf! No! Oh no!' It was too horrible to take in. As she stared, a second splash of blood hit her cheek. Wilf was dangling from the beam by a wire noose which had almost severed his head. His eyes were bulging and his tongue was lolling out. Mel fell to her knees and vomited. Who could do a thing like this?

She began to shake. It wasn't real. In a moment she'd stop hallucinating. But at last she forced herself to look up again at Wilf's poor bloodstained body swaying gently to and fro in the wind. She couldn't leave him like that. There was a platform ladder against the wall. She dragged it out with trembling hands and climbed up. Her hands became sticky with blood as she tried to unfasten the wire. It was no good. She needed something to cut through it.

A pair of old secateurs was lying on top of a lawn mower. She seized them and climbing up again began to hack away. There was a crash as at last Wilf's heavy body tumbled to the ground. Mel almost fell with it. She knelt beside him, trying to straighten his poor mutilated neck, stroking his long grey fur in a last act of affection. A piece of old sheeting was rolled up against the wall. She pulled it out and covered him then stood for a moment bewildered by grief and shock.

The sudden slamming of the barn doors made her look round in panic and she held her torch in front of herself like a weapon, peering into the darkness beyond. It must have been the wind. But then it dawned on her. Whoever had done this might still be here ... They might even be in the barn, watching her. Mel's skin began to prickle with fear.

She ran to the doors and threw herself against them. They swung open and she stumbled outside, taking great gulps of cold air. Then she was running for the house as fast as she could. She slammed the back door shut behind her and drew the bolts with trembling fingers.

What should she do? She couldn't stay here alone. She grabbed the telephone and dialled Hamish's mobile: he must be somewhere on the road between Inverness and Wrath. But it was no good – an electronic voice told her his mobile was out of range. Mel put the receiver down again. The once-comforting silence now seemed laden with menace. She must get out of here.

Heart beating fast, she ran upstairs to her room and threw a few warm things into a bag. But she grudged even the few moments that took. Back in the hall again she scribbled a note to Hamish telling him where she was going.

Then she hurried out into the night. Her heart was in her mouth as she dashed to her car. At any moment she expected to feel a knife at her throat. It took her three attempts to open the door and then she half-fell in, dragging her bag with her and gasping with relief. Then she put her key in the ignition and drove jerkily down the drive, wheels churning up the gravel. In the mirror she could see the house behind her, empty and dark.

It was so cold that a white frost was already riming the edge of the road. She forced herself to slow down: the last thing she needed just now was an accident. After fifteen minutes she pulled up by a gate. It was a very clear night and she found her way easily along the track to the abandoned bothy she'd noticed the night she'd gone to St Malcolm's Priory and seen Hamish and Laura on the beach. She tugged the old wooden doors open and looked inside. There were no gaps in the thick walls and the roof was still intact. The outbuilding next to it was big enough to take the car if she could get it down the track. She certainly couldn't leave it where it was on the road.

Ten minutes later the MGF was safely out of sight and Mel carried her bag into the bothy. She shone her torch around the derelict building. What had made her choose it as a refuge? She wasn't sure now. Somehow it had been instinctive. She pulled out a blanket, wrapped it round her and sank down against one of the walls. She was still in a state of shock and it was hard to focus on anything except the image of Wilf's body dangling puppet-like from the beam. She switched off the torch and sat cocooned in the merciful darkness.

She woke, cold and stiff, and it took her a moment to recall where she was. Then, as it all came flooding back, she thought she heard something – footsteps slithering and scraping about outside the bothy. Straightening up she stood absolutely still, listening. Perhaps it was an animal blundering about, a sheep broken loose from its fold or a cow? But it was too deliberate and purposeful.

It must be Hamish! At the thought her heart began to pound. She groped on the cold ground and her fingers closed over her torch. She was about to flick it on when something stopped her. She didn't know for sure it was Hamish. Anyone could have seen the note she'd left for him. The footsteps were getting closer as someone strode along the front of the bothy. Then she heard a hand on the catch and the door swung open. Light from a torch blinded her.

'Mel?' His deep voice echoed around the small stone room. His face in the torchlight was tight with anxiety.

Relief flooded through her body and she stumbled towards him. He pulled her into his arms, but after a moment she gently pulled away. She'd decided now. She didn't care what Harry and Everett had said. She was going to tell Hamish everything – the Iraqi agent, the strange pattern of activity at the plant, the submarine radiation readings – the works. But first she had to tell him about Wilf, and that was going to be the hardest part . . .

Chapter Nineteen

Mel woke with a start. Hamish was squatting naked by the peat fire he'd made for them, jabbing at it with a stick. His face looked grim even in the soft orange light of the flames which highlighted his muscled thighs and torso. He had every appearance of a Red Indian warrior preparing for the warpath.

'Hamish?'

'It takes a very sick bastard to murder a dog like that,' he said slowly. His voice sounded choked. 'I still can't get my head round it. I was given Wilf when my life was a mess. For a while he was the only living creature I could relate to. I loved him.' He turned to her, eyes very bright.

'I'm sorry, so sorry,' she whispered. 'And it's all to do with me. Whoever killed him was getting at me. If I hadn't turned to you, Wilf would still be alive.' She opened her arms to him. 'Come here.'

Wrapping a plaid rug round himself, Hamish came and knelt down beside her. 'You're sure you've told me absolutely everything? It's important. Think back. Even something that seems insignificant might be the key.' His voice was very gentle. He wasn't blaming her, but she felt so wretchedly guilty.

'There's nothing else,' she said. 'I've been over everything again and again in my head. The only thing I'm sure about is that the murder of the Iraqi, Sean's disappearance, whatever's going on at the plant, and now Wilf . . . they're all connected. But I've no idea how or why?'

'And Fergus – how does he fit into the equation?'

'Fergus?' She stared at him. 'He had an accident. Everyone knows that.'

'Do they?' Hamish moved closer and Mel rested her head against his chest. The strong, steady pump of his heart was reassuring but he'd raised new spectres in her mind. She gazed into the flickering centre of the fire, trying to keep calm.

'Laura said Fergus never took stupid risks with that bike,' Hamish went on. 'She thought it inconceivable he'd have lost control and gone over the cliff like that.'

'But why murder *him*?'

'Perhaps he had found something out. He was obsessed with the Iraqi's death – you told me that.'

'But he didn't know he was Iraqi. He thought he came from Pakistan.'

'At first, yes. But maybe Fergus discovered the truth. He fancied himself as an investigative journalist. Perhaps he was too successful for someone's comfort.'

'But who? That's what I keep coming back to.'

'You tell me. You're the one with all the theories.'

'Like you being a drug smuggler? Or about some drugs syndicate using the Cape Wrath plant?' She smiled wryly. 'It's humiliating. I've been wrong about almost everything from the day I arrived in Wrath. I misread all the signs, all the people. Even now I know I'm missing the obvious: that's what frightens me. If there *is* something odd going on at Cape Wrath involving the Iraqis, I've no idea what it is or who's behind it. It could be Everett, or the Director, or MacDonald – or maybe even Sean. Or someone I don't even know. But ever since I came to Wrath I've sensed that somebody's deliberately confused and blinded me. They've made a real fool out of me.'

She thought again about that cryptic entry in Sean's diary: *He's playing God.* Even lying cradled in Hamish's arms, her face against his warm chest, she felt a black, nagging fear inside her. 'I should never have told you about any of this. It could be so dangerous for you,' she whispered.

Hamish stroked her hair. 'What worries me most is the thought of you living in this ruin. You can't burn a fire in the day-time or someone might see the smoke. You'll freeze. I wish you'd come back with me to the house.'

'I can't, at least not yet.'

'But I can't be here all the time.'

'I feel safe here – I can't explain why, I just do. No one knows I'm here but you. You must go before it gets light so no one sees your car. And if you don't come back till after dark no one will be any the wiser.'

'What about your American friend. Won't he come looking for you?' Hamish kissed the base of her neck.

'Tom? I doubt he ever wants to see me again.'

'That's good – but I still don't like it.'

'It won't be for long, I'm sure. Whatever it is, it's getting close. It's going to happen soon and then I'll know – we'll both know. This is something I've got to do. I owe it to myself and to people I let down in the past. I might have been able to save Daniel if I'd seen what was coming. And afterwards . . . even then I still couldn't get any justice for him or for Simon. It's haunted me. But now I have a chance to see something through – to have some justice – and then maybe I can reconcile myself to the past and to me as I am. Does that make any kind of sense?'

'OK, OK.' He could feel her body shaking. 'I understand why it matters so much. I'm not going to argue with you because I'm not such a fool. But we'll go through this together, you and me. What exactly are you expecting?'

'If Iraqi fuel *is* reaching Cape Wrath it must be arriving by sea. The mother ship is out there somewhere.'

'So that's what you're going to be doing out here, is it? Spying?'

'I suppose so. If anything happens, it will probably be at night but I just want to lie low and watch. Hamish,' she tried one last time, 'I don't want you to get too involved in this.'

'It's not negotiable,' Hamish said gruffly. 'I can be just as

312

stubborn as you. That night you came to my house ... I'd never seen anyone look so frightened. I'm not going to let that happen to you again if I can help it. And there's something else. I'm a Highlander. This is my country and if there's some crap going on, I want to know. I'll be with you every night.'

He lifted her face gently to his. 'And remember this, Miss Public Relations, in spite of your best efforts I still don't approve of Cape Wrath's official activities. So I'm not going to be tolerant about any extracurricular freelancing on behalf of Iraq or anybody. The whole thing stinks – and somebody at Cape Wrath is going to have to answer for it. And so is the bastard who killed my dog.'

Mel nodded. He was right. He *was* already involved.

'What time is it?'

She could just make out her watch-face in the half-light. 'It's four-thirty, why?'

'I was just checking how long we've got before it gets light.'

'Why?'

'Stop asking questions just for once, please?' He threw aside the plaid, pulled her round and his mouth closed on hers. Quickly, very quickly she was becoming lost to everything but this moment, here, with him. Nothing else mattered. Fear seemed very far away as slowly, rhythmically he began to make love to her again, his shadow huge against the walls in the dying light of the fire.

So many days and nights of keeping watch along the shore near the bothy, hiding in the shadows, and she hadn't seen any sign of a ship or of anything unusual. Of course, it might make its approach from the west but that was less likely; there would be much more chance of detection. But was she just dancing through the dark? What did she have to go on? Guesswork? The logic which had failed her so often? Intuition?

At least the weather had improved. Although it was the

313

middle of December the skies were a pale, translucent blue and the sea was silkily calm. The coarse grass in the sand dune where she was lying prickled her. It was hard to believe that anything malign might happen along this wild and lovely stretch of coastline. The effects of the sunlight on water were spectacular, but although it was barely three o'clock the light was already fading. Mel turned and began to retrace her steps from the shore, the binoculars heavy on their strap around her neck. But something out on the far horizon caught her eye. She sensed something moving before she saw it and stopped. She trained the binoculars on the thin line where sky met sea. Nothing. She swept the binoculars through a wider angle, searching. She must have imagined it. Or maybe it had just been a flock of birds swooping and wheeling far out to sea.

But wait a moment . . . Yes, there was something and she had it right in her field of vision. An elongated sliver, but of what? For a moment she wondered whether it was a whale. She adjusted the sights on the binoculars and gasped. It looked like an inflatable boat about twenty or thirty feet long and, as far as she could tell in the failing light, it was a dark, gunmetal grey.

The inflatable was travelling fast towards Cape Wrath, moving parallel with the shore. As she watched it took a sharp turn, rearing up out of the water, almost vertical. For a second she could make out six or seven figures in dark clothing and wearing helmets that seemed to cover their entire heads.

Then the craft came down again, plunging deep into the water. She waited for it to resurface from a cloud of spray but there was nothing. Minutes passed and still nothing. It was as if she'd witnessed a mirage. Darkness was falling so quickly there was no point staying any longer. She hurried back to the bothy, lost in thought. What on earth had she just seen?

'You're absolutely sure about it?' Hamish kicked the fire

with his foot, trying to put life into it. For some reason it hadn't caught properly and the bothy was filled with peaty, acrid smoke.

'It was hard to spot at first because of the colour, but once I'd got a fix on it I could see it clearly, including the people sitting inside. What I don't understand is how it could just vanish like that unless it had sunk or capsized, but in that case something would've floated to the surface. But there was zilch. It was like someone had waved a magic wand.'

'It sounds like a submersible to me,' Hamish said after a moment.

'What's that?'

'A kind of inflatable boat that can be flooded so that the crew's heads, the engine air intake and the exhaust pipes stay just above the surface. Or it can be fully submerged like a submarine and tied up on the sea bed. The crew can exit and return as divers.'

Mel stared at him fascinated. 'How do you know that?'

'Believe it or not I saw one used in a shoot for a rock video. The director had a brother in the Navy. He got the idea of stuntmen dressing up as the band and diving under the waves and persuaded his brother to lend him the submersible for a day.'

'What was the song called?'

'*When I'm with you I feel like I'm drowning* . . . or something like that. The director thought he was being witty.'

Mel looked at him suspiciously for a moment. 'You're not making this up, are you?'

'Only the name of the track, which I've forgotten. But the boat was exactly as I described. It was an amazing piece of engineering.'

'Who would want to use something like that here? The Iraqis?'

Hamish frowned. 'Unlikely. If they wanted to run a shipment of nuclear fuel into Cape Wrath, they'd need something stronger than an inflatable, wouldn't they?'

315

Mel thought back to the shipments of fuel she'd seen arrive in Wrath Harbour. 'That's right. Spent fuel has to be shipped in special flasks to prevent radiation leaking out. A flask would be too heavy for a boat like that.'

'And the whole point of a submersible is really to take other vessels by surprise. It's designed for surveillance and interception.'

'The sort of thing the Police or the Customs and Excise might use?'

'Exactly.'

'Or maybe it was from Anderson Base?' Everett might be liaising with the Base through Tom. They'd certainly have the skills to intercept anyone trying to land a shipment of illegal nuclear fuel.

'It's possible.'

Mel looked at Hamish. 'But if they were out there today – practising or maybe getting ready to go into position – it must mean something's going to happen soon, mustn't it?' Maybe tonight was the night. A tremor of panic ran through her. This wasn't the moment to be afraid but a cold tension gripped her stomach.

They looked at each other in silence then Hamish enfolded her in his arms and held her tight against him. Gradually her body stopped shuddering as, slowly at first and then more urgently, they began to make love. Tonight could wait.

The moon was very nearly full, hanging over the towers and domes of Cape Wrath. The silvery light created the illusion of something more exotic than an ageing industrial plant. Why should the Iraqis choose a night like this to make their drop? Perhaps they needed the light. This stretch of coast with its needle-sharp rocks and powerful currents was no picnic. Lying in the tussocky grass, jeans tucked into thick socks, Mel's mouth felt dry and her heart was thumping. Here on the cliffs near the site they'd have a ringside view if anything happened.

316

A blade of grass tickled her face and she pushed it aside, then looked around for Hamish. He was about twenty yards further along the cliffs, between her and the plant. They both had an excellent view of the silver sand below and of the moonlit sweep of sea beyond. The lights of Wrath, hidden by the headland, were sending a pale apricot glow into the sky. Where the road from Wrath turned into the main approach to the site, Mel could see red and green lights winking on a giant Christmas tree. Well, it wasn't Santa they were waiting for tonight.

She glanced at her watch. Already two o'clock in the morning. The night shift in the plant would have crossed back over the radiation barriers for a tea break to recruit their energies for the final stint until 6 a.m. when the day shift would arrive. How many of them knew what was going on? Perhaps at this very moment one or two were inventing an excuse to disappear for a while? Or was the job being managed by someone who wasn't on shift tonight, someone who, like her, was out here in the quiet, watching and waiting?

Involuntarily she glanced over her shoulder, then looked towards Hamish for reassurance. She could just make out his tall figure squatting down and the red glow of a joint as he took a long pull. At least the wind was blowing off the sea. The smell wouldn't reach any watchers on the beach. Only Hamish could smoke dope at a time like this, but maybe he was right. She herself felt as uptight as a coiled spring. Being honest, it would be a relief if she was proved wrong, if, after all, nothing happened tonight. The gnawing fear inside her was like a physical pain.

The noise was barely discernible at first. A low hum almost indistinguishable above the breaking of the waves on the shore. But it was growing louder, more persistent. For a split-second, Mel had a vivid memory of that night in Tenango and how she'd listened to the jeeps rumbling closer, dazzling her with their headlights.

317

Raising her head, she thought she saw a pinprick of light. It was still far out to sea but drawing nearer all the time. Hamish had seen it too and was stubbing out his joint. So ... it was beginning at last. Mel closed her eyes for a moment, willing herself to be strong. Maybe all those weeks and months of being fooled and duped and frightened were about to end.

Cautiously Mel crawled closer to the edge of the cliff, then breathed in sharply. Two figures dressed in protective suits and helmets were trekking slowly and deliberately along the beach below. One of them was holding a torch on a low beam. He seemed to say something briefly to his colleague then, turning the torch full on, he began to swing it rhythmically up and down and side to side, over and over again, signalling to the boat. Keeping low Mel dodged over the coarse grass to Hamish and pointed. Their eyes met.

'Stay here. I'm going to find a way down to the beach,' he whispered.

'Hamish, don't! Leave it for the police and the security men.'

'I would, but I don't see any.' He smiled and ran a finger along her cheekbone.

Hamish was right. She scanned the rest of the beach and the clifftop, but they were quiet and empty as far as she could tell in the darkness. Not a glimmer of a torch or a crackle of a two-way radio from the site perimeter. The only sound was the mournful hooting of an owl and a pathetic squeak as it swooped on its prey in the tussocks behind them. All the time the boat was getting closer, its foaming wake glinting in the moonlight. Surely Everett must have made surveillance arrangements? The figures on the beach were still there with their torch. Up and down. Side to side. Quietly confident. Telling the boat that it was safe.

She could see it now – a powerful speedboat aiming for a gently shelving stretch of sand about fifteen feet wide between two long protective fingers of rock: a perfect landing spot. The driver was wearing a balaclava. Behind him was a rectangular metal flask with two men, also in dark camouflage, on either side of it. A fourth scanned the sea from the stern. The weight of the flask was pushing the nose of the boat high out of the water.

The driver cut his engines and turned his boat sideways onto the shore. It was slick and professional. What she was watching had happened before, she was sure. Mel glanced around for Hamish but he was gone from her side. She strained anxiously into the darkness. Then she heard a scrabbling sound and showers of stones and pebbles fell onto the beach below. The men heard it as well and glanced up. Mel flung herself to the ground, praying they hadn't seen her. She lay for a moment, face crushed against the gritty surface, fists balled, breathing ragged. But she couldn't bear not knowing what was happening. Slowly she raised her head and wriggled closer to the edge.

No, please, please no! It was an effort not to scream out to him to stop. Somehow Hamish had slithered down to the beach and was running towards the boat, his giant body hurtling through the air like a rugby player intent on a try-saving tackle. His face was contorted with anger and he was shouting something she couldn't catch. And then it became like watching something in slow motion. Hamish splashing through the shallows, hair flying out behind him like something out of Highland history – grandly, magnificently, stupidly heroic. And what happened next seemed so inevitable.

There was a shout from the driver of the boat as he saw Hamish. The man grabbed the controls and there was a roar as he let in the throttle and the boat veered away from the shore and back out to sea. Alerted by the shout, the two men in protective suits looked round and the taller one raised a gun fitted with a silencer. There was a noise barely louder than a sigh. Hamish flung up his arms as he fell forward into the surf, his hair ebbing and flowing with the seaweed at the water's edge. A terrible emptiness came over Mel and then something else began to pour into the void inside her – a primeval, unadulterated desire for vengeance.

The two men were running along the beach towards the steps leading up to the shaft. They were moving clumsily because of the heavy suits. One of them was still carrying the torch, sending light arcing out in front of them. Mel hesitated, then fumbled in the pocket of her fleece for her own torch. Thank goodness it was still there. Summoning up her last reserves of courage she half-ran, half-stumbled along the edge of the cliff and at last she found it – a narrow track that led precipitacely to the beach below. Sobbing with grief and anger she hurled herself down, feet slithering on pebbles and small rocks, tearing her hands on sharp pieces of rock as she tried to stop herself tumbling head-long. Not that she noticed or cared a damn. The real pain was deep, deep inside as she thought of Hamish sprawled in the sea, just like that other body. Bile rose in her throat but she fought the urge to throw up.

She quickly reached the wire that marked the perimeter of this remote part of the Cape Wrath site. Luckily it was there as a marker rather than to keep anybody out. No one was supposed to climb down from the cliffs as she and Hamish had done. She lay as flat as she could and wormed her way underneath, feeling the barbs catch at her, but then she was through and free.

As she watched, the suited figures disappeared up the steps to the shaft. Somehow she wasn't surprised. In her heart of hearts, wasn't the shaft where she'd always expected this to end? She yelled something, anything. She wasn't sure what, but they couldn't have heard her. Clouds were running across the moon and it was starting to drizzle as she ran after them and began to climb the steps. Her mind was a confused jumble of images. She hardly knew who or where she was as she flung herself upwards, not caring for the consequences. Anger was driving her on. Anger for cruel, thoughtless, inhuman loss of life. Anger at the waste of everything.

It was raining harder now and her feet slithered on wet

stone. There was a stitch in her side, making her breathing loud and ragged. But she wasn't trying to hide any more.

And there they were. The two of them were standing by the shaft which was lit by a powerful camping lamp. They had their backs to her. Without thinking, she took a couple of steps forward.

'Who are you?' Her voice sounded high and cold, her frosty breath spiralling into the air, hanging like a cloud between them.

They looked around, startled, but said nothing, just exchanged glances, and she took a step towards them, trying to make out the faces behind the thick Perspex visors in the light of her torch. It was no use. The helmets completely hid their features. But she must know.

'For God's sake tell me who you are!' she repeated. Her voice sounded shrill now, hysteria just a hair-breadth away. 'Sean?' What had made her say that?

After a moment the shorter man stepped towards her. Slowly he pulled off his headgear and she blinked in disbelief. John MacDonald's face was waxen and sweaty, his violet irises black pinpricks. She tried to take in what she was seeing but somehow she couldn't make her eyes connect with her brain. MacDonald . . . John MacDonald. Just like Sean had tried to tell her.

'So you want to see Sean, do you? That can easily be arranged. He's here.'

Mel breathed in sharply. John MacDonald's face was still pale but now he was smiling in a way which made her go cold. She felt her heart judder against her ribs.

'I don't understand.' She stared at him, trying to understand, seeking answers to questions she could hardly bring herself to think about. So it had been the two of them all the time – John MacDonald and Sean Docherty – the final stage of a twisted relationship. The two of them spinning a web of lies and deceit, pulling the wool over everyone's eyes.

321

'Why did you and that hippy friend of yours have to interfere? Have you any idea just how important this is?' MacDonald's tone was petulant, indignant.

But she ignored him and turned instead to the other man still hidden under his helmet. For some reason tears were filling her eyes, choking her voice. 'You bastard, Sean,' she managed at last. 'Everything you told me was a lie, wasn't it? You made me feel sorry for you. I wanted you to be alive so much.'

She turned away, the sense of betrayal overcoming anger, plunging her into a terrible blackness. They'd done this to her and now they'd taken Hamish. What was the point of anything anymore?

'I don't think you quite understand.' MacDonald's clipped tones cut into her thoughts. 'You're making assumptions again. It's a bad failing of yours.'

'What assumptions?'

'Just listen,' MacDonald went on. 'It's taken us two years to set this up. We were almost there. Tonight would have been the last time.'

'The last time . . . ?'

'Yes. We only needed another few kilos of enriched uranium.'

'Who needs it – the Iraqi Government?'

MacDonald gave a grunt of impatience. 'The Iraqi Government? Saddam Hussein? Don't be absurd. We've been using the facilities at Cape Wrath to reprocess spent reactor fuel belonging to an Iraqi *dissident* group.'

'Dissidents?' So that was it. 'But why? What's the point?'

'To give them enough material to construct a nuclear device so they can get rid of Saddam Hussein. They came to Cape Wrath because they knew we had the skills and the plant to do it. It was our chance to do something world-class again – something that matters.' His face was flushed with pride.

'Does the UK Government know what's going on?'

MacDonald shook his head impatiently. 'No, of course

they don't. D'you think they would have allowed it for one moment? But it was all so easy. The material came in at night and we stored it here in the shaft until we were ready for it. I had to have helpers, of course, but that was no problem. I told the men it was a special contract for the Government. No one queried it or cared. They're loyal to me, you see. Not to the plant, or to the Director, but to *me*.' He flung her a look inviting congratulation.

'Shut up.' Sean's voice was muffled by the helmet. He began to undo the clasps on the shaft-lid. He was even whistling a little tune under his breath.

'There's no point opening the shaft. You've been stopped. There isn't anything to hide inside it.' Her voice sounded high and nervous.

He paused. 'Wrong again.'

Some awful presentiment began to creep over her. Her hands grew sweaty and she glanced behind her towards the steps. Surely someone would come in a moment – the police or Everett's people – but she could hear nothing. Just the sound of Sean quietly working away. Now he was attaching the hook on the crane to the ring in the middle of the concrete plug.

She took a step back as the fear began to build. The temptation to run was suddenly overwhelming.

'Don't do that.'

She heard a click and saw that he was now holding a gun in his hand.

'You asked to see Sean and see him you shall. In fact you can help. Come over here.'

'But . . . aren't *you* Sean?'

'MacDonald told you not to make assumptions. Over here – *now*!'

Mel walked slowly towards the man, watching the revolver in his hand.

'Help me turn this.'

She stood next to him and took one side of the rusted metal wheel in both hands while he took the other. At first nothing happened, then with a groan it shifted and the lid of the shaft began to lift. Although the crane was hydraulic, her arm muscles ached with the effort.

This must be a nightmare, standing here in the drenching rain as the lid on this dreadful Pandora's Box began to open. In a moment she'd wake up and realize all this was just an illusion. Hamish would be there beside her.

Hamish . . . The memory of him falling, tumbling down into the waves returned, overpowering her. She closed her eyes for a moment and reached out in front of her blindly, tumbling towards the edge of the open shaft. She felt the man grab her.

'Not yet. I promised you a good look at Sean first.' He pushed her to her knees and forced her head forward so she was looking down into the blackness of the shaft. She couldn't see anything and tried to twist away, but his grip on the back of her neck was like a vice.

She heard a click and then the shaft flooded with light.

'Look!' He pushed her head forward viciously as he played the torch over the surface of the shaft – the pieces of fuel casing, the carcasses of old gloveboxes, all the bits of unwanted industrial nuclear detritus that had been tossed inside over the years, protruding out of the inky water. And something else that she didn't want to look at.

'Open your eyes! Pretty, isn't he? Or at least he used to be.'

Mel forced herself to look down into the circle of light at the grotesque, oozing features of Sean Docherty.

'Charlie?' she whispered brokenly. 'It's Charlie.'

The man gave a bark of laughter. 'You've been so stupid – so very stupid. Charlie's down there all right, but his body's under about ten tons of debris. And yet you were all so ready to believe that this was him – you and your dumb, credulous colleagues in the police.' He released her and stepped back, then turned to MacDonald.

'Drop her down the shaft and close the lid. We need to get out of here.' The man gestured towards the shaft with his gun. Mel turned shocked eyes on MacDonald. He stared back at her then looked at his companion, sweat breaking out on his forehead.

'I don't think that . . .' MacDonald began, then tailed off. 'You don't think what? That you can do it?' his companion said, and raised his gun. Mel flinched, waiting for the bullet. Time seemed to expand fantastically. How long was a second when you were waiting to die? She closed her eyes and at that very moment heard the soft phut of the gun. But she was still breathing, still living – but MacDonald wasn't. As she opened her eyes again she saw him buckle and slide to the ground, a bubble of air escaping from his mouth in a low moan. There was a small neat hole in the middle of his forehead and a look of surprise on his face.

Mel shivered violently as the second man began to pull off his gauntlets with quick neat movements. She saw his strong wrists, the long slim fingers, suddenly so familiar. Then very slowly he pulled off his helmet. His pale blond hair was almost white in the lamplight and he looked like an avenging angel.

'Well?' Tom took a step towards her. 'You don't look very surprised.'

Mel shook her head helplessly. She was beyond trying to understand anything anymore. And yet she couldn't accept the evidence of her own eyes. Maybe Tom had just been stringing MacDonald along. That was it – he'd been working undercover, pretending to go along with MacDonald to find out the truth. But no. He'd just murdered two men – shot them like vermin without a moment's thought.

She looked steadily into his cold blue eyes, impassive behind the steel-rimmed glasses. What she saw blew the chill wind of reality through her fuddled brain. It had been Tom all the time and she'd never guessed a thing.

'Just tell me why, Tom,' she whispered. Rain was pouring down, she felt the drops running down her face, or were they tears? She didn't know or care. Pain, humiliation, anger were

325

welling up inside her. She was almost choking with emotion. 'You want to know why? That's simple. Because it's the right thing to do. There's a group of us in the CIA who believe the Gulf War failed; it finished too early. Operation Desert Storm should have pushed on to Baghdad and terminated Saddam Hussein. All this pussyfooting around with so-called sanctions and UN weapons inspectors and letting Saddam call the shots makes us sick to our stomachs. So we made contact with dissidents to see how we could help them undermine the regime. When we discovered they had nuclear material stolen from the Osirak research reactor in Iraq after the Israelis bombed it we came up with the idea of giving them a nuclear capability – the one thing Saddam Hussein doesn't have. But the problem was where to reprocess it.'

'So you chose Cape Wrath?'

'Sure. We needed a plant which had the capability to reprocess but which was remote. Cape Wrath was perfect. Crazy as fuck in its own little way, but perfect. I chose it and I chose MacDonald.'

'What did you do? Give him money?'

'Believe me, it wasn't very hard to persuade him. That man was an ego on legs. The sad little jerk was actually flattered.' Tom gave the inert body a contemptuous prod with his foot, rolling it over so the face was hidden. 'It was going great until the Iraqi Government got wind that something was going on at Cape Wrath and sent an agent.'

'The waiter?'

Tom nodded. 'Correct. He was just a boy. Killing him was easy. Except that you almost caught me leaving the body on the beach. If you'd been just a couple of minutes earlier you'd have walked right in on it.'

Mel stared at him, remembering the green flash of the jeep tearing towards her minutes after she'd found the body. Tom holding her in his arms, comforting her, taking her back to Anderson Base when all the time he was the murderer.

'But surely, killing the boy must have made the Iraqi

326

Government even more sure there was something going on,' she said after a moment.

'No. My friends back in Washington used a double agent to put up a smoke-screen that he'd been killed for sleeping with another man's wife in Wrath. Cutting a man's throat is mild compared with what they do to adulterers back home.' Tom's voice hardened. 'But what I didn't bargain for was MacDonald's stupidity and arrogance. Sean Docherty began to suspect something was going on. One night he blundered into the arrival of a shipment. I had to kill him, of course. I cut his throat too. I was well taught in Vietnam. It's quick if a bit messy. MacDonald threw up and started crying. When he'd pulled himself together we weighted Docherty's body and put him down the shaft.' He looked at Mel with cold detachment.

'But then of course you had to go snooping. You wanted to find Docherty. Well, you did. That was him you were looking at when you had your little secret trip to the shaft. But I wasn't worried. I knew the story about Charlie from MacDonald – it's part of the folklore. I knew that if anyone reported anything the police would assume it was poor old Charlie. And they did.'

'So that was Sean all the time?' Mel whispered. 'And Fergus? I suppose that was you as well.'

'Yes, and I've you to thank for telling me Fergus was asking too many questions about the waiter. In fact, you were a real help, confiding in me, letting me know what you were thinking, giving me Sean's diary. I didn't ask you for it too soon, in case you got suspicious.'

'You just used me.'

'Perhaps. But at one time I hoped you might understand. I thought you and I might see the world the same way, that we might be soul mates. Then I called up your file on the CIA database and read all about you running around Guatemala with those revolutionary hippy dopeheads. I was very disappointed in you, Mel. But I used it; I told Everett. His own security people had never picked it up. That's why he rescinded your security clearance. I hoped you might just clear out after that, especially if I dumped you. But oh no, by then you were getting cosy with that Braveheart lookalike.' He paused, his expression bleak. 'I tried to warn you . . .'

'Wilf?'

'Yup. Believe me, by then I'd have killed you just as happily, but I was worried that the body count was getting a bit high. Your police aren't the greatest, but even they might have started to suspect something.'

'And now, here I am,' Mel said bitterly.

'Yes, here you are.' He came towards her again and she could see his face tauten. 'Because of you we had to bring the consignment forward. And because of you we had to make it a big one. We knew it was too risky to carry on with a series of small shipments. Tonight was going to be the last operation and we'd have had enough material. But don't worry. It's over as far as Cape Wrath is concerned, but we'll find somewhere else.'

'And murder more people, and all for some twisted, dangerous political game that makes you feel good. You're no better than MacDonald.'

'I told you I don't expect you to begin to understand.' His voice was very quiet and very detached. 'I wanted to satisfy your curiosity but now time's run out. Goodbye, Mel.'

Mel felt too numb, too drained to react. She watched dully as he took a step torwards her and raised the gun. Memories of Daniel, Sean and Hamish flickered through her consciousness. She felt she was with them already. She could even hear their voices. Or what was that sound? She saw Tom look round, and turning her own head thought she saw Everett and Connor at the top of the steps, right arms outstretched, elbows supported by their left hands as they trained their guns unwaveringly on Tom. They were on the rim of the pool of light cast by the lamp, half in shadow and standing very still.

'Drop the gun, Schultz.'

But even as Connor spoke Tom ducked and lunged forward and his gun went off. Something hot grazed Mel's temple and spun her over onto the ground. At the same moment there was a muffled sound and she saw Tom drop the gun and fall to his knees, clutching at his stomach. Blood seeped through the white fabric of his protective suit and dribbled through his fingers. A sharp, searing pain in her head made her gasp and she closed her eyes, thankful to fade out of the scene before her. Someone gently touched her wound and felt her pulse as she drifted into blackness.

How long had she been unconscious? The same voices were still talking around her. Tom, Everett and Connor seemed to be arguing about something.

'I thought you were one of us, Connor.' Tom's voice sounded bitter.

'I'm a patriot, not a maverick. Didn't you guys learn anything from the arms to Iran/Contra affair? No, I guess not. You're too damned arrogant. And by the way, your Iraqi pals out at sea have been picked up thanks to our British friends in the Special Boat Service. And for the record I briefed Everett all about you. He never believed any of that baloney you spun him.'

Opening her eyes again Mel saw Tom struggle to his feet, blood from his stomach still oozing through his fingers. He was looking accusingly at Everett.

'You at least should understand after everything you went through in the Gulf War . . .'

A tremor crossed Everett's face and he looked away. 'I'll call the medics.' He pulled a mobile from his pocket and began punching in numbers.

'Don't bother. You can just record me as missing in action.' Before Everett or Connor could react Tom pulled another gun – a small pistol – from his pocket and backed towards the shaft. His expression was a mixture of triumph and contempt as he put the gun in his mouth and pulled the trigger. There was a sickening thud as his body caught the

329

side of the shaft and then smashed into the water and debris below.

The shaft looked huge, even cavernous in the artificial light. A great maw waiting for sacrificial victims, thought Mel, feeling her face contort into a smile that had nothing to do with mirth. Her head was throbbing again and she closed her eyes to blot out the world.

'We'd better get her out of here. And ourselves before we pick up any more radioactivity from that damned thing.' Everett's voice was distant.

'How is she?' she heard Connor ask.

'OK. The bullet just nicked her temple. I think she's unconscious but she should be all right.'

There were a few moments' silence broken only by the cry of a lone seagull as it flew out to sea on some nocturnal quest. Then Connor spoke again, his voice thoughtful. 'In a way I guess we should have let Tom kill her. We could hush this up if it weren't for her. I mean, who's going to believe this wasn't a Government-sponsored plan all the time? We'll have the world's media crawling all over us and questions in the Security Council. It won't help my people and it sure as hell won't help yours. Bill and Tony aren't going to like it.'

'What are you suggesting?' Everett's clipped voice was non-committal.

'I think we both know, don't we?'

She couldn't quite believe what she was hearing. God Almighty, they were wondering whether to kill her. After everything she'd been through. Something Sean once said came back to her: *Everything and everyone at Cape Wrath is corrupt.* In their own way Connor and Everett were ideologues just as much as Tom. Well, she wasn't about to become their victim. Mel forced herself to open her eyes and to raise herself up. They were a few yards away from her, heads together, not even looking at her. Summoning all her will-power she managed to stand and back away from them towards the steps. Did she have the strength to get down them quickly enough?

But then she heard something. A convoy of Nuclear Police jeeps, blue lights flashing, was beginning to make its way down the beach. If she could only get down the steps where they could see her, she'd be safe. Everett and Connor whipped round as she flung herself towards the stairs. She half-slipped, half-fell, expecting a bullet between her shoulders at any moment. But it didn't come and she tumbled down onto the beach, landing on her hands and knees. She struggled up and began running towards the lights, waving her arms and shouting.

Then she saw something else. It couldn't be true. She daren't let herself believe it. In the headlamps of the first vehicle, through the mist of rain, she could see a tall figure limping along the shore towards them. A tall figure with long hair that was streaming out behind him in the wind. Hamish . . . He was limping but he was alive.

She ran along the sand towards him, sobbing with happiness and relief. As she got closer she saw that his scarf, tied roughly round his thigh, was soaked with blood and that his face was bruised. She stumbled into his arms and clung to his soaking body, unable to find any words at all. He stroked her wet hair and ran gentle fingers over the graze on her temple, rocking her in his embrace. Then, behind her she heard Connor and Everett's footsteps on the wet sand and her body went rigid. Hamish felt it at once.

'What is it, Mel?'

She shook her head despairingly. How could she begin to explain right now? But she didn't need to. The look in her eyes was enough. Hamish stepped in front of her, shielding her from the two men with his body. He looked at them for a moment then held out his hand to Mel. Silently they turned to walk away down the beach towards the slowly approaching convoy. Mel felt the eyes watching them, boring into their backs. With Hamish beside her she felt safe, yet for how long? She resisted the temptation to glance back. Perhaps one day in some dark alley or faraway place there would still be the final act to play out. But she and Hamish couldn't live their lives like that, dodging through shadows because they knew too much.

Then it struck her – she was holding the trump card. If she could get the story to the media quickly they'd be safe. It's only secrets that can kill, she thought exultantly. New energy pulsed through her as she dug in the pocket of her fleece for her mobile phone.

'Mel? What the hell are you doing? This is no time for making phone calls.'

'Oh yes, it is.' She smiled as she tapped in the number of the Press Association. 'It's absolutely the right time.' She was about to do the PR job of her life. The shaft was about to become world-famous.